The Write Man For Her

Christie Walker Bos

Cerridwen Press

What the critics are saying...

∽

5 Lips "*The Write Man for Her* by Christie Walker Bos is a truly wonderful story about the healing power of love. Brant and Jessica each have their own walls to scale to true love as each has been hurt by those they loved. I found their relationship very powerful and evoking the dreams we all have to find that one person who accepts us for who we are and love us no matter what. I think *The Write Man for Her* is a story of hope as much as love and this is a tale that will be with me for a long, long time. The passion between these remarkable people is stirring and well written, and with just the right touch of humor to make this book truly deserving of the Recommended Read award." ~ *Two Lips Reviews*

5 Angels "*The Write Man for Her* is a delightful and charming contemporary romance with a rare hero and a determined heroine. […] The plot is solid and very well put together. The story flows smoothly and is entirely enjoyable and engrossing. […] Christie Walker Bos has produced a gem that is unique and exceedingly appealing, not to mention very thought provoking. *The Write Man for Her* is surely a story that any romance fan would enjoy." ~ *Fallen Angels Reviews*

A Cerridwen Press Publication

www.cerridwenpress.com

The Write Man for Her

ISBN 9781419957611
ALL RIGHTS RESERVED.
The Write Man for Her Copyright © 2007 Christie Walker Bos
Edited by Kelli Kwiatkowski.
Cover art by Elphaba.

This book printed in the U.S.A. by Jasmine–Jade Enterprises, LLC.

Electronic book Publication July 2007
Trade paperback Publication May 2008

Cerridwen Press is an imprint of Ellora's Cave Publishing, Inc.®

Also by Christie Walker Bos

ʂͻ

Magical Man List

About the Author

ʂͻ

When looking for her soul mate, Christie Walker Bos made a "man list" with 65 items, created a "magical" ceremony and buried the list in the mountains. Two months later, her "magical man" appeared with 63 of the 65 required traits, so she had no choice but to marry the guy. Now she lives with her soul mate Robbie and golden retriever Simba in a mountaintop community in California surrounded by pine trees, crazed squirrels and an orchestra of birds.

A hopeful romantic, professional photographer, multi-published non-fiction and fiction author of books and articles, editor for the optical industry, professional jewelry maker, peace advocate (www.nurturepeace.com), environmentalist and feminist, Ms. Walker Bos has embraced her love of romantic comedy with plans and outlines for dozens of new books in the years to come.

"I just love a good romantic tale, especially with a liberal dash of humor. I want to laugh, cry and fall in love with the characters in every novel I read and write."

Christie welcomes comments from readers. You can find her website and email address on her author bio page at www.cerridwenpress.com.

Tell Us What You Think

We appreciate hearing reader opinions about our books. You can email us at Comments@EllorasCave.com.

THE WRITE MAN FOR HER

ॐ

Trademarks Acknowledgement

ᔕᕓ

The author acknowledges the trademarked status and trademark owners of the following wordmarks mentioned in this work of fiction:

AOL: AOL LLC LTD

Atlanta Falcons: Atlanta Falcons Football Club, LLC

Baywatch: Baywatch Production Company

Crock-Pot: JCS/THG, LLC LTD LIAB CO

Diet Coke: The Coca-Cola Company

Dockers: Levi Strauss and Co.

Dodgers: Los Angeles Dodgers LLC LTD

FedEx: Federal Express Corporation

Frisbee: Wham-O, Inc.

Internet Explorer: Microsoft Corporation

Jack Daniel's: Jack Daniel's Properties, Inc.

LA Weekly: Los Angeles Weekly, Inc.

Lion King: Disney Enterprises, Inc.

Los Angeles Lakers: The Los Angeles Lakers, Inc.

Macy's: Macy's Department Stores, Inc.

Mail Boxes Etc.: Mail Boxes Etc. USA, Inc.

Marriott: Marriott International, Inc.

Mustang: Ford Motor Company

Old Navy: Old Navy (Apparel) Inc.

Palm Pilot: Pirani, Amin

Porsche: Dr. Ing. h. c. f. Porsche Aktiengesellschaft Corporation

Post-it: 3M Company

Ritz-Carlton: The Ritz-Carlton Hotel Company

Rolex: Rolex Watch U.S.A., Inc.

Saab: Saab Automobile

San Francisco 49ers: San Francisco Forty Niners

Sapporo: Sapporo Holdings LTD

Superman: DC Comics

Tiffany: Tiffany & Company

Trader Joe's: Trader Joe's Company

Ugg: Ugg Holdings, Inc.

Chapter One

ဘ

Oblivious to the sounds of the office kicking into high gear for the day, Jessica Anne Singer, account executive for McMannon & Fitch Advertising Agency, sat at her old oak desk trying to get her fingers to keep up with the thoughts in her head. Jessica gave a quick glance at the antique clock on the wall. She had a half-hour before her client meeting. If she typed faster she would be able to write everything down before she forgot what she wanted to say. Normally she only worked on her budding novel at home, but on the way to work she'd had a great idea and needed to get it down before it was gone like steam rising out of a kettle.

Jessica's heroine, Lady Anne of Erindale, was in a precarious situation. She had just escaped from Stommin castle, where the sinister Simon LeStrand had been holding her prisoner. The only thing between her and freedom was a cold swim across the shallow inland sea that separated the castle from the mainland. Jessica's fingers were a blur as she rushed to bring Lady Anne to the safety of the far shore before she had to stop typing and go to her meeting.

Cold and not just a little scared, Lady Anne pondered her choices — take a cold swim or risk being recaptured by the guards of Simon LeStrand. The thought of his lecherous smile, cold hard eyes and what he would do to her if she were recaptured made Lady Anne shiver more than the cold night air.

"I can't be caught," she whispered through chattering teeth.

With renewed determination, she stripped off her dressing gown and rolled it into a bundle. With her clothing held over her head, Lady Anne carefully waded out into the salty water, trying not to

*think about what creatures moved silently about under its inky
surface. The seawater was more than five feet deep in some spots,
which brought the cold liquid over her lips several times. Her arms
grew tired from holding her gown up and her teeth chattered
constantly, but she could see the beach and freedom, so she told her
legs to keep moving, even though she couldn't feel them anymore.*

*Lady Anne shook her head, aware of a faint ringing sound
coming from somewhere across the water...*

"Ms. Singer? Do you want me to get the phone?"

No response.

"Ms. Singer?"

It took a while before the muffled sound of her assistant's
voice coming over the intercom registered in Jessica's brain.

"Sorry, Kim. I'll pick up."

Jessica hit the save command on her computer before
picking up the receiver.

"McMannon & Fitch, this is Jessica Singer."

Jessica recognized the shaky voice of her father and
slipped out of business mode.

"Hi Dad. Everything all right?"

"Not really. Your brother is having a bad day again. He's
taken the car and didn't tell me when he'd be home. Probably
going to hang out with those hoodlum friends of his. They all
need to get jobs."

Jessica took a deep breath before answering, raking her
fingers through her thick blonde hair.

"He's fifty-six years old, Dad. I'm sure he'll be fine. He
always comes back, doesn't he?"

"Well, I guess, but..."

"Isn't it Tuesday? Doesn't Matt go to group counseling
with his friends on Tuesday?"

"I think so. But I'm almost out of creamer and you know I can't drink my coffee without my creamer. Your mom made sure I never ran out. Now I don't even have a car and I'm going to run out by tomorrow."

Jessica could hear the panic rising in her father's voice as his words came faster and faster. Reminding him that he hadn't driven the car in seven years wouldn't help the situation, so she tried another approach.

"I'm sure Matt can run out and get more creamer as soon as he gets back," Jessica said in a calm and reasonable tone.

"What if he doesn't come back? You know sometimes he doesn't. What happens then? Could you stop by after work and bring me some?"

"I walked to work today, Dad. Do you have enough to last until morning?" she asked. *It's only creamer, for goodness sake.*

"I suppose," he said like a spoiled child who could tell he wasn't going to get his way.

"I'll leave for work early tomorrow and pick some up. I'll make you breakfast, too. How would that be?" Jessica looked up and saw Kim standing in her doorway tapping her wristwatch. "Dad, I gotta run. I have a meeting in five minutes. I'll see you tomorrow morning."

"All right. Just make sure you get French vanilla. I only like French vanilla. And I don't like runny eggs for breakfast, either. You never cook the eggs enough. Your mother made perfect eggs every day for me, every day."

"I know, Dad. I know. I'll see you tomorrow."

Jessica hung up the phone and cradled her head in her hands. Her mother had died ten years ago and her father had never been the same. She looked up at Kim and forced a smile.

"The O'Brien account, right?"

Kim nodded and gave her a sympathetic smile in return. "You asked me to let you know five minutes before they were due to arrive. They should be here any minute."

"Okay, thanks. When they get in, bring them to conference room B and take orders for coffee, tea, whatever. Just keep them happy and smiling until I get there. All right?"

"No problem," she called over her shoulder as she returned to her desk.

Kim was a five-foot-tall dynamo with short dark hair and a mischievous smile. At forty-five, she had decided to reenter the job market after a particularly brutal divorce. Jessica had liked her immediately and had hired her on the spot, even though she'd had no recent job experience.

Jessica took one more look at the story she'd been working on before closing the file. She jiggled the side drawer of the antique desk until it finally gave way and opened begrudgingly. She pulled out a tortoise-shell mirror and a three-year-old tube of lipstick, applying a thin layer of Dusty Rose to her lips. Reaching back into the drawer, she pulled out a small, matching tortoise-shell brush that she raked through her shoulder-length hair in long hard pulls. She checked her teeth in the mirror to make sure there was no lipstick and then practiced a quick smile. Satisfied that she looked presentable but not overly made up, she placed the brush and mirror that used to belong to her mother back into the drawer. Then, making sure no one was at her door watching, she snuck a peek at the eight-inch crystal ball sitting on her desk.

"Want to tell me how this is going to go?" she asked the ball of glass. When it didn't respond or show her the future, she shrugged her shoulders. "I knew you'd say that."

The old leather chair creaked as Jessica stood and slipped her arms into her black knee-length suit jacket. She scribbled a quick note on a bright pink Post-it—"Buy Dad creamer"—and stuck it on the middle of her computer monitor before leaving the office, storyboards tucked under her arm.

As she approached Kim's desk, she noticed the five red client folders Kim had prepared for the meeting and grabbed them as well. Walking down the hall with long casual strides, Jessica felt relaxed and confident. This was where she shined. This was what she was good at...the presentation, working with clients, selling them on her vision. As she neared the end of the hallway, her steps slowed and she could feel her chest tighten under her green silk blouse. The doors leading to the conference room were across from the office of Simon Fitch, one of the firm's partners and Jessica's boss. Simon's heavy oak doors were closed and Jessica felt herself exhale in relief.

Just as she arrived at the conference room, one of the doors swung open and Kim emerged. The clients were all seated around an oblong oak table with fresh cups of coffee, chatting amongst themselves.

"Thanks, Kim," said Jessica.

"Go get 'em," Kim said softly, so she wouldn't be heard inside the conference room.

Jessica nodded and smiled. As she stepped into the room, she flashed a brilliant smile that rose into the corners of her deep blue eyes.

"Good morning, gentlemen," was the only thing Kim heard before Jessica closed the door behind her.

Forty-five minutes later, the doors opened and five smiling men emerged, each clutching a red folder. Jessica came out last with the president of the company, Harold O'Brien. Both were engaged in friendly chatter as they walked down the hall to the reception area.

"I'll have a contract drawn up this week," Jessica was saying.

"Sounds great. I think this campaign is just what we've been looking for—a real winner," Mr. O'Brien said with a smile.

Everyone shook hands in front of the elevator and continued to chat until the doors slid open.

"I'll call you on Monday," Jessica said as they stepped in.

She stood there smiling until the doors closed before heading toward her office. Kim's head came up from her work when she heard Jessica's approach.

"Well?" she asked.

"We got the account."

"Congratulations! Simon will be pleased."

"I highly doubt that. Simon is never pleased with anything."

Once back in her office, she removed her jacket and threw it over the back of the brown leather guest chair before dropping into her own, which gave a welcoming moan as the leather molded itself to her body. She wiggled opened a desk drawer and stretched out her long tan legs, propping her feet up on the open drawer. She glanced at the wall clock and noted the time, deciding to give herself five full minutes to relax and enjoy her success before moving on to the next project.

She tilted her head back until it rested on the top edge of her chair, letting her hair cascade over the back. Then she closed her eyes, letting her mind drift to the beach by her home where she pictured herself sitting on a towel on the sand, the sun warming her smooth skin. She imagined herself scooping up a handful of sand and letting it slowly slip through the gaps between her fingers. She could almost hear the laughter of children playing at the water's edge and the cry of the seagulls soaring overhead. She took a deep, cleansing breath before opening her eyes.

Just as she pulled her feet off the drawer and repositioned herself at her desk, Simon Fitch rapped three times with his knuckles on the open door and came in without waiting for an invitation.

Simon was tall, lean and always dressed to perfection, his hair cropped short to his head everywhere except on the top, where it lay flat as a table. Jessica often stared at his hair in meetings when he wasn't looking, wondering if it was glued in place. Light bounced off his impossibly perfect snow-white hair, creating a disquieting halo effect that didn't match his personality. She had found his steel-gray eyes attractive at first, until they had been turned on her like a predator about to rip into its prey.

"Heard you closed the O'Brien account. Did you get a signed contract?" asked Simon in his clipped, sharp manner.

"Paperwork is being drawn up this afternoon. We should have a signed contract by the end of the week," Jessica replied, making sure to keep the irritation out of her voice.

"Should have and do have are two different things. Make sure you follow through until the contract is signed."

She didn't bother to respond because Simon never waited for a response.

Simon looked around Jessica's office in disgust. Stacks of cardboard boxes containing brochures, stationary, annual reports and other printed materials were grouped together by client, with bright pink Post-its stuck to the sides of the boxes. Storyboards leaned in layers against three of the four walls surrounding the desk, making the office a foot smaller in three directions.

"So when are you going to clean up this mess?" Simon asked, picking up a miniature pewter dragon with a red crystal in its mouth. "You don't bring clients in here, do you?"

Jessica spoke with care, as if talking to a child. "Simon, please put that down. And no, clients don't come into my office. I use the conference rooms for presentations and meetings."

"Thank God for that," Simon spat out. "Why don't you let us get you a new desk and chair? This old stuff looks like it came from a thrift shop. Not exactly the image we want to create here."

"The desk and chair belonged to my dad. They're comfortable and I like them," Jessica said, trying hard not to let her anger show as she watched Simon discard the dragon on top of a stack of client folders.

Simon caught sight of the crystal ball on Jessica's desk. "And what's this for?" he asked, reaching out to pick it up.

Jessica intercepted his hand and grabbed the ball first. "It's my crystal ball. It's how I decide what presentation to show to my clients," she said with a straight face, knowing the answer would make him crazy.

"You can't be serious?" Simon threw his hands up in the air and without warning turned to leave. As an afterthought, he called over his shoulder, "Good job", before disappearing out the door.

Jessica picked up the little dragon and cradled it in the palm of her hand. Jessica's mother had collected all kinds of pewter figurines and when she'd died, Jessica had saved them all. Just looking at them brought a smile to her face no matter how bad her day bumped along or how annoying Simon managed to be. She set the precious dragon back on its feet next to the miniature wizard with his own crystal ball. She wished she had the magical powers of a wizard so she could make one Simon Fitch disappear.

Simon treated the employees of McMannon & Fitch like his own personal chattel. In his first year as partner, he went through fifteen administrative assistants in a single eleven-month period—most of them leaving either in tears or in a rage, none of them giving two weeks' notice. Simon was the second reason Jessica was considering a career move—the first being she was ready to write something other than ad copy.

When Jessica first came to McMannon & Fitch it was just McMannon Advertising. John McMannon was a fatherly-type boss, a real mentor, always concerned about his employees. He was a large, robust man in his mid-sixties with a snow-white beard, deep blue eyes that twinkled when he smiled, a small button nose and rosy red cheeks. He had a penchant for wearing designer reading glasses perched on the end of his nose. He was proud of his Scottish heritage, and often wore a vest under his suit jacket in his family's red and green plaid tartan.

One day, when accompanying her boss in the elevator, four kids and their mother had gotten on at the sixth floor. For the entire ride down, the children had just stared at John. When everyone finally got off on the first floor, the youngest of the four children walked up to John McMannon, president of McMannon Advertising, and tugged on the edge of his suit jacket, asking, "Excuse me. Are you Santa Claus?"

John had let out a deep, hearty laugh that sounded suspiciously like "Ho, Ho, Ho" before walking away. When Jessica had looked back she saw all four kids talking excitedly, pointing at her boss. They knew Santa when they saw him.

About two years ago, John had had a mild heart attack, and decided after his recovery that he needed a partner to take care of the day-to-day workings of the company. Enter Simon Fitch, a well-educated, experienced, clean-cut, professional jerk.

With John almost out of the picture and Simon running the show, Jessica found herself thinking more and more about getting out of advertising and pursuing another career — writing fantasy adventure stories, romances and even a novel or two.

Jessica had been writing stories since the age of ten. Twenty-eight years ago her stories tended to be about dragons and unicorns, magic princesses and mysterious wizards. Jessica had used her mother's pewter figurines as characters, sometimes acting out the plot by moving the figures around and giving them each a unique voice. The stories of her childhood evolved into tales of teenage angst and moody poetry. In college, her interest in writing became the focal point of her studies, leading her to a career in advertising and public relations.

Now, at thirty-eight, Jessica longed for the whimsical writings of her youth, full of emotion and magic, instead of the plastic hype that made her clients smile and her nauseous.

A year ago at a client dinner meeting, Margery Wexler, the wife of orange juice magnate Walter Wexler, mentioned a night class she was enrolled in through UCLA's extension program. At first Jessica feigned polite interest, but when the woman continued on with a glowing report of how interesting the experience was and how she could attend class via the internet at her own convenience, Jessica's mock interest became genuine. This led to an hour-long discussion between the two women, during which time Mr. Wexler tried to interrupt on three separate occasions only to be shushed by his wife.

By the end of the evening, Jessica and Margery had exchanged email addresses and were sharing stories like old school chums while everyone else stood around with their hands in their pockets.

The next day, Jessica had been called into Simon's office and reprimanded for ignoring the client. That same afternoon, Margery had emailed Jessica to tell her what a wonderful time she'd had at dinner. It was the first time she could remember anyone listening to *her* at one of her husband's business dinners. She urged Jessica to take action and pursue her dream of writing more than just "boring ad copy".

The following morning, Jessica had been called into Simon's office once again. Without preamble, Simon got right to the point.

"Apparently Mrs. Wexler has more clout than we thought. I just received an email saying we have their orange juice account, and if all goes well, their entire line of juice products. This was all on one condition—that *you* personally oversee the account."

Jessica had tried to suppress her smile and remain focused. She could tell that handing over this account was as painful as a root canal for Simon, and she enjoyed every second of it.

Besides landing the Wexler orange juice account, her conversation with Margery Wexler had led her to UCLA's online extension program, where her dream of writing whatever her heart desired was only a few classes away. In her daydreams she envisioned herself tapping away at her keyboard, bringing together ladies who were tired of waiting and impossibly handsome knights for great adventures.

Not too long ago, her daydreams had also included a loving husband who allowed her to write, four rambunctious, giggling children, a big shaggy dog and of course Merlin, her cockatiel, all living together in some idyllic little cottage along the coast of Malibu. In her dream world she saw herself looking out the window to watch her kids playing in the sand, while her dog slept in a patch of sunlight on the hardwood floor.

After her divorce and years of dead-end dating, she had downsized her dream to just writing fantasy novels and having Merlin as her only male companion.

She glanced at the clock. She had enough time to squeeze in one small project before her lunch meeting with the art department. Unlike Simon, she showed her appreciation for a job well done and liked to build good working relations with the people she depended on every day. She had to admit she also enjoyed sticking Simon with a hefty lunch bill every other week. So whenever there was a new project to discuss, Jessica scheduled a lunch "meeting" and took the three illustrators out to lunch to go over concepts. Today would be more of a congratulatory lunch for landing the O'Brien deal. She knew it took the creative talent of her illustrators to bring her ideas and concepts to life and never took full credit for her successes.

Grabbing a stack of client folders off the floor next to her desk, she began reviewing the status of each account, making "to do" notes on Post-its and sticking them on each file folder. She knew it was odd in this age of computers and Palm Pilots to be so dependent on little pieces of sticky paper, but everyone has a system, she reasoned, and this was hers.

The rest of the morning flew by without a hitch. Lunch with her illustrators ran a bit over the allotted hour but since Simon was even later, there was no one at the office to make a fuss. The afternoon disappeared just as quickly as the morning and for once she left the office at closing time.

Most days she didn't care when she got home since there was no one waiting for her but Merlin. But tonight was different. Tonight was the first class of her online extension course, Creative Writing 235. According to her counselor, this class was a bit different from most, with a videotaped lecture available for viewing twice a week. The first class had been available online since ten o'clock that morning. There had been more than a few times at lunch when she found herself itching to rush back to the office for a quick preview, but had forced herself to wait. She had been on a waiting list for over six months for this class before she was contacted via email about a last-minute cancellation. Now the wait was over and she couldn't walk home fast enough.

Her office building was on the corner of Broadway and Sixth Street in downtown Santa Monica. Jessica had an easy walk down Broadway before turning left on Fourth Street. Sometimes on her way home she would take a detour into Santa Monica Place, a huge indoor mall, and window-shop for an hour before continuing home. But not today. Jessica passed the mall and made her way over the bridge spanning the freeway, past the Civic Center until Fourth Street narrowed and changed into a residential area.

It was a perfect Southern California day, with a light onshore breeze rattling the leafy green palm fronds of the tall trees that lined the street. As she walked past the park at Hollister and Fourth, she saw one of her neighbors tossing a Frisbee to her golden lab, Skipper, and called out a greeting.

Her neighbor waved back before wrestling the Frisbee from the dog's mouth to throw it again.

Jessica turned up one block to Fifth Street and rounded the last corner. She had to resist the urge to sprint, so anxious was she to get home.

The narrow tree-lined street in the quiet residential area of Santa Monica was filled with unique little cottages overgrown with flowers, ferns and small patches of lawn. In front of Jessica's house was a huge Malaluka tree with its strange papery bark and a white picket fence in need of a fresh coat of paint. Keys in hand, Jessica hopped over the two small steps to her narrow walkway and then took the four steps up to her front door two at a time. Entering her rent-controlled bungalow like a small tornado, she dropped her satchel and purse the moment her feet crossed the threshold. The crash of leather meeting hardwood startled Merlin and made him squawk and screech.

"Same to you," she answered as she went to turn on the computer that sat on a small antique desk in a corner of her living room. While she waited for the computer to do its start-up calisthenics, she kicked off her heels and tossed her jacket on the over-stuffed burgundy sofa. Then with a trick she learned as a summer camp counselor, she pulled her bra off through the sleeves of her blouse in one fluid motion.

"Ahhh," she sighed in relief, free of the cruel lace restraint. Then she hurried into her bedroom, plopped onto the bed and pulled off her pantyhose so fast that she ripped them.

"Shit," she said, examining the giant hole she had caused before tossing them in the general direction of the white wicker wastebasket. The pantyhose missed the wastebasket on the floor entirely and instead fluttered down over a dozen little pewter statures of wizards and fairies sitting on her dresser.

Jessica unzipped her skirt, let it drop to the floor and grabbed a pair of men's plaid flannel pajama pants off a hook behind the door. Hopping on one foot to keep her balance, she pulled them on during her trek back to the living room. Comfortable at last, she made a quick check of the computer and found it ready for her password. She typed in "jessthemess", a nickname she had had since childhood, and hit enter. In four quick steps she was in the kitchen grabbing a beer from the fridge, a jar of peanut butter from the cupboard, and a long wooden spoon from a jar filled with dozens of wooden spoons before returning to her computer.

She entered the address of the extension homepage and waited for the start of her new career to begin. Her hand froze over the mouse, almost afraid to make the final click.

"Here goes," she said, her voice just loud enough for Merlin to hear, who squawked his encouragement. With one final click of the mouse, Jessica started the video lecture and suddenly the image of Professor Brant Wilson stared out at her, followed by his deep, rich voice filling her living room.

"Welcome to Creative Writing 235, or as I like to call it, Writing from Your Heart."

"Hello," Jessica blurted out in surprise at the image on her computer screen.

Professor Wilson was a lot younger than Jessica had expected. Instead of a sixtyish, gray-haired, stodgy old intellectual, here sat a man who looked to be in his early forties with an engaging smile and chocolate brown puppy dog eyes. His hair just touched the top of his button-down pale blue collar and he wore a deep blue tie with what looked like stars and planets floating around in space. Jessica tipped her chair back and took a long, slow pull on her beer as the toes of her bare feet curved around the edge of her desk.

Now this is the way to take night classes, she thought.

For the next hour, Jessica didn't move except to take tiny nibbles from the glob of peanut butter on the wooden spoon. The more she listened to Professor Wilson, the more she wanted him to talk. She watched as he rolled back and forth on an old-fashioned oak swivel chair behind a red mahogany desk, bringing books into view and making suggestions on what the students should read.

His voice was smooth as melted butter and exuded confidence.

"My class is a little different in that I provide this live video instruction as well as plain text lectures. I think it makes the class more interesting, although that could be my ego talking."

The way he looked into the camera made Jessica feel as if he were talking one-on-one, just to her. She leaned forward and ran her finger over her monitor as if she could actually touch his thick, wavy brown hair.

"If I spill my water, say something foolish or ramble on like a complete bore, the way only truly educated people can, then you will see and hear it all as it's happening. No retakes, no second chances—just like in a real classroom." Professor Wilson smiled into the camera lens.

Each time he chuckled at his own little jokes, she could feel the hairs on her arms leap to attention. When the lecture was finished, Jessica looked at the clock on her computer in surprise. *That was an hour?* Then she realized she hadn't even taken notes. It was a good thing she could replay the entire class whenever she wanted. Just another advantage of taking classes online.

After watching the class for a second time, this time taking notes, Jessica had her first class assignment.

"What I did on my summer vacation," she said out loud. "What summer vacation?" she asked Merlin. She hadn't taken off more than an occasional three-day weekend in years.

After her divorce, Jessica had thrown herself into her work. While this had helped her career blossom, it had wreaked havoc on her personal life. Not only hadn't she been on vacation in the last four years, she hadn't been on a date for over two years. And as her best friend Cath often reminded her, she wasn't getting any younger. Between work and running interference between her widowed father and her unpredictable brother — who were now sharing a house together — Jessica didn't have the energy to add dating into the mix.

Maybe I should write a fantasy piece on what I wish I'd done on my summer vacation.

Jessica carried a yellow writing pad, a pen and Merlin over to the couch and got comfortable. She made several false starts, each time crumpling the paper into a yellow ball and tossing it at a wooden wastebasket near the computer desk. Merlin found this very exciting and every time she made a toss, he would run back and forth across the top of the couch and whistle.

When she finally got one in the basket she said, "Merlin, you're supposed to say 'two points' when I do that. Come on, say it…two points, two points." But Merlin just squawked.

"Fine. Be that way. See if I ever take you to a Lakers game."

After an hour of false starts she had an idea that seemed acceptable and began to write. As she worked, Merlin hopped onto her shoulder and played with strands of her hair, but even that didn't distract her — she was in the zone. The words were flowing and she couldn't stop. Working purely for herself and not some client, she smiled as she wrote — a new experience for Jessica — and the words just kept pouring out of her. Merlin made his way down her arm and tried to bite at the moving pen in her hand, but Jessica was so focused she didn't even notice. An hour later she was done with her first draft.

Moving to the computer, Merlin now on her shoulder, she clicked over to her word processing program and began typing. Twenty minutes later, after a few revisions, she was done. She printed out a copy and, grabbing another beer from the fridge, returned to the couch to read it over one more time before sending it off.

"What I Did on My Summer Vacation"

By J.A. Singer

Eyes closed, face tilted up to the sky like a giant sunflower, I let the sun spread over me like my grandmother's patchwork quilt – heavy, warm and comforting...

Chapter Two

ॐ

Eyes closed, face tilted up to the sky like a giant sunflower, I let the sun spread over me like my grandmother's patchwork quilt – heavy, warm and comforting. A heavy sigh escaped my lips. It was two o'clock on a Friday afternoon and I had just escaped to the roof of my twenty-story office building. My colleagues were still debating the qualities of whitening toothpaste as I sipped ice water from a giant plastic cup. I set the cup back down on the pebbled asphalt roof and felt the heat rising from its black surface. I stretched out on Fred Dryer's old lounge chair like a lone sentinel keeping watch over the surrounding landscape of air-conditioning units, protruding pipes and electrical boxes.

Small beads of sweat appeared across my forehead like popcorn popping in a hot skillet – pop, pop, pop – until several beads joined forces to form a single drop that rolled off my forehead, back into my hair. Smaller beads of perspiration emerged above my upper lip, collecting in that little divot below my nose.

I wasn't dressed for this – black jeans and a white collared shirt, standard casual-Friday attire – and the sun knew it. Attracted to the black fabric, it beat down on my legs and made them feel deliciously weak and lethargic. I knew the kind of sunburn I would get through the cotton weave of my pants – mottled and patchy – but didn't care. The sun baked away my concerns, pressed down on my chest and forced me to breathe slowly and deeply.

As if in a trance, I sat up and pulled my shirt over my head and placed it behind me to act as a towel, leaving me in a white lace bra. Ahhh, *a voice inside my head sighed.* That's better. Sun on bare flesh is the best, *I thought. One by one, droplets of sweat began to form in the concave valley between my breasts and then united to create a large droplet that rolled lazily down my stomach, splashing into the pit of my navel without fanfare.* **Ahhh.** *The mental sigh floated through my brain again.*

A low hummmm *began to build in intensity, disturbing my peace. It took a second to realize the disturbance was coming from my pager, which jumped around on the tarred roof like a kid who had waited too long to go to the bathroom. Without opening my eyes, I reached down, groping for the buzzing June bug, until at last I grabbed its vibrating body. I brought the electronic leash up to my face, shielded my eyes from the sun with one hand and cautiously opened one eye. McConnelly – the toothpaste meeting was ready to resume. Damn. My summer vacation was officially over.*

Or was it?

I turned my head to the right until I could see the red lip of the cup sitting next to the lounge chair. Clutching the buzzing pager in my hand, I swung my arm out over the edge of the chair and lined up my hand with the target. Relaxing my grip, I let the annoying reminder of work slip out of my hand. **Bombs away,** *I thought, right before the satisfying sound of splashing water reached my ears.*

Stretching out like a fat tabby in front of a sunny window, I closed my eyes again, interlaced my fingers and placed them like a pillow under my head.

I had just bought myself five more minutes of summer.

Interesting, thought Brant, as he finished reading the short story from one of his new students. He flipped to the first page to find the name—J.A. Singer. Then he hand-wrote his comments on the title page of the paper. "Nice imagery. Clever interpretation of a 'vacation'. Kept my interest throughout."

Then he turned the paper over, picked up the next story and began to read.

"What I Did on My Summer Vacation", by Cory Smith. *This year's annual Smith camping trip to Yosemite started out the same way it does every year – with a family argument. The type of argument that can cancel trips, sever family ties and create hard feelings more lasting than the granite of Yosemite's Half Dome.*

The word "argument" unexpectedly triggered the memory of the last one he'd had with his wife, over six years ago. He involuntarily shuddered as the entire scene came rushing back, unbidden, razor-sharp—sharp enough to still cut deep, as if it had happened only yesterday.

It was an unseasonably warm Sunday afternoon in early October. The windows of their small Westwood townhouse were all open and a warm breeze made the sheer white curtains dance in undulating waves. Linda, Brant's wife, was in their bedroom talking on the phone to her friend Catherine and Brant dozed off in front of the television as the San Francisco 49ers battled the Atlanta Falcons on the gridiron. Somewhere in his sleep he heard his name being called, a soft whisper coming from far away. He didn't stir.

"Brant," he heard again, this time a little louder.

Brant jerked awake. "What?" he asked, sounding confused, as if he didn't know where the voice had come from. He pushed himself up to a seated position.

"I can't do this anymore," Linda said, standing in the doorway between the living room and their bedroom.

"Do what?" he asked, still confused, still half asleep, rubbing his face with one hand.

"This," she said with a sweeping gesture, indicating the entire living room. "All of this. You and me. I just can't do it. I'm not that strong. I want more. I want children. We had a dream together and now it's been shattered. I still want the dream, Brant. I'm so sorry…I want a divorce."

Brant was stunned. Had he heard her right? Did she say divorce? Suddenly he was wide awake.

"You're kidding, right?"

She didn't say a thing. She just started to cry in soft hushed sobs and mouthed the words "I'm sorry".

"Come over here and sit next to me, babe," he said as he patted the space on the couch beside him. "Come and sit. We'll talk. It'll be okay. You'll see."

"I don't want to talk. There's nothing left to say. Talking won't change a thing, not one bloody thing, and you know it."

The sobs were coming faster now, choked out between the words.

"Please, Linda. Just come and sit with me. It will be okay," he said, even though he knew that was a lie. Things would never be okay again. Never.

But she wouldn't budge from her position, not physically or verbally. She clung to the doorjamb, using it to support her weight and her sorrow. Brant felt an overwhelming sense of helplessness. He didn't know what to do or say to make things better. Everything he said just made her cry more, until there was really nothing left to say.

She went back into the bedroom and disappeared for about ten minutes before coming out with two packed suitcases.

"I'll send Catherine over for the rest of my things. I think it will be easier that way. I'm so sorry, Brant. I know this hurts but I have to do this. I would end up hating you in the long run if I stayed."

Sensing it was over for real this time, Brant spoke between clenched teeth. "I'll hate you if you go."

"I'm so sorry, Brant."

The sound of pity in her voice was more hurtful than her words, breaking through his restraint, releasing his anger in one cold blast.

"If you're going to go, just go—but don't ever come back, ever."

"Brant," she pleaded, asking for forgiveness with that one word. But the cold look in his eyes let her know that forgiveness or understanding wasn't being offered.

She moved toward the front door, head down, watching her feet as they slid across the hardwood floor. Setting down one of the bags, she opened the screen door and used the bag to keep it open. Turning back, she took one last look at her husband and hesitated.

"Can I at least give you a hug goodbye? A final kiss for luck?"

"What kind of luck would that be?" he asked, not even looking at her—feeling paralyzed with anger. "Just go."

And so she did. The anger that had been building inside Brant seemed to come to a head at the exact moment the screen door slammed. He grabbed the reading lamp on the end table next to the couch and flung it at the door. It hit the screen and bounced back, hitting the wooden floor with a crash, shattering the ceramic base into a hundred jagged little pieces, just like the pieces of his heart.

That was the last time Brant had ever seen his wife. Her best friend Catherine came by a week later to grab a few things. Brant didn't say one word to her as she walked from room to room with a list that Linda had given her. He didn't care what she took—personal possessions didn't mean anything to him. His divorce papers had arrived by registered mail and he just signed anywhere there was an X. He just wanted the whole thing to be over with.

Now, six years later, the memory of that day was still as sharp as the lamp shards that had stayed on his living room floor for over a week.

I have to find a way to get over this, he thought, as he inhaled the salty air in an attempt to calm himself. With a sudden splat, something large, white and wet landed on page one of Cory Smith's essay.

"Shit," he exclaimed, leaning back, repulsed. Then looking up at the sky he yelled, "Ha! You missed me you winged rat," as a huge white seagull with black wing tips made his escape. Looking around, he couldn't find anything within easy reach so he used the last page of the previous story to clean off the bird crap.

It really didn't matter since his students would never see the pages. With every batch of assignments he received online, he printed them out so he could take them outside to read. Sure, he could have used a laptop, but the pleasure of putting red pen to white paper was somehow lost on a computer screen. After he read each assignment, making comments on the title page, he transferred his handwritten notes into each student's private computer file, usually in the evening when it was too cold to sit outside.

Out on his deck the ocean breeze tickled the hairs on his arms. The air felt so thick and salty he could actually taste it. On foggy mornings he waited for the low clouds to burn off before moving to the deck, bringing coffee, papers and pens with him. He would sit outside for hours—reading, writing and devising new assignments to ignite the creative fires within his students. When he looked up from his work he could watch the comings and goings of his neighbors, occasionally shouting a "hello" or a "how's it going", or even catch a squadron of pelicans out for their morning maneuvers.

Most mornings Brant was outside when one of his neighbors, Frannie Martin, delivered his mail. Frannie was just over five feet tall, with short, dark-brown hair with bright blonde streaks that made Brant think of a zebra. Frannie was one of those people who were always in a great mood. She always found time to chat for a few minutes before going home to her place. Brant guessed that Frannie was in her mid-twenties, although she was married to Steve, who was at least forty.

Lucky man, thought Brant.

Every other day or so, Frannie would pick up Brant's mail when she picked up hers at the Mail Boxes Etc. store and then drop it off at Brant's place on her way home. Brant had his groceries delivered on Thursdays from Grocery.com. The delivery guys had their own key to the security gate and never seemed to be in much of a hurry. They brought the groceries he ordered inside the house even when Brant sat outside on the deck. One young girl even brought him a cold drink from time to time, sitting with him for a while and talking about her job, boyfriend and how things were at school.

Working at home was a solitary experience and while Brant enjoyed his time alone and the convenience of it all, he did appreciate the occasional human contact with the outside world. Except for his Saturday morning cruise around the marina, his Sunday morning basketball game and visits to his local coffee shop for a latte, Brant didn't get out much. And for now that suited him just fine.

With his UCLA baseball cap to shade his eyes from the sun, polarized wrap sunglasses to eliminate the glare coming off the white pages in his lap and a Hawaiian print shirt, Brant looked more like a beach bum than a college professor. Sipping from a tall plastic tumbler of iced tea, Brant refocused on the soiled essay and began to read again.

So far his ten o'clock class showed signs of occasional talent, heavy at times, even with a few glimmers of brilliance. There were a few students who appeared clueless—his challenges—but for the most part they were all starting out on equal ground. As he finished the Yosemite camping trip story, he was already formulating the next writing assignment he would give his students. He really enjoyed stimulating his students' creative juices and then reading the fruits of their labors.

What he liked most about teaching virtually was that he didn't have to deal with his students in person, especially the female ones. For the two years he had worked on campus, Brant had discovered that being a good-looking college professor could be an occupational hazard. The female students, staff and, to Brant's surprise, even some of the male students, weren't shy about showing more than just casual interest. Sometimes requests for a student-teacher conference ended up feeling more like a date than a consultation. The harder he tried to keep things professional—even to the point of being aloof—the more interested they became.

One of his female students had tried to persuade him to give her a better grade by alluding that she would reward him with sexual favors. When he had refused, she had become so infuriated that she threatened to go to the Dean and file sexual misconduct charges against him. She never did, but it had scared Brant enough that he never had another student conference in his office, meeting students in public places like the cafeteria instead.

The virtual classroom suited him just fine, as did his solitary lifestyle. His life had settled into a predictable routine. His days of letting women—wives, students or lovers—put him through hell were definitely over.

And Brant Wilson was happy with that. Or so he thought.

Chapter Three

Monday morning was a blur of frenetic activity with three different client meetings, two staff meetings, three calls from her dad before noon and a business lunch. It wasn't until two-thirty in the afternoon that Jessica collapsed into her chair and kicked off her shoes. She had to move several Post-it notes off the screen of her laptop in order to find the Internet Explorer icon. Several clicks later she accessed her personal file for her writing class.

She had been dying to find out what her professor had to say about her essay but just hadn't had time. Under "Assignment One" there was a new entry.

"Nice imagery. Clever interpretation of a vacation. Kept my interest throughout."

Well, that's encouraging, she thought. She scrolled down to the end of the comments page looking for the letter grade and found none. Odd. She'd have to ask him about that. Why not now?

Dear Professor Wilson,

Thank you for your comments on my essay. I have a quick question for you. What grade did you give my piece? Looking forward to class tomorrow.

J.A. Singer

Just as she hit SEND, Simon rapped three times on her door, making her jump.

"Did I catch you playing on the 'Net or something?" he asked with a grin that could have been mistaken for a snarl as he walked in uninvited.

"Just catching up on some email," she said without expression, and then waited for him to get to the point of his visit.

There was an awkward five-second lull where they just stared at each other before Simon broke the silence.

"We're having a meeting in the conference room in ten minutes and I want you to bring the O'Brien boat account materials, including the storyboards."

"I'll be there," she said with a brilliant fake smile.

Jessica wondered why he felt the need to tell her about the meeting in person instead of picking up the phone. She was sure there was some other reason why her boss found it necessary to physically deliver these little messages. Sometimes his mannerisms suggested he was trying to catch her at something. But what? Once she had found him standing at her desk, reading all her Post-its. When she had come in he'd acted a little guilty, but then made some comment about how the computer has electronic notes that might be more efficient and look a hell of a lot more professional. She got the distinct feeling that he was building a mental file, if not a physical one, against her.

Note...Jessica Singer, unprofessional.

But today she felt he was in her office for another reason. Like he wanted to ask her something but didn't know how. He kept shifting his weight from one foot to the other. That wasn't like him. After another period of silence, he shoved his hands into his pockets and turned to leave, saying as he left, "And put your shoes on before you come. We have an image to maintain."

"Somebody save me, please," Jessica whispered under her breath.

"I heard that," he said without turning around and disappeared out the door.

"Prick," she mouthed.

Wonder if you heard that?

The big important meeting was nothing but a review of last month's successes. Each account rep gave a ten-minute summary of what they accomplished and what they had planned for next month—very boring and self-congratulatory. Jessica had the impression that this was Fitch's way of showing McMannon how great he was at running the company. The older, and obviously wiser, McMannon looked as bored as Jessica felt.

She hated these monthly rah-rah sessions. The only good thing about the meetings was that they brought John back into the office and gave her a chance to reconnect with her mentor. After her presentation of the O'Brien account, Jessica stopped paying attention. She let her mind take her to the edge of the water where poor Lady Anne of Erindale stood wet and shivering from the cold, waiting for Jessica to get on with the story.

At least now she had a hero in mind worthy of her heroine. She pictured her professor standing in the deep shadows of the trees, a tall man in black breeches, a silver breastplate and a black cape with deep brown eyes—just the type of man to help Lady Anne out of her predicament. Picturing her professor in medieval garb brought a contented smile to her lips. She even let out a small sigh, which caused the coworker next to her to give her an odd look. But Jessica didn't take notice. She was too busy scripting out how the brave Sir William would react when he saw Lady Anne emerging naked from the water.

Sir Brant William stood at the edge of the woods scanning the water's edge for boats and castle guards. His focus changed when a bit of movement in the water caught his eye. What looked like a large white ball seemed to float two feet above the water, moving toward the shore. The white ball caught the light of the waxing moon as it bobbed eerily above the water. As Sir William watched, the ball began to rise higher and higher out of the water until he could see what held it up – a naked woman, glistening with a thousand sparkles of moonlight.

Sir William stole a quick glance at the drawbridge but none of the soldiers appeared to have seen the woman. When he looked back, she was gone.

Impossible, *he thought.* Was it a vision? The Lady of the Lake come to warn me of treachery?

His thoughts overwhelmed him and kept him rooted where he stood, like the silent tree he leaned on for balance. He shook his head to dispel the image but just as he began to look away, movement at the water's edge caught his eye once more. The woman or goddess or spirit now stood on the beach, and this time he knew what he must do. He raced out silently through the knee-high grass to meet her.

"Jessica," Simon snapped.

Jessica shook her head in confusion before turning to face Simon.

"Yes?"

"I asked you to bring us up to date on the Liman account."

"No problem. I was just thinking where to begin," Jessica replied before launching into a brief review.

The remainder of the day dragged on. When it was time to go, Jessica walked with rapid strides to the elevators. Simon came out of his office at the same time and walked to the elevators, making sure he stood right next to Jessica.

"Leaving a bit early today, are we?" he asked, looking at his gaudy Rolex.

"Right on time, I believe," answered Jessica without looking at him.

"Must be nice to have all your projects under control."

"I'm taking work home," she lied. She *did* have a large black portfolio held under her arm. The fact that it was empty would have been of interest to Simon.

"How very admirable," he replied without an ounce of sincerity.

Just then, the elevator dinged and the doors slid open. An empty torture chamber waited to trap Jessica with her boss for ten agonizing floors.

"Excuse me. I've forgotten something," Jessica mumbled as she turned away from the open doors.

"I'll hold it for you," he offered, sensing her foreboding.

"No thanks. This might take a few minutes," she called over her shoulder as she rushed back down the hallway.

Simon shrugged and entered the elevator alone.

That was a close call, she thought.

When she made it back to the elevator a few minutes later, there were several people waiting and she was happy to squeeze in with the crowd.

A bright blue sky greeted Jessica as she emerged from her office building and a gentle ocean breeze whirled around her as she made her way home. It was a perfect September day, warm like summer without all the tourist traffic. Jessica resisted the urge to pop into the mall as she made her way past Santa Monica Place and turned down Fourth Street. About a mile later she was home, Merlin squawking his greeting as her keys jiggled in the lock.

"Miss me?" she called out, as she headed for her bedroom to change into faded blue jeans, a blue Old Navy sweatshirt and five-year-old jogging shoes. When she reentered the living room, Merlin was all talkative and excited—bouncing from one perch to another.

"Hold that thought," she told him. "I'll be back before dark."

She locked the front door, listening to Merlin scream at her from inside, and took off jogging toward Pacific Coast Highway and the Santa Monica pier. A short jog down Ocean Park Boulevard brought Jessica to The Promenade, a pedestrian-only sidewalk that paralleled the beach and ran all the way from Santa Monica to Venice Beach. As she approached the pier, foot traffic on The Promenade became more congested so she slowed to a walk. The concrete walking path was a shimmer created from thousands of small pieces of abalone shells that caught the sunlight, illuminating their mother-of-pearl colors to highlight the blues and greens. Once she'd climbed the steps up to the pier, she could see Cath sitting on the pier railing up ahead. She would have waved but Cath was too absorbed in her favorite pastime—guy watching...and letting guys watch her.

Cath was hard to miss. With her mane of strawberry-blonde hair that tumbled around her shoulders, bewitching green eyes and perky little nose, Cath was an Irish leprechaun tempting men with her very own pot of gold.

It had been the first day of her senior year at UCLA when Jessica first met Cath. She'd been perched on a desk with her feet on the seat, surrounded by five guys drooling over her. Jessica instantly hated her. From her petite nose to her perfect B-cup breasts to her lilting laugh, she was everything Jessica wasn't. Women like Cath always made Jessica feel large and clumsy.

Jessica had taken a seat as far away from her as she could but that didn't seem to matter. Once the professor walked in, Cath had hopped down from her throne, glanced around the room, spotted Jessica, and walked right over and plopped down next to her. Jessica almost groaned out loud.

"Cath McLean," she said as she sat down. "And you are?"

"Jessica Singer," she forced out.

"Looks like we're the only good-looking women in this class, which means you get half the guys and I'll take the other half. Deal?"

Jessica turned to look at her like she was an alien and was greeted with an elfish grin.

"I'm not here to pick up guys. I'm here to learn," Jessica replied, the coolness of her voice apparent.

Cath chose to ignore Jessica's tone. "Here to learn, are you? Well then, you won't be disappointed because there's plenty to learn about the men in this class. I've taken it three times already and I've learned something new each time."

"What?" Jessica couldn't believe this girl.

But before Cath could explain, the teacher cleared his throat, signaling the start of the lecture.

Cath leaned over to Jessica and whispered, "Let's have coffee after class and I'll bring you up to speed."

When Jessica tried to reply with a negative, Cath just put her finger to her lips, motioning with her head to the professor who was scribbling illegible notes on the blackboard. After class, Jessica had tried to make a clean getaway but found Cath right on her heels, struggling to keep up with Jessica's long strides.

What Jessica found out over the course of that semester, besides the history of men attending Modern Advertising 504, was that once you got past Cath's intimidating good looks, she was a bright, witty woman with a lot more going for her than her physical assets. It didn't take long for them to form a friendship that would see them through three marriages and three divorces—one for Jessica, two for Cath—one miscarriage—Cath's—and dozens of dead-end dates.

Now at thirty-six, Cath was as full of energy as ever, but Jessica forgave her this fault as only a best friend can. Jessica was almost standing next to Cath before she realized her friend was there.

"Did you see that guy?" she asked, looking down the pier at a deeply tanned college kid in board shorts and no shirt.

"A little young, don't you think?"

"No harm in looking. Come on, let's walk. Can't wait to hear all your news. You sounded so excited on the phone. Is it a new guy?" she asked as she hopped down off the railing.

Jessica laughed. With Cath, if you were happy it had to be because of some guy. They left the pier and joined other walkers on The Promenade, heading south toward Venice Beach. They walked at a good clip, talking the entire way. Cath stopped talking for just a moment as they passed a class of lifeguard trainees getting ready to go for an afternoon swim around the pier. During the brief moment of silence, Jessica enjoyed checking out the pairs of old men playing chess on tables with built-in chessboards under the palm trees next to the walking path. On the ocean side of The Promenade, the South Bay Bicycle Path was almost as busy as the local freeways. Bicycles of every description, from beach cruisers to tricycles, raced up and down the curving pathway, along with rollerbladers, joggers and skateboarders.

With seagulls screaming overhead, Jessica told Cath all about her night class and her first writing assignment. She explained how her fantasy novel was beginning to take shape, and how ever since she started taking the class the story just seemed to write itself. Cath was only mildly interested in Jessica's writing experiences until she mentioned her professor.

"So what does this professor look like?" Cath asked with a twinkle in her green eyes. "Anyone I'd be interested in?"

"Let's see—he's male and has a pulse, so yeah, you'd like him."

"Hey! I'm not that bad, am I?" Cath protested.

"No," Jessica softened. "But I think you'd like Professor Wilson. From what I've seen—and mind you I've had two whole classes—he's witty, intelligent and not bad to look."

"How 'not bad'?"

"To start with, he looks like he could be the all-American poster boy—clean-shaven, tan, strong jaw, deep brown thick hair that's kind of wavy and cut short, but not too short, dark brown eyes that twinkle when he makes a joke but are otherwise soulful."

"Damn. Sounds good enough for me. We need to meet this guy."

"He's not a guy. He's definitely a man...*all* man."

Just then a very fit young man on rollerblades glided by wearing nothing but a pair of very short cutoff blue jeans and a large black cat draped around his neck like a scarf. His tanned muscles flexed as he skated and as he passed Jessica and Cath, he did a one-eighty to check them out. He broke into a full radiant smile before doing another one-eighty and skating on.

"Nice," purred Cath in appreciation.

"That guy should be on the bike path," Jessica muttered.

"So what about the professor's body? Can it live up to that?"

"Hard to tell. I've only seen him via video and he's always seated behind a desk. His upper body looks like it's in great shape and I don't think he has a gut, but who knows from the waist down."

"We'll just have to find out about that later. Married, single, divorced?"

"How would I know?"

"Is he wearing a wedding ring?"

"I didn't notice," answered Jessica as she turned her head to take in the full expanse of beach stretching out from the bike path to the water's edge.

"Tsk, tsk. We *are* slipping. First thing you look for is a ring or the shadow of a ring," reminded Cath. After years of dating, Cath was very perceptive about these kinds of things.

"Look, he's my professor, not a potential boyfriend. I'm taking this class to get my creative juices flowing again — start writing fiction. And it's working. I can't seem to think about anything else. Today in the boardroom during one of Fitch's dreadfully dull meetings, I wrote an entire chapter in my head."

"Professor, schmessor. You need to get more than just your creative juices flowing again."

"What?"

"It's not like you're twenty-two and he's forty, like when we were in school. This guy is most likely our age right?"

"I'd guess in his early forties."

"Right. So he's fair game. So how are you going to meet him? What's the plan?"

"I meet him every Tuesday and Thursday night and we have long, meaningful conversations," Jessica said, drawing out the words "long" and "meaningful".

Now it was Cath's turn to be confused. "Really?"

"No. I see him every Tuesday and Thursday night for class."

"That's not good enough. He doesn't see *you*. And you can't count viewing a video as meeting someone, otherwise I could say I know Kevin Costner, Mel Gibson and Pierce Brosnan and have long, meaningful conversations with them every night, too."

"There's a chat room that he hosts on Wednesday nights. I could talk to him there."

"Well, it's a start. A pathetic start, but a start nonetheless."

"Don't know why you're always so keen on me hooking up with every man I meet."

"Not every man. I would never want you to get together with that boss of yours, that Fitch guy," Cath said with a shudder. "He gives me the creeps. He's always sneaking looks at you. Checking out your legs when you're not looking."

"He is? How do you know that?"

"Remember last year's Christmas party and how every time we turned around he was there?"

"Yeah, but I thought he was stalking you, not me."

"Me too, at first. But when I left for the bathroom he didn't follow, and when I came back I caught him staring at you from the bar, pretending to talk to some brunette."

"Oh great," Jessica moaned. "That could explain why he's always popping into my office to deliver simple little messages. I thought he was out to get me fired."

"He's out to get you all right, but not fired. I'd watch out for him."

"Great," she sighed again. "Enough about me and my nonexistent love life. Let's hear about Chad the movie mogul."

Now it was Cath's turn to sigh. "What a mess."

"Oh goody," Jessica said with glee. "Another great story from the Cath files of disaster dates."

"You don't have to sound so happy about it," Cath said, only half joking.

"Cath, darling, if it wasn't for all your adventures into dating hell and back, I'd forget all the things I hated about dating and start going out again."

"It wouldn't kill you, you know. Look at me. I survive. I'm barely singed at all. You had better get back out there or you're going to end up with someone like Fitch."

"Nice try. I think we were talking about you, not me. Back to Chad and Malibu. And don't leave out the juicy details—they're my favorite."

For the next hour and a half as they walked along the beach trail and back, Cath regaled Jessica with tales from Malibu, pretty boy Chad, his fabulous body, his tiny mind, and the antics of rich drunken people who think they're somebody but are just as much a nobody as everybody else.

"So, when Chad fell over the balcony into the sand below —"

"Oh my God! Was he hurt?"

"Nah. He did a nice somersault and landed on his back. Knocked the wind out of him, though. Some *Baywatch* wannabe rushed down and began giving him mouth-to-mouth while he was still breathing. Then they started kissing. I was so relieved. That was my excuse to get the hell out of there."

"How did you get home?"

"Now the story gets interesting. I had called a cab and was waiting out front when this guy named Pete came out to leave. He asked me if I needed a ride and I said sure and off we went. Turns out he's a highway patrol officer and rides a motorcycle. He told me wonderful stories of all the weird and wacky things he catches people doing when they should be concentrating on driving. We ended up sitting outside my apartment talking for three hours until two in the morning."

"Talking? Just talking?"

"Amazingly so. Not so much as a playful grope the entire time."

"That has to be the most amazing part of the entire story. So are you going to see him again?"

"As a matter of fact, I am. This Friday we're going to the opening of a new little gallery in Venice. Gives me an excuse to go buy something trendy and/or bizarre at that little thrift shop I love so much."

"Any excuse to shop," agreed Jessica.

They were back at the junction of Ocean Park just as the sun dropped down to kiss the ocean goodbye for the day.

"Don't forget to call me Wednesday night after your chat room date with the professor," said Cath over her shoulder as she headed for her car.

"It's not a date," shouted Jessica after her, but Cath only smiled and waved, pretending she couldn't hear her.

"It's not a date," Jessica said again to herself and started jogging home.

Cath could be pushy when she thought it was in Jessica's best interest. Anytime Jessica showed the slightest interest in a man, Cath started pushing her like it was her last chance at finding love.

But as Jessica jogged on through the streets of Santa Monica in the fading light of day, she realized that she too had looked at her last relationship as her only chance of finding love and happiness. She had been so desperate to make it work she had almost fallen into the trap that so many desperate women do—changing herself into the image of what the guy wanted. When that relationship had failed as well, she had given up on love. She turned to writing about love instead—and even that hadn't produced any results.

Chapter Four

ॐ

The new semester was underway, with assignments and critiques taking up most of Brant's time. But it was the chat room sessions on Wednesdays that were the highlight of Brant's week. It was his one opportunity to "talk" with his students and pick their brains. From the way they expressed themselves, along with their chatty writing styles, Brant could usually guess their age within a year, their ethnic background and even the socio economic group to which they belonged.

Brant recalled with clarity the first chat session of the semester, when one of his students, a J.A. Singer, had taken him to the boards over a poem. After Brant had made what he thought was a very eloquent interpretation of the work, J.A. had made an opening salvo.

"With all due respect, Professor Wilson, I think your analysis is way off-base. Your perspective—white male, middle-aged, affluent American—has obviously tainted your view."

After reading the first set of assignments, Brant had looked up J.A. Singer in the registration file and knew that J.A. stood for Jessica Anne.

Jessica wasn't finished yet.

"It's quite understandable and probably correct to view the work of Nerada from the male perspective, seeing as the author is male, yet his culture, the time period in which the poems were written and his impoverished lifestyle might suggest a different meaning.

"I think Scott," she continued, referencing a fellow student, "might have a valid point on his symbolism, and

47

while Scott is also an American male, I think he hits closer to home in his analysis."

This had started an intense discussion between Professor Wilson and Jessica in which the other students had to fight to get in their opinion. The aforementioned Scott was on the J.A. side of the argument, as were about five other students. Brant had closed the session with a comment about everyone having a right to their own opinion, with no one person's opinion carrying more weight than another's. Several students jumped onboard with the professor, and by the end of the discussion, only Jessica and Scott had held their ground.

At first Jessica's comments had annoyed him. As a rule, his students didn't challenge him. Then as he started paying attention to what she was saying, he had to admit she made some valid points. Jessica's comments were insightful and well thought out, almost as if they had been researched ahead of time, which was possible considering the topic of the discussion was posted on Monday. Most students just showed up and gave their opinions and comments off the tops of their heads.

Jessica was most definitely different. Based on her comments and references, Brant was pretty sure Jessica was older than most of the students in this class. His guess was mid-thirties.

While not seeming to care whether or not she pissed him off in the chat room, Jessica had been extremely interested in his comments on her assignments and insisted he label each piece with a letter grade. Their first dialogue had been via email, in which Jessica had requested a letter grade for her first piece and he had refused, saying this was a pass or fail course only. After being bombarded with an email every day, Brant had finally given in and sent her a letter grade—a C.

"There," he had said to the computer monitor as he hit the SEND key. "Bet this isn't the grade you expected."

After three weeks of engaging in verbal warfare with Jessica during the chat room sessions and arguing over her grades each week, there was a period of silence. For two Wednesday nights in a row Jessica hadn't logged on. To Brant's amazement, he found he was disappointed. He had begun making a habit of being extra-prepared for these sessions, with reference materials at hand and extra research under his belt. So when Jessica didn't show up, there was no one left to challenge his opinions or ask him probing questions. The sessions had seemed boring, with everyone just going along with everything he said. He had even made a couple outrageous comments and not one student took the bait.

"J.A. would have been all over that statement," he had prodded them. "You can't let that slide. Someone out there must have something to say."

The bulletin board had remained empty for almost thirty seconds before Scott came up with a semi-lucid reply. Brant found himself missing the witty comebacks of his chat room opponent.

So a week ago, Brant had given Jessica's class a special assignment—write a short story based on personal experience. Brant would select one story and discuss it in next Wednesday's chat session. The story would be posted Monday morning to give his students a chance to read it before the chat began.

Of course, no matter *what* J.A. wrote, that would be the selected story for the night, Brant decided. A student critique was a surefire way to bring Jessica back into the chat room.

* * * * *

"You're getting boring," Cath complained when they were out to dinner at their favorite Italian restaurant. "All I ever hear is Professor Wilson this and Professor Wilson that and some gibberish about a Lady Anne and her knight.

"I just think he's fascinating," Jessica shrugged. "And as for the gibberish about my novel, it's not gibberish. Besides, you never pay attention to what I say anyway, unless it's about a man."

"Your professor Wilson is the first man I've heard you talk about with any real passion for years."

Jessica sighed. "You call it passion, I call it...I don't know what. He just has a way of getting under my skin, especially during chat room discussions. And then we're always going 'round and 'round about my grades. Everything I do, he gives me a C. I know my work is better than that."

"Why don't you ask for a student-teacher conference? Talk to him face to face," suggested Cath.

"He won't meet with me. It seems the reason he teaches online is so he doesn't have to meet with students. I asked — no, *demanded* that he meet with me to discuss the whole grade thing and he said no — end of story. And anyway, why would I want to meet with him? Haven't you been listening? He makes me so crazy with his writing analysis that I can't type my responses fast enough. Meeting him would be a disaster. I suggested an assignment on writing a fantasy scene and he said it wasn't relevant to his curriculum. Writing from Your Heart? I think he should change the name of his class to Writing What the Teacher Tells You."

"At least you're having an intelligent conversation with a member of the opposite sex."

Jessica closed her eyes and put her face in her hands. The closest thing she had to a steady relationship with a male was Merlin. When she lifted her head up at last, the waiter, a nicely-built young man with long hair pulled into a low ponytail, brought them their antipasto salads and walked away, but not before giving Cath a sexy smile. Cath still had it. Guys of all ages still swarmed around her like mosquitoes to a bug zapper — and most of them got zapped. Jessica felt more like a wilted flower that couldn't even attract the tiniest of bees.

After her divorce and several botched attempts at dating, Jessica found it easier to write about a knight charging out of the forest to rescue her than to venture out onto the cold stone ledge of dating, risking another devastating fall. It wasn't as if she wasn't interested or didn't find men attractive, but like the waiter, men just seemed to look right through her. Now her dream of a home with a husband and children and a sunny window seat for writing her novel looked about as possible as one of her fantasy stories. Why couldn't she be as brave as the characters she invented? Jessica took a deep drink of her Chianti and as she set her glass down, a sigh escaped her lips.

"What's the big sigh about?" Cath asked, reaching over and squeezing Jessica's hand.

"I just didn't think I'd be here at this point in my life."

"What? At Francesco's? I thought you loved this place?" Cath poked, trying to get Jessica to lighten up.

"You know what I mean—a single, childless career woman. It's not what I wanted. It's not what I planned."

Jessica took another long drink of wine and emptied her glass.

"So why not do something about it?"

"Like what?"

"Well for starters, you could look up this professor you're always going on and on about. See if he's as annoying in person as you find him via email."

"Even if I wanted to, which I don't, it would be impossible. Remember, he won't meet with students in person. And besides, if he were destined to become anything more than just my teacher, he would have agreed to meet with me. So there. I tried and fate has stepped in and said no."

"Sometimes fate needs a swift kick in the ass to get it jump-started. Just meet with him once and then you can let fate take it from there. What have you got to lose?" reasoned Cath.

Jessica considered what Cath said. She didn't want to be alone forever, did she? And she did find him attractive, intelligent and sometimes witty, although infuriating. She *would* like to see what he was like in person, if just to prove to Cath that she had done her best to come out of hiding. If nothing came of it, fine. She would be right back where she was now.

"If I did want to find this man," Jessica began, "how would I begin?"

"Now we're talking," Cath said with glee. "Let's finish up here and head over to your place and see what we can learn from his video class."

An hour later they were seated side by side in front of Jessica's computer with Merlin perched on Cath's shoulder, playfully pecking at her dangling earring.

"Take a look at his clothing. What does it tell you?"

"I have no idea," Jessica replied, already bored with Cath's detective game. "I think you watch too many of those profiler-murder cases on TV."

"Look," she said, pointing at his tie. "He's very conservative except for his collection of crazy ties. He must have a sense of humor if he can wear these ties," Cath concluded after reviewing six classes.

"Not that *that* will help us find him, but an interesting observation," said Jessica.

Cath considered it a good sign that Professor Wilson didn't wear a wedding ring or have a shadow of one. Of course, that wasn't infallible proof that he was available—he could be engaged, separated, married but ringless or in a steady relationship—but Cath was encouraged even if Jessica seemed distracted.

Cath and Jessica scrutinized the floor-to-ceiling bookcase positioned behind Professor Wilson's mahogany desk, which held an impressive collection of American literature. Then they spotted two works of erotica by Anais Nin.

"Very revealing," said Cath, lifting her right eyebrow for emphasis. "Maybe we can use this to somehow lure him out."

"How?"

"What if you write something a little erotic? Something that will pique his curiosity about you? Make him want to meet with you in person," Cath said with a wicked smile.

That gave Jessica an idea.

"I could do an erotic fantasy with a fairy princess and a unicorn…"

"Too weird," Cath vetoed. "Stick with something contemporary."

"He'll just give me another C. That, or it will terrify him and he'll burrow in even deeper."

Cath held out her finger to Merlin and transferred him to the desk.

"Just make it super hot. If he doesn't respond, then he's not a red-blooded male and you should just stick with Merlin here," she said as she stroked the feathers on the back of the bird's head.

"I don't know…this seems a little far-fetched to me."

"For once, just go for it, will you?"

* * * * *

When Brant started receiving the student stories, he reviewed each one briefly before printing them out. When Jessica's short story arrived, he printed it out, poured himself a cup of coffee and went out on the deck to read.

"Eating Rice"

By J.A. Singer

The sushi bar was packed with the usual lunch crowd. All the booths lining the walls were full, as were the tables running down the center of the restaurant. It was going to be tough to find a table for three people, so Maddy gave her order to Jane and Cindy so she could scout the place for an opening. Every Wednesday it was the same. They would say they were going to leave work early to avoid the crowd but they somehow always ended up walking through the restaurant door right at noon, along with thirty other people. Today the crowd and lack of a place to sit was more irritating than most Wednesdays. After the morning she'd had, Maddy just wanted to sit and eat in peace. She had almost bowed out of their weekly lunch, feigning a headache, but her friends would have none of that. Jane had dug around in her purse and come up with two aspirins before Maddy could think of another excuse.

"Here," she had said as she handed Maddy the pills. "Hit the drinking fountain on the way out and your headache will be gone before we even get there."

It wasn't a suggestion, it was an order, and the next thing she knew she was taking two aspirins she didn't need before being hustled into the back of Cindy's blue Mustang.

Cindy and Jane were three people away from the front of the line when Maddy spotted a table about to become available. An older gentleman was making all the motions of finishing up at one of the center tables — wiping his hands and face with a napkin, gathering up the trash around him and stacking it on his tray, searching his jacket pockets for his car keys. Yep, this was the table. Maddy saw a group of four eyeing the table as well and moved in closer. She wanted that table and she was going to get it. She casually walked over just as the gentleman slid to the edge of the bench seat to stand up.

"Let me help you with that," she said in her sweetest voice, and took the tray from his shaky hand.

He looked at her, taking in her shoulder-length brown hair and warm honey-brown eyes, and smiled.

"Why thank you, young lady. You have a nice day now," he said as he used his free hands to push himself up from the bench.

In four quick moves, Maddy dumped the contents of the tray into the trash, placed the tray on top of the trash container, tucked her skirt under her and slid into the bench seat, claiming the table for herself and her friends. Her competition had barely taken one step in her direction before Maddy had moved in.

Amateurs, Maddy thought with smug satisfaction. Now that she wasn't going to have to sit on a cement planter outside the restaurant with her meal balanced on her knees, she began to feel a whole lot better. Two minutes later, Cindy and Jane showed up with plates of sushi, California rolls, rice and large red cups filled with Diet Coke.

"Good job on the table," Jane said as she slid in across from Maddy. "I thought we were going to be outside perched on the planter wall."

"I knew Maddy would get us a good table. She has good table-getting karma," added Cindy.

"Not as powerful as your parking-space karma, though," said Maddy. "It's almost uncanny."

This set the direction of the conversation for the remainder of lunch. Somewhere between parking karma and reincarnation, Jane and Cindy lost Maddy. She was off in her own little world, eating rice with a pair of chopsticks and making noises to feign participation. Jane and Cindy were so deep into their conversation they didn't even notice.

Maddy stared straight ahead, looking blindly at the space between Cindy and Jane, which had become empty when three people vacated the table behind them. Without warning, a strikingly handsome young man came into view in the space between her friends. He sat alone at the table directly behind them and was now positioned in front of Maddy. Cautious at first and then a little bolder, Maddy stole glances in between bites of sushi and adding halfhearted comments to the conversation.

Whenever his attention was drawn elsewhere, Maddy examined him like one would examine a fine piece of sculpture. He had thick, dark brown shoulder-length hair with a natural wave that kept it out of his eyes. The color of his eyes were like dark chocolate, yummy and rich, framed with impossibly thick eyelashes. On his baby face grew a stubble of beard that only served to accentuate his delicious lips. His lips were the thing that fascinated Maddy the most. They were full, warm, inviting – slightly parted when not eating – sensuous and moist. Maddy found herself wondering what it would feel like to be kissed by those lips.

Twice she got caught checking out the young man and both times she held his gaze. She stared right into his eyes without flinching. He was always the first to break eye contact. This made Maddy smile in triumph.

He's such a boy, she thought.

Maddy guessed his age to be around twenty-four or -five, which made him at least eight years younger than her. Just as Maddy finished her last California roll, the young man began to eat from his rice bowl. He sprinkled the rice with soy sauce before absently bringing the first forkful to his mouth.

At first Maddy was disappointed that he wasn't going to use chopsticks but that was soon forgotten when she saw how slowly he moved the fork of rice to his mouth. She was riveted. It was as if she had a telephoto lens zoomed in on his mouth and the camera was rolling at half speed.

The fork descended again into the rice bowl and then crept up with several grains of rice stuck to its tines. As the fork made its way from bowl to mouth, his lips parted in anticipation.

What I'd give to be that fork, thought Maddy, as she watched the hard, cold stainless steel slide into his mouth.

The thought sent a shiver down her spine and gave her a most unexpected jolt of pleasure. Next he picked up a piece of sashimi, moist pink salmon nestled on a tablet of white rice. He ate it deliberately, his pink tongue reaching forward to meet the succulent fish. He took two torturous bites before turning the page of his magazine. Then without looking, he found the fork again and dipped it into the bowl of rice.

Each time the fork made the journey to his mouth, Maddy's body would coil up like a spring, her breathing all but stopping as she moistened her lips with a quick flick of her tongue. Maddy was so *completely focused on the fork and mouth that the face and eyes of the young man became a background blur.*

As the fork approached the mouth, the lips snapped into focus, moist and ready to accept the offering. Maddy opened her own mouth just a little, mimicking his actions with hers. His mouth opened and the fork slid in and disappeared, the full, warm lips closing around the metal for just a moment before releasing it from their grasp.

Maddy imagined what it would be like to have those lips wrapped around very specific parts of her body, grasping gently before releasing her. She had to bite her lower lip to stop from moaning aloud, and that's when she saw it – the faintest of smiles dancing around the corners of his mouth.

He knew she was watching him. And now she knew that he knew.

He picked up another piece of sashimi, this time with his fingers, and slid the entire morsel into his mouth ever so slowly.

He waited, what seemed like an eternity to Maddy, before taking another bite of rice. Because he knew he was being watched, Maddy was afraid he would stop altogether. But eventually he picked up his fork and plunged it once more into the bowl.

As the fork rose once again to his waiting lips, Maddy had to remind herself to breathe. When he brought the fork to his mouth, Maddy could feel the dampness gathering between her legs, making her even more aware of how aroused she was becoming. His motions hypnotized her. Every time he wrapped his lips around a morsel of food he was wrapping his lips around her. Maddy felt flushed and tingly all over and was surprised that Jane and Cindy were so oblivious to the erotic electricity in the air.

If he keeps eating like this I'm going to lose it right here at lunch, *Maddy thought.*

The next time the fork found itself surrounded by those delicious lips, it stayed a while longer. He slid the fork in and out of his mouth, caressing and licking it with his delicious tongue. For the second time, Maddy caught the traces of a small smile at the corners of his yummy mouth. There was no more eye contact, just an intimate connection between his mouth and Maddy's eyes.

As if from a long way away, Maddy heard her name being called as Cindy attempted to get her attention.

"Maddy. Are you all right? You haven't said two words all lunchtime."

"What?" asked Maddy, confused about where she was and what she should be doing.

"It must be the headache," reasoned Jane. "I guess the aspirin didn't work."

"Actually," said Maddy, snapping out of her trance, "I feel great. Are we going already?"

Jane and Cindy looked at each other, puzzled.

"We thought you were in a bad mood or the headache was bothering you," said Cindy in amazement. "It's like you were in another world."

"I'm in a great mood. Never felt better." Maddy beamed as she gathered up her trash and slid out from the table. By the time Maddy cleared her tray, Jane and Cindy were already halfway to the exit. As she moved in the direction of the young man, every nerve ending from her head to her toes tingled with excitement.

As Maddy reached the man's table he stretched out his hand and grabbed her by the wrist before she could walk by. The place where their flesh touched exploded with a burning heat. Maddy stopped and looked directly into his eyes. This time he held her gaze with a strong and steady determination. He pulled her closer so he could whisper in her ear. His breath caressed her and made the hairs on her neck stand at attention.

"Let's do dinner. We'll have rice together...again."

Then he placed a napkin in her hand. When Maddy looked at it she saw his phone number written in blue ink. Maddy smiled and closed her hand around the napkin before walking away. She walked out of the restaurant as casually as her shaky legs could carry her.

Brant found he was flushed when he finished reading Jessica's story and the idea of taking a cold shower crossed his mind. He was surprised at how the story had gotten to him.

He couldn't remember the last time a student's story had turned him on. Even if he hadn't already planned on selecting Jessica's story for the chat session, now, after reading it, he decided he would have selected it anyway. This would get his students talking—and Jessica back into the thick of things.

* * * * *

Jessica ate lunch at her desk while checking her email. When she read the notice that the featured short story for the chat session was to be "Eating Rice", Jessica flushed a deep red. Without wasting a moment, she was on the phone to Cath.

"He picked my story! What am I going to do?" she blurted.

Cath didn't miss a beat.

"Perfect. He's taken the bait. Now you've just got to reel him in."

"But I don't want to 'reel him in'. He's going to rip my story apart in front of the whole class. Why did I let you talk me into this?"

"Oh, stop it. Your story is great. It got me hot and horny. I read it to Pete over the phone and he came rushing right over, sirens blasting."

"You need to come over Wednesday night and help me during the chat room session. You got me into this. You owe me."

"I guess I could…"

"You could feed me some great lines," suggested Jessica. "You could be a female Cyrano de Bergerac."

She knew Cath wouldn't be able to resist that.

"I'll come over, but I don't think you need my help. You don't have to say much. Just let everyone else do the talking. That will keep the professor on his toes."

"That suits me just fine," agreed Jessica. "I still don't see how this is going to help. Why don't you come over early and we'll have dinner first?"

"You're not going to try to cook are you?" Cath asked, remembering Jessica's last cooking disaster that she had politely eaten.

"No, your stomach can relax. I'll order takeout and pick it up on the way home," Jessica reassured her.

"Great," said Cath with enthusiasm.

"You could try and mask your happiness and relief a little."

"Why? You suck at cooking. I know it, you know it and anyone who has ever been your dinner guest knows it."

"Gee, thanks."

"You're welcome. See you Wednesday," Cath said before hanging up.

Chapter Five

ഇ

The Wednesday evening chat session was only a couple hours away and Jessica couldn't sit still. While working on her novel in her head, she cleaned the bathroom, rearranged the six items in her fridge and ate three spoonfuls of peanut butter right out of the jar. "Eating Rice" had been chosen as the sacrificial lamb for the evening's discussion and after missing two Wednesdays in a row due to business meetings with clients, Jessica had to admit if only to herself that she had been looking forward to resuming her sparring sessions with her professor. But now that the chat session was going to be centered on *her* story, she was almost afraid to log on.

With the other two chat sessions she had attended, she had made sure she was well prepared. She enjoyed the mental sparring that took place with her professor. The fact that she could say whatever she wanted without being distracted by body language or raised voices made her feel safe. If she allowed herself to think about it—which she rarely did—she *did* want to meet this man. She sensed they were making a connection, but were limited by the electronic medium through which they conversed.

She had already written him into her novel, making him the knight, of course, who would rescue Lady Anne and save the day. He was beginning to show up in her dreams as well, erotic, sexual dreams, from which she awoke hot, wet and restless.

What she wanted more than anything was his approval of her writing. She was dying to show him the novel, but was afraid his criticism would squelch her enthusiasm. She wondered how someone she had never actually met could both inspire and frighten her at the same time.

She found that all she wanted to talk about was his class, his lectures, his eyes, his assignments, the protracted arguments they had shared during chat room sessions. Even though Jessica wasn't ready to acknowledge her feelings to Cath, her friend had picked up on the fact that something was there, something that hadn't been there before. Something worth pursuing.

On the way home from work, Jessica had picked up sushi, rice and two large silver cans of Sapporo Japanese beers in honor of her story. When Cath knocked, Jessica leapt up and ran to the door, tripping over her discarded high heels in the middle of the room. Between gulps of beer and forkfuls of rice, Cath discussed their strategy and reread Jessica's story out loud so they would be prepared for any questions. At ten to seven, they polished off the last of their beers and turned on the computer.

"I think you should stay in the background during the session if you can. Your comments should be short. Make him want to know more. Make him want to talk with you in private later over a cup of coffee, maybe," said Cath, thinking out loud while Jessica signed into the chat room. Three students were already there and as soon as Jessica signed in, she began getting comments.

"Loved your story, J.A. Did this happen?"

"No comment," Jessica replied.

"Nice imagery with the food. Had to take a cold shower."

"Obviously from one of the male students," snickered Cath.

"Did you write this? It sounds familiar," wrote a Margie Strous.

"Jealous?" asked Cath, talking to the monitor.

Professor Wilson signed in at seven and got the session going with a little commentary on the work. "I chose this story for tonight's discussion for a number of reasons. It had good descriptive passages that gave you a clear picture of what was going on in the mind of the protagonist, the plot or story line in this little tale kept you interested, and it stood out from the rest by venturing into the rich world of erotic literature, if somewhat tentatively. Let's open the chat room discussion with a few words from the author, J.A."

Jessica wasn't ready to review her own work and turned to Cath in a panic. "What should I say?"

"Divert the question. Say something like, 'Thanks for choosing my story for tonight's discussion, but I'm more interested in hearing what my peers have to say about it'."

Jessica typed in Cath's response and hit SEND. The screen erupted with a flurry of activity—questions and comments flying back and forth. Professor Wilson didn't get a word in all night. Jessica tried a couple of times to redirect questions to the professor but inevitably a fellow student would fire off an answer faster. The session went on longer than normal and by eight-thirty, Jessica felt drained.

"That was a waste," she sighed as the session ended.

"No it wasn't," said Cath with a smile. "It went exactly as planned."

"It did?"

"Yes. Answer me this. How do you feel right now?"

"Tired, frustrated, drained," said Jessica.

"Perfect! And I bet our little professor is feeling frustrated, too. I'm sure he's dying to talk to you in person since he couldn't talk online. Send him a separate email, expressing your frustration at the way the chat session went, and see if he suggests you meet to discuss your work further. I bet this will work," said Cath with confidence.

Jessica clicked on the email icon and began composing a short note to the professor.

Dear Professor Wilson,

While I was pleased that you chose my short story for the session tonight, I was a little disappointed that there wasn't enough time to get your insights and comments on my work. The comments of my peers are nice, but it's your feedback that I find most valuable...

"That last part is good—stroke his ego a little. Very nice," commented Cath, as Jessica read the email out loud.

"Should I sign it J.A. or Jessica?"

"I think it's time to drop the J.A. I don't understand why you used it in the first place," Cath said before taking another mouthful of rice from the takeout container.

Jessica typed in, *Sincerely, Jessica Anne* and hit SEND.

They both just stared at the computer monitor, waiting for a reply. After nothing happened for five minutes, they began clearing away the remains of their takeout mess.

"I guess we were a little optimistic to think he'd be online right now and would answer you right away," said Cath a nanosecond before the computer pinged to let Jessica know she had mail.

Both women flew back into the living room, stumbling over each other. Jessica grabbed the mouse and clicked on the new email.

I would be happy to discuss your work in more detail. Would you like to set up a private chat?

Professor Wilson

"A private chat?" moaned Cath. "That's just lame. Email him back. Say, 'How about a chat in person over coffee?'"

"I can't say that. It's too forward for me."

Cath looked at her hard and pointed at the keyboard. "Type."

Jessica sent out the next message already knowing what the answer would be.

Ping.

He replied instantly. Jessica opened the new email.

I'm sorry, Jessica. That would be impossible. Let me know if you are still interested in an online *chat and I will set it up.*
Professor Wilson

"Damn," said Cath. "I thought we had him. He's not going to cooperate, is he?"

"I tried to tell you," said Jessica, her voice relieved. "So that's it then."

"You'd sure make a lousy detective—giving up after our first attempt. We've just started. This just means we've got to be more devious, that's all."

"How devious?" asked Jessica, wondering what her friend had in mind now.

"Just devious enough."

* * * * *

It was Thursday morning at nine and Jessica sat at her desk surrounded by familiar yellow Post-its. A bright pink square stood out in the sea of yellow with the words, "Call the college!" written in Cath's clear, neat handwriting.

The plan was a clever one, or at least they had thought so after those Sapporos. First they had found a P.O. Box address listed on the UCLA website for contacting Professor Wilson, which seemed too easy. So the question was how to get a physical address so they could find out where he lived. As Jessica lifted the receiver off the phone, doubt flooded her like a swift cold current and she almost put the phone back in its cradle.

What am I doing? How could I have let Cath talk me into doing this?

Just then Simon wrapped three times on her door and let himself in.

"Busy?" he asked, walking toward her, seeing she was on the phone and ignoring it.

Today, Simon looked a little spiffier than usual—navy blue suit, pale blue button-down shirt and maroon tie.

Jessica put down the phone. "Not anymore," she said with a forced smile. "Was there something you needed?"

"Just wanted to chat," he said, making himself comfortable in the only chair not piled high with paperwork.

"Chat?" Jessica repeated, half question, half statement. "What would you like to chat about?"

"Oh, I don't know. Why don't you start," he smiled and just sat there.

"All right," she said. "Nice weather we're having."

"That's the best you can come up with? 'Nice weather'? How about, 'How are you, Simon? What have you been up to lately?'"

Jessica stared right at him and repeated without expression, "How are you, Simon? What have you been up to lately?"

"So glad you asked," Simon said, ignoring Jessica's monotone. "I just got tickets to the *Lion King* and I'm taking my top employees to see it. And you, Jessica, are one of my top employees."

Here we go, she thought.

This was the second time Simon had invited her to some event. The first had been a Dodgers game with clients, only the clients hadn't shown up, leaving Jessica stuck with Simon for nine long, boring innings. Well, she wasn't going to fall for that one again. She pulled her day planner out from under a stack of papers and opened the book before looking up.

"When's the show?" she asked without showing any emotion.

"December 15th," Simon said with satisfaction.

Jessica flipped to December and looked at the empty square and then at Simon.

"Sorry. I'll be out of town that weekend. Maybe another time," she said, before snapping the book shut.

Simon rose to his feet.

"That's too bad. The *Lion King* tickets were in lieu of your Christmas bonus, you know."

Jessica shrugged. "Guess I'll just have to buy the CD."

Simon gave her a grimace of a smile and then left.

Jessica didn't believe for a moment that the tickets were her Christmas bonus, especially after what Cath had told her. Now she was thinking that Simon's odd behavior was some form of courting ritual and that the tickets were a thinly disguised request for a date. Jessica buried her face in her hands.

Is this what I'm destined for? Why are the wrong men always the ones who're interested? I've got to turn my life around before it's too late.

When she raised her head the pink Post-it seemed to glow in reply—"Call the College!"—and she reached for the phone with new determination. Cath's comment about giving fate a swift kick ran through her head as the line rang. Sick of sitting back and waiting for her new life to begin, Jessica was ready to take a chance and go for it. The phone line connected and a young female voice answered.

"UCLA Extension Information, Carrie speaking."

Jessica took a quick breath and began. "Hello. This is Mable Tetters with Federal Express. We have a delivery for a Professor Wilson but were only given a post office box number. We can't deliver to a P.O. Box. I'm calling for a street address. Can you help me?"

"I'm sorry. I can't give out a teacher's home address. Maybe you could deliver the package to the college address," Carrie suggested.

"I'm afraid that would be impractical. We're delivering a mattress. I'm pretty sure Professor Wilson would prefer to have that delivered to his home," lied Jessica. "Do you have a home address for him?"

Jessica held the phone so tight her fingers began to go numb.

"I see your point," said the voice slowly as she thought of what to do. "Let me get my supervisor. I'm just a student worker and don't have access to that information."

A few seconds later, an older female voice came on the line.

"This is Mrs. Vanderpole. Can I help you?"

Jessica told her lie again but Mrs. Vanderpole had a ready reply.

"That shouldn't be a problem, Professor Wilson's post office box is at a Mail Boxes Etc. store and they accept FedEx there. I'm sure with a mattress, they will contact him to have someone run over and pick it up," Mrs. Vanderpole explained.

"I see. Thank you. You've been most helpful," Jessica said, trying to keep the disappointment out of her voice. After hanging up, she immediately picked up the phone and called Cath.

"No luck. He picks up his mail at a Mail Boxes Etc."

"Okay…"

Jessica could almost hear the gears working in Cath's brain.

"On to plan C," Cath announced.

"What's plan C?"

"You'll see," Cath purred innocently.

"I don't like the sound of this."

* * * * *

Two days later, they were parked in the public launch parking lot next to Mindanao Way and Basin G in Marina Del Rey with coffee, donuts and binoculars.

"Why did you bring donuts? Neither one of us has had a donut in years," asked Jessica.

"All the detectives and cops in the movies have coffee and food on stakeouts, and donuts just seemed right," she said before taking a bite of a glazed donut. "It's sinfully delicious. Try one."

Jessica peered over the pink lid into the donut box as if a snake might pop its head out and bite her.

"Explain to me again how you got his address."

"I told you about Pete, right? The CHP officer? I just asked him for a little favor—track down and find your professor Wilson. It's not like he's in hiding like criminal types so I figured it would be pretty easy. Just punch his name into a computer and there he'd be. Turns out it wasn't that easy. His license expired about four years ago and he hasn't renewed it, same thing with his car registration—nothing current. He used to live in Westwood but Pete had to call in some help to find his current address. Not having a driver's license could be a red flag you know. That's what Pete said."

"Nothing like invading the guy's privacy. Couldn't Pete get in trouble for doing this 'little favor' for you?"

"I guess. But you know how guys are. Until they marry you, they'll do almost anything to impress you," Cath said happily.

Jessica braved the pink box and selected a cinnamon twist donut before staring out the windshield across the parking lot.

Apparently Professor Wilson lived on a boat, at slip 618 to be exact, within the Santa Monica Yacht Club. Locked gates between the boat docks and the packed parking lot made it impossible to just stroll up and down the docks to find his slip. So the two amateur sleuths sat in Cath's '65 dark green Mustang parked four rows back from the dock gates, waiting and watching, deciding their next move. It was ten o'clock on Saturday morning and there was a bustle of activity around the docks—a grocery delivery service, groups of people meeting friends for a day cruise, boat repair men, even a guy in a wheelchair—all coming and going in and around the yacht club docks and riding along the bike path that cut through a shipyard and went around the parking lot.

"If you're done chowing down donuts, let's get a closer look at the area," said Jessica, as she watched seagulls circle then land on an open garbage can in the middle of the parking lot. "There's a park at the end of Mindanao Way. Let's at least enjoy this beautiful day."

So Cath and Jessica walked across the parking lot and down the street to Burton W. Chace Park. Asphalt paths weaved around areas of grass with picnic tables shaded by plenty of older trees. A light onshore breeze made their hair dance around their faces and surrounded them with the smell of saltwater and seaweed. When they reached the end of the park they had a great view of the main channel and the entire marina. When they walked back along the north side of the park they tried to figure out which slip was 618.

"We can't hang out here all day," said Jessica. "He could be gone for the weekend or out for the day. What are our chances of just happening to catch him as he's coming or going?"

Cath just shrugged. She was too busy checking out a handsome young man in a pair of swim trunks and no shirt washing down one of the boats with a hose.

"Let's go. This is ridiculous. Why did I ever let you talk me into this?"

* * * * *

The following Saturday, Jessica sat alone in her white SUV, cursing her best friend Cath as she sat waiting for Federal Express outside the Mail Boxes Etc. store. Cath had bailed out at the last minute, leaving Jessica to stakeout Brant's mailbox alone. As it got closer to ten, Jessica started to get nervous and couldn't stand sitting any longer.

She left the car and went inside the store right before the rumbling sound of the Federal Express truck signaled its arrival. Jessica pretended to be looking through a rack of greeting cards when the driver came in with the package. Cath had had the brilliant idea to send the professor a package and then wait at the store to run into him when he showed up.

Jessica had her doubts. If he wasn't expecting a package, why would he just show up?

But Cath had called the store two days ago, telling them she had sent an overnight package and wanted to know how the professor would know it had arrived. The very helpful store owner had explained that they called their customers when important overnight packages arrived, since not everyone picks up their mail every day. And so the plan was set in motion. Cath had found a funky tie at a comic book store with an illustration of Superman on a sky blue background. Cath had even wrapped it up so all Jessica had to do was send it out.

While Jessica looked at the cards a petite brunette with bright blonde streaks came into the store and was greeted by the clerk.

"Hey Frannie, Professor Wilson just got a package. Are you picking up his mail today or should I hold it for him later?" asked the clerk.

At the sound of Professor Wilson's name, Jessica's attention shifted to the woman called Frannie.

"Sure, I can take it. Might as well give me all his mail," she said as she moved to unlock her box and pull out her own mail.

Jessica went outside and got back into her truck and waited for Frannie to leave, wondering how this was going to turn out now.

Frannie was on a bicycle, which would have made it difficult to follow her had it not been for the fact that Jessica already knew where she was going. She drove out the driveway of the Marina Waterside shopping center and could see Frannie just getting on her bike. Driving down Admiralty Way, she caught the light and turned left. Parking on the street, she ran down to the walkway that snaked alongside the rows and rows of docks, getting there just before Frannie's bike came into view.

Using a key to get through the gate, Frannie walked her bike down the long gradual ramp to the docks, turned left and made her way to a boat, a huge wooden sailboat with a tall mast. She removed her helmet and left her bike next to the sailboat, walking down three more slips to a funky old blue and white houseboat.

Jessica stood out of sight, watching the door to the houseboat, anticipating Professor Wilson's arrival. She imagined him as he would look in casual clothing, his muscular arms barely covered in a thin white T-shirt and his fine legs hidden in a pair of stonewashed jeans. She pictured him tan and athletic, the perfect captain of his vessel, such as it was, wearing the traditional leather deck shoes or maybe even barefoot. Her body began to warm to the idea of meeting him in person. Thoughts of evenings strolling along the beach hand in hand watching the sunset came unbidden to her mind. Then the scene changed and it was Sir William carrying Lady Anne away from the treacherous LeStrand to the safety of his castle.

The sound of a clanging ship's bell brought Jessica back to the real world. Frannie had pulled a cord tied to a light post on the dock and was talking to someone on the boat, out of Jessica's line of vision. As she shifted her position, a flash of white drew her attention as the professor came into view.

Jessica was stunned.

This changes everything, she thought as she stood there staring.

Eventually she turned around and walked slowly back to her truck, all her musings of a few minutes ago coming back to haunt her. Sitting in her truck, staring out at the marina and all the boats gently bobbing up and down, Jessica wondered how she had let herself fall into the same old trap of basing all her hopes on fantasies. She fumbled in her purse for her cell phone and hit the speed dial button for Cath.

She just couldn't believe it. Professor Wilson, her very own knight in shining armor — the man who was going to sweep her off her feet, take long romantic walks along the beach and inspire her to write the next best-selling novel — was in a wheelchair.

Chapter Six

℘

While waiting for Cath to pick up the phone, Jessica's mind was trying to make sense of what she saw and felt. She kept trying to match the man in the wheelchair with the man behind the desk teaching Writing from Your Heart. After what felt like eons, Cath picked up the phone.

"Cath, I'm at the marina and I've just seen Professor Wilson. You're not going to believe this, but Professor Wilson is in a wheelchair," she blurted out.

"He's in a what?" asked Cath. "You're breaking up."

"A wheelchair. The professor is in a wheelchair."

Cath didn't say a thing at first, leaving Jessica to wonder if she had lost the connection.

"Cath? Are you still there?"

She heard a heavy sigh.

"Well, that explains it, doesn't it," said Cath.

"Explains what?"

"Everything. Why he teaches virtually, why he never meets with students, why he's such a recluse. It explains it all," said Cath, with a hint of sadness in her voice.

"Maybe he has a broken leg or something," said Jessica, grasping at straws, not wanting to believe that the man she had cast in the leading role of her life was in a wheelchair.

"Was he wearing a cast?"

"No. Nothing like that."

"So much for finding the perfect man," sighed Cath.

"I guess so," said Jessica, somehow feeling that she was letting this man down.

Jessica clicked off her cell phone and stared out the window. Professor Wilson is in a wheelchair. How can this be? What kind of knight would be in a wheelchair?

Like most women, Jessica had wondered what the professor's fatal flaw would be. Would he be an arrogant know-it-all? Would he be tongue-tied in person—only able to express himself in front of the camera? Would he have a temper or a cruel streak, be a lousy lover? All of these thoughts had entered her mind, but never once the possibility that he'd be damaged goods, a cripple.

A cripple. What a horrible word. Jessica was sure that there was a politically correct word or phrase that would be more appropriate, and she desperately wanted to use that word, but "cripple" kept flashing in her mind like a grotesque neon sign in Las Vegas.

"This is ridiculous," she said out loud. Looking into her rear-view mirror, she gave herself a good talking-to. "Good God. You're acting like you've just lost your best friend. What is your problem? You don't even know this man. It's not as if he's dead, just in a wheelchair. He can still be your teacher and help you with your novel. Isn't that the real reason you're trying so hard to meet him?"

An older man walking a dog across the parking lot cut a wide berth around the crazy woman in the truck having an argument with herself in the mirror. Jessica caught him staring cautiously at her as he walked past.

Yes, I'm a lunatic, she thought.

Only crazy people make up imaginary stories about how life will be with people they have never even met, and then get disappointed when things don't turn out the way they've planned. Jessica put the keys in the ignition, started her truck and drove home, trying to reconcile the real Brant Wilson with the one she had made up.

* * * * *

Right after her visit to the marina, things got crazy at work. Jessica made a concerted effort to control the chaos by staying late every night for two straight weeks. Unfortunately, this kept her away from her computer and her writing class as well. By the time she got home she was so exhausted that all she did was slip into bed each night. The computer sat sulking in the living room, feeling as neglected as Merlin. She hadn't written one creative word in weeks and poor Lady Anne was stranded in the woods with a knight in a shining wheelchair.

But even excessive work couldn't dissipate the blue funk Jessica found herself in. Simon was driving her crazy by popping into her office unannounced for various ridiculous reasons that he seemed to make up as he went along. The holidays were creeping up on her like they always did, making her feel inadequate for not having her gifts purchased, her plans made, her cards picked out or her house decorated. On Thursday, Jessica had taken dinner to her Dad and brother only to find Matt playing cards with three of his veteran buddies, one of which was in a wheelchair. Even when Matt introduced her to Shay, Jessica could only smile and nod before using the excuse of getting the guys more beer as a means of escaping the room. Jessica had a dozen questions she wanted to ask Shay but just couldn't bring herself to say a single word.

For two weeks Cath tried to make contact with Jessica. She'd left countless messages and emails and Jessica hadn't offered a single response. Cath wanted to talk about their annual Orphans' Orgy for Thanksgiving, when all their friends who didn't have family nearby gathered to celebrate the holiday together. Cath thought they should get the ball rolling and asked Jessica to call the usual suspects to set up their planning lunch. Even this minor responsibility felt like a heavy weight pulling her down.

On Friday evening of the second week, Jessica heard a knock on her door. Already dressed in her pajamas at six,

Jessica cautiously looked through the peephole to find her best friend standing on the porch. She opened the door and before she could say a single word, Cath pushed past her into the small apartment.

"What's going on?" asked Jessica, concerned with Cath's behavior.

"That's what I'm here to find out," Cath said, plopping down on one of Jessica's overstuffed chairs. "Sit," she commanded.

Jessica was so shocked that she did as she was told.

"Now talk," said Cath, leaving no room for arguments.

"What should I talk about?" stalled Jessica, knowing darn well what Cath wanted to know.

"How about, for starters, why you haven't returned any of my phone calls or emails?"

Jessica tried to get away with a simple answer. "I've been busy."

"Bullshit. You've never been that busy before. I want to know what's going on. You look awful. Is that Fitch guy giving you a hard time again? If he is, I'll go right on over to his swank little office and give him a piece of my mind."

"It's not Fitch. He's the same jerk he's always been," Jessica said, grabbing a pillow off the floor and pulling it to her belly for comfort.

"If not Fitch, then what? The holidays? What?"

"It's everything. Fitch. The holidays. Professor Wilson."

"What about Professor Wilson? He's in a wheelchair. End of story."

"This is why I didn't want to talk about it. I knew you wouldn't understand," Jessica sighed.

"Try me," Cath prompted.

"The man inspired me. I've never written so much and so well since I enrolled in his class. My novel, the one you're not the least bit interested in, is practically writing itself. Or it was. Now I'm blocked. I used to look forward to Tuesday and Thursday classes—listening to his voice, watching his face as he presented the material. I lived for his comments on my articles, poems and short stories. He seemed to care. Our email arguments were the most stimulating conversations I've had in years. We connected somehow, even through email. I know it sounds odd, but I miss him. I feel like I've lost my best friend."

"So what does that make me?" asked Cath, trying to break Jessica's mood. "I thought I was your best friend?"

"Of course you are."

"Then you should have called me. You know I would listen to you no matter how insane you sound."

Cath got up and went over to Jessica's chair, leaning down to give her a big hug.

"So you've quit your writing class, then?" asked Cath, as she walked into Jessica's kitchen to look for some wine and glasses.

"I haven't quit. I've just been so busy at work that I've missed two weeks. I doubt that he's even noticed," Jessica said with pity in her voice, which elicited an "oh brother" from Cath in the kitchen. "There are only two classes left anyway, so what's the point? I guess I can retake the class next semester."

"Here's what we're going to do," said Cath as she brought two very large goblets of red wine back into the living room and handed one to Jessica. "First, take a huge drink of this. Second, we're going to turn on your computer and see if you have any messages besides mine. And third, you are taking a shower, getting dressed and we are going out."

"Number three sounds more like a three, four and five to me," said Jessica, already feeling a little better now that Cath was taking charge.

"Drink, smartass. Now give me your hand," Cath insisted, and pulled Jessica to her feet. "Turn on your computer and let's see if Professor Wilson has 'even noticed' your absence."

At the thought of Professor Wilson, Jessica's heart began to beat faster. She hadn't looked at his image on the computer since she discovered he was in a wheelchair. She was afraid he wouldn't look the same or sound the same or that she wouldn't have the same physical reaction to his voice. As if in a trance, Jessica clicked on the prompts that would take her to her email. Within seconds her screen was populated with over seventy-five messages. Cath stood looking over her shoulder.

"You can skip the fifteen messages from me. They all say basically the same thing—'Where are you?'. There," she said, pointing to a message halfway down the screen. "And there," she said again, pointing to another message.

There were at least five messages from Professor Wilson.

"So open one of them," prompted Cath.

Jessica sat frozen in front of the screen. She just might have sat there all night staring at the monitor if Cath hadn't intervened. Reaching over Jessica's shoulder, she placed her hand over Jessica's on the mouse, moved the cursor to the first message and clicked. Up popped a note from Professor Wilson.

Dear Ms. Singer,

I have noticed that you haven't turned in two of your assignments and haven't been attending the Wednesday night chat sessions. Is everything all right?

Professor Wilson

"There, you see? He did notice. Feel better now?" asked Cath, giving her girlfriend a squeeze around the shoulders. "Let's see what else he has to say."

Cath moved again to click the mouse but this time Jessica beat her to it.

Dear Ms. Singer,

I am concerned about your lack of "attendance" and your missing assignments. If you're planning on dropping the class, please let me know. If there are extenuating circumstances we should talk about, just send me an email and maybe we can work something out.

Professor Wilson

As Jessica read all the messages, a smile began to spread across her face.

"Sounds like he misses you," said Cath. "Guess you better start showing up at class again."

"Guess so."

"Now for steps number three, four and five. Go take a shower and get dressed so we can go out. I'll try and straighten up this mess you call an apartment while I'm waiting. Now go."

Jessica got up and gave Cath a big hug and a sheepish grin.

"Thanks. I needed this."

"Yeah. I know. Now get going. I don't want to be stuck here all night."

* * * * *

An hour later, Cath and Jessica were pulling into the parking lot of a trendy hot spot in Malibu.

"Why this place?" complained Jessica, looking at the line for valet parking and another line to get in.

"Because I know someone here who can get us in and you need to get out of your dreary mood. You remember Pete? Well, he knows the bouncer here. He helped him out of a tough spot once. I meet Pete here a lot."

"Why don't I know these things?" asked Jessica, feeling like she had walked into the middle of a movie.

"You would, if you opened your email every once in a while."

When they pulled to the front of the valet line, a kid who didn't look old enough to drive opened the door for Cath.

"Nice wheels," he said, first admiring the Mustang and then Cath.

"Thanks. Make sure you park her in a good spot. She's my baby," Cath purred.

Jessica just shook her head and headed toward the rear of the line.

"Hey. Where are you going? We don't need to get in line," she said, waving Pete's CHP business card in the air.

With that, both women walked to the front of the line, where Cath showed the bouncer Pete's card and they were let in, much to the distain of the thirty people waiting. When the red padded leather doors opened, the women were hit with a blast of music and warm air. The interior was dark, the music was loud and the place was packed with all the beautiful people. Jessica felt out of place and alone.

Why do I let her talk me into these things?

Jessica squeezed past guy after guy who had no problem blatantly checking her out. At the bar, Cath stood on tiptoes and leaned in to ask the bartender a question. He pointed to a far corner of the room and Cath grabbed Jessica's hand and dragged her deeper into the lion's den.

When they got to the back area, there was a doorway that led into another room that was a little more insulated from the music. Two pool tables filled most of this area, with only a handful of pool players gathered at each table holding pool cues and nursing their drinks. Other people sat around on high barstools, watching the games and checking out the players as they bent over to make their shots. Cath spotted

Pete at one of the corner tables and waved. Jessica watched as Pete's face lit up like a Christmas tree.

Poor guy. He likes her. Hope he's used to getting zapped.

Cath introduced Jessica to Pete, who asked what they wanted from the bar and then disappeared back through the crowd to fetch their drinks. Jessica turned around and surveyed the room. There were lots of guys in their mid-twenties and early thirties, most of them checking out all the young, thin, underdressed twenty-two-year-olds. Not one person looked her way. If this was supposed to make her feel better, it was failing.

Just then Pete returned with her drink—Malibu Rum and pineapple juice. She downed it like it was fruit punch. On top of the wine she'd had earlier, she figured she would have a nice little buzz in about thirty seconds.

Jessica, Cath and Pete played a couple games of pool before Pete suggested they have a late dinner at a quiet little restaurant up the coast. The next thing Jessica knew, she was driving Cath's Mustang, following behind Pete's Saab and cruising along Pacific Coast Highway, wondering once again why she had come. Thoughts of Brant crept back into her mind and she found herself smiling as she remembered his email messages.

So he had noticed.

She felt a rush of pleasure that made her sigh. She decided then and there that she was going back to class. Maybe she could still salvage a passing grade. As soon as they got to Duke's, a Hawaiian restaurant right on the beach, Jessica told Cath she wanted to leave. Cath protested until she saw the stubborn look in Jessica's eyes and gave in. The maître d' called a cab and thirty minutes later she was back in front of her computer, ready to confront the image of her professor with the new knowledge of who he really was.

When the video started, Jessica almost jumped. There he was—just as handsome as ever. His voice still resonated deep in her soul and her heart still skipped a beat when he made one of his corny jokes. She sat there and listened and watched as he went through his lesson plan, gliding in and out of the picture on a wheeled office chair to retrieve some book. He laughed as he read something funny, smiling into the lens of the camera as if he could see right through the monitor into her eyes. For the first time since she had seen him at the marina, Jessica forgot that her professor was in a wheelchair.

When the lesson was over, she sat and stared at the blank screen. Then clicking on her search engine, she entered "paraplegic" and hit ENTER. Up came thousands of sites on paralysis—some sites medical in nature, some personal. She started reading and at ten o'clock Saturday morning, she awoke with a start to the sound of Merlin squawking. She had read as much information as her brain could absorb before falling asleep at her desk.

With a major kink in her right shoulder from sleeping slumped over, Jessica headed for the shower to wake up. With her shower done, she pulled on her running shoes, a pair of shorts and an old UCLA hooded sweatshirt, grabbed her purse and keys and headed for Marina Del Rey for the third time.

Chapter Seven

ജ

Once again, Jessica found herself lurking around slip 618, leaning against the metal railing and staring down at the blue-green water, wondering what kind of lunatic she was becoming. A seagull screamed overhead, white wings extended as it soared on the ocean breeze over the tall masts of several sailboats. This time she was there of her own choosing, not from Cath's pressuring. She tried calling Cath at home, but only got her machine.

"I know you're not going to believe this, but I'm hanging out around the yacht club waiting for Professor Wilson to make an appearance. Call me when you get this message. I need a shot of courage."

As she left her message she noticed a white balloon floating past her in the water. Another balloon floated by a second later. Looking closer, she discovered they weren't balloons but jellyfish—translucent white inverted bowls with long tentacles floating like clouds on the rising tide. Jessica watched, entranced by their soft forms and the way they moved without effort past the boats in their moorings.

Movement down at the far end of the dock jolted Jessica out of her trance. She watched Professor Wilson come wheeling up the long incline of the dock ramp to the gate. He leaned forward at the waist to grasp the metal gate handle and pushed it open with a powerful shove. Then he wheeled himself through the opening and headed off down the walkway.

Jessica walked toward him, watching as he weaved his way around obstacles until he came to the bike path. He put some muscle into his strokes and was off before Jessica could approach him. Jessica was amazed at how fast he pulled away from her and had to start jogging to keep him in sight. As the bike path snaked its way through a shipyard, she lost sight of him several times. She kept going, hoping he would still be on the path when she rounded the next corner. Just as she came around a sweeping curve, Jessica glimpsed the professor making his way off the bike path and heading across the street into the parking lot of the Marina Waterside shopping mall, where the Mail Boxes Etc. store was located.

Jessica slowed her jog to a walk so she wouldn't be out of breath when she caught up to him. The professor had slowed his pace as well as he weaved in and out of parked cars. By the time Jessica made her way across the parking lot, Professor Wilson was coming out of the Mail Boxes Etc. store with letters wedged between his legs. He turned left on the sidewalk and rolled three doors down to a coffee house called Jane's Addition.

As Jessica reached out her hand to open the glass door of the coffee shop, her mind went into overdrive, questioning why her body had brought her to this place. The next thing she knew, she found herself standing in line behind Professor Wilson.

For the first time, Jessica was up close with the real Brant Wilson, not the two-dimensional video image. His hair was a deeper, richer brown than what appeared on the monitor and his shoulders were broad and strong.

Since she still couldn't think of what to say, she turned her attention to the menu board on the wall in front of her. Some part of her brain heard Professor Wilson say thank you for his large mocha latté and make a small joke. The young female barista laughed brightly as she leaned over the counter to hand him his coffee. She called him by his first name and smiled warmly.

Jessica was still in a daze when she stepped into the spot vacated by the professor and his chair.

The young woman cleared her throat after a few seconds and asked, "Can I help you?"

Jessica continued to stare at the board. She shook her head and asked, "What *am I* doing here?"

"I hope you're here to order coffee," replied the girl with jet-black hair, a nose ring and a purple ruffled blouse.

Jessica was jarred to attention. "What?"

"You asked, 'What am I doing here?' I'm hoping you want to order something."

"Oh, yes. A chai tea latté, medium please." *Snap out of it, Jessica.*

After paying for her tea, Jessica looked around the small living room-type setting for the first time. Overstuffed chairs and antique floor lamps with beaded shades were sprinkled around to form small gathering spaces. A large green corduroy sofa with huge orange throw pillows sat against the far wall, over which hung a batik print of a pair of green and peach lovebirds.

A young couple shared an intense conversation in earnest whispers in the corner farthest from the front window. Professor Wilson had moved his chair over to an open spot near the lace-curtained picture window that looked back across the street toward the bike path and the ocean.

Jessica grabbed a copy of *LA Weekly* from the wooden coffee table in front of the sofa, and made her way to a chartreuse velvet chair. Opening the newspaper and pretending to read gave her something to do while she planned her next move. Every few minutes she took a sip of her tea and glanced around the room, letting her gaze rest just for a second on her professor, a mere six feet away from her.

He was even better looking in person. Thick brown hair cut right at the edge of his collar, warm brown eyes, a delectable mouth, a healthy tan and strong muscular arms all melded together to create one fine-looking man. His legs sat motionless with feet resting on two metal platforms at the front of the chair. And then there was the chair itself—a black canvas seat balanced over two huge black wheels that were tilted in at the top, with metal framework and padded armrests, also in black. It was an SUV of a wheelchair, not like the one used by her brother's friend, Shay.

Brant was also reading the paper and had it spread open across his lap. He held his coffee in his left hand, sipping occasionally, and turned the pages with his right.

Now what? Just be casual and say hi. And don't stare at the chair.

She just wanted to act normal, whatever *that* meant in this situation.

Hiding behind her newspaper, Jessica took several deep breaths.

Just stand up, you big coward, and go say 'hi'. It's not that difficult.

With tea in hand, she bolted upright and took her first step before looking where she was going. Professor Wilson was wheeling his way past Jessica when she ran into the side of his chair. Hot tea flew into the air and Jessica cried out as her shin slammed into the side of the wheel—and she fell face first across the professor's lap. The young couple in the corner turned to see what had happened and the professor let out a surprised gasp.

For one long interminable moment Jessica didn't move—whether out of shock or pure mortification, she wasn't sure. Her shin throbbing with pain was nothing compared to the fire of embarrassment that was rushing up her throat and across her face. Then she felt his warm hand on her arm and heard his voice next to her ear, his hot breath making the short hairs around her face dance.

"Are you all right?"

As Jessica regained her composure she pushed herself back to an upright position.

"I'm fine," she said, trying not to put her full weight on her right leg and wincing in the process. "I am sooooo sorry," she continued. "Are *you* all right?"

"Didn't feel a thing," smiled Brant as he wiped a drop of tea from his forehead.

Jessica tried to smile back, acknowledging his little joke until she noticed his previously white T-shirt.

"Oh, my God. Look what I've done! You have tea all over you. Let me get some paper towels or something."

Jessica limped over to the counter and retrieved a handful of napkins.

Brant moved alongside her. "I think you should sit down so we can take a look at your shin before we worry about a little tea," suggested Brant, as he looked at the bloody gash on Jessica's right leg.

"My shin?" asked Jessica, stretching out her leg to see a line of red blood running down onto her white jogging shoes. "Oh dear."

Jessica looked back up and caught the girl behind the counter trying not to laugh.

"Hey, Nicole. Would you wet me a couple of napkins? And how about some bandages? We seem to have an injury here."

"Sure thing," she said as she left to find what Brant needed.

"I can't believe this." Jessica limped over to the sofa and sat down.

Brant wheeled over and moved the coffee table to the side so he could maneuver in front of Jessica.

"Why don't you put your leg up on the table so I can have a better look?"

Moving her leg with care, Jessica lifted her leg and set it on the table.

"How bad is it?" she asked, hoping it wasn't as bad as it felt, but not daring to look.

"I think you'll live. Take a look."

"I'd prefer not to. I'm not very good with blood, especially my own. This is awfully nice of you, considering I ran into you."

Brant was so close she could hear his breathing as he bent over at the waist, examining her bloody shin. She took the opportunity to study him at close range. He was wearing a white T-shirt that hugged his arms and chest in all the right places. His neck and cheeks were smooth and tan, with no stubble. His hair fell down over his forehead, blocking her view of his eyes. The hair on his arms was sun bleached to a golden brown and his tanned skin was pulled taut over well-defined muscles. Sunlight from the window revealed golden highlights in his hair and she had to resist the urge to reach out and run her fingers through his thick locks. As soon as he sat up she turned her face to the window, pretending to be interested in a mother pushing a baby stroller.

Nicole brought a stack of wet napkins and a first-aid kit over to the table. "Here you go, Dr. Brant," she said with obvious amusement, before heading back to wait on a customer who had walked in.

"You have no idea how embarrassing this is. As if it wasn't bad enough I threw my tea all over you and fell across your lap, now you're stuck cleaning my wounds."

"Actually, it's my pleasure," Brant replied, as he wiped up the lines of blood that ran down Jessica's tanned leg.

The cold wet napkins felt wonderful on her leg and when he pressed them over the gash it made the throbbing stop. With Brant absorbed in his doctoring, Jessica could watch how carefully he cleaned her leg then patted the area dry with another napkin before covering the wound with two small bandages.

"There, you can look now," he said, looking up at Jessica.

Leaning forward, Jessica checked out her injury. She was going to make some comment about how much blood there was for such a tiny cut when she lifted her head to look directly into the chocolate-brown eyes of her professor.

In that moment, words left her. Something electrifying flowed between them as their eyes locked on one another for the very first time. Seconds ticked away and neither of them moved. A flash of heat moved from Jessica's face, across her breasts and down lower, making her flesh feel on fire. Jessica lowered her eyes and pulled her leg off the table, pulling her knees together and placing her hands on her lap. There was an awkward silence. Not in control of her vocal cords, she mouthed the words "thank you".

Finding her voice at last she whispered, "I have to go now," and stood up to leave.

"I'm sorry. What?"

"I have to go. Again, I am so sorry."

"And again...it was my pleasure. It isn't every day that a woman falls into my lap," he said with an innocent smile, as he backed his chair away from the sofa to give her more room.

As she walked to the door, Jessica tried not to dwell on what a mess she had made of their first meeting. Then without thinking, she looked back and said, "Thanks again, Professor Wilson," opened the door and left. It wasn't until she was across the street and heading back to her truck that she realized her blunder.

Now he knows that I know him, she thought. *I am such an idiot.* She looked back to see if he was following her but there was no one there.

* * * * *

Brant's warm smile turned into a quizzical look the moment the woman said his name. She had called him Professor Wilson, which meant that she must know him from school. She was wearing a UCLA sweatshirt, although it was one of the older styles from years ago, so maybe she'd been a student back when he was teaching on campus, or even someone from the English department.

She knows me but I don't have a clue who she is, he mused.

The whole situation made him feel uneasy. Then there was the physical attraction—an unnerving experience. Why had the touch of her skin under his fingers sent shivers up his arms? When she had looked into his eyes he had stopped breathing. She had aroused not only physical feelings in him, but something more. Something he had been so careful to bury deep down where no one would ever find it.

But even more amazing was the look in *her* eyes—he had aroused *her*. He just knew it. After all, he was paralyzed, not blind. He could see it in the blush of her cheeks, the sudden softening of her mouth and the twinkling in her eyes. He had made her so flustered that she had fled.

At first he wanted to go after her, but the moment it occurred to him to do so he suppressed the urge. How pathetic, chasing after her in his wheelchair. That image stopped him cold. *What kind of woman would be interested in me?* He turned his chair away from the door and packed the contents of the first-aid kit back into its plastic container. Then he took the kit to the counter, said his goodbyes to Nicole and headed back to his boat. He worked out his frustration on the way home, pushing himself hard until he was covered with sweat and his arms throbbed with a dull ache, one that matched a mysterious new feeling in his heart.

* * * * *

Jessica sat in her truck trembling. Her shin throbbed from her cut and her heart raced from walking back so quickly. But her trembling had nothing to do with her shin or her walk and *everything* to do with one Professor Wilson.

If she closed her eyes she could still feel his gentle touch as he washed away the blood from her leg. Every time his fingers brushed against her skin it had sent shivers up to her belly. When their eyes had finally met it was like a door opening, letting in a gust of warm summer air filled with promises. It had taken away her ability to speak and so she had left as quickly as possible. But on her walk back, her mind had been working faster than her feet, first berating herself for being such a klutz and then congratulating herself on coming up with a truly original way of breaking the ice, and almost her leg.

Staring across the parking lot at the moored boats, Jessica replayed every moment—his casual manner, the ease with which he took charge, his careful cleansing of her injury. The more she thought about the whole experience, the more pleased she became. Pleased until she thought about what she had accomplished—not a darn thing. She knew where he lived, had met him in person, even gazed into his puppy dog eyes. But he hadn't met *her*. Sure, he had met some clumsy woman who had literally fallen all over him, but he didn't know it was her—J.A., Jessica Anne Singer, UCLA extension student, career woman and stalker of college professors.

What had this meeting accomplished? Even if he did want to get to know her—and after today's fiasco she highly doubted it—he didn't even know her name.

As that thought tumbled across her mind, something on the bike path caught her attention. Professor Wilson was moving fast along the path about twenty yards from where her truck was parked. This would become a complete waste of time if she didn't do something and do it fast. Jessica got out of her truck and hobbled across the parking lot, managing to get to the dock gate just as Brant was pulling out his key.

"Professor Wilson?"

He turned his upper body around to look up at the woman who had fallen across his lap. His face lit up with a broad, honest smile.

"I thought a more formal introduction might be in order. I'm Jessica Singer," she said, hoping he would recognize her name from class.

When he didn't react immediately, Jessica rushed on.

"You know, J.A.? From your writing class? Jessica Anne Singer. I wrote that piece about eating rice and other illustrious compositions. I must apologize again for running into you like that. I'm usually more careful."

Brant's smile faded as Jessica kept talking. When she finally took a breath, Brant was able to jump in.

"So, Ms. Singer, what brings you to Marina Del Rey? A happy coincidence or were you looking for me?"

For just a split second, Jessica considered lying — making up some imaginary friend she was to meet at the coffee shop. But she opted for the truth instead, knowing it was easier to remember later on.

"Actually, I was stalking you," she said with a playful smile, looking directly into his upturned face.

"Really? I don't know whether to be flattered or scared. You're my first stalker," he said, amazed that she would admit to such a thing. "I must say, I'm at a loss as to what happens next."

"Actually, so am I."

Silence hung between them for what seemed like forever. Jessica cracked first.

"Guess I should go then. Nice meeting you," she said softly as she turned to leave.

"No, wait," Brant called out a little louder than he'd intended. Before he had time to think about what he was saying, Brant had invited her to join him for tea on his boat. As he led Jessica down the long ramp to the dock and his boat slip, he was already beginning to question his decision.

This was a bad idea, inviting a student onto the houseboat.

What had come over him? She hadn't been to class for the past two weeks, so maybe she wasn't technically a student anymore. Since she had tracked him down, maybe she was a kook, even dangerous, and now he was inviting her into his home.

Brilliant maneuver, Professor, he thought as he approached the short gangplank that connected the dock to his boat.

Once they arrived at slip 618, Jessica got her first real look at Professor Wilson's houseboat. The long rectangular box was painted blue with a flat white roof and sat on top of dual pontoons. The sides of the house were dotted with windows of various sizes, with the larger windows near the front of the boat to provide a view of the marina. The house part sat in the middle of the boat, with a wheelchair-width catwalk around the outside perimeter.

A wide gangplank with a deeply grooved surface and raised side edges connected the boat to the dock. Tilting his wheels up slightly, Brant popped his chair up onto the ramp and then with smooth, long strokes, propelled himself along the catwalk between the bow and the stern. Holding on to the rope railing, Jessica followed.

"Why don't you have a seat on the aft deck and give me a few minutes to change into something a little less sweaty."

"Sure," she replied and headed toward the front of the boat.

"Aft is that way," Brant said with a smile, pointing to the back of the boat before moving down the catwalk to the bow and then disappearing around the corner.

Jessica made her way to the back of the boat, where she found it was shaded by a canvas awning. There was a bench seat with a covered cushion that ran along the entire width of the boat. A mini barbeque was secured out over the railing on one side and a storage box was on the other. A sliding glass door separated the cabin from the aft deck, with mini-blinds blocking the view of the interior.

Jessica scanned row after row of sailboats, yachts and motorboats berthed in the marina all around her. The houseboat was close enough to the end of the dock to afford a great view of the main channel and the rest of the marina across the way. Several slips down, a young woman in the tiniest of string bikinis came out onto her deck, drink in hand, and made herself comfortable in a deck chair. She lifted her hand to shield her eyes from the sun and peered across the water at Jessica. It was unseasonably warm for early November and there wasn't the slightest of breezes.

Just then Brant opened the mini-blinds from inside, slid open the door and rolled out. On his lap he balanced a teak serving tray with two glasses of iced tea, a sugar bowl and a spoon.

"Thought you might be thirsty, since you didn't get to finish your tea earlier," he said with a twinkle in his eyes. "Thought *iced* tea would be safer for me, though. Hope it's okay."

"Iced tea is great. Thank you," she said, ignoring his poke at her clumsiness. She noticed that he had changed into a short-sleeved, plain khaki shirt that showed off his tan just right. The top three buttons were undone and she caught a glimpse of his muscled chest and a tuft of dark brown hair as he bent forward to hand her the glass. He looked fresh and clean and absolutely yummy.

"Sugar?"

"Tons," she said, taking the spoon from the tray and helping herself to four heaping teaspoons.

"I see you like a little tea with your sugar."

"I like it sweet," she smiled, as she swirled the grains of sugar around and around in her glass until they began to disappear.

Brant watched her, fascinated not by the swirling sugar but by the fact that he had a living, breathing woman sitting on his boat, sharing a glass of tea like it was something he did every day. In his four years living on the boat, he had never had a woman onboard, except for Frannie and the occasional delivery girl, and they didn't count. Now here was this woman he barely knew, a student no less, drinking tea and acting like this was perfectly natural. With her first sip, Jessica let out a satisfied, "Ahhhh."

"Just right," she said as she drank down half the glass before she realized that the professor was staring at her. "Guess I was thirstier than I thought. How about you?" she asked, holding out the spoon. "Take sugar in your tea?"

He took the spoon, placed it on the tray and then placed the tray on the bench seat next to Jessica.

"I'm a purist when it comes to tea—no sugar, no lemon, just tea."

He picked up his glass and took an equally large gulp that practically drained the glass.

"So, Ms. Singer, what's on your mind? What's so important that it couldn't be handled in the usual manner?" he asked, setting his glass down and folding his arms across his chest, waiting for an explanation for her bewildering presence.

"For starters, why don't you call me Jessica?"

"I don't think so. You're a student of mine and according to the student-teacher handbook, I must call you Ms. Singer and you must call me Professor Wilson. You *are* still one of my students, aren't you? I noticed you've missed two weeks of class assignments."

"Yes, I'm still officially enrolled in your class. I've just been overwhelmed at work lately. But things have slowed down a little so I'll try and catch up on the missed assignments." She looked out over the marina to break the intense eye contact.

Brant waited for her to continue and when she didn't, he asked, "So why *are* you here then?"

"That's a really good question…" Jessica stalled.

Why am I here? I could tell him about my novel, but then he'd say I could have emailed it to him.

Thinking aloud, Jessica continued, "I guess I was intrigued by the mysterious professor who refuses to meet students in person and hands out Cs no matter what I turn in."

"Over the years," he began slowly, "I've had a few students who have wanted to meet me face-to-face, but I was always able to dissuade them with a couple well-worded emails," he said, a little harsher than he wanted to.

Suddenly Jessica felt very uncomfortable sitting on her professor's deck. She stood up to go.

"Please, sit down. I'm sorry," Brant said, gently grabbing her wrist to stop her from going any farther.

There it was again—that rush of electricity at the touch of his skin to hers. She looked down at his hand just to see what it looked like touching her, and he immediately released it. She wondered, as she sat back down, if he had felt it too. Just then a call came from across the water that washed the moment away.

"Brant. Yoooohoo! Brant. Over here. It's Mitsy."

Jessica swung around to see the young thing in the string bikini standing at her railing, showing off her perfect body and waving her arm in their direction. Brant waved back.

"Do you want to come over tonight? Scott and the boys will be home around seven and we're going to cook up whatever they've caught today."

"Sounds good, Mitsy. See you around seven." Brant turned back to Jessica. "Neighbors."

"Yes, you have quite the neighborhood here. A most amazing backyard and fabulous scenery. This boat is pretty unusual as well. Custom-made?"

Jessica hoped the change of subject would get him talking, because suddenly she didn't know what to say.

"Yes. It was an old houseboat that I had gutted and redesigned to fit my particular needs." Feeling self-conscious as soon as he mentioned his disability, he quickly changed the subject, not wanting to talk about himself. "So where do you live? Somewhere close by?"

"In a small rent-controlled cottage on Fifth Street in Santa Monica. Pretty close to the beach, but nothing like this," she said, gesturing at the water surrounding them.

They talked about living on a boat for a few minutes before Brant decided to ask the question that had been on his mind since the moment she had told him she was a student.

"Tell me. How did you track me down, Ms. Singer? I thought I was pretty well hidden away, at least from my students."

Jessica explained how she had obtained his address and staked out the Mail Boxes Etc. store, using the delivery of the package to finally pinpoint him to an exact boat.

"You really are a stalker. I thought you were kidding," he said, laughing at her ingenuity. "So Ms. Singer…"

"Jessica."

"Ms. Singer," he said deliberately. "Now that you've found me, what do you think?" he asked, doing a three-sixty in his chair. "Not what you expected, am I?" he said with a bit of an edge to his voice.

"You can say that again," she said, without realizing that what she said could be taken the wrong way. "Your sense of humor is much drier in person, your eyes are much darker and you are definitely more alive than on the monitor."

"And the chair?" he asked, not willing to let her duck around the issue of his confinement.

"I admit, the wheelchair was a surprise," she said as she really looked at it closely for the first time. "I think I saw you the first Saturday we were here, but I didn't recognize you as

Professor Wilson, just some guy in a wheelchair on the bike path."

"So now you know everything there is to know — I live on a boat, I'm a paraplegic, I race my chair up and down the bike path like a madman, I drink mocha latté and iced tea with no sugar. Your curiosity should be satisfied, right? Is there anything else you need to know?"

Jessica could hear a mocking tone that for some reason had crept into his voice. It was like he expected her to get up and leave now that the issue of the wheelchair was out in the open.

"I'd have to say," she said, "that if anything, my curiosity has been piqued." Then she surprised herself with her boldness. "What I'd really like to know is whether or not you'd like to get to know me better?" she asked.

If Jessica had surprised herself it was nothing compared to the shock Brant felt.

"You're asking me out on a date?" he asked incredulously, not really believing what he had heard.

"Well, I guess I am. Why not?" Jessica suddenly felt up to the challenge. Their conversation was taking on the same tempo and flow as their chat room discussions, with Jessica challenging everything Brant said. It felt comfortable and familiar and gave Jessica the courage to speak her mind.

"I could think of a dozen reasons why that would be a bad idea," Brant sputtered.

"Start naming them," Jessica replied, calling his bluff.

"For one, I don't date students."

"I'll drop the class," she answered. "Name another."

"I don't even know you," he protested.

"Hence the reason for the date — to get to know each other."

"Ms. Singer — "

"Jessica," she insisted.

"Ms. Singer. You have no idea what you would be getting yourself into."

"So why don't you tell me," she dared him, looking straight into his eyes.

Brant moved his chair in closer, his knees touching hers. Jessica felt the contact but Brant didn't. He leaned forward and spoke barely above a whisper.

"Look. You came here expecting to meet one kind of man and found another. This chair and all it represents doesn't surround me like some 'thing', it has *become* me. You can't separate us. There's no point getting to know me without getting to know this," he said, patting the wheel of his chair. "In my experience, I've found most people, women people in particular, just aren't up to it."

"What if I am 'up to it', as you put it? What then?" she asked, leaning forward and placing both her hands on the arms of the chair.

When Jessica touched the chair Brant reacted like he'd been stung. He moved his chair back with such a jerk that it startled Jessica. They stared at each other as the sound of water lapping at the hull of the boat created a soothing background for their raging thoughts.

Jessica stood to leave for the second time. *This has been a mistake.*

"Chair or no chair, I wanted to get to know you better. But I guess you're not going to give me that chance, are you?"

Brant was speechless. He wanted to say something but he didn't know what—his tongue was as paralyzed as his legs.

"See you in class, Professor," she said, and then walked along the catwalk back to the gangplank and let herself off.

Way to go, Brant scolded himself. He had just scared off the first woman who had shown interest in him, chair and all, in over four years. If he could have kicked himself he would have.

Chapter Eight

ଔ

Finding it hard to concentrate, Brant pushed himself away from his computer and rolled out to the deck. His attempts at scripting his next lesson plan were interrupted by visions of Jessica—Jessica as she lay across his lap, Jessica as he nursed her warm, tanned leg, Jessica as she stirred enough sugar into her tea to cause a dozen cavities and finally, Jessica as she marched off his boat and out of his life.

His mind had created a running argument that he couldn't stop from repeating over and over again. Feeling very melodramatic, Brant went into the galley and poured himself two fingers of scotch, neat, and returned to the deck. He held the glass tumbler aloft and looked through the amber liquid catching the late afternoon rays of the sun. He flashed on the skull scene from Hamlet and began to speak out loud.

"To pursue or not to pursue, that is the question. Is it nobler to suffer the slings and arrows of outrageous doubt or take action and pursue, embarking upon a journey—a sea of troubles, that is sure to end in tragedy?"

He waited a moment, looking to the sky as if expecting an answer from somewhere, before downing the scotch.

For years Brant had taken great pains to avoid personal relationships with women. He lived on a boat. He worked through the anonymity of the internet. He didn't attend school functions, meetings or social gatherings. Women he met at the marina were always friendly, like Mitsy and Frannie, but were never interested in him as anything more than a friend. He had become one of those "interesting characters" people always talk about meeting around boat docks.

He had lied to Jessica when he said email had always been enough for his students. Once, during his first year as a virtual professor, he had let his ego be tempted by the advances of a young coed who had responded to his above-the-waist good looks. She was so insistent that he finally caved in and agreed to meet her at a restaurant. Her emails had been so very flattering and sexy that for a moment he had almost forgotten about being confined to a wheelchair and believed that he could go on a normal date.

It was an Italian place with red-and-white-checkered tablecloths and a bottle of Chianti on every table. He had arrived early and was already seated at the table, with instructions left with the maître d' to escort the young woman to the table. The place was dimly lit and when Carolyn arrived she didn't notice the chair right away. Her face was alive and she spoke with animated pleasure at meeting the "mysterious" Professor Wilson. It wasn't until he moved his chair back to retrieve a napkin that had flown from her hand during a particularly passionate gesture, that she finally saw the chair.

That shut her up. For the first time since she'd arrived, Carolyn was speechless. Brant knew the exact moment of the discovery—had anticipated how awkward it would be, but wasn't prepared for how much it would hurt. That moment of silence told him everything he needed to know. He would never be anything but a man in a wheelchair. He would never go out on a date again. He would never have an intimate relationship with a woman.

When Carolyn had regained her composure and the conversation resumed, the subject of the chair never surfaced. From that point on, her speech lacked that little spark of flirtation that makes conversations between men and women so exciting. By the time dessert was served they had run out of topics, and the evening ended with her apologizing for having to eat and run. More like eat and flee, Brant had thought.

Brant's logical side kept bringing up images of that humiliating night—freeze-framing the images like posters from some horror movie.

It will happen again. You'll be hurt. You're happy with things the way they are. Why rock the boat? he thought as the boat beneath him rocked ever so gently on the tiny swell of a passing dingy.

But then thoughts of Jessica's bare leg under his touch would bring back memories of the electricity that had passed between them. And, he reasoned, she had already seen the chair and all that it implied and didn't turn and run. Well, actually she *had* run, but that seemed to be more out of embarrassment from falling on him than anything else. And she had come back, he argued on. Only to leave again…

Yeah, but that was my fault. I practically shoved her overboard. She probably thinks I'm a rude jerk — a crippled, rude jerk.

But then his mind recalled the moment she had touched the arms of his chair. It had been a deliberate act, meant to show acceptance. Yet somehow it had been a violation of his personal space and he had reacted to that touch as if he had been struck.

How he wished he could take that moment back. But honestly, he couldn't even guarantee that he wouldn't react the exact same way in the future.

His mental battle raged on with no winner in sight.

"You are a hopeless fool," he said under his breath, as he forced himself to go back into his office to finish his script for next week's class.

Back at his desk, he gave the internal argument a break long enough to flesh out some new ideas for class. Eventually Brant the professor kicked into gear and the material for his lecture just flowed smoothly from brain to fingers to keyboard to screen. Within thirty minutes he was done and scrolled up to quickly review his work before saving and printing the outline. With that out of the way, he put his mind to the task of what to do about one J.A. Singer—student, woman and possible date.

A date.

The thought sent shivers down his arms and back until the feeling stopped abruptly at his waist. Brant hadn't been on a date in ages. He had to admit he did miss the touch, the scent and the sounds of having a woman in his life. Before the accident, Brant had had it all—a beautiful wife, a great job teaching English at UCLA, an overpriced townhouse in Westwood and the promise of children within the next year or two, something both he and Linda had talked about almost since the day they met. Both of them wanted a big family, with Brant wanting a couple girls and Linda talking about a couple boys. The accident had changed all that.

It had been the first week of summer break. Linda and Brant had decided to take an evening bike ride along the path starting at the Santa Monica Pier. They parked their car in the beach parking lot and unloaded their bikes. It was a warm, clear night with not a sign of June gloom that often shrouded the coast at that time of year. Brant thought it would be nice to have coffee and dessert so they headed north along the beach bike path. They would stop several miles up ahead at Back on the Beach Café, where they would enjoy their dessert before making the return trip.

The happy couple rode side by side, talking as they pedaled while the sun made its way toward a dip into the cool waters of the Pacific Ocean. Midway to the café, they had to get off their bikes and walk over to the street since a large section of the bike path was under repair. On Highway One, the road was narrow and congested, and they had to ride single file for about a half mile. Brant was anxious to get off the highway and back to the bike path where it was safe, and so he pedaled a little faster, pulling ahead of Linda.

Suddenly there was a blaring of horns. A truck driving in the southbound lane swerved over the line into oncoming traffic, causing a car in the northbound lane to make a radical swerve to avoid a head-on collision. The driver missed the truck but swerved right into Brant, sending him flying into the air like a rag doll. He landed with a sickening thud on a stack of two-by-fours that were lined up alongside the road for a construction project.

Brant heard, more than felt, a disconcerting snap before his head slammed into the boards and he was knocked unconscious. When he awoke in the hospital it was to the sound of Linda's hysterical crying. It was the nurse who noticed that Brant was awake and she tried to bring it to. Linda's attention, but she was inconsolable and had to be taken from the room. Brant lay there confused and alone. After what seemed like an eternity, a doctor appeared and gave Brant the news that would change his life forever.

Linda stuck by his side like the good wife until he was home from the hospital. She waited another six months before bailing out of the marriage. So much for "in sickness and health", Brant had thought bitterly. Even though Brant still could have fathered a child or two, or even six, he would never be the kind of father Linda had wanted for her children. A father who could teach them how to swim, chase them around the yard and play baseball in the park. And so, after six months, she had left.

Brant was bitter for a long time. He eventually sold the townhouse, quit teaching and threw himself a giant pity party that lasted two and a half years. Most of his friends had been Linda's friends, too, and when Linda left, so did everyone else. He figured he made everyone uncomfortable.

His family back East was very supportive and offered to move him back home, but that was the last thing he wanted — to be back under his parents' roof to be coddled or, even worse, pitied.

One afternoon when he was drowning his sorrows at the closest bar, he ran into a boat captain who was halfway through a six-martini lunch. Through an exchange of equally pathetic tales of woe, they each discovered that they had something the other person needed. Brant needed a new place to live where he was removed from the everyday nuisances of city life. Captain Jeremiah Barkley needed cash—and lots of it—to pay off a little gambling debt that had gotten out of control and might just end up getting him killed. If he didn't pay up in full by Sunday, he was, as he so eloquently put it, "going to be shark bait".

Captain Barkley owned a dilapidated houseboat in Marina Del Rey that nobody in their right mind would consider buying. But Brant wasn't in his right mind, and so a deal was made.

Brant used some of the money from the sale of his home to buy Captain Barkley's boat, sight unseen. The next day, cash in hand, Brant took a cab to the Santa Monica Yacht Club to meet with Captain Barkley and draw up the paperwork. The yacht club manager collected the fees and assisted with the sale but was skeptical about Brant living on any boat—and that boat in particular. But Brant assured him that everything would be just fine and paid him five years' slip rental fees in advance. He also offered to pay to have a handicap-accessible dock ramp installed, which went a long way toward convincing the man that Brant would be a good tenant.

Over the next six months, Brant hired and supervised a bevy of workers as they refurbished the piece of crap he had bought and turned it into a livable, seaworthy vessel, fit for someone in a wheelchair. It wasn't easy, but eventually things came together. After months of living at a motel, Brant moved onboard.

Brant had been well liked at the university and had had good reviews from both students and faculty before the accident, so when he reapplied at UCLA as an online teacher he was given the job almost immediately.

With a place to live that kept him out of the spotlight and his career back on track, there was only one major void in his life—one he didn't know if he could ever fill. Not having the use of his legs was bad enough but he got used to it. Not having a woman in his life to love and share his joys and pains was something he had resigned himself to a long time ago. That was a problem he couldn't fix with pure determination. He needed the cooperation of a member of the opposite sex — something he just couldn't control.

Women, at least the ones he had met so far, were terrified of the whole chair thing. Sure, he had women who would talk and flirt with him, like Nicole at the coffee shop or Frannie his neighbor, but whenever he had asked someone on a date, they couldn't back away quickly enough.

So after several botched attempts he had simply given up. He had convinced himself that he was happy with his career, his friends on the docks and his Sunday morning basketball buddies. He didn't need anything more.

Then along came Jessica Singer, and everything he'd thought he understood about himself went right overboard. He found himself needing to apologize to this woman he barely knew and somehow convince her to give him a second chance — a second chance at exactly what, he wasn't sure.

A smile began to spread across his face as he thought of a clever, if not subtle, way to apologize to Jessica for his behavior. He would pursue this woman after all. He'd have to wait until after the semester ended before he could take her out officially, but somehow he would work that out. If he got hurt again, he could always hide out for another four years until he got over it.

With that settled, he turned off the computer, shut his eyes and let his mind take him to images of Jessica on the back of his boat, bare legs and all. Then, like any red-blooded male, he began to imagine Jessica in a tiny bikini, like the ones Mitsy seemed to wear year-round. From there it was only a short stretch of the imagination to remove all her clothing.

Thinking about the touch he had already experienced and Jessica standing before him naked was enough to cause a mild tingling in his groin. He opened his eyes and looked down at his dead legs and the area where they joined. The fabric revealed the results of his sexual imaginings and he smiled with pride.

"I'm glad someone is still up for a challenge," he said out loud, and then laughed for the first time in months.

* * * * *

Jessica had spent the first half of the drive from Marina Del Rey to Santa Monica blaming herself for botching the entire day. From running into Brant's wheelchair to somehow offending him by touching it, Jessica felt she had pretty much screwed up the whole thing. On the second half of the drive, she decided her professor had played some part in ending the day on a less-than-perfect note, too.

He seemed a little moody. One minute he was all nice and accommodating, and the next he came across as harsh, bitter and a little skittish.

He had been friendlier when he hadn't known she was a student. Even though she wasn't a young co-ed in the traditional sense — young, naive, innocent and vulnerable — she was technically his student and maybe there was more of an issue there than she understood.

The wheelchair was obviously another sensitive area. She assumed it was a fairly recent event, not something he had grown up with, which would explain why he wasn't comfortable talking about it and why he'd reacted like she'd shot him when she placed her hands on the arms of the chair.

Funny, he didn't have a problem touching me, she thought, as she walked up to her front door.

Merlin greeted her with a flurry of feathers and a squawking "hello".

"How's my big boy? Ready to get out of that cage and stretch your birdie legs?" she asked as she kicked off her shoes, dropped her purse on the sofa and crossed the room to Merlin's wire cage.

Opening the little door, she stuck her hand inside with her finger extended and Merlin stepped right on. She brought the bird to the hollow between her breasts and began gently scratching the back of his neck, pushing the gray feathers up toward the top of his head. Merlin responded immediately to the mini-massage and closed his eyes as if in a trance.

"If only men were as easy to please as you," she sighed.

As if he understood her, he opened his eyes, swiveled his head around and affectionately pecked at her finger.

Jessica placed Merlin on her shoulder and walked to the fridge to find something cold to drink. Opening the avocado green relic revealed a lot of empty space containing one beer and a half-finished can of soda that had lost its carbonization. She grabbed the beer and closed the door, reading the pink Post-it on the freezer that read, "Buy groceries".

She pulled the note off the fridge and walked it over to the front door, where she placed it on the doorjamb so she'd have to look at it every time she left the house. Then she grabbed the portable phone and settled into her favorite corner of the sofa and dialed Cath. As she waited for her friend to pick up, she took a long draft of beer.

The first mouthful of beer always went to her head. The second always crept down lower until it settled nicely between her legs, giving her a warm, sexy glow. She took her second mouthful when Cath picked up.

"Hey," Cath answered. "Helloooo?"

It took Jessica a second to finish swallowing.

"It's me," Jessica finally answered. "I was drinking. Sorry."

"What's up?" asked Cath, as if her best friend hadn't just called her four hours ago from the stakeout.

"Did you get my message?"

"Oh, my God, yes. Sorry I didn't call. Pete was still here. Tell me everything."

Jessica proceeded to replay, analyze and dissect every detail of her haphazard encounter while Cath interjected questions and comments. An hour later they were still talking.

"I really don't think it went that badly, considering how it all started. I think if anyone blew it, it was him. He seems a little oversensitive about the whole wheelchair thing," said Cath.

"The 'wheelchair thing'? You mean the fact that he's paralyzed from the waist down? That thing?" Jessica asked with not a small dose of sarcasm.

"I know this is very heavy. Nothing to make light of," Cath backpedaled. "I'm sure it's a perfectly horrible way to have to live. I just meant that I would have thought he'd be used to it by now."

"Maybe it was a recent accident, not something he's had to live with forever."

"True," Cath agreed, falling silent for a moment.

Suddenly, Jessica started laughing.

"What's so funny?"

"Merlin is playing with my earrings and tickling my neck and earlobe in the process. Okay, enough of that," she laughed as she pulled the bird from her shoulder and placed him on the oak coffee table where she had her feet propped up.

"I was thinking…" Cath began.

"That's dangerous."

Cath ignored the comment and continued, "I wonder how paralyzed he is? There are different degrees of severity, you know. I wonder if he can have an erection, for instance."

"Jesus, Cath."

"Don't give me that. You can't tell me you haven't already thought of it, especially after all the sparks that were flying."

"I confess, I thought of it almost immediately. I even spent hours online reading up on all the different types of paralysis, including sexual function. Does that make me some kind of a perv?"

"No, just normal. Now, that boss of yours, he's a perv."

And the next thing Jessica knew another hour had passed before she finally hung up to work on an assignment for class. She put Merlin back in his cage to the sound of protesting squawks, flicked on the computer and was halfway to the fridge for something to eat before she remembered the fridge was empty.

Sitting back down in front of the computer, she pulled up last week's assignment, due in one day, and tried to concentrate. But not a single word would come to her. The only thing of interest that popped into her mind was Brant Wilson.

Jessica was nervous about seeing Professor Wilson on online. Would he look different? Act different? Or would he just seem different since she had met him face-to-face, fallen all over him and even asked him out on a date, of all things. It was so not like her, but after six years of celibacy, maybe she was ready to get back into the game. By the reaction of her body to Professor Wilson's touch, she knew her body was raring to go, even if her mind was holding back.

Shaking her head, Jessica placed her hands on the keyboard and tried to focus once again on her assignment. If she wasn't careful she was going to blow the class just like she botched the meeting with her professor.

Chapter Nine

ℵ

Brant had taken a little extra time dressing for Tuesday's lecture, making sure everything was in place. Since this was new material, he had notes stacked neatly in front of him on the leather blotter. He was seated on his rolling desk chair and glided back and forth with ease behind his desk, gathering books from the shelves behind him. At nine fifty-five, Brant hit the switch for the lights, checked his hair one last time, checked the computer connection and then hit the camcorder switch. Just like the camcorder, he was instantly on.

"Welcome back, everyone. Hope your weekend was as interesting and full of surprises as mine," he said with a mischievous twinkle in his eyes as he adjusted his new Superman tie.

"Today's lecture I've aptly named, 'Between the Quote Marks & More'. We're going to focus on dialogue—the exchange of information between your characters, the stuff found between the quotation marks. Amateurs will string a series of he said, she said lines together and call it a conversation. The professional uses dialogue to reveal character. Dialogue grows from the character and from conflict, and in turn reveals the character and advances the plot."

Brant was excited about the material he presented and it showed in his enthusiasm for the topic. He began pulling out books, one by one, and reading passages of dialogue he had marked with yellow slips of torn paper.

"A dialogue between two people isn't always made up entirely of the words between the quotes. Often what's outside the quotes is just as revealing. It's here that you can convey tone, emotion and body language. Let's look at the following simple conversation between Dick and Jane."

Brant pulled out the sample he had prepared and reached for his reading glasses. If it had been a live class, he would have heard his female students sigh with delight as he looked over the top of the glasses into the camera and smiled before starting to read. Somehow the tortoise-shell half-frames made him look younger and even sexier.

"Dick, please wait. I have something I want to tell you," said Jane.

"I can't. I'm already late. Can't it wait until tonight?"

"I guess. But it will only take a minute."

"Well, all right. What is it?"

"I'm..."

"Let's call that Version A — just the exchange of dialogue. Now in Version B, we will use the same exact dialogue but add information outside the quotes."

"Dick, please wait," Jane pleaded with a hint of desperation in her voice. "I have something I want to tell you."

Dick looked annoyed. He glanced at his watch to emphasize his impatience. "I can't. I'm already late. Can't it wait until tonight?"

"I guess," Jane replied, her bottom lip starting to quiver. "But it will only take a minute."

"Well, all right," Dick sighed in exasperation, knowing nothing Jane ever wanted to talk about lasted a minute. "What is it?"

"I'm..." Jane broke into tears, unable to go on.

"Sometimes the entire conversation takes place outside the quotes, without a word being said. In person, that would involve facial expressions, body language, and nonverbal signs and gestures. In writing, it takes detailed descriptions."

Brant swiveled his chair around and reached for the stack of books he had prepared for the lecture. He spent the next forty minutes reading examples of dialogue, both verbal and nonverbal, from Emerson, Hemmingway and Miller, with comments on each passage. When he finished, he took off his glasses and looked into the camera.

"And now for the part you've all been waiting for…this week's assignment. I want you to create two characters, give them something to argue about and then drop me, the reader, into the middle of the conversation. No lead-in, no intro, just the argument. Think of it as getting on a bus and sitting next to a couple who are having a fight. By the time the argument is settled, I should have a good idea how these two people tick, what their relationship is to one another and what kind of people they both are.

"Have fun with this assignment. Look up some of the examples I read today and study up on how the masters handle dialogue. Remember, I want this between two people, no internal dialogues this time. We'll tackle that next week."

Brant gave them a deadline of next Tuesday and a preview of Thursday's class. When he checked the clock he was five minutes over. At least in a virtual classroom, no one gets up and walks out after the allotted sixty minutes.

Turning off the camera, he allowed himself a moment of reflection before preparing for his noon class.

I wonder how Jessica will react to that intro, he thought as he subconsciously played with the tie she had sent him. Something like anticipation crept into his mind but he couldn't identify it right away. It had been so long since he'd even entertained thoughts of a woman or cared what a woman thought of him, that the whole process was as foreign and forgotten as running for a touchdown.

There was another new emotion that danced about his subconscious along with anticipation—and that was hope. Although he was too scared to acknowledge it, hope had entered his life and her name was Jessica Singer.

* * * * *

Tuesday had been quite enjoyable right up until Simon had stuck his head into her office and commanded, without preamble, "My office in five." He hadn't even given her a chance to respond. Grabbing a yellow notepad and pen, she forced herself out of her chair and headed for Simon's office. When she passed Simon's assistant, Claire, she whispered, "Know what this is about?"

Claire shrugged but didn't say a word. Claire was Simon's newest assistant and seemed to be well on her way to breaking the longevity record, having already survived three months.

"Close the door and have a seat," Simon said as she stepped over the threshold.

Jessica stiffened and felt the hairs on the back of her neck rise up.

Once she was seated, Simon made her wait while he shuffled papers around his oversized desk. He looked up at Jessica, seated with her legs tightly crossed and her skirt pulled down as far as possible. He gave her what she considered a lecherous grin and then began.

"I have good news for you, Jessica. I found you another client. A good one."

"Sounds interesting," Jessica replied without getting too excited. With Simon, there was always a catch.

"This is a Canadian company that's opening a branch office in Los Angeles. They're going to need a full marketing campaign—advertising, both local and national—the works. Are you up for the challenge?" he asked, scrutinizing her every expression.

It sounds too good.

"Of course. Sounds like a winner," she said, unwilling to say more. She was still waiting for the catch.

"It's settled then. I'll send over the complete file tomorrow morning."

"Great," Jessica said with a smile as she stood to go.

If I can just get out the door right now, everything will be fine.

She almost made it. Her hand was on the brass door handle when she heard his voice coming from behind her.

"Oh. And one other thing, Ms. Singer."

Here it comes.

"We'll need to take a trip to Vancouver to seal the deal. The head of Tyler, Inc. is a woman and has insisted on working with a woman. I've taken the liberty of booking our flights for this Friday morning, eight a.m., LAX. Hope you didn't have a date for Friday night. We won't be back until Saturday morning," he said with a triumphant smile.

Jessica couldn't believe it. This was low even by Simon's standards. The only word that escaped her lips was a tight, "Fine," before she opened the door and marched out.

She spent some time trying to get out of the trip to Canada, and when that didn't work, spent the rest of the afternoon doing some quick research on Tyler, Inc. before heading home.

She stomped up the steps to her front door, got frustrated when the key wouldn't turn easily in the old lock and entered her house in a foul mood. She was glad Merlin was a bird and not her husband because she didn't have to apologize for shouting "Shut up!" the moment she came in the door. It wasn't until she had kicked off her shoes and changed into a tank top and a pair of oversized boxers left behind by some forgotten date from her distant past that she began to feel human again. Merlin whistled for her attention and this time she responded and let him out of his cage.

"Sorry about biting your head off," she cooed to the bird. "I've had a rotten day."

She went to the fridge for a cold beer and found it still empty. She leaned back far enough to see the front door and looked at the Post-it on the doorjamb. Disgusted with her own forgetfulness, Jessica plopped onto the sofa and flicked on the television. She was content to be hypnotized by the drone of the news anchor until something about UCLA made her think of her writing class. She jumped up, startling Merlin into half flying, half falling off her shoulder onto the couch.

Moving to her desk, she hit the power button and waited for her system to boot up. As the start-up routine went through its drill, Jessica began to notice she felt nervous. How could she have forgotten her class? Especially considering what had transpired over the weekend. The homepage for UCLA's online extension courses appeared on her screen and with three clicks she was ready to begin.

"Here goes," she said, as she made the final click that would run the video lecture.

And there he was, wearing her tie, smiling right at her. The tense lines on her face began to relax and everything softened—her lips, her mouth...her entire body.

When he made a comment about an interesting weekend, she thought she had misheard him at first. She stopped the program, turned up the volume and started the lecture over again from the beginning.

Sure enough, Professor Wilson had alluded to her little visit. It had to be that. She watched the rest of the lecture with half a brain. The other half was busy trying to decipher why he was wearing her tie and what, if anything, she should do about it.

* * * * *

After a long day at the office, Jessica reluctantly skipped class on Thursday night. She spent the evening packing for her last-minute trip to Canada with her devious boss. She had attempted to change her seat assignment but the flight was booked and all seats were spoken for. She did manage to change her seat assignment on the flight home—at least that was something.

Friday morning found her at the airport at six a.m. holding onto a steaming cup of chai tea latté like her life depended on it. Simon was, of course, right on time and dressed to impress. Jessica had an uneasy feeling he was dressed to impress *her* and not the client. He was in an unusually chipper mood and wouldn't stop talking. As they stood in line to board the plane, he went on and on about what a great client this was going to be and how they were going to make such a good team. Jessica nodded at the proper places and used the sipping of her tea as an excuse not to respond.

Jessica's seat was next to the window, Simon's next to hers in the middle. She looked at the seating arrangement and a feeling of dread came over her. She was going to be trapped. Before she took her seat she headed for the bathroom, hoping to avoid having to get up and push past Simon later in the flight. When she got back, Simon was already seated and comfortable. The gentleman in the aisle seat had the good manners to get up and let her in but Simon just smiled and pulled his legs in as far as he could.

Bastard!

Jessica sucked in everything she had to try to avoid touching even the smallest part of Simon's body. During the flight, Simon continued talking away and used the excuse of looking out Jessica's window as a reason to lean across her. Once he even placed his hand on her thigh, as if to steady himself, when he leaned across. His gestures were so sneaky she figured he would proclaim innocence if she protested.

Although the flight was only a few hours long it felt like an eternity. If they hadn't been scheduled to see the client within an hour of arriving she would have entertained the notion of getting good and drunk.

The cab ride to the client's office was a lot quieter. She took the opportunity to pull out her research on Tyler, Inc. and do a quick review before they arrived.

The sales meeting went smoothly, with both Simon and Jessica giving top-notch presentations. After the two-hour meeting everyone was famished and so the topic turned from business to lunch. The lunch lasted another two hours, with lively conversation and plenty of business talk to actually warrant the write-off it would later become.

On the drive to the Marriott Pinnacle in downtown Vancouver, Jessica had to admit that Simon had been brilliant. She began to see why McMannon had hired him. He was slick, sure, but he also came off as sincere to the client, something she hadn't seen in him before. This didn't mean she liked him any better, but she respected his work a little more.

Simon was in a great mood after nailing the presentation *and* getting a signed contract at the end of lunch. While Danielle Tyler signed the contract, Simon had taken the opportunity to look at Jessica and smile very deliberately, as if to say, "See. You get the contract right away." He never missed an opportunity to poke.

Jessica was deep in thought, gazing out the window as the cab sped through the streets of Vancouver toward their hotel, when Simon interrupted her thoughts.

"I feel like celebrating," said Simon. "How about after we check in we meet in the hotel bar for a drink before dinner?"

She could hardly deny him a little self-congratulatory celebration. After all, he had earned it—they both had. Between her extensive research and his presentation, they had wowed them.

"All right. I'd like a few minutes to freshen up, though. Let's meet in half an hour."

Simon beamed and nodded. Just then the cab pulled up to the front of the Marriott and the doorman opened Jessica's door. She looked up at the tall, impressive structure, which seemed to be nothing but hundreds of windows held in place by a crosshatch of steel. The hotel stretched up and up until it seemed to kiss the clouds.

Jessica's heels and the wheels of her luggage made a musical click-clack, click-clack sound as she made her way across the highly polished marble floor of the lobby. Trying to avoid a heavyset couple having a heated discussion as they walked, Jessica had a run in with one of the leafy potted palms placed around the lobby.

"Careful," Simon spat out, as Jessica pushed aside palm fronds and continued walking.

At the registration desk, Jessica was relieved to find that Simon had booked them two separate rooms on the tenth floor—no trickery there—although they were joined by a shared wall. A horrible picture of Simon using a water glass to listen through the wall flashed in her mind and she had to physically shake her head to dislodge the image. They shared an elevator to the tenth floor and arrived at their rooms without incident.

"See you at the bar in thirty minutes," said Simon as he swiped his key card and opened his door.

Jessica nodded and then did the same. She had a corner suite, with huge windows offering breathtaking views of both the mountains and the Vancouver shore. Jessica tested the bed by falling back like a board, her body bouncing on the mattress. She found the bed comfortable enough, with lots of extra pillows just as she liked. She quickly unpacked a few items and then went into the bathroom to brush her teeth and redo her hair. She decided to wear the same clothes and just change into more comfortable shoes. Lying back down on the bed, she tried her mind trick for total relaxation. For five minutes she placed herself, mentally at least, back at the beach in Santa Monica, seagulls circling overhead and the sound of water lapping against the side of a boat.

That's not right.

She realized she had mixed her vision of herself at the beach with her time spent on Brant's boat. Thoughts of Brant filled her mind and before she knew it, her decompression time was gone. She found herself arriving late to the bar, with Simon already holding a spot for her at a quiet little table in one corner. He stood when she approached and like a true gentleman, pulled her chair out for her.

"I've taken the liberty of ordering you a drink," he said, as he signaled to the waitress that he was ready.

As if by magic, the waitress appeared with two martini glasses, a bucket of ice and two shakers. Like a magician, she performed her magic of turning liquor and ice into cold, flavorful martinis. Simon had ordered a Cosmopolitan for Jessica and a dirty martini for himself.

"How did you know I liked Cosmos?" asked Jessica, sipping on the sweet, cold drink.

"I pay attention," Simon replied with a knowing smile.

From anyone else that would have been a compliment, but when Simon said it, memories of him following her around at the Christmas party gave her the creeps.

In an attempt to fill the silence, Jessica started asking Simon questions about his interests and activities outside work. She learned he had a penchant for racing fast cars and found himself at the speedways whenever he could. He had even raced in a few amateur races with the likes of Tom Cruise, Paul Newman and other celebrity racers. He loved the adrenaline rush of the race and the excitement of hobnobbing with fellow enthusiasts.

Jessica tried to listen attentively but found her mind drifting back to a marina and a certain professor. After two martinis and no food since lunch, Jessica began to feel the effects of the alcohol on an empty stomach. When she mentioned she needed something to eat, Simon jumped at the opportunity to suggest dinner at a fabulous little restaurant he knew across town.

"Across town" was the red flag Jessica needed to snap out of her stupor.

"I'm not in the mood to get back in a cab again," Jessica started to explain.

"We could stay here then. I hear the Showcase restaurant in the hotel is quite nice."

"Oh, I couldn't possibly make it through an entire dinner," she continued. "I'm exhausted. I just want to go to my room and order room service and relax. We have a morning flight and I want to get a good night's sleep."

With that she rose from her seat, expecting Simon to remain seated, but instead he jumped up as well.

"Sounds very pragmatic. I think I'll do the same."

Now she had no choice but to let him walk with her to the elevators and up to the rooms. Simon made small talk as they rode up to the tenth floor. Then he said good night before slipping into his room, leaving Jessica to sigh in relief. Once inside her room, she looked over the room service menu and ordered a Caesar salad, bread and butter and a glass of Merlot before changing into flannel pajamas that had white clouds floating on a blue background. There were two queen-size beds in the room and she used one as a place to throw her clothes. She pulled on a pair of warm, oversized socks, rearranged all the pillows from both beds into a comfy backrest against the wall, flicked on the television and started channel surfing, stopping to check out any movies or programs that looked interesting. She finally settled on the movie *Sleepless in Seattle,* even though it was forty-five minutes into the film. She had seen it so many times, it didn't matter that she had missed the beginning.

A knock at the door and a call of "Room Service" had her jumping out of bed and grabbing her purse. When she opened the door, there stood Simon Fitch behind a silver cart with white tablecloth.

"Hope you don't mind, but I thought it would be nice to eat together. So I took the liberty of having your order placed on my room tab," he said, as if nothing made more sense than that.

Jessica was speechless at first and Simon took that as an invitation to start pushing the cart into her room. He made it halfway through the door when Jessica came to her senses and put both hands on the cart to halt its forward motion.

"What are you doing? I thought you were hungry," Simon said full of innocence.

"I am hungry, but I prefer to eat alone, thank you," Jessica replied, failing to keep the anger out of her voice.

"You don't have to get all upset about it. It was just an idea," Simon backpedaled. "I'll just wheel the cart into your room and then I'll leave."

Simon attempted to push the cart again, but since Jessica hadn't released her grip, the cart didn't move an inch.

"You're being ridiculous, you know," said Simon, acting as if Jessica's behavior was out of line. "Just let me wheel this in and I'll go."

"Thanks, but no. I am more than capable of handling it myself," Jessica replied, and jerked the cart into the room, causing some of the wine to slosh out of the glass.

With the cart now in the room, Jessica moved back to the door to close it but not before Simon stepped inside. Jessica reacted with a quick intake of breath and backed herself up against the wall. Simon moved in close, placing his hands on the wall on either side of her shoulders. For a second neither one spoke as Simon stood looking directly into Jessica's eyes. There was something different about this Simon. Gone was all the poise and reserve she had seen at the business meeting.

Gone was the indifference and cold façade he paraded around the office for everyone to see.

The look in Simon's eyes could only be described as lust-filled — and it scared the hell out of her.

She tried to duck under his arms but he grabbed her and pinned her against the wall.

"I've been wanting to do this since the moment I first laid eyes on you, Jessica Singer."

And without further explanation, he bent his head and tried to kiss her full on the lips, his mouth slightly open and his breathing ragged.

Jessica's reaction was instinctual. With her arms held tight against the wall her only weapon was her knee. She brought it up hard and fast, catching Simon in the groin. This not only ended the kiss but also brought a loud shout from Simon as he released his grip on Jessica's arms. Then she grabbed his doubled-over form and pushed him out the door into the hall with all her might, before slamming the door shut and putting on the security chain. It wasn't until the chain had stopped swinging in place that she stepped away from the door.

Adrenaline coursed through her veins as her heart raced and her breathing came in hard, fast gulps of air. Soon, anger replaced shock as she played the situation over and over again in her mind, trying to figure out what had just happened.

If he thinks I'm going to let that go, he's in for a big surprise.

Ignoring the food, she went to her briefcase and pulled out her laptop. She hooked it up to the internet at the desk in the corner of her room and connected to her company email system, where she shot off two letters — one to McMannon and one to HR — regarding the incident.

About twenty minutes later there was a knock at the door that connected her room to Simon's.

She approached the door as if it might burst open at any minute. She was about to put her ear to the cold surface when the knock came again.

She jumped back and shouted at the closed door, "Go away, Simon." Through the door she could hear him talking to her. It was muted but she could make out phrases like, "I'm sorry" and "It won't happen again".

Damn straight.

Jessica went to the phone and called the front desk, asking to change rooms. At first the clerk wasn't uncooperative, but when Jessica told her the situation she changed her tune. A new room suddenly became available on the eighteenth floor and a bellman was sent up to help her move her luggage and make sure she wasn't followed.

Once safely relocated, she called the airport and changed her flight home. Instead of the eleven a.m. flight, she found a seat on a plane leaving at nine a.m. and booked it. After everything was taken care of, she picked up the phone and ordered room service again. When the knock came this time, she looked through the peephole first before opening the door. When she asked for the bill to sign, the young man explained that it was on the house and again apologized for her troubles.

The wine helped her relax and the ending of *Sleepless in Seattle* put her in a mellow mood that allowed her to slip off to sleep around eleven p.m.

The next day, she slipped out of the hotel, boarded the plane without incident and by one in the afternoon, she was home in front of her computer, looking forward to "seeing" her professor.

She reviewed Tuesday's class and wrote down the assignment. Then she watched Thursday's class as well and noticed that Brant was still sporting her Superman tie. She wanted to send him a quick little email saying "Nice tie" or something, but instead she decided to concentrate on her assignment. She had no intention of dropping the class but if she didn't turn in her assignments on time, she would certainly fail. She reviewed the assignment one more time and then smiled.

"So he wants an argument, does he?" she said out loud to Merlin, who danced around her desk fighting with the pencils sticking out of a cup. "Well, I'm just the woman to give him one."

Her head was filled with voices arguing back and forth. She used her anger from last night to fuel her emotions and soon the words were pouring out of her. She acted the scene out loud, shouting out words and phrases, much to Merlin's fascination, as her fingers tried to keep up with the torrent of emotions that flooded her mind.

Chapter Ten

ᔓ

Fall had arrived overnight, with temperatures dropping from the seventies during the day into the low sixties. Brant felt the difference Sunday morning as he reached over to shut off the alarm. As he sat up, his blanket fell away and the cold air hit his exposed upper torso and a gaggle of goose bumps formed along his arms. Pushing down with his hands, he scooted to the edge of the bed before swinging his lifeless legs over the side. Even though his legs and feet didn't feel the cold, he still needed to keep them warm. He pulled on a pair of dark green sweatpants and his Ugg boots, which had been sitting at the end of his bed, before using his arms to lift himself into his chair.

He rolled to the built-in dresser and selected a long-sleeve T-shirt and pulled it on over his head, followed by an extra-heavy gray sweatshirt. Once dressed, he rolled over to the closet-sized head, where he had just enough room to back his chair in alongside the toilet. Using bars secured to the wall, he lifted himself from his chair to the toilet in one easy motion, before pulling his sweats down to his knees. There was no door on the head, since he was the only one who ever used it, and so he stared out into his bedroom while he took care of business.

Once back in his chair, he moved to the lowered sink attached to the wall to wash up and brush his teeth. There was a small nautical mirror attached above the sink that looked like a brass porthole and he used it to examine his stubble with his fingertips. He thought about shaving but decided to wait until later. First things first, he needed his morning coffee.

He rolled out of the bathroom and straight to the galley for his first cup of coffee of the day. The clock in the galley said he had fifteen more minutes before he had to be off. Grabbing his coffee, he headed out to the deck where he found the Sunday paper that was tossed there for him by Sammy, his neighbor. He used his fifteen minutes to sip coffee and survey the news before heading out for his Sunday morning basketball game.

He had to wheel himself over a mile to get to the park where the guys all met. He considered it a good warm-up for the game itself. About twelve guys in wheelchairs usually showed up—sometimes a little more and sometimes a little less. They were all athletes, very competitive. If you were expecting mercy or sympathy, you had come to the wrong place.

The game was as tough and hard-hitting as any other, and by about ten a.m. they had a small crowd watching. The sound of bodies smacking into each other was replaced with the sound of metal on metal as chairs collided in an attempt to get the ball.

Even though it was a cool sixty-one degrees, everyone on the court was sweating. About fifteen minutes into the game, Brant had a great breakaway and thought he was going to be alone under the basket when Wally slammed hard into the side of his chair. Brant still managed to get the shot off and score.

Racing down to the other end of the court to work defense, Brant got caught up in a three-way jam of chairs that found his hand smashed between his chair and Wally's. He looked down for just a minute to see that his flesh was torn and that blood flowed freely. He had to pull himself out of the game long enough to clean up and bind the wound. By the time he got back into the game they were down by six points.

Brant decided to turn up the heat a little and rushed Wally as he moved the ball up court. Brant shadowed Wally like a boxer and when he saw his chance, cut him off with his chair and intercepted Wally's pass. Immediately he was swarmed by the opponents in what looked like a major pileup on the 405 Freeway. Three players, including Brant, somehow ended up on the ground with their chairs tipped over. A couple people who had been watching the game started walking onto the court to help, but one look from Wally sent them back. Between the guys, they righted the three chairs and helped get everyone seated again. The message was loud and clear—we can take care of ourselves. Brant's team ended up losing by one basket, but once the game was over no one seemed to care who won.

Several guys left the group to join their wives or girlfriends who had been watching from the sidelines, while Brant and Wally wheeled off to Jane's Addition to lick their wounds and warm their hands with a cup of Joe. Brant loved his Sunday morning battles on the basketball court even when he did end up with an injury or two. But he couldn't help but be envious when he saw some of the players wheeling over to waiting girlfriends and wives for a congratulatory hug. It tugged at his heart as he watched them wheel away—one hand pushing their chair along and the other holding that of a loved one. For some reason, this morning it struck him particularly hard and he had to turn away. These guys found women to love them, chair and all.

Will that ever be me?

The image of Jessica Singer came to mind and that foreign feeling called hope crept into his thoughts.

* * * * *

Jessica had slept in Sunday morning before calling Cath and asking her to meet her at the pier for a walk along the beach. Writing out the argument had done wonders for venting her rage. When she had read it back she realized that her anger wasn't about Simon at all, but about Professor Wilson. The assignment had turned into a not-so-subtle argument for why he should get off his ass, figuratively of course, and ask her out on a date. Her own audacity shocked her—it was so Cath-like—and she had toyed with the idea of picking another subject, but couldn't decide. So she thought she'd consult Cath on whether or not she should send the assignment in or spend the rest of the afternoon working on something new. She had printed out a copy and had it folded inside her sweatshirt pocket.

This morning they decided to walk north of the pier along the bike path with the intention of ending up at the Back on the Beach Café for coffee and toast. They talked the entire way, mostly about the disastrous trip to Canada and what she should do about Simon. It wasn't until they were seated at the café with hot cups of coffee and tea in their cold hands that Jessica pulled out the assignment and handed it to Cath.

"Here. Read this and tell me what you think. It's my assignment that's due on Tuesday," she explained.

Cath took the paper without comment and started reading. Only a few lines into it she looked up in surprise.

"Oh, my. Someone is laying it on pretty heavy," Cath said, going right back to the story.

"I know. That's why I wanted you to read it and tell me if you think I should send it or not. It might be too bold."

"Too bold like a blow to the head, maybe," Cath said. "If this doesn't knock the indifference out of him, I don't know what will."

Cath finished reading the argument in silence and then put the papers aside before resting her elbows on the table and cradling her chin in both her hands.

"So? Should I send it or not?" asked Jessica.

"Oh, I would definitely send it. You'll get an A for sure. The dialogue was very believable."

"That's not what I mean and you know it," Jessica prodded. "Do you think I've stepped over a line somewhere? Am I being too aggressive?"

"Yes and yes. But this is progress for you. You are *finally* — and did I emphasize finally enough? — coming out of your protective shell. I think your dialogue is just as much about you being brave as it is about him. If I can quote your own character, 'Safe is very, very sad.' Although I still don't understand why you're pursuing this particular man."

"Okay, I'll send it," Jessica declared with a confidence she didn't feel, ignoring Cath's comment. "So what should I do about Simon?" she asked, changing the subject.

* * * * *

Jessica dreaded going to work on Monday morning and considered calling in sick. But then she remembered all the work piled up in her office and knew that wasn't an option. She would have to face Simon someday. When the elevator doors opened her body tensed up, bracing for the worst, as if Simon was going to be standing right there waiting for her. But he wasn't. She made it to her office without a sign of him. It wasn't until lunchtime that she found out *he* had called in sick. After that she was able to relax.

John McMannon had responded to her email regarding the Simon Incident, as he called it, and suggested they meet at three in his office. He had made a special trip for the meeting, which told Jessica he was taking this seriously. When she walked into his office she was surprised to see Albert Driscol, the company attorney, as well. John McMannon rose and walked around his desk to greet her when she stepped into the office.

"You know Mr. Driscol from legal, don't you?" he asked, nodding in Driscol's direction.

"Yes. I've worked with him on some projects," she smiled.

"I'm sorry this isn't a project this time," Albert replied without getting out of his chair.

"Come. Sit down, Jessica," John said, motioning to a huge, overstuffed leather chair in front of his desk. Then he stuck his head out the door and asked his assistant to hold any calls, before closing the door and returning to his seat.

Jessica crossed her legs at her ankles and folded her hands in her lap, sitting on the edge of the chair, trying to act calm. Inside, her stomach was in turmoil.

"We each have a copy of your email but we would like to hear what happened from you, if that wouldn't be too upsetting." John said, the kindness and concern evident in his voice.

"Not at all," Jessica said and then began relaying all the details, starting with Simon's visit to her office and ordering her on the trip.

Both Albert and John listened attentively, Albert taking notes and asking a few questions. When she was finished they were all silent for a few moments before John spoke.

"I've asked Simon to take the week off while we decide what to do about this. I didn't want you to be uncomfortable in the meantime. I will be meeting with Simon tonight to hear his side of the story. He seems a little more humble than usual, so I don't think he'll be denying what you've said. Do you want to file a sexual harassment suit against Simon or the firm?"

"No," said Jessica, thinking how that would just prolong the entire ordeal. "I just want to be able to do my job without being harassed. And I hope you understand that I will never agree to go on a business trip with Simon again," she said a little more forcibly than she'd intended.

"Of course, that is completely understandable," nodded Albert.

"Jessica, you are one of my best account executives and I don't want to lose you, so whatever you need to feel comfortable is a priority for me," reassured John.

"Thanks. I appreciate that. As long as he keeps his distance for a while, I should be fine. And," Jessica added, "tell him he needs to knock on my office door and *wait* for an acknowledgement from me before bursting in. It's unnerving."

"Sounds reasonable," John agreed. "Anything else?"

"I'm good for now. Thanks for being so supportive," Jessica said as she stood up. "I didn't know what to expect. This has never happened to me before."

John, and this time Albert, too, stood up.

"Again, on behalf of myself and the company, I am so sorry you had to endure Simon's ridiculous behavior and I can assure you it will never happen again or Simon will be walking the streets looking for a new job."

With that Jessica left the office, feeling much better knowing that not only did she have a Simon-free week ahead of her, but Simon would be out should he try something like that again. The thought of him in his preppy clothes standing on a street corner with a sign that read, "Will work for food", made her mouth curl up in a delicious smile and put a new bounce in her step.

* * * * *

When Brant opened his email the following Tuesday morning, his first impulse was to head straight to Jessica's assignment, open it and devour every word. He had such nervous anticipation that he felt like he had butterflies in his stomach. But instead, he forced himself to go through his standard routine of opening each email, printing out the assignments before starting to read them. He did sneak a peak at Jessica's opening salvo as it slid out of the printer.

"You are such a coward, William Anthony Garber," she said with such force that Will took a step back as if he had been struck.

After reading the first line, Brant placed the paper back in the pile and waited for the rest to finish printing, even though he was dying to continue reading. Once done, he grabbed the stack and rolled into the galley where the heater kept things nice and warm. He had a great view of the marina out the sliding glass door that opened onto the aft deck. Rows of sailboats bobbed in the gentle tidal surge, their masts standing like a forest of trees against a deep blue sky. A cool breeze caused flags to flutter and seagulls to work a little harder when flying into the wind. Brant glanced at his watch—eight forty-five. He had a good hour before he had to get dressed for class. Everything else was all set up and ready to go, so he took his first sip of coffee and began to read.

"You are such a coward, William Anthony Garber," she said with such force that Will took a step back as if he had been struck. "What are you so afraid of?" she demanded, as she tossed her fiery red hair to one side and placed her hands squarely on her hips.

Obviously she expected an answer and expected it now. Will was glad she had closed his office door before laying into him.

"Well, I…" Will began, not knowing how to continue. What WAS he so afraid of?

"Well?" Susan asked, trying to sound patient but failing miserably. "I can't believe my big brother is going to let one bad relationship scar him for life. It's been five years. You must be over it by now. Trish is such a nice girl, nothing like…what was the loser's name?"

"Margie. Her name is Margie and she was almost your sister-in-law. At one time you said she was a 'nice girl' too," he said, arms folded tightly across his chest. "She's not a loser."

"See, that's what I mean. The girl cheats on you, breaks your heart and yet you're still defending her after all these years. Get over it!"

Now Will was getting mad.

"I don't know why you think you know what's best for me," he barked right back at her. "Ever since we were kids you've always bossed me around. I'm thirty-five years old and I don't need you telling me what to do," he said with finality, hoping that would end the conversation. But he should have known better. Susan was a pit bull when she thought she was right. And she always thought she was right.

Susan decided to take a different approach and let her arms drop to her side before shifting her weight to one foot. "I know I'm a bit bossy at times..."

"A bit?"

"Okay, so I'm very bossy. It's my nature. But I'm just trying to help. I don't want to see my brother all alone forever. You're not an alone kind of person."

Will just nodded and let her continue.

"Trish is such a nice person and all I'm suggesting is you come out of your hermitage for one night and go out with us. Just one little date. No pressure."

"Ha," Will snorted, not believing her for one moment.

"Look. It will be the four of us. You don't even have to pick her up or anything. We'll meet at Sandy's Sports Bar, have dinner, a little conversation and that's it. No big deal. If you like her great, then you can take it from there."

"I wish it was that easy," Will whispered, sadness evident in his voice.

"It can be," said Susan as she walked up to her brother, stood on tiptoes and kissed him gently on the forehead. "Baby steps, Will. That's all I'm saying." She wrapped her arms around his waist and leaned her head against his chest.

Will responded by wrapping his arms around her petite frame.

"I know it shouldn't be a big deal but it is. I haven't been on a date for over five years," he confessed.

Susan could hear his heart beat and his deep voice reverberate in his chest.

"You asked me what I'm afraid of? Well, everything, if you must know."

His words came pouring out in a torrent of emotion that Susan hadn't heard from him in years. All she could do was hold him even tighter so they wouldn't be swept away.

"What if I can't remember how to act in front of a woman? I work with men all day and then I go home. Except for you, I haven't had more than a one-minute conversation with a woman in years.

What if I just sit there all night like a fool? What if she hates me? Or even worse, what if she likes me? Then what? What if I like her and she likes me and we start going out and I fall in love again and then everything goes to shit and I get my heart broken? Why would I want to do that? It's safer to do nothing."

Susan sighed and pulled back enough to look up into Will's face.

"You're right. A million things could go wrong. But maybe, just maybe, it will be a nice dinner, some great conversation and the beginning of a new friendship. It's not safe. But Will, safe is boring. Safe is sad — very, very sad."

Will gave her a big brotherly hug before pulling out of her embrace.

"Fine. What have I got to lose but my heart...again," he said with a sheepish grin.

"That's the spirit," she said with glee. "Roger and I will swing by here after work on Friday and pick you up. Bring something a little trendier to change into, like that navy shirt I bought you last Christmas. It makes your eyes look even bluer."

"Are you going to tell me what shoes and socks to wear, too?" he teased as he walked around behind his desk and sat down.

"Only if you want me to," she replied, acting all innocent. "You know I never give unwanted advice."

"That's it. Get out," he said playfully. "I do have work to do."

Susan blew him a kiss and headed for the door.

"See you on Friday. Try to smile, will ya? This is going to be fun."

"Fun for you," he mumbled under his breath.

"I heard that," she sang out over her shoulder as she walked through the door.

Will watched as his sister walked down the hallway with a bounce in her step. At least someone was happy.

Brant flipped over the last page of Jessica's assignment and sat back in his chair. It was only after finishing that he realized he had leaned forward over the pages, taking on some of the tension of the scene. Now he took a deep breath and tried to relax.

So she thinks I'm a coward, does she? She thinks I'm hiding away, afraid to go out. She doesn't even know me. Maybe I just don't like you, Jessica Singer.

But he knew that wasn't true. He liked her just fine, although he didn't quite understand why. He only knew her from her writing, their chat room bantering, their meeting at the coffee shop and her brief visit here on the boat. Aside from being a little klutzy and a possible stalker, he didn't know much about Jessica Singer at all. He had to admit she was an interesting woman…someone he ordinarily would have asked out on a date if he had met her casually.

But life was anything but ordinary now. He looked down at his lifeless legs. Balling up his hand into a fist, he brought it down hard on his right leg just above his knee. He felt his hand impact a solid object and felt a slight vibration from the hit as the movement passed up to his waist, but if his eyes had been closed he wouldn't have known something had hit his leg. Both his legs, from the waist down, were completely without feeling.

Brant turned over Jessica's assignment once again and started reading it for the second time with the intention of making some comments. Her dialogue was good, very good — so he made comments on that point. But what struck him most was how she had used this assignment to communicate with him — at least that's what he *thought* she was doing. The words coming out of Will's mouth could have easily come out of his own.

"What am I so afraid of?" he asked out loud. The sound of his own voice startled him.

He looked at the argument in his hands and found Susan's words—"Safe is boring. Safe is very, very sad."

I'm turning into a sad, pathetic shadow of a man, Brant thought.

Brant wheeled his chair around and headed for his study. There, he clicked over to his email program, pulled up a new email and began typing. After two minutes, he addressed the email to Jessica Singer and then paused a moment, wondering what the hell he was getting himself into, before hitting SEND.

* * * * *

Tuesday night, Jessica ended up taking a cab home since she'd worked until ten and didn't feel like walking home in the dark. Not having to worry about being left alone in the office with Simon had freed Jessica to work late. It wasn't until he was gone that she realized how much she had let his presence affect her work habits. Even though she had worked from eight until ten, she felt light and carefree. She even had the cab stop at the corner liquor store for a six-pack of beer and a pint of ice cream. No one would ever accuse her of being a health nut.

Once she was settled into her flannel pajamas, she took a bowl of ice cream over to the computer. But before she could get to her class, her email kicked in with a ping, alerting her that she had mail. Clicking on the icon, she scanned the list and was surprised to see a message from Brant Wilson—not Professor Wilson from UCLA, but a Brant Wilson from AOL.com. Her heart began to beat a little quicker and she took a huge spoonful of ice cream before clicking on the message.

For an English professor, I'm sure having difficulty finding the right words for this email. I've tried several different approaches — cocky, humble, bold, forthright and clever — and they were all terrible. So looks like I'm going with the formal approach...

Dear Jessica,

Would you do me the honor of dining with me this Friday evening at the 12 Washington restaurant in Venice Beach? Please email or call at your convenience.

Sincerely,

Brant Wilson

Fool, professor, poet

555-4331

"Well I'll be damned. Merlin, my professor just asked me out!"

Chapter Eleven

∽

Jessica parked her truck in the public lot on the corner of Venice Boulevard and Pacific Avenue. It was the closest place she could find to the restaurant on a Friday night. Clutching her coat around her tighter to fend off the cold onshore breeze, Jessica filled her lungs with the cold salt air. She hurried along Pacific heading toward Washington Boulevard, where 12 Washington was nestled in amongst cafés, skate shops and a sushi bar. The high tide brought the sound of crashing waves even closer to the shore, intensifying the sound of water hitting sand. Jessica stopped and turned toward the ocean just as one particularly loud crash echoed off the buildings. She welcomed the wind that hit her full in the face and made her hair dance in the breeze like autumn leaves. She used the moment to try and calm herself before crossing the street and making her way to the restaurant. At the end of Washington was the Venice Beach Pier and even though it was November, crowds of people were still walking around, spilling out onto the sidewalks from the cafés, bars and the Mercedes Grill, giving the area around 12 Washington a carnival atmosphere.

The restaurant's red brick exterior and gray-shuttered windows with matching flower boxes reminded Jessica of something she might find in New Orleans. The gray head of a huge gargoyle was mounted between the two second-story windows and gazed down at her with a large gaping mouth that revealed two sharp teeth. Outside the restaurant was a small enclosed patio area that Jessica imagined would be the coveted spot to sit on a warm summer night, but tonight all the chairs and tables had been brought inside.

The soft light from the interior poured through the windows, giving Jessica enough light to see the little gray gargoyles perched on the wooden ledges above the door and windows. As she pulled the door open, a wave of warm air greeted her and the delicious aroma of garlic reminded her how hungry she was.

The maître d' was expecting her and led her to a table in the back where Brant waited. Burnt-orange glass globes hung from wrought iron sconces mounted on the walls, and brass chandeliers with red flame lights flickered high overhead. The walls had been painted in shades of Tuscany ocher, with a webwork of fake brown cracks giving the impression of age. On the center of each round wooden table was a large red candle held in place by a twisted metal ivy vine. Covering most of the available wall space, mounted in antique gold frames, were old mirrors in a variety of shapes and sizes reflecting and multiplying the warm light. As Jessica approached Brant's table, he turned his chair and graced her with his amazing smile.

"Hope you'll excuse me if I don't get up," he joked as she moved to the seat against the wall.

"Sorry I'm a little late. I couldn't find a place to park anywhere near the restaurant," she said as she grabbed her napkin and placed it on her lap.

She looked up and found Brant staring right at her. It was pleasantly unnerving. For weeks that same face had stared at her from her computer monitor and now it was right in front of her — the same only different.

"That's one of the advantages of taking a cab, I guess."

"Do you have a car?" she asked, wondering how he would drive one if he did.

"I thought about getting one of those customized vans with the hand controls, but then I thought about the traffic on the freeway and how often you need your hands for explicit gesturing and thought I'd skip it for the time being."

Imaging Brant flipping someone off made Jessica laugh, which broadened Brant's smile even more.

"I know what you mean. You can't drive in L.A. without hand gestures. It would be like an Italian trying to talk without his hands. My ex-husband was Italian. Being in a conversation with that family could be physically dangerous, what with all the hands flying around. It's addictive, too. After a couple dinners, I found myself talking with my hands as well. After I knocked over a glass of wine with one large sweeping gesture, I took to sitting on my hands."

"You *are* a little klutzy," teased Brant, referring to the incident in the coffee shop.

"One little accident and I'm branded for life."

"Two little accidents—tea and wine—maybe it's just a liquids thing." Brant took a sip of water. His mouth was so dry he feared his lips would stick together. "So you've been married before, also? You seem too young to have already been married and divorced. Did you get married at twelve?"

"I acted like a twelve-year-old, does that count? How about you? When did you get divorced?"

"Six months after the accident. My wife thought of me as damaged goods."

There's that phrase again, thought Jessica.

It made her feel sick all over, if only for a second or two.

"My marriage ended for similar reasons," Jessica said, looking down at her lap, remembering how her hot-tempered Italian husband had thrown that very phrase at her before he stormed out.

Brant was curious as to what that could mean but before he could ask, the waiter arrived to take their drink orders. Jessica turned down the offer of a cocktail in favor of wine with dinner. Brant followed her lead and asked for the wine menu, from which he selected a red wine from Napa Valley.

"Any idea what you want for dinner?" he asked, picking up the menu.

"I have no clue. I'm starving though, so I'm sure anything would taste wonderful. Have you eaten here before? Do you want to recommend something?"

"I've eaten here a couple times, a long time ago. I remember that the Pacific red snapper was excellent. I'm glad you came hungry. I don't understand those women who eat before a date and then pick at their food during dinner. Why they think this will impress anyone is beyond me. It makes me feel odd to be wolfing down a meal in front of someone who has trouble finishing their salad."

"No problems here. I may not be much of a cook but I sure know how to eat."

The waiter brought the bottle of wine and performed all the proper rituals before taking their order. Then he disappeared, leaving Brant and Jessica alone.

"Do you mind if I ask you a personal question?" Brant ventured, watching Jessica's face for clues in her reaction.

"I guess that will depend on just how personal." She took a sip of her wine for fortification.

"Fair enough. Here goes. Why did you still want to go out with me even after you found out I'm a para?"

"A what?"

"A paraplegic. We've just shortened it. Makes it sound cooler, don't you think?"

Brant's face had lost its smile, but was still soft and kind. Jessica took in that face long and hard before answering.

"You go right to the hard stuff, don't you?"

"Might as well get it out of the way."

"I could say that you being a 'para' isn't a big deal, but that would make me a liar or very naïve and I'm neither. I found myself fascinated by the witty, intelligent guy on my computer monitor. That's who intrigued me. You are still that guy, aren't you? Or do you have an evil twin?"

That brought the smile back to Brant's face.

"I wish I had an evil twin, it would be easier than being stuck in this chair for the rest of my life."

"To finish answering your question, once I found out that you were in a wheelchair, I have to admit I was unprepared for that possibility. Of all the things I had imagined you could be—arrogant, a snob, a jerk, short—"

"Short! Now that's funny. You were worried about me being short?"

"Can I finish?"

Brant nodded and took a drink of his wine.

"Yes, short. How can you tell how tall someone is when you've only seen them sitting down?"

"I'm six four when stretched out on a bed and about four-five when sitting in this chair."

"Cute. Anyway, when I thought about it, what I liked about you hadn't changed. So here I am. Satisfied?"

"Good answer, J.A. Singer. I give you an A-plus."

"Well that's a first…"

"No talking about school, okay? I'm still feeling odd about you being a student of mine. I think we're breaking some rules here."

"First," she replied, "I'm not some college coed you're taking advantage of, and second, class will be over soon and then that issue goes away."

"Good point."

"Now it's my turn to ask some hard questions. Why did you change your mind and ask me out?"

"I don't like hard questions. Pick another one." His brown eyes caught the light and sparkled.

"I don't think so, Professor," she said, matching his playfulness. "I had to answer your question now you have to answer mine."

"That's fair. I have to admit it was your argument."

That drew a blank look from Jessica, so he went on.

"You know. Your assignment to write an argument?"

"Oh, right. The Susan and Will dialogue."

"I don't know if you intended to or not, although I have a strong suspicion you did, but the dialogue struck a little too close to home for comfort. If I had a sister, I'm sure those exact words would pour out of her mouth. And Will's replies could have been taken from the soundtrack that runs night and day in my head. It was kind of creepy, how you seemed to know what I would say. If, of course, that had been me."

"So it was like having the argument with me but without me there, right?"

"I guess so."

"And I obviously won and that's why we're here now, right?" Jessica asked with a small smile.

"It's more than that, but yes, that was the last straw that broke down my resistance."

"I'll have to remember this for the future. Any time I want to get my way, I'll just write up a story and make it happen."

"I wouldn't count on that happening again," Brant replied, just as the waiter brought their soup.

The conversation took on a lighter quality and the rest of the meal flew by with Jessica having only one minor mishap. At one particularly lively point in the conversation, Jessica made a gesture with her hand while holding her fork. The tiger shrimp on the end of the fork flew off and landed in a water glass two tables down, making a nice little splash. The owner of the glass looked around, not knowing where the mystery shrimp had come from. Brant had trouble containing his laughter while Jessica wanted to slide under the table. The waiter brought the unfortunate recipient of the flying shrimp a new glass of water and Jessica tucked her hands under her legs.

Both Brant and Jessica refused the dessert tray, deciding instead that a walk along the beach would be better for their health. Brant rolled out from the table and made his way to the door. Arriving first, the maître d' opened the door for both of them as they moved out into the night. The wind had died down a little, so it didn't feel as cold. Jessica pointed in the direction of her car and they headed north along Ocean Front Walk. Jessica had her hands stuffed deep into her pockets to keep them warm while Brant had put on leather gloves without fingertips for pushing his chair along.

"Do you want me to push you so you can keep your hands warm?" asked Jessica, thinking that his fingers had to be freezing.

"No, I'm fine. I do this all the time. Because they're working, they don't get cold. Here, feel," he said, pausing to raise his right hand off the wheel.

Jessica pulled her hand out of her pocket and reached over to grab Brant's hand. As she lightly squeezed his fingers, which were warmer than hers, a rush of electricity surged up her arm and made her whole body tingle. Brant gave her hand a squeeze before going back to pushing his chair along.

"Your hands are warmer than mine," Jessica managed to spit out, while her body concentrated on recovering from the contact.

Why does just a touch from this man send me into sensory overload?

She wondered if it had the same effect on him.

"There's a café on Pacific," Brant said. "A small hole in the wall. Let's duck in there and warm you up a bit. They have great coffee and sometimes someone is reading poetry or playing the guitar. It has the ambiance of an old beatnik hang out."

Jessica agreed and they turned down Twenty-fifth Street toward Pacific and headed down the sidewalk to Barbara's Beans. The place was alive with an eclectic group of people providing the pulse—a young guy with dreadlocks wearing a purple vest and pants that looked like they were made out of brocade upholstery material. His girlfriend in a long flowing purple velvet dress, with long blonde hair pulled back in a single braid. An elderly couple with snow white hair and heavy wool coats sitting in overstuffed chairs, clutching their coffees close to their faces to keep themselves warm. A group of three teenage girls—all wearing far too much makeup and not nearly enough clothes to be warm. A guy in his mid-twenties who looked like a Poindexter-type scientist, complete with round spectacles, plaid shirt and a red bow tie. Jessica couldn't decide if he dressed like that as a joke or if that was his normal attire. He even had a white plastic pocket protector with an assortment of pens and mechanical pencils sticking out the top.

"Why don't you go find us a place to sit and I'll order us something warm. You prefer tea, right?" Brant asked as he moved himself closer to the order counter.

"Chai tea latté, no whip. Thanks."

Jessica took a look around the small room and found a spot with one open chair and enough space for Brant to slide in. There was a floor lamp next to the chair and Jessica moved it back so Brant would be able to sit next to her. A few minutes later, Brant rolled over with a tray on his lap and two ceramic mugs filled with steaming hot coffee and tea. He had also bought two small cinnamon stick cookies that were on a paper doily on a hand-painted antique saucer.

"That looks dangerous," Jessica commented, watching the hot liquid come close to splashing over the edge of the mugs.

"Not as dangerous as it would have been if you were the one carrying the tray," Brant teased.

"I'm not even going to dignify that with a response." Jessica took her tea off the tray, being extra careful not to spill even a drop.

Brant did a slow one-eighty in his chair and then backed it into the spot Jessica had created.

"You're very good at that," she said. "I'm afraid I would be running into things and knocking stuff over all the time."

"Trust me. I did at first. You think *you're* klutzy."

"I'm not klutzy."

"You should have seen me when I got my first chair. It was one of those big, heavy steel things, with wide metal wheels and heavy-duty everything. It was unwieldy. I hated it with a passion and took great pleasure in ramming into walls and scraping past doorjambs. It wasn't until I got this sleek, sporty model that I began using any finesse."

Brant studied Jessica as she listened to him talk about his chair. If she was uncomfortable with the topic, she was an expert at hiding it.

"This doesn't bother you at all, does it?" he asked her.

"What doesn't bother me?" Jessica asked, knowing full well what he meant.

"All this talk about my chair. It makes some women very uncomfortable," he said, taking a sip of his coffee.

"I guess I'm not 'some women'. Your chair is part of your life, so it's interesting to me...*you're* interesting to me, as well."

"Hmmmm," Brant said with what could only be described as a devilish look. "I wish you would explain that to the rest of the female population."

"I don't think so. Why would I want to help other women get to know you better and create competition for myself? They have to figure it out for themselves."

Just then, a young man who had been curled up like a cat in a beanbag chair in the corner of the café got up and approached Brant and Jessica. He was tall and very slender, his oversized denim jeans falling down past his hips. He had a drawing pad tucked under his arm and a charcoal pencil tucked into his hair over each ear. His long black hair was thin and in need of a good shampooing, but his eyes were bright and his smile sincere.

"Hey guys. Mind if I draw a portrait of the two of you?" he asked when he came to a stop in front of them. "You have great energy. I can see it, you know. It's pulsing out around you like radio waves. Not everyone has that, you know."

Brant and Jessica looked at each other and then at the young man. Jessica shrugged her shoulders. "Doesn't matter to me, as long as it won't take too long."

"Sure," Brant agreed. "How much is this going to cost me?"

"If you like it, twenty bucks. If you don't, it won't cost you a cent," he said, confident they would like it. "Mind if I arrange you a little?"

"Arrange away," said Brant, giving Jessica an amused look. "I believe in supporting local talent. Hope you don't mind?"

"Not at all," she said, not sounding quite as convinced as the young man took her hand and helped her to her feet.

"If you could just sit on his lap facing into the light of that lamp..."

"I don't know about this," Jessica said slowly, looking at Brant for help.

Brant patted his lap. "It's okay with me."

"Of course it is," she said as she carefully lowered herself onto Brant's lap with her legs hanging to the side.

"Are you sure this isn't going to hurt you?" she asked, not wanting to put her full weight on him.

Brant gave her a "you've got to be kidding" look before reassuring her. "Can't feel a thing," he said, even though he could feel a pleasant pressure weighing down on him and the beginnings of a delicious stirring.

"Could you lean back into him? Maybe rest your head against his chest?" the young man asked, as he stepped back to look at the scene from a different angle.

Brant moved his right arm around her shoulders and rested his hand on her forearm.

"Did you pay the kid to do this?" Jessica asked, finding it difficult to relax.

"No. But I will," Brant chuckled.

Jessica could feel his laugh reverberate in his chest.

"Okay, just relax now. This should only take about ten minutes. I'm very fast."

Ten minutes! she thought. *How am I going to just sit here like this for ten minutes?*

Then Brant took his left hand and began stroking her hand. As the warmth of Brant's body began to seep into hers, Jessica began to relax. His touch was soft and light and was more than a pleasant distraction. Tucked in under his chin and up against his chest, she could inhale deeply and be filled with his scent—a subtle mixture of sea air and some sort of aftershave that smelled like a forest after a rain—she relaxed so much that she just naturally closed her eyes. She tried not to think too much about what Brant might be thinking.

"That's good! Keep your eyes closed. I like it even better that way," the young artist said encouragingly.

"This isn't a bad way to end a first date," Brant whispered into Jessica's hair. He took the opportunity to brush his nose and lips across the top of her head. He could almost taste her. Jessica answered with a murmured consent.

Finally the artist announced he was done.

"That *was* fast." Jessica pushed herself to an upright position and stood up, leaving Brant to readjust himself in his chair. She walked over to where the young man had perched himself on the edge of a coffee table and looked over the top of the drawing pad at the charcoal and pencil portrait.

"Wow. You *are* good. May I?" she asked, reaching for the pad.

She walked the pad over to Brant and turned it around for him to see.

"Yes, very nice," Brant agreed, examining the portrait of Jessica leaning into him, eyes closed with a peaceful expression on her face. "Looks like you were almost asleep."

"Any longer and I would have been," Jessica said as she turned the portrait back around to look at it again. "Look how he captured you here with just a few strokes. Amazing."

Brant pulled his wallet out of his jacket pocket and gave the young man a fifty-dollar bill.

"Hold on. I'll get change from the cashier," he said, turning to take the money to the counter.

"Keep it," Brant told him. "It was worth it."

The young man's smile spread even wider across his face.

"Let me roll that up for you," he offered, as he took the pad away from Jessica and carefully tore off the sheet of drawing paper. Then he rolled the paper before pulling a rubber band out of his pocket and securing the tube.

"If you can, I would spray the thing with a fixative so it doesn't smudge. Charcoal does that, you know," he said, handing Jessica the rolled-up portrait.

"Thank you, I will." Jessica turned to Brant, "Shall we go?"

"Sure, let me just finish my coffee and we're out of here."

A few minutes later, Jessica was making her way toward the door. The place was even more crowded than when they had arrived. The young artist had approached another couple, who were shaking off his offer of a portrait. He looked up long enough to wave goodbye before approaching the three teenagers who were bunched up together on a lumpy couch

151

against the far wall. When Jessica turned around, Brant was right behind her.

"My car is a couple more blocks. Do you want to call your cab now?" she asked, holding the door open for him.

He wheeled past her on to the sidewalk and waited for her to catch up before speaking.

"I'll walk you to your car and then call a cab, if that's all right." Now that the evening was coming to a close he began to feel self-conscious.

He started to think about what he should say when they got to her car. Should he ask her out again? She was technically still his student until the end of the semester. Maybe he should wait. He could say that he'd call her sometime. But that was so vague. What about kissing her good night?

How in the hell can I kiss someone from this bloody chair?

Jessica would have to lean down to him like a mother bending over to kiss her child, and he certainly didn't like the way that would look or feel. A kiss, if there was to be one, would have to wait until another time, another date. Those ten minutes with her sitting on his lap, head leaning against his chest, had been wonderful. It was the closest he'd come in contact with a woman since the accident and it felt good — warm, intimate, comfortable. With all these thoughts racing around his brain, he hadn't spoken one word as they moved past shop after shop down the street to Jessica's car.

Jessica might have spoken up sooner had she not been equally absorbed in her own thoughts. Her entire body had felt pleasantly languid as she stepped out of the café. She could still feel the touch of Brant's fingertips caressing her hand. Thoughts of him touching her all over in that same way made heat rise up her throat, and she cast a quick glance at Brant to make sure he couldn't read her mind, but he seemed lost in his own little world as well.

"A quarter for your thoughts," she ventured.

"A quarter? I thought it was a penny."

"Inflation," she joked.

They walked a little farther in silence before Jessica, using the portrait as a pointer, said, "We turn here. I'm in the parking lot across the street." They crossed the street and entered the lot.

"You should have this," Jessica said, extending the portrait roll toward Brant.

"I bought it for you. You keep it."

"I think you should keep it," she countered. "You paid for it and besides, I can pull an image of you up on my monitor every Tuesday and Thursday. Do you want me to wait with you until the cab comes?" she asked, not liking the idea of just leaving him sitting there all alone.

"No. I'll be fine. I'm going back to the café and I'll wait there. I took one of their cards so I could give the cab company the address. By the time I get back there, I shouldn't have to wait long."

"Pretty smart," Jessica stalled.

"I *am* a professor."

She knew it was time to get in her truck and go, but it didn't seem right to just leave. Normally, at this point, a good-night kiss would have been the perfect ending to a perfect evening, but she just couldn't think of a way that wouldn't feel awkward.

"Well, I should go. Here's the portrait. I assume you will hang it in a suitable place, framed and all," she said, handing him the drawing.

He pulled the roll from her with his left hand and grasped her hand in his right. He pressed her fingers up to his lips, lingering there long enough for Jessica to feel the warmth of his breath against her cold fingers. After a moment he released her hand.

"Thank you for a wonderful evening, J.A. Singer. We'll have to do this again sometime," he smiled, and then before she could reply, whipped his chair around and took off.

Jessica wanted to say something witty and charming, something that he would remember, but she couldn't think of a single thing so she unlocked her car and climbed in. She didn't start the engine right away, but sat there savoring the moment and the feeling of his lips pressing against her hand. Driving home she didn't even turn on the radio so that her mind could replay, uninterrupted, the entire evening from start to delectable finish.

As she often did, she wove pieces of her evening into her fantasy tale of Princess Anne, using her experiences in real life as fuel for her imagination. Before she knew it, she was home with an entire chapter ready to go. Even though it was late, she turned on her computer and began writing, the words flowing like a river running down a mountain. By the time she got everything typed up, it was three a.m. She shut off her computer and crawled into bed.

Her last conscious thought before drifting off to sleep was a question. *How long will Professor Wilson wait until he asks me out again?*

Chapter Twelve

ဢ

The week that Simon came back to work should have been stressful, but Jessica was surrounded by a fuzzy warm glow that not even Simon Fitch could dispel. She hadn't had to wait long for Brant to contact her again. On the Saturday morning after their date, she had turned on her computer to work on another class assignment when the chime rang out, signaling that she had mail. In addition to messages from Cath asking when they were meeting to discuss Thanksgiving, and Sandy, another friend from her UCLA days, there was a message from Brant. With one double-click, she was reading.

Dear Jessica,

Thank you for a most wonderful evening. The best I've had in a long, long time. I hope you'll consider going out again sometime.

Take Care,

Brant

P.S. The portrait looks quite nice taped to my refrigerator.

Jessica hit REPLY and began typing.

Dear Brant,

I, too, had a wonderful time. What did you have in mind?

She had signed it "J.A.", with a postscript of "The refrigerator? I see you found a place of honor".

Emails had gone back and forth for an hour—nothing too serious—always ending with a postscript about the portrait on the fridge. Jessica spent Sunday catching up on the assignments she had missed and working on her novel. By the time Monday rolled around, Jessica had forgotten that Simon was due back to work.

Jessica was sitting at her desk, shoes kicked off, sorting through a dozen Post-it reminders when a timid knock at her open door caused her to look up. There stood Simon, waiting for her to give him permission to enter.

"We need to wrap up some details on the Tyler account. I thought we could meet in the boardroom a little later?" Simon called out from the doorway.

Several seconds passed before Jessica responded.

"I don't think that's necessary. Why don't you email me whatever it is and I'll take care of it from here. After all, it is my account."

With that, Jessica looked back down at the work in front of her. Without another word, Simon turned and left. Jessica heard the creak of his leather shoes as he walked away and only then did she look up, a triumphant smile spread from her lips to the corner of her eyes.

Looks like my Simon Fitch problems are over.

Back in his office, behind the closed door, Simon was throwing darts as hard as he could at the cork dartboard hung on the back of his door. Claire, his secretary, counted each dart—one, two, three—as they made impact, and then his five steps to and from the dartboard as he stomped over to retrieve the darts before starting all over again. Self-preservation told Claire that now was not a good time to disturb her boss.

* * * * *

It was less than two weeks before Thanksgiving when Cath, Dennis, Sandy and Jessica met at the Rose Café for lunch to discuss their annual Orphans' Orgy. The traditional planning meeting was really just an excuse to get together.

Each year, all of Cath's and Jessica's single friends without family in the area gathered to gorge themselves on turkey and all the trimmings, watch football and drink too much. Since the death of her mother, Jessica's dad and brother preferred to go out for Thanksgiving dinner or eat turkey sandwiches from the deli as they watched football for hours. So Jessica had joined the ranks of the orphaned.

Jessica parked her truck on the street and walked to the café. Painted on the walls surrounding the entrance were two larger-than-life, fully opened roses, one rendered in deep reds and the other in shades of pink. Jessica stood to the right of the door waiting for her friends to arrive, admiring the last of the real roses in the garden that ran along the sidewalk up against the building.

Dennis was the first to arrive, a bear of a man with wild brown hair and a short beard. He gave Jessica a huge hug, lifting her off her feet.

"You look as beautiful as one of these roses. Things must be going well for you," commented Dennis, admiring the rosy glow in her cheeks.

"Things are good," she offered, all she was willing to tell him for now.

Cath and Sandy came walking around the corner after parking in the back lot. Sandy was tall and thin with long straight hair that fell just above her waist. Even in her boots, Cath didn't even come up to her chin. After more hugs, all four friends entered the café together. They decided to sit out on the patio since the weather was still mild and the heat lamps were turned on. A tall, dark-haired waiter named Miguel ushered them to a table next to a Chinese Elm and a planter filled with miniature palm trees. Cath gave Miguel "the look" and was rewarded with a sexy smile in return. Once they were all seated and drink orders were taken, the group settled in and caught up on each other's lives. The conversation stopped long enough for Miguel to take their orders. When the conversation got around to Thanksgiving, Dennis reminded everyone that it was his turn to host the event and cook the turkey.

"Do you even know how to cook a turkey?" Cath asked, not altogether jokingly.

"How hard can it be? Jessica did it," Dennis threw back.

"I believe my culinary abilities have been insulted. No wait. Let me check." Jessica looked at Dennis.

"What culinary abilities?" Dennis couldn't resist.

"See? Insulted." Jessica faked a pout.

"Jessica's turkey came out fine," Cath said in her friend's defense. "Even if she *did* forget to take out the giblets from the neck cavity and sewed up the bird with fishing line, which melted. Aside from that it was perfect."

"Cath, next time you feel like rushing to my defense, don't bother."

"Just trying to help," Cath said with a sugary sweet smile.

"I thought Jessica's turkey was terrific," Sandy added between mouthfuls of her salad.

"Okay. Enough. I think I can handle the turkey. What size should I get? Do we have a headcount?" asked Dennis.

"I emailed everyone already and came up with ten people. Cindy and Jim can't make it this year. They're flying back East to have Thanksgiving with Cindy's folks," Sandy said with a knowing smile.

"She's going to introduce Jim to her parents? They must be getting serious," Jessica said.

Dennis shook his head. "Poor guy. When her nice, Midwestern family gets a look at Jim's dreadlocks, it should make for interesting dinner conversation. Bet they've never seen a white guy with dreads. Too bad we can't be at *that* dinner."

"You just thrive on controversy, don't you?" Jessica poked.

"That's why I hang out with you guys—guaranteed drama, better than primetime."

Both Cath and Jessica leaned in and gave him a playful punch in the arm.

"You girls need to do something about your violent tendencies."

They punched him again.

Cath winked at Jessica before saying, "We know you love it, Dennis. It's the only female contact you get."

"Ouch. Low blow, ladies. Low blow," Dennis said while rubbing his arms as if their punches had hurt.

"So back to the headcount, are we good?" asked Sandy.

"Well...I might be bringing someone," offered Jessica, taking a long drink of her iced tea to avoid saying more.

"Really? Are you going to say who or do we have to guess?" asked Dennis, sensing the opportunity to turn the spotlight on Jessica.

"His name is Brant and I haven't asked him yet. I don't even know if he's an orphan or whether or not he has plans. I just thought I'd warn you."

"Brant. Sounds like a yuppie name to me," poked Dennis, trying to get a rise out of Jessica. "Do you think he'll fit in with our little family of misfits?"

Cath, for once, didn't say a thing and just let Dennis have his fun.

"We let *you* in, didn't we?" countered Jessica.

"Ouch again."

"All right you two. Let's get back on track. We've got ten, maybe eleven people. Dennis is cooking the turkey, God help us, and Jessica will email everyone his or her cooking assignments. And remember, don't let Roger bring anything he has to cook," Sandy said. "Remember last year when his potato salad almost killed us all?"

"Right," Jessica nodded. "I'll have Roger bring drinks and I'll bring the football snacks. That way the two non-cooks won't threaten the health of their friends."

The four friends finished up their plans and divided the lunch bill before each one rushed back to work. As Jessica made her way to her car, she was thinking about the best way to ask Brant about his plans for Thanksgiving. She didn't even know him well enough to know whether or not he had family in the area. As she maneuvered her car through the streets of Santa Monica, she decided the best way to find out was to ask him.

That's when she realized that she was hoping he was just as alone as she was.

That evening, sitting in front of her computer, Jessica agonized over what to say and how to say it. After an hour of deleting clever messages, she opted for the direct approach.

What are you doing for Thanksgiving?

She sat there and stared at the sentence, trying to decide if it was too bold or daring.

Why am I so worried about this? After stalking the poor man, this is nothing.

So before she could change her mind, she hit the SEND key without even signing her name. Then she shut down her computer and turned on the television, afraid she would get an immediate answer — an answer she didn't want to hear.

* * * *

It took Brant two entire days before he replied to Jessica's question. It wasn't that he hadn't seen the message right away.

As a matter of fact, he was sitting at his computer the moment it came in. It was amazing to him how such a simple question could throw him into such turmoil, and bring up feelings and emotions he thought he had succeeded in burying a long time ago.

What am I doing for Thanksgiving?

Same thing he'd done every year since the accident and divorce — watch football, drink himself into a stupor and eat a turkey sandwich from the deli while he felt good and sorry for himself. Brant couldn't stop his thoughts from drifting back to a Thanksgiving sixteen years ago.

It had been a scene right out of a Norman Rockwell painting. Linda's family sitting around a huge table covered with a white linen tablecloth and piled high with bowls of mashed potatoes, stuffing, corn bread and green beans. Mr. Stanford, Linda's dad, stood behind the golden brown turkey, carving knife in hand, while Linda's mom snapped the annual turkey-cutting photo. It was family tradition that Mr. Stanford cut the first piece of turkey and sample it. After making a big show of chewing and swallowing — while everyone sat in silent anticipation — Mr. Stanford would pronounce, "This bird is done", and everyone would raise their glass of wine, water or milk, turn to Mrs. Stanford and sing out, "God bless the cook." It was a hokey tradition and Brant just loved it.

Thinking back now, Brant wondered whether he had fallen in love with Linda's family or with Linda. Two years later, when he decided to propose, Brant knew that he would pop the question at the Thanksgiving table, right after the toast to the cook. He had rehearsed his lines on the flight up to Seattle with the engagement ring sitting heavy in his jacket pocket. After what seemed like the longest day, it was time for dinner and the family settled in around the table. As soon as the toast had been finished, Brant pushed back his chair and stood up.

"I have something to say," he shouted in his excitement.

Even Linda's two brothers, Stanley, age ten, and William, age seven, sensed that something important was about to happen and sat still for once, staring at Brant.

Trying to keep his voice from cracking, Brant began. "This is my third year around the Stanford dinner table, and I just want to thank you all for allowing me to be a part of this amazing family. While you already feel like family, I thought I should make it official."

Linda's eyes had widened as Brant reached into his pocket and pulled out the black velvet ring box. Linda's mom gasped and covered her mouth, while Linda's dad kept his eyes fixed on his daughter to gauge her reaction. The only ones who didn't know what was coming next were Linda's brothers.

Brant pulled his chair farther away from the table, went down on one knee and opened the ring box to reveal a small but brilliant diamond in an old-fashioned setting that had belonged to his mother.

"Linda, you would make me the happiest man on earth if you would marry me."

Tears filled Linda's eyes as she pushed back her chair and stood up. Brant stood up to meet her, the ring box still in his hand. Reaching up to encircle her arms around Brant's neck, Linda pulled him against her and whispered, "Oh, yes, oh, yes," into his ear.

Linda's mom burst into tears and the two boys looked around bewildered. Even Mr. Stanford wiped a tear from the corner of his eye when he thought no one was looking.

"What's going on?" asked Stanley. "Why's everyone crying? Did someone die?"

"Your sister's getting married," Mr. Stanford managed to say without his voice cracking as he walked over to shake Brant's hand.

"Oh. Is that all?" Stanley replied, sounding disappointed. "Can we eat now?"

No one answered, since they were too busy hugging each other — mother and daughter, father and daughter, mother and son-in-law-to-be. On that Thanksgiving Day, they broke tradition and had a second toast, a toast to the happy couple.

Now with a week to go until Thanksgiving, Jessica had opened the door to old memories and emotions. He'd been asked to join neighbors and friends for dinner before but had always said no. After a few years, they just stopped asking and that was fine with Brant. Now along comes Jessica Singer, opening up old wounds she didn't even know he had. Brant sat staring at his computer screen for fifteen minutes before deciding to shut it off.

Two days later, he sent a short email to Jessica.

* * * * *

It was the Wednesday before Thanksgiving and Jessica had taken her car to work so she could stop at the store on her way home. Halfway down the cracker aisle her cell phone rang.

"Hey Jess, it's me," said Cath. "What are you doing?"

"Picking up the munchies for tomorrow, why? You need something while I'm here?"

"No thanks. I took care of all my shopping last night. Did you ever hear from Brant?"

"Yeah. He said he had other plans," Jessica said, the disappointment evident in her voice.

"That's too bad. I was looking forward to meeting this guy. Why don't you send him one more email, say something like, 'In case your plans fall through, here's Dennis' address and phone number.'"

"I guess I could do that," said Jessica as she selected two boxes of crackers and dropped them into her cart. "But his email was kind of short and I haven't had another since."

"It's up to you. Anyway, I thought I'd pick up some fresh flowers for the dinner table at Andrel's before she closes tonight. What time are you showing up?"

"By the start of the first game," Jessica said while maneuvering her cart to the dairy section, where she picked up a selection of cheeses.

"Okay. I'll see you then. I gotta run."

Jessica finished shopping, drove the four blocks home and found the last parking spot on her street. Three trips later, she had all the groceries in the house. Out of habit, she turned on her computer as she passed her desk on the way into the kitchen.

With Merlin out of his cage and running up and down the kitchen counter looking for crumbs, Jessica put together a quick salad for dinner and poured herself a small glass of red wine.

Holding out her finger for Merlin, Jessica moved the bird to her shoulder, grabbed her salad and wine and sat at her desk. She had a dozen emails, mostly from everyone getting together for Thanksgiving, but nothing from Brant.

She must have hit a nerve. Jessica twirled her hair around her finger as she tried to decide whether or not to send the email Cath had suggested. Their first date had gone well, at least that was the conclusion Cath and Jessica had come to after a lengthy dissection of every detail. Then there had been their playful banter before she had ended it all by asking about his plans for the holiday.

"Stop it, Merlin," she chastised, as he pecked at her silver hoop earring. Taking the bird off her shoulder, she set him on the desk, where he proceeded to walk all over her keyboard, pecking at several keys before she could grab him.

"You're being a naughty bird. Back in the cage you go."

When she came back to the computer, a blank email was staring back at her with Brant's address already in the "send to" spot. Jessica looked from her computer screen to her bird, who was protesting his imprisonment with loud squawks.

"You trying to tell me something you little wizard?" she asked.

Turning back to the computer, she muttered, "What the hell?" under her breath and began typing.

Chapter Thirteen

ॐ

Thanksgiving morning dawned clear and cold—a chilly Southern California cold of fifty-two degrees. Jessica threw her hair up with a tortoise-brown claw and pulled on a pair of faded jeans and an oversized UCLA baby blue sweatshirt, which accentuated her blue eyes. Making sure Merlin had plenty of fresh water and seed, she attached a honey millet spray to the inside of his cage.

"Happy Thanksgiving, Merlin. Enjoy."

Twenty minutes later she was carrying bags of chips, dips, crackers and cheese up the four steps to the front door of Dennis' cottage-style house in Venice Beach. From the porch, Jessica could hear the pregame show for the first college game of the day blasting out of the six surround-sound speakers. She banged on the door several times before peeking in the window. Dennis was sitting dead center on a huge oversized sofa, his back to the front door, soaking in the splendor of his audio-visual wet dream. Jessica set her bags down on the porch, turned the doorknob and walked in. She walked right up to Dennis and punched his shoulder. He jumped and screamed.

"Jesus Christ! Don't do that."

"What?"

Dennis reached for the remote on the coffee table in front of the couch—the only other piece of furniture in the living room—and turned down the volume.

"Were you trying to give me a heart attack?"

"Are you trying to blow out your ear drums?" Jessica retaliated, relieved he had turned down the volume.

Just then there was another knock at the door, followed by a weak "hello", indicating another guest had arrived. It was Holland, and he was struggling with three cases of beer. Jessica walked back to the door and held it open for Holland before scooping up her bags off the porch and making her way through the living room to the kitchen. In the time it took her to do that, the guys had already opened a beer each and were sitting on the kitchen counter, legs dangling.

"You two don't waste much time," Jessica commented as she placed all her bags on the kitchen table that sat in front of a large bay window. The two guys just gave her big grins, raised their bottles and saluted her before their next swig.

The kitchen was filled with the aroma of baking turkey and Jessica bent over to peer into the oven.

"Don't touch!" Dennis barked out as her hand reached out to open the oven door for a better look.

"Geez. I was just going to sneak a peek," Jessica complained, standing back up. "What's all this?" she asked, indicating the four large pots, one on each of the four stove burners.

"One's potatoes, one's green beans," he said, pointing to each pot. "Corn on the cob and gravy."

Jessica lifted one of the lids to discover the pot was empty. So were the other pots.

"Cath's bringing potatoes and green beans to cook here and Wendy is bringing the corn and will make the gravy," Dennis explained. "I had to borrow three of the pots from neighbors and had no where else to put them. It's all high-tech cooking stuff that you wouldn't understand."

Holland and Dennis clinked bottles as if to say "good one". But before Jessica could think of a clever comeback, someone was knocking at the front door again. Acting disgusted with their childish behavior, Jessica turned her back and walked out of the kitchen.

Cath was at the door with a half-dozen bags and a bouquet of flowers. Roger was walking up the steps behind her with more beer. After exchanging hugs and greetings, Jessica helped Cath bring in her stuff and joined the guys back in the kitchen. More hugs were exchanged before Cath started pulling items out of her bags and Jessica went to work putting chips in bowls, making dips and shuttling everything out to the coffee table. The guys followed Jessica and the food into the living room like rats following the Pied Piper.

"What's a girl have to do around here to get a beer?" Cath called out from the kitchen.

"Ice chest," Dennis, Roger and Holland replied in unison, and Jessica chimed in with a "me too". Cath came out holding two beers and made the guys move over on the couch before passing Jessica her beer.

Cath looked around Dennis' living room.

"When are you going to get some more furniture for this place and put some pictures on the walls or something?"

"As soon as I pay off the TV and audio system," he answered, his eyes never leaving the image of a crimson and gold blur weaving his way to the end zone. When the running back crossed the goal line, the guys erupted into cheers.

Jessica looked at the screen.

"That's S.C. You don't even like them."

"I know, but I have a hundred dollars on them and that touchdown just covered the spread."

Cath couldn't have cared less about the game and looked around the room again.

"This couch is big but it'll never hold ten people. You have any chairs hidden around here?"

"In the garage," Dennis managed to say before yelling "idiot!" at the kicker, who just missed a routine extra point.

"Come on, Jessica. Help me get out some chairs."

Once in the garage, it was quiet enough for Cath and Jessica to have a normal conversation.

"So? Did you send him another email?" Cath asked as she wandered around the garage looking for chairs.

"Yes," Jessica said as if it didn't matter in the least.

Cath dragged two overstuffed chairs out from behind a ping-pong table that was folded in half and standing near the rear wall.

Looking back at a trail of stuffing, Cath asked, "You don't think Dennis wants us to use these, do you?"

Jessica looked around the garage and spotted a tower of white plastic patio chairs stacked in a corner. "Let's grab these."

Cath abandoned the two chairs destined for the dump in favor of the stack of plastic.

"Ugly but utilitarian," Cath pronounced as Jessica handed her three chairs stuck together.

Before they started dragging chairs into the house, Cath had one more question.

"What is it with you and this guy, anyway?"

"What guy?" Jessica played dumb.

"Don't be coy…the professor."

"I don't know what you mean," Jessica lied.

"You have to ask yourself, where could this possibly go? Do you want to have to care for this man for the rest of your life? Who knows if he can even get it up? Maybe that's dead, too. Have you thought about that?"

"A little blunt, aren't we?"

Softening her tone, Cath continued, "I'm just a little concerned about where this is heading. You've had so many dead-ends and each time I see how they chip away at you. I'm just looking out for my friend."

Jessica put down her stack of three chairs and hopped onto the top. Cath followed suit. With both women sitting atop the chairs like royalty, they continued their conversation.

"So, are you going to answer my questions? Why are you pursuing this? Do you feel sorry for him or something?"

"No," Jessica said a little too fast.

"Ah ha! Now we're getting somewhere." Cath was like a hound on a blood trail. "It's a pity date. Once you learned he was in that chair, you couldn't change your tune without it looking like you were a terrible person."

"That's not true!"

Cath wasn't buying it.

"Look. You went out on a date and it was fun but you can tell him it didn't work out. Happens all the time. That's what dating is for. You gave the guy a shot—chair or no chair—and now you can walk away guilt-free. No one would think any less of you."

Part of what Cath was saying struck a chord with Jessica, but just part of it. She *did* find the man fascinating and had wanted to get to know him. But once she had seen him in that chair she'd had to override the urge to just walk away. She just didn't like the kind of person that would have made her—a little too much like her ex-husband Lee.

The first six months of her marriage to Lee Gulliano had been wedded bliss. Both were in love and ready to have children right away. Lee came from a large Italian family with six brothers and four sisters and cousins, aunts and uncles enough to fill a park. While Jessica's brother, Matt, was her only sibling, Jessica still had dreams of a large family, although not quite as large as Lee wanted. They had compromised and agreed to have four kids.

When six months of unprotected sex didn't produce results, Lee started to get anxious. Why wasn't Jessica pregnant yet? Every time her period came, he'd throw up his hands in disgust.

"What's za matter with you? Most girls get pregnant if you look at 'em cross-eyed."

"Maybe it's you," Jessica had retorted, only to be laughed at.

"No way. I come from a long line of Italian studs. Eleven kids in my family, two in yours. You do the math."

After a full year of monthly torture sessions during which Lee accused Jessica of being sterile, she had finally convinced him that they should both be checked, not just her. After a series of tests, it was determined that while both of them had healthy levels of sperms and eggs, there was a problem with the delivery system. The doctor suggested in vitro fertilization, but Lee would have no part of it.

"It's just not natural. If I can't get you pregnant the good old-fashioned way, then I'm not interested. What would my family say? It's just not right. Besides, I don't care what that quack of a doctor said, I still think there's something wrong with *you*, not me."

And to prove his point, he'd had an affair with his secretary and "knocked her up" on the first try. On the day he told Jessica that he was filing for divorce, he was strutting around the house like a proud cock. He even bragged about fathering the child and having the affair. The last words out of his mouth before walking out in a flurry of hand gestures were, "I told you it wasn't me. You're damaged goods."

The phrase "damaged goods" had reverberated in her head the first time she saw Brant in his wheelchair, and it made her feel ashamed. She remembered how she had felt for months after the divorce whenever she saw a mother with a baby. The phrase would slip into her consciousness like a thief in the night, robbing her of self-esteem, making her turn away in shame from scenes of maternal bliss.

"Here's the deal," Jessica said. "I do find him attractive, interesting and intriguing. Our date was very nice —"

"Nice is such a blah word."

"Let me finish. You know what Lee did to me. I never want to do that to anyone—ever. So if Brant is interested then I'm interested. If it doesn't work out, then it'll just be like one of my other relationships that haven't worked for one reason or another. But I'm not going to walk away just because he happens to be in a wheelchair."

"And what happens if one of you falls in love? What then?"

Jessica jumped down from her throne.

"That's always the question, isn't it? Guess we'll just have to take our chances like everyone else." Jessica let out a sigh before changing the subject. "Enough of the twenty questions. Let's go watch men in tight pants run around a football field knocking the crap out of each other."

Cath knew when to drop a topic. She slid off her chairs until her toes touched the ground. "Works for me."

* * * * *

By noon, the living room was packed to capacity with bodies wedged onto the couch, some opting for the floor and others gathered in groups of two and three on white patio chairs. The coffee table, covered with chips, dips, beers and crackers, looked like a child's finger painting. With the game on, people talking in different groups and the occasional shouting for exceptional plays, it was a miracle anyone even heard the phone ring, let alone found it buried under one of the couch cushions. Sandy felt the vibration of the ringing handset more than heard it, since she was sitting on it.

"Orphans' Orgy, head orphan here," Sandy announced into the phone.

Sandy heard a very masculine laugh on the other end of the line.

"This must be the place," the man said. "I'm Brant. Jessica invited me."

"Great. When are you coming over? Do you need directions?"

"I'm kind of already here. I'm out front. Could you please tell Jessica?"

Sandy was a bit confused but answered with a "sure" before shouting out to Jessica, "Hey Jess. Some guy named Brant is on the phone. Says he's out front."

At the sound of Brant's name, Sandy had not only gotten Jessica's full attention, but Cath's as well. Jessica walked over to Sandy and took the phone. Placing a finger in one ear, she moved toward the front door as she spoke.

"Brant?"

"I decided to come after all. I'm outside in front of the house."

By now Cath was at the front window looking out. Brant was sitting in his chair at the base of the steps with a six-pack of beer, a bouquet of flowers and a shopping bag from Trader Joe's. Jessica shut off the phone as she walked out the door, a huge smile spreading across her face.

"Thought you had other plans?"

"They fell through. Hope it's not too late to take you up on your offer?"

"Not at all. I'm glad you changed your mind."

A blast of cheers could be heard coming from the house, indicating another touchdown had been scored.

"Sounds like a rowdy bunch. Think I'll fit in?"

"I don't know. Do you like football or football?"

"I love football. Used to play the game before I switched over to basketball."

"Darn. I was hoping you'd be one of us girls."

Just then the door flew open and three guys came bounding down the stairs.

"Looks like you could use a little help there," Dennis said. He introduced himself and extended his hand to Brant. "Welcome to the annual Orphans' Orgy and my house. Let me help you with this stuff."

With that, Dennis grabbed the beer, the bag of food and handed Jessica the flowers. Holland and Roger introduced themselves and then without warning, each grabbed a side of Brant's chair and carried him up the four steep steps leading to the front door. Jessica followed behind and noticed Cath still watching from the window. Cath gave her the thumbs-up sign before stepping away.

As soon as Brant was in the house, Dennis announced, "Hey everyone. This is Brant, a friend of Jessica's."

Everyone turned, said quick hellos and turned back to the TV just in time to see a spectacular tackle.

"Good thing you brought your own chair. Dennis has no furniture to speak of," said Cath as she came over to meet Brant for the first time. "I'm Cath, Jessica's cohort in crime. I've heard so much about you."

"Really?" A curious smile brought up the corners of his mouth.

Jessica felt like kids were doing somersaults in her stomach as her best friend sized up Brant. Jessica stepped between them.

"I don't think I want you two to become friends. It could be very dangerous for me. Come on," she motioned to Brant with a tilt of her head. "I'll show you where they hide the beer."

Jessica headed toward the kitchen. Once there it was a little easier to hear each other.

"I'm happy you decided to come," Jessica told Brant as she plunged her hand into the ice and pulled out a beer.

"So am I."

Electricity filled the space between them, causing a tingle to run down Jessica's neck to the tips of her toes. The moment hung in the air like a soap bubble before it was burst by Sandy and Holland's entrance into the kitchen.

"Oh. Are we interrupting something?" Sandy asked, grabbing Holland by the shirt, getting ready to pull him back out of the kitchen.

"We were just getting a beer."

Holland pulled himself free from Sandy's grip and gave her a confused look before moving to the ice chest as well.

"It's halftime," he said, as he twisted off the top of his beer. "If you want a good seat for the second half, I'd get in there now if I were you."

"Sounds like a plan," Brant agreed before taking his beer from Jessica, turning his chair around and heading for the door.

Jessica grabbed a fresh beer for herself and followed Brant into the living room. He was able to pull his chair up alongside the couch and Jessica tucked herself into the corner. The halftime commentary was playing itself out without sound and someone had turned on a Dave Mathews CD instead.

"Your friends all seem very easygoing," commented Brant before taking a long pull on his beer.

"They are. Not a single jerk in the entire bunch."

"A few nutcases, maybe," interjected Cath, as she joined the conversation by pulling up a plastic chair and sitting in front of Brant.

"Speak for yourself," Holland chimed in as he was walking past them.

Not letting Holland's comment distract her, Cath continued, "Jessica says you live on a boat in Marina Del Rey. That must be a challenge in a wheelchair."

Jessica's expression of dismay had no affect on Cath, who never saw it. She was watching Brant intently with a radiant smile on her face.

"I had the boat retrofitted to accommodate my chair and me. I bought it dirt cheap from a drunken old sailor. It saved us both—gave me a place to live and gave Captain Barkley enough money to pay off a serious debt and start over."

Jessica was relieved Brant hadn't been offended by her question.

"Even though I've only seen the outside decks," Jessica added, "it seems like you're able to get around pretty easily."

Brant turned the full power of his smile on Jessica. "You'll have to come back for a full tour sometime. I'll show you my office where I film the class."

Jessica's entire body responded, growing softer and warmer with every second of Brant's attention. For five wonderful seconds, Jessica forgot Cath was sitting with them until she heard her next question.

"I hope you don't mind my asking, but what happened? Were you in an accident or something?"

"Cath!" Jessica blurted out. She couldn't believe Cath had just come right out with it. She hadn't even had the courage to ask Brant that question. Cath had always been bold and brutally honest, even to the point of being rude, but this was just too much.

"Hey, if I had walked through the door wearing a cast or hobbling on crutches, everyone would want to know what happened to me. So why should this be any different?" Cath asked with a sheepish grin.

"It's okay. It doesn't bother me, Jessica," Brant reassured her, before answering the question.

Jessica just shook her head, still not believing that Cath would blurt out such a question.

"I was riding my bike along PCH when a car hit me and sent me flying. It wasn't the flying that hurt me, it was the landing."

Jessica cringed as she pictured Brant's athletic body being tossed into the air by the impact.

"That happened about seven years ago and I've been in a chair ever since, and will be for the rest of my life."

Cath leaned in closer to Brant and asked in a whisper, "Can you still have sex?"

The whisper was loud enough for Jessica to hear.

"Jesus Christ, Cath!" Jessica jumped to her feet. A couple of her friends glanced at her quizzically before turning their attention back to the football game.

Brant was laughing as he said, "It's okay. It's probably the number one question I get, especially from other guys."

Grabbing Jessica by the wrist he coaxed her to sit back down. When Jessica saw Brant was laughing, she knew it was going to be all right. Brant turned to face Cath, winked and mouthed the word, "yes".

Cath broke into a big smile.

"Cool. Just looking out for my best friend's interests, here. I'm getting another beer. Want one?"

"Sure. If the Spanish Inquisition is over," he laughed. He polished off the one in his hand before handing the bottle to Cath.

Cath looked at Jessica.

"I think I need something stronger," Jessica exhaled and slumped deeper into the corner of the couch.

"A little early for the hard stuff, don't you think?" asked Cath.

"Not if you're going to keep interrogating Brant like that."

Cath laughed and squeezed Brant's shoulder.

"He's a big boy. He can handle it. Besides," Cath said, directing her comment to Brant, "I always grill all of Jessica's boyfriends. Just thought you'd want equal treatment. Someone has to make sure she doesn't end up with another loser."

"*Go!*" Jessica commanded, pointing forcibly toward the kitchen. "I apologize for my ex-friend's behavior," Jessica said as soon as Cath had left the room.

"No need. I think she's great. Most people tiptoe around my injuries and the whole chair thing like it's something to be avoided at all costs. It's like having an elephant in the room that no one admits is there."

"So you're not upset?"

"Not at all."

"That's a relief..." Jessica was going to say more but someone switched back on the TV sound and everyone started coming back into the room.

Brant fit right in with the football-crazed crowd. But while his attention was on the game, he continued to hold Jessica's hand, toying with her fingers and stroking the back of her hand with his thumb. Jessica couldn't have told you who was playing. Her thoughts kept going back to the conversation and Cath's outrageous questions.

So he can still have sex, Jessica thought, as she enjoyed the touch of his fingers on her hand. *Not a bad thing to know before you get serious with someone.*

* * * * *

Dinner was a huge success. After moving the couch against the wall, the guys had brought in a couple old doors and set them up end to end on top of four wooden crates in the middle of the living room. Once the whole thing was covered with a couple tablecloths, it looked like the perfect medieval banquet table. Jessica, Cath and Sandy had made short work of setting the table and Brant's and Cath's flowers added the finishing touches. The food was plentiful and delicious and no one walked away hungry. Once the aftermath of the feast was cleared away, everyone sat around the huge table finishing off the wine and talking about family, work and friends.

It was then that Jessica felt a familiar melancholy descend upon her like a warm blanket. She remembered how her mother had always spent the entire day in the kitchen while she, her brother and father would play football in the street with the neighborhood kids. When her mother died, her father made no effort to continue their family traditions. Without his wife, holidays didn't mean much to him any more, so he refused to celebrate them. Her brother Matt wasn't celebrating holidays either, except for Veterans' Day, when he threw a huge barbeque for all his war buddies.

Sensing the shift in Jessica's mood, Brant reached under the table and grabbed her hand.

"A quarter for your thoughts," he said in a tone to match her mood.

"I thought it was a penny," she replied, recalling the dialogue from their date.

"Inflation," he whispered as he squeezed her hand.

"I still miss my mom, especially around the holidays."

Brant waited for Jessica to continue.

"She died ten years ago—cancer—and my dad has never been the same since. Sometimes I really feel like an orphan. How about you? Where's your family today?"

"They all live in Connecticut, a little town called Weston. I'm sure they're having the traditional feast with all the cousins, aunts and uncles. They always invite me, of course, but I always refuse. Too much of a hassle..." Brant's words trailed off.

Now it was Jessica's turn to squeeze Brant's hand.

"It's getting late. I should be going. I'll just call a cab," he said, pulling his hand away and reaching into his pocket for his cell phone. Jessica gave him the house address when he asked. "He'll be here in about ten minutes."

Cath was making the rounds with the coffee, so Brant lifted his cup to indicate he wanted a little more.

Once Cath had moved out of hearing range, Brant asked, "So. What would you think about coming over to my boat sometime next week for that tour? Class is over for this semester, so you aren't technically a student of mine anymore."

"Speaking of being a student, when do we get our final grade?"

"Not the grade thing again. You passed, okay? That's the only grade you need to know."

"Did I just barely pass or did I pass with flying colors?"

"Flying colors, banners waving, trumpets blaring, the works. Happy now?"

"Yes! Ecstatic. Do you think I need to take another class?"

"Take all the classes you want, just not from me," he said, looking very serious.

"Why not from you?" Jessica asked, a bit taken aback.

"Because then we can't see each other, can we?" This made Jessica break out into a smile. "Besides, you know how to write just fine. All you need is the time to do it. You almost didn't pass because you missed some assignments. So make writing a priority and just sit down and do it."

"Sounds like you've made that speech before, Professor."

Cath pulled up a chair next to Brant. "So how did you like the tie we sent you?"

"It was fun. I didn't have that one."

"How many ties do you have?" she asked.

"Counting the one you sent, two hundred and thirty-one."

"Wow! That's quite a collection. Why ties?"

"It's my nod to fashion. My mother always says everyone collects something. So I decided to pick something I could use. Then once people find out you collect a certain thing, you receive that for every occasion. Once I got ten ties for Christmas."

Cath laughed. "Maybe I should start collecting something."

"You have a collection," Jessica poked. "Broken hearts."

"Not true."

Jessica couldn't resist putting Cath in the hot seat for once. "Where's Pete? Did you dump him already?"

"He had to work. A lot of drunks on the road today," Cath replied, not giving Jessica the satisfaction of looking the least bit ruffled by her question.

The sound of three taps on a horn came from out front.

"That's my cab. You guys want to give me another hand down those steps?"

"No problem," Dennis answered as he stood up.

Holland stood up, too. Jessica and Cath followed the guys to the door. The guys carried Brant and his chair down the stairs and then slapped him goodbye on the back.

"Hope to see you around again," Dennis shouted over his shoulder as he headed back up the steps.

"I'm going to say goodbye now," Cath added, bending over to kiss Brant on the cheek. "It's cold out here." And then she took the steps two at a time back into the house, leaving Jessica and Brant alone on the sidewalk.

"Thanks for inviting me. This was one of the nicest Thanksgivings I've had in a long time."

"I'm glad your plans fell through, then," Jessica smiled, knowing he hadn't had any.

"How about next Saturday," Brant blurted out, before he lost his nerve.

"Next Saturday?"

"Why don't you come over? If you're free, that is. I'll make dinner."

"Sounds wonderful." Jessica watched as Brant expertly jockeyed his chair into position before pulling himself into the backseat of the cab. The driver folded up his chair and placed it in the trunk while Brant rolled down the window. "So, Saturday it is. What time?" Jessica asked as she crouched down alongside the cab and rested her forearms on the window ledge.

"How about six?"

"Okay. Depending on traffic, I'll either be early or late."

Brant reached out the window and put his hand at the nape of Jessica's neck, pulling her forward until her face was inside the cab. The touch of his hand to her neck sent shivers down her spine as she anticipated what was going to happen next. Before she had time to think, Brant's lips were touching hers and their mouths melted together in a long, slow kiss. Brant pulled away, looking deep into her eyes before speaking.

"See you at six, then," he whispered, not willing to break the mood.

All Jessica could do was nod as delicious sensations continued to wash over her.

The cabdriver took that as his cue and put the car in drive. Jessica pushed herself to a stand, using the car window for balance, before the cab pulled away from the curb.

I'm in so much trouble, Jessica thought as she made note of her body's reaction to Brant's kiss. She couldn't wait to get home to add another chapter to her novel. She had a feeling Lady Anne and Sir William would be having an intimate encounter in the very near future.

Chapter Fourteen

છ્ર

As Jessica drove the twenty minutes from Santa Monica to Marina Del Rey, her mind was playing pinball with a dozen thoughts—from work to Simon to Brant to Cath and then back to Brant again. Images from her novel kept mingling with images from her life, making it difficult to concentrate on either.

The week after Thanksgiving had started out slow at work, but like a rock rolling down a hill, had picked up speed so that by Friday the place felt like a zoo run by the monkeys. In an attempt to catch up, Jessica had gone into the office Saturday morning, only to run into Simon. They had come face to face in the coffee room. Jessica had just finished making herself a mug of hot tea when she turned around to find Simon in the doorway. Her body flinched as if she had been hit.

"Simon. You startled me. I didn't know anyone else was here today."

"Me either," he said, his voice neutral.

Jessica wanted to head straight for her office but Simon wasn't moving from the doorway. They stood in silence, Jessica looking at the steam rising from her mug and Simon looking at Jessica. When Simon started talking, he began slowly with measured words but started building momentum and volume as he tried to explain.

"Jessica, I'm sorry about how I behaved on our business trip. It was inexcusable. Really. It's just that I find you so attractive…"

Jessica looked into the face of a Simon Fitch that she'd never seen before. Gone was the cold gleam in his eyes and the arrogant smile that usually curled his lips. Gone too was the crisp, manicured appearance. Today he wore a pair of faded jeans and a white polo shirt.

"Ever since McMannon brought me onboard I've been fascinated by you, but I didn't know what to do about it."

"So you try to force yourself into my room and kiss me?"

"I know. That was the wrong way to go about it. It's just that…I haven't had much luck with women, especially beautiful women, and I just didn't know how to approach you."

"You could have just asked me out like normal guys do."

"Would you have said yes?"

"Well, no. You're my boss, Simon. I would never date my boss. It's just not smart."

"What if I wasn't your boss? Would you have said yes then?"

Jessica wanted to say no, but he looked so pathetic and lost that she softened just a bit.

"Maybe…but you *are* my boss. So it's just not going to happen."

Simon crossed his arms and leaned against the doorjamb.

"So if I were to quit the company, take a position with another agency…you would consider going out with me?"

Jessica didn't like the direction this was heading. The walls of the break room felt like they were closing in and Simon was blocking the only exit.

"I need to get back to work," she said and began moving toward the door, hoping he would get the hint and move.

For just a second, it didn't look as though Simon was going to move aside, but when Jessica was a step away, he backed into the hallway and let her pass without saying a word.

As soon as Jessica's back was turned, the corners of Simon's mouth turned up into a triumphant smile.

If I were no longer Jessica's boss, he reasoned, *then she would go out with me*. He could fire her, but that would probably piss her off and then she'd never go out with him. He could give up his position, but that was out of the question. There must be another way. He just needed to make it happen.

Simon walked back to his office, his mind poring over possible solutions.

* * * * *

Jessica had stayed at work long enough to gather up materials to take home. She hadn't felt comfortable staying alone in the office all day with Simon creeping around.

Trying to work at home hadn't been such a great idea, either. She had answered a dozen phone calls before she decided to let the machine take over.

Brant called to tell her where to pick up a gate key from the dockmaster so she could get onto the dock. Hearing his voice on her machine brought Jessica more pleasure than she would have thought possible. She picked up the phone before he could finish his message.

"Hey. I'm here."

"Screening your calls?"

"Actually, yes. I'm trying to get some work done and the phone has a mind of its own."

Brant gave her directions to the dockmaster again and reconfirmed the time.

"Want me to bring anything?"

"Nope. Everything has been taken care of. You might want to bring a sweater or something warm. It gets damp down here at night."

"Sure. See you at six."

When she hung up, the smile on her face had spread to her entire body. Two minutes later, her smile turned to a frown as she listened to Cath recount the details of her last date with Pete.

"You know, I thought this one might be a keeper and then he goes and pulls a stunt like this."

Jessica couldn't tell if Cath was hurt, pissed or both. "I'm sorry."

"We had planned on going to my company's Christmas party next Saturday and now that's not going to happen. I bought a new dress and everything. I just don't get it. There we were having a great time when without reason he gets all macho on me and starts acting like a jealous husband, just because I'm flirting with the bartender. You know me. I always flirt with the bartender—you get better drinks that way. It's never bothered him before, and then bam! He slams his beer down on the bar, makes a big scene and storms out, leaving me stranded."

Jessica could hear Cath sniffing and guessed that she'd been crying. This was a first for Cath. She had always been the one who pulled out of the relationship first. Two divorces and dozens of dates—all ended for one reason or another by Cath. On one hand, Jessica felt bad for her friend, but on the other, maybe this would be good for her—let her see how it felt to be on the receiving end for once. Of course Jessica could never say that to her, but she thought it.

Cath wanted to come over, go for a walk and then get dinner, but to her amazement, Jessica said no.

"Sorry Cath. But I have plans for tonight. I'm going out with Brant."

"Oh...that's right. I forgot. You could call him..."

"You'll be fine. Do what I always do—cuddle up with a good movie and a glass of wine and bawl your eyes out. Things will look better in the morning. I'll call you tomorrow and we can take a walk then."

Cath hadn't been very happy with the suggestion but Jessica figured she'd get over that as well.

As she pulled into the parking lot after getting the key from the dockmaster, Jessica tried to turn off all the thoughts that were bombarding her. She tried her mind game — imagining she was at the beach, sand sifting through her hand, gulls circling overhead — but after a minute her eyes popped open. She was too antsy to continue.

Grabbing her purse, Jessica climbed out of her truck and walked over to the gate. It was a cool evening with a slight breeze and Jessica was glad she was wearing a heavy sweater. She'd taken the time to curl her hair so that it cascaded in soft curls around her face, and had even applied a touch of lipstick. A big improvement, she hoped, over her Thanksgiving Day hair-up-in-a-claw-no-makeup appearance. Sticking the key into the lock, Jessica was overcome by a sudden case of nerves.

What am I doing here? she asked herself

She paused at the gate, hand frozen on the handle. Thoughts rocketed around her head, ridiculous thoughts. What happens if she falls in Love? What if she does and he doesn't? Will he want to get married? Would they live on a boat? She could never live on a boat. Could they have children? Would he want to? What about his health? Why did she find him so fascinating? Why him?

"Stop it," Jessica said out loud, and then looked around to see if anyone was watching the crazy person talking to herself.

You're always jumping ahead. This is just a date. Now relax. You can do this, Jessica Singer. Just because you're dating someone, doesn't mean you have to marry the guy.

Her pep talk worked and she turned the key in the lock and opened the gate. Walking along the dock, Jessica noticed how Brant's boat looked out of place amongst the sailboats and yachts that belonged to his neighbors. The houseboat would have been more at home on the bank of a river or on a lake. When she stood at the bottom of the gangplank, she remembered the pull-string that Frannie had used, and reached over and gave it a yank. She heard a sliding door open and close and the sound of his wheels rolling along the deck as he moved around the catwalk. Then he was there.

"Permission to come aboard?" she called out.

"Permission granted."

Brant noticed how firm her legs looked in her skin-tight jeans as she made her way along the gangplank with long graceful strides.

"Glad you're here," Brant said, as he offered her a hand, assisting her onto the deck. "Follow me."

He led her to the stern of the boat, where there was a sliding glass door similar to the one at the fore. When the wheels of his chair hit the mat in front of the door, the door slid open.

"Automatic," Brant explained. "There's a slight ramp, so watch your step."

Stepping across the threshold, Jessica felt her body relax. The warm teak wood walls were illuminated in a soft golden light emanating from brass lanterns placed along the hallway.

"I'll give you the twenty-five-cent tour," Brant said over his shoulder as he rolled down a hallway that was just wide enough to accommodate his chair. "This room is my office," he said, pointing to a doorway on his right. He reached inside and flipped on the wall switch for the light.

Jessica stuck her head in the doorway.

"I recognize this," she said, stepping into the room. She admired the bookcase-covered wall and the huge desk sitting in the middle of the room. Looking at the books on the top three shelves, she turned to Brant.

"How do you reach all those books?"

"I don't. Those books I've already read or never plan to. Many of them are old college textbooks. Everything I use is on the bottom three shelves. Go ahead and sit," Brant said, pointing to the desk chair on wheels.

Jessica moved behind the desk and sat down, while Brant wheeled his way into the room and over to the camera mounted on a tripod opposite the desk. He flipped a switch, which turned on the video lights.

"Wow. That's bright. Maybe I should wear sunglasses." Jessica rolled the chair back and forth behind the desk just like she'd seen Brant do a dozen times. "How do you start and stop the camera from here?"

"Over there to your right." Brant pointed to a stack of books on the desk. "See the remote control hidden behind the books. Just hit the red button."

Jessica hit the button.

"Now look into the camera and imagine you're talking to a hundred students."

Jessica shielded her eyes from the lights so she could see Brant then tried to see the camera.

"It's not on, is it?"

"You just turned it on," Brant said matter-of-factly.

"Well how do I turn it off?" Jessica asked, picking up the remote.

"Don't tell me you're camera-shy? I didn't peg you as the shy type, what with stalking me, writing a hot little story about eating rice..."

Jessica blushed.

"I'm not a stalker and writing a story in privacy is one thing, being on camera is another. Now please, how do you turn it off?"

"Push the red button again," Brant laughed. "Guess I'm just used to it. Come on. I'll give you the rest of the tour."

Brant backed into the hallway and waited for Jessica to come out of the office before switching off the light.

"This," he said, pointing to his left, "is my bedroom. It's also where the head is located. Since I live alone and the chair is tough to maneuver in such tight quarters, there's no door. So if you need to use the head just close the bedroom door. It's a sliding pocket door."

Jessica didn't go into the bedroom but looked in from the doorway. The walls were paneled in teak wood just like the hallway and the queen-size bed was covered with a deep burgundy comforter. Brass porthole windows let in the soft lights coming from the other boats around them. A single piece of furniture, an antique dresser, stood against one wall. On it sat a number of small pewter frames arranged in parallel lines to one side. Jessica would have loved to pick up each one and examined the photographs, looking for clues to this man's life. Instead she let her gaze continue around the room, moving over to a built-in shelf next to the bed that held a brass table lamp and a clock radio. An open closet revealed Brant's clothes hung in perfect rows at waist level, with a special rack for his ties.

"Your tie collection?"

"Over two-hundred ties and counting," Brant said, shrugging his shoulders. "Kind of goofy, I know."

Jessica noticed how all his shirts were grouped together by type—long-sleeve, short-sleeve and T-shirts. Not at all like her closet—a riot of clothing all fighting over three feet of space.

"Everything is so neat and orderly," Jessica said in awe.

"It has to be in such small quarters," Brant said, trying to cover his natural neatnik tendencies. "Come on. I'll show you where we're having dinner."

Jessica followed Brant farther down the hall until it opened up into one large room.

"Welcome to Chez Brant—the smallest French Bistro this side of Pacific Coast Highway. Tonight," he said with his best cheesy French accent, "for jour dining pleasure, ve vill be serving Coquilles St. Jacque, a verrry special carrot soup, French bread and of course, a lovely little Cabernet Sauvignon."

"I didn't know you spoke French."

"Obviously, I don't," Brant laughed, dropping the accent. "I know we should have white wine with shrimp, but the red is so much better. Hope you're not picky about that sort of thing."

"Beer is my drink, so what do I know?"

"Fabulous. Won't you be seated, miss?" Brant gestured with an exaggerated flourish of his hand to the single chair in the room.

Jessica eased herself onto the padded dining room chair and looked around the cabin. Like Brant's bedroom, the galley was a study in neatness, with clean, smooth white countertops, teak wood cabinets all lowered to chair height and a modern refrigerator and oven tucked into the cabinetry. A smile spread across her face when she saw their portrait from the coffee shop held to the refrigerator door with a couple of tacky Las Vegas magnets.

The galley table sat in the corner of the room with a view looking out over the back of the boat through the sliding glass door. Barely large enough for two people, Jessica could see how it was the perfect height for someone in a wheelchair. She ran her finger around the rim of the blue ceramic plate in front of her that looked like it had been handmade. When she leaned into the middle of the table to smell the dusty pink roses that were artfully arranged in a small white porcelain vase, she almost caught her hair on fire on one of the dozen votive candles that surrounded the flowers.

Jessica glanced over at Brant. Thank God he was too busy gathering the wine and glasses to see the near miss. With his back turned, Jessica could let her eyes linger over his broad shoulders. She noticed how the candles' flickering light painted Brant's wavy brown hair with golden highlights. As he pulled the cork out of the wine bottle, her eyes were drawn to his muscled arms, exposed from the elbows down by the pushed-up sleeves of his rusty-brown sweater.

"Would you like a glass of wine?" Brant asked over his shoulder.

"That would be great. Want me to help with anything?"

"Your job is to sit there, relax and look beautiful, which I must say you do very well."

Jessica blushed at the compliment. "After the day I've had, I was hoping that was all I'd have to do, just sit and relax."

At Thanksgiving she had looked a slob, hair up, baggy sweatshirt. Tonight she had tried a different look and she was pleased he had noticed.

Brant brought the two wineglasses and the bottle of wine over to the table and poured them each a glass.

"Bad day?"

"Let's just say I'm so happy to be here."

Brant handed Jessica her glass and raised his for a toast. "Here's to having a wonderful, relaxing evening."

Jessica raised her glass and clinked it against Brant's. The wine went down easy and created a warm sensation that spread south from her throat.

"Why don't you tell me about this bad day of yours?" Brant suggested as he wheeled his chair around to the stove where the carrot soup was simmering.

Jessica filled him in on her day, leaving out the conversation with Simon, which still made her shudder just to think about. By the time she finished her carrot soup and her first glass of wine, Jessica was feeling more and more relaxed.

"Mind if I take off my sweater? It's pretty warm in here."

"Not at all. You'll need it later if we go out on the deck. I'll put it in the bedroom for now."

Brant watched as Jessica pulled the bulky sweater up over her head to reveal a white silk blouse that was unbuttoned enough to show a hint of cleavage—a hint that Brant admired as he took her sweater. When Brant came back he refilled their wineglasses before dishing up the Coquilles St. Jacque. After several mouthfuls, Jessica had to force herself to stop eating long enough to comment on the food.

"This is incredible. You made this?" she asked in amazement.

"Sure. It's very simple. I just followed the recipe out of *The Joy of Cooking.*"

"You make it sound like it's no big deal. I'm not much of a cook. I've been known to burn water."

"There has to be one dish you do well. What's the best dish you've ever made—your specialty?" Brant watched as Jessica took a piece of her hair and twisted it around and around her finger. He loved watching her talk. It gave him an excuse to stare at her face without being rude.

"I think the question *should* be, what's my most famous cooking disaster? There are literally dozens to choose from."

"Name one," Brant challenged.

"Let's see…there was the time I made French onion soup and tried serving it in cold crystal bowls that ruptured the instant the hot soup hit the glass, or there was the time I tried to make quiche but didn't know you needed to squeeze the water out of the spinach first and ended up with quiche soup, and then there was the turkey fiasco."

"I heard about that one from Holland, something about melted fishing line…" Brant laughed.

"Yes. It was quite funny. For me, cooking is a necessary evil."

"But you love to eat?"

"Yes, especially when someone else does the cooking." Jessica took several more bites of the Coquilles, savoring the creamy sauce and the delicious morsels of shrimp. "It's a good thing I don't cook," she managed to say between bites. "I'd be as big as a whale."

"Don't stuff yourself on the shrimp. You'll need to leave room for dessert."

"Dessert? Don't tell me? Just a little something you whipped up this afternoon."

"What else have I got to do?" Brant backed his chair away from the table and rolled over to the kitchen counter, where he pulled out a covered, frosted glass cake pedestal. When he brought it over to the table, Jessica's eyes widened with pleasure.

"Double chocolate cheesecake with raspberry sauce," Brant announced as he removed the cover.

Jessica moaned in appreciation as she took in the chocolate perfection before her.

Brant set the lid down as he watched Jessica stare at the cheesecake as if it had descended from the heavens. He liked the way her eyes sparkled with delight as she admired his chocolate masterpiece. He let his eyes wander farther south to her smooth throat and farther still to the opening of her silk blouse. The shiny fabric fell across her breasts in soft folds, leaving little to Brant's imagination. His body responded and he had to reposition himself in his chair. Just looking at her made him feel inexplicably happy.

"Ready for a piece or do you want a little more Coquilles?"

"There you go with the difficult questions." Jessica took one more piece of shrimp, another sip of wine and then called it quits. "The chocolate is calling and I must respond."

"I'll just grab the raspberry sauce and some small plates," Brant said, backing away from the table, unwilling to take his eyes off Jessica until the last moment.

With a tray on his lap, he had two small plates, two clean forks, a cake cutter and the raspberry sauce. When he turned back to the table, Jessica was standing right in front of him, one hand holding their plates and the other her half-filled glass of wine. Brant stopped short of running into her but not before the sudden movement of his chair spinning around had caught her by surprise.

Jessica succeeded in not dropping a thing but the sudden jerk of her arms sent red wine flying — with the majority of it landing on her white blouse.

Staring down at her blouse, Jessica let out an exacerbated sigh.

"It's ruined. I guess I *am* a bit of a klutz." She walked around Brant and put the plates and her wineglass on the counter.

Brant put the tray on the table. "Take off your blouse."

Jessica turned around and looked at Brant, a little shocked. "What?"

"If we run it under cold water right away, we can probably save it."

Jessica studied his face. "This isn't a sneaky way of getting my clothes off, is it?"

"You're the one who spilled the wine," Brant reminded her. "I'll get your sweater, okay?" Brant moved down the hallway to retrieve Jessica's sweater and when he came back, found Jessica sitting at the table in a white lace bra, arms folded across her chest. Her blouse was bunched into a ball on the table. Brant rolled toward Jessica, her sweater in his lap, his heart racing as each turn of his wheels brought them closer together.

"Maybe I won't give you your sweater after all. You look more delicious than my chocolate cheesecake."

Jessica could feel the color rising up her neck and into her cheeks. Brant's eyes bore into her, releasing a flood of emotion and desire. It had been years since a man, a man she was interested in, had looked at her with such desire.

"Hand over the sweater or I'll be forced to—"

"To what?" Brant picked up the sweater and held it out beyond Jessica's reach. He had her trapped—his chair blocking her way to the sweater.

"Let's trade," Jessica suggested. "One soiled blouse for one sweater."

"Sounds fair," Brant agreed, bringing the sweater back within reach.

Jessica had to unfold her arms to make the trade and Brant was rewarded with a perfect view of her breasts cradled in sheer white lace. He caught just a hint of nipple before Jessica pulled her arms back in.

"Hope you enjoyed the view," Jessica teased, as she pulled her sweater over her head and adjusted her hair.

"Oh, I did. Thank you," Brant said with utter sincerity before taking her blouse over to the sink. Finding it hard to concentrate, Brant tried focusing his attention on the task at hand. "We're going to need more than water to get out these stains. In the bathroom medicine cabinet, you'll find a bottle of hydrogen peroxide. Could you grab it?"

Jessica walked down the hall to Brant's bedroom and reached in the doorway to switch on the light. Moving her hand up and down the wall, she found the switch at waist height. The bathroom switch was also lower. Brant's bathroom was as neat as the rest of his home. She half expected the items in his medicine cabinet to be alphabetized. On the second shelf she found the brown bottle of hydrogen peroxide and, resisting the urge to snoop among his things, closed the cabinet and returned to the galley.

"Here you go. This gets out wine stains?"

"You don't pour it directly on the stain but mix it with water first. It takes the red out," Brant said, showing her the red marks still visible on her blouse.

"So let's see...you cook amazing meals, keep your home in ship-shape and know how to get red wine out of silk blouses. Is there anything you can't do?"

"Well, walk for one thing."

"Funny. I'm being serious," Jessica laughed. "I can't even boil water without burning the pan, my house looks like it's been hit by a tornado half the time and I would have thrown that blouse away."

Brant finished with the blouse and held it up for Jessica to see. "Voilà. Zee stains, zey are gone."

Jessica applauded as if Brant had just performed a magic trick.

"Let's have dessert out on the deck. I'll bring the cake and some port if you'll grab one of the heavy Mexican blankets out of the hall closet. It's there on the right," Brant motioned toward the hallway.

When Jessica returned, Brant was already outside and seated on the padded bench seat where Jessica had sat on her first visit.

"Hope you don't mind if I join you up here. This way we can share the blanket."

"Sounds perfect. I see you lit the tiki torches," she said as she sat next to him and pulled the heavy blanket over both their legs.

The bench was a little too short for two people, which caused their shoulders to touch. Brant reached over to the tray he'd set down next to the bench and picked up a plate and fork with a thick wedge of chocolate cheesecake, drizzled with raspberry sauce.

"May I?" he asked, holding a forkful in front of Jessica's mouth.

Nodding her approval, Jessica opened her mouth like a little kid. Brant moved the fork up to Jessica's lips, teasing her with it before sliding it past her lips. Jessica made appreciative yummy noises as she savored the mixture of flavors. Brant couldn't help thinking of Jessica's erotic story of the fork moving in and out of the young man's mouth. He let himself imagine her lips around a specific part of his body and his hand began to tremble.

"This is incredible," she mumbled, using her tongue to swipe chocolate off her teeth.

"Glad you like it," he managed. "Here. Taste the port. It brings out the taste of the raspberry sauce." He handed her a small glass and watched as she took a sip of the sweet, rich wine.

"Mmmmmm. How do you know all this stuff?"

"I took a cooking class online and another class on matching wine with food."

"I'd ask for the recipe but with my cooking skills, there's really no point."

Brant shifted his body slightly, turning his upper body more toward Jessica.

"No need. I'll make it for you whenever you want." Brant reached over and took Jessica's chin in his hand, turning her face to his. He hesitated for a moment, staring into her eyes, before leaning in and kissing her. The kiss was warm and sweet, tasting of port and chocolate. Brant pulled away to ask, "Is this okay?"

"It's just like your cooking…delicious," Jessica whispered before leaning in and kissing Brant, opening her mouth to his.

They kissed on the back of the boat, Brant's strong arms wrapped around her, his hands moving up and down her spine into the hair at the nape of her neck. When he moved his fingers, massaging her scalp and grabbing and releasing handfuls of hair, it sent shock waves down to Jessica's toes.

Brant couldn't believe how wonderful she felt in his arms, how she went all soft at his touch or how her body pressed into his—warm and yielding. He loved the feel of her hair tangled in his fingers and buried his face in her neck, filling his lungs with her scent. The image of her sitting in the galley in her jeans and bra danced through his mind as he reached up under her sweater to run his fingers across her back. She didn't tense up as he worked his hands around to her waist until he was caressing her stomach with the tips of his fingers. Waiting for any negative reaction before moving higher, Brant kissed her more deeply than before, trying to say with his kiss what he couldn't yet put into words.

A soft whimper escaped Jessica's lips as Brant reached up even higher under her sweater and cupped her breast gently in his hand. Brant found her breast to be just as he imagined it— firm yet soft. He ran his fingers along the exposed flesh pushed up by the lacy bra. He felt Jessica shiver at his touches as he teased her with his tongue, then bit and pulled gently at her bottom lip, eliciting a deep throaty moan.

Jessica's hands weren't idle as she explored his mouth and lips. Her hands ran over the hard expanse of his back all the way up to his broad shoulders and down his muscled arms. When her hands moved down and found their way inside Brant's sweater, she wasn't ready for how hot his flesh felt. Jessica was startled as Brant's entire upper body jerked and his mouth broke away from hers.

"My God! Your hands are freezing," he said as he took both her hands in his and started rubbing them briskly.

"I hadn't noticed."

Jessica watched as Brant continued to rub her hands. Then she pulled one hand away and presented it to his mouth, brushing her fingers against his lips. "I can think of a faster way to warm up my fingers."

Brant accepted her offering and opened his mouth enough for Jessica to slide in her index finger.

"Two down, eight to go," she sighed, as Brant sucked first on her finger and then on her thumb.

Pulling her hand away, Brant again grasped both her hands in his. "I think we should go inside," Brant managed to say as Jessica leaned in and kissed his throat.

Cold hands or not, Jessica was unwilling to go inside and break the connection of their hands and hearts. Brant let go and cradled her face, drawing it in for a deep, soulful kiss. Their tongues danced around each other, driving up the heat of the moment and causing Brant's arousal to push hard against his jeans. The kiss flowed and evolved, finding a rhythm of its own, moving from a soft, slow flitter of tongues to a hard, penetrating, lusty plunge, leaving their lips tender and bruised. When they came up for air, Jessica was shaking all over.

"That does it. I'm taking you inside," Brant said with authority. With that he pulled away the blanket, pulled his chair alongside the bench and slid over onto the seat.

"I'm not cold," Jessica protested, even though her hands were like ice and once separated from Brant's lips, her teeth chattered uncontrollably.

Brant patted his thighs. "Come on, I'll give you a ride."

Jessica laid the blanket aside and lowered herself onto Brant's lap. As she wiggled into place, she was very aware of his erection pressing against her. Brant rolled his chair up to the sliding glass door, which opened automatically when his wheels hit the mat. As soon as they were in the cabin, Jessica turned herself sideways and leaned into him. Brant's arms encircled her as they reenacted the pose of their portrait hanging on the refrigerator.

"This has been a wonderful evening, Professor. But I'm afraid I should be going."

While her mouth said she should go, her body ached to stay, her fingers playing with his thick wavy hair.

Brant didn't speak but took the opportunity to nuzzle his nose into the side of her neck, inhaling deeply as if trying to commit her scent to memory. His hands moved up and down her arms with long, loving strokes. Jessica cuddled deeper into his arms, happy to stay a few moments longer. They sat like that for ten minutes, Jessica listening to the beating of Brant's heart and the soft lapping of water against the side of the boat. Brant held onto her like a drowning man until reluctantly Jessica pushed herself up straight.

"It's late. I should go." Even as she said the words, Jessica's mind went back to Brant's bedroom, tempted by the warm burgundy comforter and thoughts of sleeping with this man.

Brant wanted to shout out, "stay!" Wanted to roll her right into his bedroom and make love to her until the seagulls started screaming with the sunrise. But he knew it was too soon, so he helped Jessica stand up.

"I'll put your blouse in a bag," Brant said—the only thing he could think to say.

Jessica found her purse and waited while Brant folded her wet blouse and placed it in a plastic bag.

"I'm walking you to your car," he said, as he tucked her blouse between his legs and began to move toward the hallway.

Once on the dock, Brant led the way up the long ramp in silence to the gate. Jessica stepped ahead and opened the gate for Brant and then let him follow her to her truck.

"Sit down again, will you?"

"This is pretty convenient, you having a chair everywhere we go," she teased as she sat on his lap again.

"Good night, Jessica Singer."

He brushed his tongue over her bottom lip, teasing her before devouring her like a starving man. He drank her in—her taste, her texture, her touch. He wanted this woman more than he wanted to walk, to run, to dance. If it wasn't for the fact that now even he was feeling the chill in the air, he would have sat next to her truck all night just kissing her.

When Brant pulled back, Jessica was breathless. Her chest was heaving and she didn't even notice how cold it was. Her face felt like it was on fire and her lips burned. Even under the harsh glare of the security lights, Jessica could see the flush in Brant's cheeks and the warmth in his eyes. She didn't want to break the moment but it was getting late. She stood up and unlocked her door.

"This has been some evening..." Jessica's words trailed off into the night as she savored their last kiss.

"Save next Saturday night for me, will you? I have something special I want to show you." And with that he whipped his chair around and headed back to the dock, leaving Jessica to wonder what next Saturday would bring.

Chapter Fifteen

ଛ

After such a wonderful weekend—Saturday night with Brant, a walk along the beach with Cath and then spending the rest of Sunday writing—Jessica was reluctant to go to work on Monday. While working on her novel, the words had flowed and flowed, making her want to call in sick so she could keep writing. But when the alarm went off Monday morning, Jessica dutifully dragged herself into the office. Once there, Jessica was happy to learn that Simon would be out all week checking out a PR firm in Portland, Oregon. The entire office let out a collective sigh of relief.

Kim gave a quick knock on Jessica's door before walking over to her desk.

"Here are those files you asked for." Kim paused, looking for an open spot on Jessica's already crowded desk.

"Set them on the floor."

Kim placed the file folders on the floor next to Jessica's desk, alongside another stack of folders. As she stood up, she looked at Jessica and didn't turn to leave.

"What?" Jessica could feel Kim's scrutiny.

"There's something different about you today," Kim observed.

"Simon's gone. Everyone has a smile on their face today, including Claire."

"No. It's more than that. Your cheeks have a flush of color and I don't think it's rouge. You're wearing your hair down, which looks great by the way, and you have a glow about you."

Jessica tried to steer her off course. "Must be the holiday spirit."

"It's a man, isn't it?"

Jessica blushed.

Judging by Jessica's reaction, Kim knew she was right. Moving aside a carton of papers from the client chair, she made herself comfortable. Jessica just looked at her, pretending not to know what she expected next, but it became obvious that Kim wasn't moving until she came clean.

"So I met this man. It's no big deal," she admitted.

"Go on," Kim encouraged her. "I'm not leaving until I find out about the guy who put that sparkle in your eyes."

Jessica proceeded to tell her about Brant and their date on the boat, leaving out the fact that he was in a wheelchair.

"Sounds like this one has potential," Kim approved.

"Compared to the losers I've dated in the past, Brant is a real prince."

Kim stood up to leave. "Just take it nice and slow and don't rush into anything. Princes have a habit of turning back into frogs."

"Kim?" Jessica's serious tone made Kim sit back down. "I think I'm falling for this one. It seems too soon, I know, but I can't help how I feel. What should I do?"

"You're asking me? I'm not much of an expert. I thought I was in love, married the guy and then look what happened — he runs off with some bimbo he met on a train. I should have known better, believing his stories about working late and out-of-town meetings…but I was 'in love'. Makes me sick to think how stupid I was."

"When a man cheats, *he's* the stupid one. Besides, I can't image Brant cheating." Jessica tried to imagine Brant picking up some blonde in a bar and the image just wouldn't gel. "Brant's kind of a recluse."

"Even hermits have a libido. You need to take it slow. Try to get to know him better before declaring your love. Hold that back until you're sure."

"How will I know? I thought I was sure the last time and look what happened."

"This time you have some experience. Use it. Being in love is intoxicating, but you have to be practical, too. So many marriages fail for practical reasons—kid issues, money, different values and different expectations. It's hard to stay in love when everything else is falling apart."

"Who said anything about marriage?"

"What's the point of love if not to marry?"

"You can fall in love without getting married," Jessica argued.

"Maybe *you* can, but I wouldn't be able to. Once I'm in love, my minds turns to marriage, sometimes even before the first date. I try on the man's last name like an infatuated teenager. I can't help myself. It's pathetic, I know. Guess I'm just old-fashioned when it comes to love."

Jessica wouldn't admit it, but she had tried on Brant's last name as well. "Can't help how I feel," she said, thinking about how memories of last night gave her a warm glow all over. "And yet there are things about this man that I'm not sure I can live with. Or to put it more accurately, don't know what impact they'll have down the road." Brant's disability would affect every part of their lives, but in what ways, she didn't know.

Kim stood up again. "Sometimes you don't get to pick who you fall in love with, love picks you. I'd say give it more time, a lot more time. You've been on what, one date?"

"Two," Jessica interjected.

"Two whole dates and you're already in love." Kim shook her head as she walked to the door.

Jessica slumped in her chair. "I don't know what to do."

"Don't *do* anything. Relationships have a life of their own. Just enjoy and see where the adventure leads. Don't force things to happen or you'll find yourself trapped in a marriage to another frog."

When Kim was gone, Jessica picked up her crystal ball and rolled it from hand to hand. Holding it up to the light, she peered into the glass globe looking for answers. Nothing magically materialized to enlighten her so she went back to work. An hour later she had a very similar conversation with Cath, only this time it was Jessica giving out the advice to the lovelorn. Cath, who on Sunday had ranted on and on about how much Pete bugged her, was now convinced he was her soul mate and that she'd lost him forever.

"So call him," Jessica suggested, knowing Cath would never pick up the phone first.

"Why should I? He's the one who left me at the bar. He owes me an apology," Cath pouted.

"What if he thinks it's *you* who needs to apologize? Are you going to lose the love of your life by being stubborn?"

"But I didn't do anything wrong," she insisted.

"You can apologize without admitting you were in the wrong."

"And how do I do that?" Cath spat back.

"You say you're sorry for making him so angry or hurting his feelings. You apologize for how your actions made him feel, not necessarily for your actions. You *are* sorry you upset him, aren't you?"

"Well sure…"

"Then call him up and tell him that. Once you two are talking again, you can discuss what made him so angry. If you like this guy, it would be worth the effort."

Jessica looked at her watch—ten to noon. "Look. I have a lunch appointment. Call me tonight if you want. Better yet, call Pete."

The rest of the week was a blur of clients, deadlines and meetings. Cath phoned Jessica on Wednesday, letting her know that she and Pete were "on again", thanks to her well-crafted apology, which had led to some great make-up sex. Besides her conversation with Cath, Jessica had two very long phone calls with Brant.

The first was on Tuesday night and lasted for over an hour. They talked about writing, career choices, office politics and how Brant managed to sidestep all the faculty politics by working virtually.

On Friday night when he called, Jessica was in bed reading a book. This time their conversation delved into more personal details. Jessica learned about Brant's family in Connecticut and how they had wanted him to come home after the accident. Jessica spoke about her mother's death and her father's withdrawal from Jessica and her brother. They each shared their thoughts on careers and families and discovered they both wanted something more than a career. After two hours, Brant had brought the conversation to a close, teasing Jessica about the surprise for Saturday night.

"Can't you give me a clue?" Jessica pressed, snuggling down deeper into her blankets.

"You'll need to dress warm and be in the holiday spirit," Brant hinted.

"So we'll be outside and it has something to do with Christmas. Are we going somewhere?"

"No more clues. You'll just have to wait until tomorrow."

Jessica yawned. "This is going to drive me nuts."

"I can tell," he said sarcastically.

"Sorry. Just a little tired. So besides warm clothes, should I bring anything? Wine, food?"

"A toothbrush?" Brant let the implication hang in the air for just a second before continuing, "Or a bottle of wine."

The toothbrush comment wasn't lost on Jessica. "See you tomorrow," Jessica laughed before hanging up.

Thoughts of a late evening—a *very* late evening—made Jessica feel all warm and fuzzy as she reached over and turned off the small Tiffany lamp next to her bed. The thought of crawling into bed with Brant Wilson, former professor and future lover, both excited and terrified her.

What am I getting myself into?

* * * * *

Jessica pulled her jacket in tight around her as she made her way to the dock gate. Brant had propped the gate open for her so she wouldn't have to go get a key. A damp ocean breeze made wisps of her hair dance around her face as she walked down the dock with her head down. Her pace slowed as she approached Brant's boat and she looked up into a glow of white light. Brant's boat was outlined in white twinkle lights from fore to stern, transforming the funky-looking craft into a fairy's palace.

As Jessica stood at the foot of the gangplank she could hear the refrain of "We Wish You a Merry Christmas" coming from inside. Despite being cold, she didn't ring the bell right away when she heard Brant's deep voice join in the singing. Her smile spread until it turned into a laugh as Brant tried and failed to hit one particular high note. Jessica pulled on the cord and the sound of the bell blended with the Christmas music. A minute later Brant appeared, wearing a forest green sweatshirt and a Santa hat.

"If it isn't one of Santa's elves," Jessica laughed as she walked up the gangplank and bent over to kiss Brant on the cheek.

"Hope you've been a good girl this year, Ms. Singer, because Santa has a real nice present waiting for you," Brant said in a booming, Santa-sounding voice.

Jessica followed Brant into the cabin and down the hall to the galley, where Christmas music was pouring out of the wall speakers.

"Let me turn this down," Brant shouted over "Deck the Halls".

Jessica looked around the cabin. "You've been busy."

Walking over to a corner of the room, Jessica took in a deep breath of pine-scented air emanating from a three-foot Christmas tree covered in white lights and old-fashioned blown glass ornaments.

"These are beautiful," she said as she turned a glass Santa in her hand. "They remind me of my childhood. We had the same type of ornaments on our tree. Where did you get them?"

"My mom sent them to me. She was so excited that I was interested in decorating for the holidays that she sent me a huge care package full of all this stuff." Brant gestured to all the Christmas decorations adorning the galley. He watched as Jessica looked around the cabin, waiting for her to spot the mistletoe hanging from a light in the middle of the room, above where he was sitting.

It took a few seconds before Jessica saw the lump of green tied with a red ribbon suspended over Brant's head.

"How did you get that up there?" She came over and sat in his lap, looking up at the mistletoe.

"Elves," he whispered in a voice full of longing, as he reached his hand around the nape of her slender neck and pulled her in for a long, deep kiss before releasing her.

A couple more kisses like that and the evening could take a very interesting turn. When Brant's pulse returned to normal, he wheeled them both over to the counter where a Crock-Pot held a steaming concoction.

"Have you ever tried spiced wine?" Brant motioned to the Crock-Pot. Jessica stood up and put her face over the pot and inhaled.

"Smells wonderful—like cinnamon and cloves."

"Good nose. It's cinnamon, cloves, a little nutmeg, orange and lemon peel, port and brandy. I'll fill two mugs, if you'll grab that Mexican blanket again. Do you remember where it is?"

"Sure." Jessica went to the hall closet and came back with the blanket. "I assume we're heading back outside again."

"That's where the surprise is."

Jessica followed Brant through the sliding glass door out to the deck, where a single chair was set up facing out into the harbor. On the chair was another Santa hat.

"I'm guessing you want me to wear this?" Jessica picked up the hat and pulled it onto her head, turning to Brant for approval.

"Perfect," he beamed. "Now I'm not the only one who looks ridiculous. Here." He handed her a mug of spiced wine. "This will keep your hands warm, the hat will keep your head warm and the blanket can cover the rest."

Brant pulled his chair alongside Jessica's and they both sat in silence for a moment, hands wrapped around their mugs, steam rising up to their faces.

Jessica tucked the blanket around her legs. "What are we doing out here besides freezing?"

"You'll see." Brant sipped the hot wine, letting the warm liquid heat him.

Then in the distance, Jessica could hear the faint refrain of holiday music floating over the water. Turning toward the sound, she caught a glimpse of moving lights coming around the corner of another dock. Voices singing "We Wish You a Merry Christmas" became clear as a huge sailboat with red and green lights strung from the top of its mast came into full view along the main channel. Jessica turned to Brant.

"Surprise! I rounded up a few hundred friends of mine to decorate their boats and put on a parade just for us," he said jokingly. "Hope you like parades."

Jessica leaned into Brant, tucking her arm around the bend of his elbow and resting her head on his shoulder. "I do now," she said as another boat came into view, this one with three reindeer and Santa's sleigh outlined in lights.

One after another, over fifty boats—from yachts to day cruisers—made their way along the main channel right past slip 618 for the annual Christmas boat parade. Shouts of "Merry Christmas" echoed back and forth over the water as the costumed boat crews waved at their audience sitting out on the boats moored in the marina. Reflections of the holiday lights danced and skipped over the rippling water, creating a kaleidoscope of colors.

"It's so lovely," Jessica murmured before lifting her head and looking at Brant. "I've always loved this time of year. How about you?"

"When I was a kid, Christmas was magical—the lights, the music, the whole Santa-with-flying-reindeer thing and all the presents that appear overnight in your stocking. I've always looked forward to creating that same kind of experience for my children…"

Jessica squeezed his arm. "Me too," she said, thinking of the children she would never have. Then to fill in the silence she continued, "When it came to all the myths of youth—Santa Claus, the Tooth Fairy, the Easter Bunny—I had a real hard time giving them all up. Even when my friends told me otherwise, I still wanted to believe. From there it was an easy transition to believing in fairy people, leprechauns, unicorns and other mythical creatures. I still love to escape into a well-written fantasy novel. That's why I want to write fiction. I have an overactive imagination."

"For the last seven Christmases, I've avoided the holiday by burrowing deep into my own little world of books and work and didn't stick my head back out until after the New Year."

Jessica understood far too well. After her divorce, Christmas had turned into a depressing series of parties and family obligations that would fill her with dread at the first signs of red and green in storefront windows.

"This is the first year I've felt like having a tree again or putting up lights since…" Brant took Jessica's hand in his and gave it a meaningful squeeze. Just as he was leaning in to kiss her, a shout came across the water, causing Brant to pull back.

"Yoooohoo! Brant! Merry Christmas," Mitsy called from the back of her boat.

Dressed in fur from head to toe, Mitsy was standing at the railing of her yacht waving at the two of them, her husband and boys busy watching the last of the boat parade glide by. "Why don't you and your girlfriend come over after the parade for a hot toddy?"

Brant waved back. "Maybe another time, Mitsy. Merry Christmas." He turned to Jessica. "Let's go inside before she invites herself and the boys over."

Jessica grabbed the blanket and their empty mugs, waved at Mitsy who was still leaning on the railing watching them, and followed Brant inside. Cold air followed them in, causing the heater to switch on.

"You hungry? I have a Chinese chicken salad ready to go." Brant moved to the refrigerator and opened the door to reveal a large glass bowl filled with lettuce, Mandarin orange wedges, almond slices and grilled chicken pieces. "All I have to do is toss in the dressing and add the Chinese noodles."

"Sounds perfect. I'm going to bring my chair in so I have a place to sit."

"What? You don't like sitting on my lap?" Brant teased.

Jessica ignored him and went outside to retrieve the chair. She stayed a moment to wave at one more boat in the parade that had created a Christmas tree out of green lights by suspending them down from the tip of the mast. When she came back in, Brant had the salad ready and on the table. She took off her jacket and placed it on the back of her chair.

"There's a bottle of wine in the rack next to the refrigerator and the bottle opener is lying next to it. See if you can open the bottle without spilling it."

"I get the distinct impression you think I'm clumsy," Jessica said over her shoulder as she expertly removed the cork and poured two glasses of red wine. She took a moment to examine their portrait still clinging to the refrigerator door.

"Picture of your girlfriend?" she asked as she brought the wine to the table.

"I think so. What do you think?"

"Looks like your girlfriend to me," Jessica laughed.

Brant brought two ceramic bowls to the table and began serving the salad. Jessica sat in her chair with her hands tucked under her legs.

Brant reached down and pulled out her left hand. "I was just teasing you about being clumsy. I think you're as graceful as a gazelle."

"And I think you're a wonderful liar—" was all Jessica managed before Brant leaned in and planted a quick kiss on her lips.

Then lifting his wineglass he made a toast. "Here's to you, Jessica Singer. Thanks for bringing the Christmas spirit back into my life."

Jessica glowed with pleasure as she took a sip of wine before removing her Santa hat and starting in on her salad. Brant removed his hat as well and pulled his chair up to the table. In between bits of conversation, they managed to each finish their salad and drink the entire bottle of wine. The heater made the cabin cozy and warm while the wine did its part to keep the conversation moving along.

Jessica removed her bulky sweater to reveal a long-sleeved V-neck T-shirt. To Brant's delight, he noticed she wasn't wearing a bra and had difficulty keeping his eyes above her neck. Every time Jessica looked away, Brant stole secret glances, causing his body to come to full attention. To distract himself he launched into a story about his days on the UCLA football squad.

During the story, Jessica sat transfixed, her chin resting in the palm of her hand as she took the opportunity to examine the laugh lines at the corners of Brant's eyes. She watched as he kept pushing aside a brown curl of hair that kept falling in front of his left eye. His lips enthralled her, the way they wrapped around each word, like the young man in her story whose lips wrapped around the fork, conjuring up erotic images for her main character. Jessica, too, found herself imagining those lips on her body and it flooded her with a different kind of warmth.

Brant stopped in midsentence and Jessica pulled her attention to his eyes, which were boring into hers.

"I'm sorry. I forgot you're not exactly a football fan."

"True. But I'm a Brant Wilson fan."

"Enough about me. I've been monopolizing the conversation all evening. It's your turn," Brant offered, his eyes never leaving hers.

"I have a better idea." This time it was Jessica who leaned in to kiss Brant.

Brant responded by moving his chair in front of her, positioning his knees on either side of her legs so he could face her. Jessica scooted herself to the front of her chair so she could get even closer. Their kiss went from tender to passionate as Brant ran his hands along her arms before moving to her waist and belly. His fingers traced slow circles on her abdomen, moving upward until his knuckles grazed the soft curves of the underside of her bare breasts. Jessica's pulse quickened as he teased her with tender touches, moving to her waist and around her stomach, brushing across her breasts as if by accident.

Jessica grabbed Brant's hands and pulled away from his kiss. "I can't keep this up," she managed to get out, her breath coming in gasps.

"I'm sorry. I thought—"

"Sitting. It's too awkward," Jessica explained before he could get the wrong idea.

Brant's expression went from one of concern to pure joy.

Jessica stood up and pulled her T-shirt back into place. "I need to use the bathroom first," she said, before heading to Brant's bedroom.

Once in the bathroom, Jessica rested her hands on the sink and bent down to look at her flushed face in the lowered mirror.

Okay, Jessica. This is it. Might as well find out what kind of lover he is now before it's too late.

She played with her hair, checked her teeth and then splashed a little water on her face.

"God, I hope he's good," she whispered to her reflection.

Brant took a few minutes to clear the dishes and put the salad back in the refrigerator. He noticed his hands were shaking.

This is it. The big test. I haven't made love to a woman since the accident. I hope I remember what to do, what to say.

"God, I hope I'm good enough for her," he whispered to himself.

Then he poured a single glass of port and rolled down the hall. When he got to the doorway he was surprised to see Jessica sitting naked on his bed wrapped in his comforter.

"I was cold," Jessica offered as an explanation.

Brant brought her the glass of port. "This should warm you up."

Jessica watched as Brant lit two candles on the dresser and then switched off the lights. When he pulled his sweatshirt over his head, Jessica got her first view of his upper body — muscular and strong, with a masculine patch of soft brown hair laying flat against his chest between his nipples. She watched as he positioned his chair next to the bed before bending over at the waist to remove his Ugg boots. Then like a gymnast mounting the parallel bars, he hoisted himself up onto the bed. Once there, he scooted himself back farther onto the bed until his feet were next to Jessica's.

"Mind sharing some of that comforter?"

Without responding verbally, Jessica pulled the comforter out from around her shoulders and spread it over the two of them. Brant watched as Jessica's breasts were revealed. His hand reached out to gently brush his fingers across the soft curves, stopping at each nipple to do little circles with his fingertips before moving on.

"Beautiful," he said like a prayer.

A moan escaped Jessica's lips and she let herself sink back into the pile of pillows stacked against the headboard. Brant reached under the comforter and removed his pants, dropping them off the side of the bed before turning his upper body toward Jessica's.

"Lie down with me," he whispered. He watched as Jessica slid farther under the comforter, moving her body to his until their hot bellies were touching.

Brant began kissing her, first along her neck and then moving down between the sweet valley of her breasts until his mouth covered her nipple and sucked it gently, pulling a sigh of pleasure from Jessica's lips.

"It's been so long," Jessica whispered into Brant's hair as he toyed with one of her nipples between his teeth.

She ran her fingers through his thick hair before pulling him away from her breasts to taste his mouth once more. For an hour they explored, tasted and immersed themselves in each other, savoring every caress, every moment, like two love-starved prisoners.

When Brant couldn't stand it any longer he pulled away from Jessica's kiss.

"Do you mind?" he asked, reaching for a condom in a little wooden box by the lamp.

Once protection was in place, he pulled Jessica toward him for another long, deep, slow kiss.

"Hope you like being on top," he managed to say between kisses, his voice husky with desire as he rolled onto his back, pulling Jessica atop him. Repositioning herself, Jessica straddled Brant and lowered herself over him, taking his full length deep inside her in one long motion. Brant groaned, running his hands along the tops of her thighs as Jessica arched her back in pleasure. Their lovemaking took on new urgency and with Jessica in control of the motion it wasn't long before Brant's body exploded in blissful release. Teetering on the brink, Jessica continued to rock back and forth until she too felt her body spasm over and over again, leaving her exhausted and weak. She collapsed onto Brant's chest, not moving until their breathing returned to normal. Only then did she slide off to one side where she could nestle in the crook of Brant's arm.

"That was wonderful," Jessica murmured in a sleepy voice.

Brant wrapped his arms around her and his hand started caressing her arm, dragging the tips of his fingers up and down, lulling her into a deep, peaceful sleep.

Brant listened as the sound of her breathing moved into the slow rhythms of sleep. He felt her warm flesh against his and the rise and fall of her chest as she lay in his arms. He pulled her in tighter for just a moment and kissed her on the forehead. Before he fell asleep, his mind tortured him with a dozen questions he couldn't answer.

Where can this possibly lead? Will she stay? Could she ever love him? Was this a huge mistake?

Just then Jessica laughed softly in her sleep, making Brant smile.

I don't care, he told himself. *I'm happy now. I'll worry about tomorrow, tomorrow. No more questions*, he told himself before drifting off to sleep.

Chapter Sixteen

ဢ

Before she opened her eyes, the aroma of frying bacon and fresh-brewed coffee seeped into her subconscious. It took her a few seconds to remember where she was and why the room seemed to be moving. She opened her eyes and sat up to find she was alone in Brant's bed. She pulled a dark green curtain aside to look out the small window at other boats bobbing up and down in their moorings. Laid out on the end of the bed was a navy blue fleece bathrobe and Brant's Ugg boots. Grabbing the bathrobe, she slipped out of bed and walked into the bathroom where she found a toothbrush—still in its box—sitting on the sink. Several minutes later, wearing the Ugg boots that were two sizes too large, Jessica shuffled into the kitchen, hair up in a ponytail and her face freshly washed.

Brant heard her coming before she appeared behind him. "How'd you sleep?" he asked while pouring orange juice into two glasses.

"Like I'd been knocked out. I haven't slept like that in years. Do you think it has something to do with the rocking of the boat?"

"Could be that...or another type of rocking," Brant teased with a triumphant smile. "You know what they say about the motion of the ocean."

Jessica couldn't think of a witty comeback so she just smiled and took one of the glasses of orange juice.

"I have water on for tea or coffee, if you prefer. I found this chai tea at the market—hope it's all right."

Jessica bent over and kissed him on the cheek. "That was sweet of you to buy me tea. Thanks."

When she bent over, the bathrobe gaped open and Brant had a tantalizing view. "No. Thank *you*," he said with a wicked grin.

Jessica stood up and pulled the robe in tighter around her. "You're terrible."

"That's not what you said last night," he winked, before rolling back out of striking range. "I don't know about you, but I'm starving. I've made bacon. Do you want some eggs?"

"Sure, but why don't you let me make them. I *can* cook eggs."

"Eggs and butter are in the fridge and the frying pan is already on the stove. I like mine over easy. I'm going to get the Sunday paper." With that, Brant took off down the hall, leaving Jessica to play in the kitchen.

When Brant came back, he rolled up to the table and spread out the newspaper. "Need any help?" he asked without looking up.

"Nope," Jessica replied, trying to sound confident as she picked eggshell pieces out of the pan with the tips of her fingernails. When the eggs were done, she started opening cupboards looking for the plates.

"Bottom left, next to the sink. Silverware is in the drawer by the stove." Brant pretended to be reading the paper while watching Jessica put together breakfast in his oversized bathrobe and huge boots.

When she knelt down to pull plates out of the cupboard the bathrobe fell to one side, revealing her leg all the way up to her hip. Brant bit his lip and buried himself deeper into his paper until Jessica brought over two plates with eggs, a separate plate piled with crisp bacon and his glass of orange juice. Jessica placed four strips of bacon onto her plate next to her scrambled eggs.

"I'm famished," she mumbled around her first bite of bacon. "I just love a big breakfast, although most mornings I don't have time for one."

"I could get used to this," Brant agreed, helping himself to several strips of bacon as well.

Both of them attacked their eggs like they hadn't eaten for days. When Jessica wasn't looking, Brant pulled a large piece of eggshell out of his mouth and hid it in his napkin. Once their hunger had been satiated, they began to slow down and enjoy their morning drinks.

"I'm heading over to the park in an hour to play basketball. Want to tag along?"

"Basketball? In wheelchairs? Sounds interesting."

Brant was doing his best to sound casual, like it was nothing special. Afraid if he let her know how much he wanted her there it would crush him if she said no. "It's basically the same bunch of guys every Sunday. We divide up into two teams and play for about an hour, sometimes two."

"Sounds fun."

"We even have a wheelchair referee on occasion."

"I'd love to come. I don't have anywhere I have to be until this afternoon." Jessica stood and cleared away the dishes.

"Why don't you go change while I clean up," Brant suggested. "Unless you want to make a bunch of horny old guys very happy by showing up in that robe."

"I could go like this..." Jessica untied the belt around her waist and flashed him, giving Brant a full-frontal view before turning around and heading for the bedroom.

"Not fair!" he shouted after her. "It's a good thing for you I'm in this chair."

He heard her call back "Good thing" as he started washing the dishes.

* * * * *

An hour later they were walking along the bike path toward Venice Beach, Brant using one hand to propel his chair and the other to hold Jessica's hand. Once at the basketball courts, Jessica joined the other spectators on the sidelines. Brant waved like a little kid, enjoying the fact that for once someone was there watching him.

Jessica was amazed at how physical the game was and how skillful the guys were at maneuvering their wheelchairs — weaving in and around each other with one hand and bouncing the ball with the other. Jessica cringed at the sound of metal on metal every time the chairs collided.

A short woman with bleached blonde hair wearing a sweater two sizes too small introduced herself as Barbara, Evan's wife. Barbara was an active spectator, yelling out encouragement to Evan, screaming "foul" when chairs collided and hooting wildly when anyone made a basket, no matter what side they were on. After one nasty crash, Jessica had moved as if to go onto the court, but didn't get far. Barbara grabbed her firmly by the arm and pulled her back.

"They can handle it," she explained matter-of-factly.

"But—"

"You're new to all this, aren't you? If he needs your help, he'll ask for it. Otherwise, just let him take care of himself. The worst thing you can do is treat him like a child."

"Well. I wasn't going to... I just thought," Jessica stammered, taken aback by her bluntness.

"Don't worry. They do this every Sunday. Someone usually ends up hurt or bleeding. It's easier to fix a few cuts than a bruised ego. Trust me." Barbara winked at Jessica before screaming, "Foul!" her attention drawn back to the game. "Foul! You call yourself a ref?" she hollered at Bernie, a Vietnam vet with both his legs amputated at the knees. Bernie gave her a huge smile before flipping her off and rolling away. Barbara just laughed.

After the game, Brant introduced Jessica to several of the guys before a bunch of them headed for a local coffee shop. Brant was tired, sweaty and the happiest he'd been in years. They gathered in a corner, their chairs arranged in a U-shape. The guys relived the game, congratulating each other on great moves and ridiculing their stupid mistakes. Jessica joined in, laughing at their jokes and jabs. Brant couldn't stop smiling as he watched Jessica joke around with his teammates. This was the first woman he'd ever brought to one of his games. He was thrilled at how she joined in—no awkwardness or reluctance to participate in the teasing and laughter. More than once, images of the night before resurfaced, causing his smile to grow even wider.

"You must be exhausted. That game was a lot rougher than I imagined," Jessica said after noticing Brant's torn sweatpants for the first time.

Brant followed her gaze. "Happens all the time. The fabric gets caught in the metal parts of the chairs. I never even notice until I get home."

"I hate to admit it, but I don't even know who won."

"Today we did, by two baskets. One made by yours truly."

"You were great," Jessica smiled and meant it.

They spent an hour in the coffee shop before making their way back along the bike path. When they arrived at the dock gate, Jessica was running late and bent down to give Brant a quick kiss before running over to her truck. Brant sat watching her, not opening the dock gate until Jessica's truck had left the parking lot. He waved at the back of the truck as it headed for the driveway and just caught Jessica's arm waving back at him before he turned to go. If he could have skipped down the dock, he would have.

* * * * *

It was the Saturday before Christmas and Jessica was spending the day at the Santa Monica Place mall, trying to find just the right dress for the company Christmas party that night. Normally it didn't matter to her what she wore but tonight Brant was going to be her date and she wanted him to see her in something other than jeans and a sweater. After three hours of frustration, she finally found what she wanted — the perfect marriage of classy styling and sex appeal in a clingy black dress with a deep plunging back.

Back at home she spent hours getting ready, including the wrapping of a Christmas gift she'd bought at the mall. Brant had offered to pick her up in a cab but once he found out where the hotel was — walking distance from his boat — it made more sense for Jessica to pick him up.

A light rain was falling when she left Santa Monica, so she covered up her dress in a trench coat and threw her umbrella on the backseat. The rhythmic swish of her windshield wipers was hypnotic, having a calming effect even in the bumper to bumper traffic. Jessica drove right up to the gate and parked illegally in the red. She was just reaching over to get her umbrella when there was a knocking on her door. Brant was sitting in his chair under a huge umbrella right outside the truck. She rolled down the window.

"Pull away from the curb and open your passenger door," he called out as he backed away from the truck.

Jessica nodded and rolled the window back up before more rain made it inside. Once she opened the door, Brant rolled alongside and proceeded to hoist himself up onto the seat using the door handle and the edge of the seat. With the truck being higher than a car, it took some doing, but since he didn't ask for help Jessica just sat there and watched. Once he was inside he let out a sigh of relief.

"That was easy," he grinned as he wiped the rain off his face. "Would you mind throwing my chair in the back? It folds in half."

"No problem." She closed Brant's umbrella and gave that to him before trying to figure out how to collapse his chair.

"There's a lever in the front and back. Press those in and then pull the wheels together. Here, give me your umbrella." Brant stuck his arm out the window and held the umbrella over Jessica as she bent over and found the two levers. Once the chair was collapsed it was a simple matter, although a wet one, to toss it in the back of the truck. By the time Jessica got back in the car her hair was covered in droplets of water that sparkled like diamonds in the glow of the car's dome light. Jessica turned the rearview mirror toward her to assess the damage.

"Don't worry. You look stunning." Brant reached over and turned her face toward him. Using just the tips of his fingers, he wiped a couple droplets off her cheeks and nose before leaning over and kissing her deeply. After that, Jessica didn't care what she looked like.

If it hadn't been raining, Brant would have met Jessica at The Ritz-Carlton Marina Del Rey. He passed the hotel often as he rode along the bike path across the street. The hotel sat on the edge of the water, sparkling like facets of a diamond with hundreds of white twinkle lights in the trees. Pulling up under the covered entryway at the front entrance, a young man in a red jacket helped Jessica pull Brant's chair out of the back and directed them to the ramp. The place was decked out for Christmas, with a huge tree covered in lights at the entrance and boughs of greenery hanging over every door. Once inside they shed their rain gear and Brant had his first look at Jessica in her new dress.

Jessica did a slow turn to show off the back of the dress. "Like what you see?"

Brant made a low appreciative whistle as he admired the plunging back and the way the front of the dress clung protectively in all the right places.

"You look absolutely stunning," Brant managed to say, unable to tear his eyes away from her curves.

"You clean up pretty nice yourself."

Jessica took a few seconds to admire the way he looked in his navy blue blazer with crisp white shirt and a navy blue tie with silver stars. His khaki pants had neat creases ironed down the front and were cuffed at his ankles just above black penny loafers.

"Good thing all those college coeds can't see their professor now. You'd be inundated with emails."

Jessica and Brant made their way down a long carpeted hall to the left of the lobby until they came to the Marina Vista Ballroom. A coat check had been set up just outside the main room inside a small reception area. Jessica was greeted by Claire, who was sitting at a small table where nametags were laid out in alphabetical order.

"Hi Jessica. Love the dress," Claire said. "Makes you look like a different person. Hate to spoil the whole thing with one of these stupid name tags."

"I don't think I need one. Everyone knows who I am." Jessica took the preprinted nametag and stuck it in her bag next to a silver-wrapped object with a red silk ribbon. "This is Brant. Brant, Claire. Guess he'll need a tag."

Claire gave Brant an appreciative once-over before replying. "Sure. Just give me a second. B-R-A-N-T?"

"Perfect," answered Brant, not missing "the look". Brant recalled how he used to get the look on a regular basis in college. He had asked a woman friend what it meant.

"It means 'yummy', as in 'I'd like to eat you up'," she had explained, to Brant's embarrassment.

He had to admit that once he knew what it meant, he'd enjoyed it and began seeing the look on a regular basis. When Linda had given him the look, he decided to take her up on her unspoken request and three years later they were married.

Brant couldn't remember the last time he'd inspired someone to ogle him, but he did know it felt damn good.

Must be the suit, he thought with a smile as he stuck his nametag over his coat pocket.

"Have a wonderful time," Claire called after them, as Jessica took Brant's hand and walked him into the ballroom.

"Boy, she was smitten," Jessica whispered, looking back over her shoulder at Claire, who was still watching them.

"I don't know what you're talking about," Brant lied with a huge smile.

The ballroom was half-filled with people all dressed to impress, gathered into small conversational groups. Large picture windows looked out to the west over the marina with its spectacular view of the moored sailboats and yachts. Windows on the south wall provided views of a terrace and garden area that were lit up with white twinkle lights. The Marina Promenade was one level down and ran alongside the docks, and if it weren't raining would have made for a wonderful evening stroll. The plush carpeting in marigold and hunter green made it difficult for Brant to propel his chair with just one hand so he let go of Jessica's hand in order to push himself forward.

Topiary trees—covered in white lights and gold bows— had been brought indoors and were lined up along the windowless walls that were covered in a caramel and satin moiré wallpaper. Most of the people were crowded around the bar area while a few groups were already seated at the round tables that surrounded a wood parquet dance floor brought in for the party. Someone from one of the tables called out to Jessica. She turned to see Kim waving her over.

"Go ahead," Brant said. "I'll get us drinks. What do you want?"

"Red wine to start. Thanks."

Brant headed for the bar and Jessica made her way over to Kim.

227

"So that's the man who put color in your cheeks and a sparkle in your eyes," Kim said as soon as Jessica was close enough to hear.

"Not what you expected, I bet," Jessica said as she sat down next to Kim.

"True, but looks can be deceiving. Why don't you two sit at my table?" Kim waved over one of the waiters wandering around with a plate of crab cake hors d'oeuvres. "Could you please take this chair away?" she asked, indicating the chair next to her.

Just as the chair was removed, Brant came up with Jessica's glass of wine and a bottle of Heineken tucked between his legs.

"I assume this spot's for me," he said as he maneuvered his way up to the table.

Jessica moved from Kim's right to Brant's left so that he sat between the two women. Kim introduced Brant to the other people at the table—Jane from accounting and Victor from the mailroom—both of whom looked completely bored.

Brant had just swallowed his first sip of beer when Kim started in with a barrage of questions designed to find out as much as she could as quickly as possible.

"So Brant, what do you do for a living?" Kim cupped her chin in her hand, her elbow on the table, and gave Brant her full attention.

Jessica let out a sigh, knowing that Brant would be occupied for the next fifteen minutes. Brant answered all her questions with a light breezy air and even managed to get in a few questions of his own. By the time the salad arrived, Kim and Brant were talking like old friends.

After the salad course, John McMannon grabbed a cordless mic from the DJ set up in the corner of the room and made his way to the center of the dance floor. Underneath his charcoal gray suit coat, John was wearing his traditional holiday attire—a red and green plaid vest with gold buttons and a deep green tie.

"Merry Christmas, happy Chanukah, happy holidays to all," his voice boomed out. "Welcome to the tenth annual McMannon Christmas Party. I'm not in the office as much as I used to be, so I'm very pleased to be able to spend this time with you tonight. We've had an excellent year and we couldn't have done it without all of you, so you'll find a little something extra in your last paycheck of the year."

With that, some of the younger members of the agency let out an enthusiastic cheer.

"Well, it's not *that* much," John responded with a chuckle. "Enjoy your meal and I hope to see many of you out on the dance floor right after dessert."

Jessica leaned into Brant and whispered, "Thank God you're here. Now I don't have to embarrass myself on the dance floor."

"I wouldn't be so sure of that," Brant whispered right back.

Jessica looked at him, wondering what he meant.

"I used to be quite the dancer…"

"Yeah, but certainly not now?"

"We'll see." Brant's eyes lit up with a devilish twinkle.

"Honestly. I hate dancing. I feel like I have two left feet."

"Maybe you'll surprise yourself."

"I don't like the sound of this." Jessica reached for her wine, aware that Kim was listening to the entire conversation.

Just then the main entrée arrived and Jessica could turn her attention to the grilled salmon, garlic whipped potatoes and steamed vegetables. Brant took on the manly chore of making sure everyone's wineglasses stayed filled. Three more people had joined their table and the wine began to work its magic on Jane and Victor, who were now sitting next to each other not quite as bored as before.

After a dessert of mini crème brûlée tortes, the music started and Jane and Victor headed for the dance floor. Kim excused herself to visit the ladies' room and the other three people headed back to the bar, leaving Jessica and Brant alone for the first time all evening.

"I can't tell you how much I appreciate you coming. In the past I've brought Cath along and then had to endure a month of questions from Kim as to why I came without a date, *again*. You were great with her."

"It was nothing. She's a nice woman who's obviously looking out for you."

"Sometimes she feels more like an older sister than my assistant."

"I can see that," Brant smiled, looking straight into Jessica's eyes.

Breaking eye contact, Jessica turned away to retrieve her bag that was hanging off the back of her chair. Sitting the bag in her lap, she opened the snap and pulled out a silver package, handing it to Brant.

"Merry Christmas," she said with cheerful glee, meant to disguise how nervous she was. Would he think her too forward for buying him a gift? Would he think that she expected a gift in return? Was it too early in the relationship for the exchange of gifts?

Jessica hated when her mind took off in a dozen different directions, leaving her grasping at words.

"You bought me a present?"

"It's okay if you didn't get me anything," Jessica jumped in, already thinking she'd made a mistake. "It's no big deal. It's kind of a joke gift. I even bought it on sale —"

Brant put two fingers up to Jessica's lips to silence her.

"It's all right, Jessica. I bought you something, too," he said. "I just wasn't planning on giving it to you tonight at your work party."

"Oh!"

"Do you still want me to open this now?"

"Sure. It's just something I thought you could use."

Jessica watched as Brant untied the red silk ribbon and slipped it into his jacket pocket. Next he pulled away each piece of tape and pulled off the paper. This certainly wasn't the way she opened gifts. Jessica watched him fold up the silver paper and put that, too, in his pocket before turning the box over. By the time he finally opened the end of the box and let the silver frame slip out into his hand, Jessica couldn't contain herself any longer.

"It's for our portrait."

"I know. The refrigerator doesn't do it justice," he leaned over and kissed Jessica first on the cheek before turning her face with his hand so he could kiss her on the lips. "I'm so glad it's not a tie."

Jessica laughed more out of relief than because of what he said. Her laughter was drowned out by the DJ's voice rising above the music.

"And now something for all those budding office romances," the DJ purred into the microphone as he brought up the volume on Billy Joel's "Just the Way You Are".

Brant backed his chair away from the table and held out his hand. "Come on. They're playing our song."

"Where are we going?" *He can't be serious about dancing,* thought Jessica as she pushed back her chair and stood up.

Brant led her on to the dance floor where five couples were swaying in each other's arms as they moved around the floor. Brant tipped his chair up and over the lip of the parquet wooden dance floor and turned his chair around to face Jessica.

"Now what?" Jessica whispered, stepping toward him.

Brant patted his lap. "Have a seat. Remember how you were seated for our portrait?"

"Oh." Jessica could feel all eyes on them. Feeling very self-conscious, she lowered herself onto Brant's lap. He wrapped one arm around her and gently guided her to lean into him. With his free arm, he slowly rocked his chair back and forth to the beat of the music.

Jessica took a deep breath and let herself melt into him. She even managed to forget that everyone from her office was staring at them as Brant ran his fingers up and down her arm while maneuvering his chair around in slow circles.

"Where did you learn to do this?" Jessica asked into Brant's shirt.

Brant spoke into her hair, taking the time to nuzzle her head with his chin. "The idea came from some old movie I saw as a kid, but the moves are straight off the basketball court, slowed down a bit to match the music."

"Well, Brant Wilson, you've made a dancer out of me, two left feet and all." Jessica burrowed in even closer and Brant gave her arm a squeeze.

A minute later the song ended and, to Jessica's surprise, everyone on the dance floor turned toward them and started clapping. Jessica stood up and looked around in amazement. Brant did a three-sixty with the chair before taking her hand and leading her off the floor just as another song was beginning.

"Want another drink?" Brant asked. "All that dancing made me thirsty."

"Sure. How about something a little stronger this time...say, Jack Daniels on the rocks?"

"Remember, you have to drive."

"Not necessarily..." Jessica gave him a wicked smile. "The company will pay for a room for anyone too inebriated to drive."

"Interesting. Should I make yours a double?" he teased, before heading to the bar without waiting for an answer, grinning from ear to ear.

As Brant wove his way through the tables he couldn't help but think how well the evening was going. First he was ogled by Claire, always good for the ego, then he'd gotten Jessica out on the dance floor for a very romantic moment which, based on the applause, had looked as romantic as it felt. And then there had been Jessica's gift—always a positive sign when a woman buys you a present.

Brant smiled to himself as he remembered the silver charm bracelet with a silver typewriter and a little book that opened on tiny silver hinges, neatly wrapped and waiting for Jessica back at his boat. He wished now that he had brought it with him tonight, especially if there was a chance they would be spending the night at the hotel.

Suddenly someone was blocking his way, someone with perfect creases in his pants and dress shoes that shined like mirrors. Brant looked up into the hard face of a man who, judging by his thinly disguised sneer, looked down on him both literally and figuratively. Without preamble, the man launched into what sounded more like a sermon than an introduction.

"I'm Jessica's boss, Simon Fitch—as in McMannon & Fitch. Nice little display out there on the dance floor. Very entertaining," he said without a drop of sincerity.

Brant kept his tone cool as he felt the beginnings of a knot forming in the pit of his stomach at Simon's sarcasm. "Glad you enjoyed it."

"I don't know if Jess has told you, but we're quite close. We go out of town on business trips all the time—*overnight* business trips, if you catch my drift," he said with a wink.

Brant's knuckles turned white as he tightened the grip on the wheels of his chair to stop himself from reaching out and hitting the man.

Speaking with a casual air he didn't feel, Brant replied, "Funny. Your name has never come up."

"She must have a good reason for keeping our relationship private, I guess, what with me being her boss and all," Simon said in a conspiratorial tone.

"Excuse me," Brant said, as he backed up to maneuver around Fitch, but Fitch moved in closer and placed his hands firmly on Brant's armrests.

"Look here, Poster Boy," he said in a low, menacing whisper, so no one around them could hear. "Jessica has great potential at McMannon & Fitch and she doesn't need some cripple like you holding her back."

Brant leaned forward in his chair until his face was two inches from Simon's. His voice was calm. Dead calm.

"Remove your hands or I'll remove them for you."

A small group of people standing nearby turned to look at the two men squaring off. Simon saw the looks on their faces and straightened himself.

"This isn't over," Simon hissed.

"It hasn't even started," Brant replied, before moving back and going around Simon in one fluid motion, leaving Simon standing alone with several employees looking at him.

"What are you looking at? Get back to work!" he said automatically, before realizing where they were.

But the phrase triggered the reaction he wanted and everyone scattered like a startled flock of birds. Simon turned around and saw Brant at the bar. Turning back, he searched out Jessica sitting at a table talking to Kim and headed her way.

If it hadn't been for the worried look that came across Kim's face like a shadow of a dark cloud, Jessica wouldn't have known Simon was standing directly behind her. She swiveled around in her seat to face him.

"Simon," was all she said.

"Jessica. Kim. Having a good time?"

Jessica didn't answer, so Kim filled in the blank space left by her silence.

"Why yes. It's a lovely party as always. Would you like to dance?" she asked, trying to rescue her boss.

"I don't think so," he said, before slipping back into his fake smile. "I wouldn't mind taking Jessica out for a spin, though," he said, holding out his hand.

"I'm not much of a dancer," Jessica replied politely.

Jessica wanted to get up and walk away but Simon was blocking her. Then she saw Brant approaching and relief flooded over her, feeling sure he would rescue her—her knight on a shining steed. Then her relief turned to real concern as she realized Brant wasn't slowing down as he approached.

Simon didn't know what hit him as something sent him flying into the table, knocking over several glasses of water and two glasses of wine. Kim jumped up to avoid the water that was heading her way. Jessica stood up as well and backed away from the table, knowing Simon's reaction would be explosive.

Simon regained his balance and whipped around, curses pouring from his mouth.

"*What the fuck?* Who's the clumsy idiot— YOU! Why don't you look where you're going in that thing?"

"I was," Brant smiled.

"Just because you're a cripple," he spat out, "you think you can bash into people and get away with it. Well not with me. That's assault! I'll sue."

Simon's voice was gaining volume and soon a small crowd surrounded them.

Jessica looked at Simon who had more color in his face than she'd ever seen before. Then she turned to Brant, who looked like he was going to burst out of his chair at any minute and strangle her boss.

"Come on, Brant. Let's go."

She grabbed her purse off the table but Brant wasn't moving and neither was Simon. She lowered her hand to Brant's shoulder and gave it a small squeeze.

"Come on. He's not worth it," she said.

Keeping his eyes on Simon, Brant backed his chair up before making a slow turn to leave.

"You must be all kinds of screwed up, Jessica Singer, to prefer this broken man to me!"

Before Brant could whip his chair back around, Jessica stomped over to Simon and slapped him hard across the cheek.

Simon's response caught Jessica off guard. In one fluid motion, Simon grabbed her by the shoulders, pulled her in violently and kissed her hard on the lips before pushing her away. Simon took a step to the right so he could look directly at Brant. What he saw was open hostility sitting in a steel trap and it pleased him beyond reason. The booming voice of John McMannon interrupted Simon's gloating.

"What's going on here?"

Jessica was stunned into silence. She couldn't believe Simon would pull a stunt like that—and in front of her coworkers.

"This man assaulted me," Simon stammered, pointing at Brant.

McMannon looked at Brant and then at Jessica.

"If anyone was assaulted, it was me," Jessica explained. "Simon just grabbed me and forcibly kissed me."

Simon looked around, remembering where he was.

"The bitch's boyfriend rammed me with that THING!" he shouted, pointing at Brant's chair like it was the most disgusting thing he'd ever seen.

"That will be enough, Simon. I think it's time for you to leave," McMannon said with authority, as if he was talking to a child.

When Simon didn't move, McMannon walked up to him and took him by the arm to lead him away. "Now," he barked, and Simon's demeanor suddenly changed. His head hung down and his shoulders rolled forward into a slump. He barely picked up his feet as he shuffled off.

Everyone watched him go, whispering amongst themselves. Jessica turned to Brant.

"Guess we should go as well."

"Sure," was all he said, turning his chair around and heading for the coat check.

Brant felt completely humiliated. Never in his life had he wanted to punch someone as much as he'd wanted to punch Simon. Fitch had pushed all his buttons and all he could think to do was ram him with his chair.

How pathetic, he thought. *Jessica must think I'm a fool.*

Jessica had hoped Brant would say something — anything — but he just sat staring straight ahead as they waited for Claire to retrieve their coats off the rack. Jessica placed her hand on his shoulder but when she felt his muscles tense under her touch, she pulled away. Once they had their coats they went to the lobby, where they waited in silence for Jessica's truck to be brought around.

Jessica knew things had turned out badly but it wasn't like she'd done anything wrong, she reasoned. She wasn't the one who'd rammed her boss for no apparent reason. Something was not right here and she was going to find out what, just as soon as she had Brant trapped in her truck. When Jessica pulled into the parking lot at the boat dock, she turned off the engine and crossed her arms to wait him out.

It wasn't raining anymore but the pavement was still wet. The truck sat in a dark area between two circles of light cast by the overhead security lamps. It was Brant who broke the silence.

"Are you going to get my chair for me?"

"I don't think so. Not until you explain what that was all about."

"What's to explain? I'm tired. Defending your virtue is hard work, especially from a wheelchair."

"Defending my virtue? What's that supposed to mean?" Jessica could feel the anger rising up into her face. When Brant didn't respond she continued, "Is that what that was, defending my honor by ramming my boss with your chair?"

Brant wondered how he had become the bad guy in all this.

"Simon is an ass, but you didn't have to hit him," Jessica continued.

Brant felt his blood pressure rising and the knot in his stomach growing tighter and larger.

"The guy calls me a cripple, tells me he's having intimate relations with my girlfriend and then kisses her for all the world to see, and I'm suppose to sit tight and take it? It's bad enough that I'm trapped in this chair and can only do so much, but I was handling the situation just fine until you had to slap him."

"So you think I'm having sex with Simon?" Jessica asked, her voice trembling with a mixture of anger and hurt.

How could he think such a thing?

"That's *not* what I said. But that's what Simon said—and *that's* why I rammed into him. I'm sorry if it's not the way you would have handled it but my options are a bit limited."

"I can't believe that guy. And then he kisses me! Of all the nerve…"

"If you had just walked away like you asked me to do, that never would have happened," Brant said.

"I wasn't going to let him insult the two of us like that and do nothing," Jessica replied, feeling once more the anger at being kissed by Simon.

"Oh. So it's okay for you to slap him but I can't ram him with my chair?"

Jessica took a deep breath. "I see your point. I was just so angry. I wanted to protect you."

"I don't need protecting, Jessica. I'm quite capable of handling myself."

"I didn't mean it that way."

"Look. We're both tired and upset. Why don't we call it a night?"

"I guess you're right. I'll get your chair." Jessica stepped out of the truck, slowly walked around to the back and grabbed Brant's chair. She pulled it open and locked everything in place before bringing it up to the door. Brant had the door open when she got there and slid out of the truck into his chair.

"Good night Jessica," he said, his voice sounding suddenly very tired and defeated.

The sound of his voice melted what was left of Jessica's anger and she stepped in front of him.

"I'm sorry Brant. We should be angry at Simon, not each other—"

Brant held up his hand to stop her.

"I'm not mad at you. I'm angry with myself for letting that ass ruin our evening."

Brant took Jessica's fingers and pulled her hand to his lips for a gentle kiss before releasing her. "Good night," he said in a whisper before maneuvering around her, leaving her standing alone in the dark.

Chapter Seventeen

✂

It was the Monday before Christmas when a startled Merlin squawked as Jessica's phone rang three times before the answering machine picked up.

"You've reached the home of Jessica and Merlin. I must be out so please leave a message."

Brant waited for the obligatory beep and then began his well-rehearsed message.

"Hey Jessica. It's Brant," he said, trying to sound casual. "Sorry I haven't called sooner but I've been scrambling to make last-minute plans to go home for Christmas. Haven't been home since the accident so I thought it was long overdue. I'll call you when I'm back in town. Have a terrific holiday. Bye."

That wasn't so bad, thought Brant. *I sounded upbeat and very natural. Just a friend calling to say Merry Christmas.*

But Brant felt like a coward calling Jessica's home when he knew she was at work. As he moved around his bedroom gathering clothes, folding and arranging them in a suitcase on the bed, his mind wandered back to Jessica's company Christmas party. Why had he let Simon ruin their evening? The guy was most definitely an ass out to cause problems. He stuffed several pairs of plain white socks violently into a side pocket of his luggage. But what Simon had said had wounded him where he was most vulnerable, causing him to doubt his feelings for Jessica and whether or not he should continue the relationship. He looked at the bed where they had made love and his heart ached for her again. Was this just the reaction of someone who had been starved for affection for years, or was it something more?

By the time he was finished packing, he was more torn than ever...happy to be leaving his boathouse and all the images of Jessica it conjured up, but sad that he would not be with her for the holiday. Sitting on his dresser was the small wrapped box with the silver charm bracelet he had bought for her. He picked it up, turning it around in his hand, weighing it and shaking it as if it were a magic eight ball. For just a moment he considered driving over to her office and delivering the gift in person before he left town, but the thought of running into Simon washed away that idea. He slipped the box into his jacket pocket and called a cab to take him to the airport.

Two hours later he was settled in a bulkhead seat absently scanning the pages of the in-flight magazine until one of the articles jumped out at him. The feature was about a group of wheelchair pilots who owned their own charter plane service. Brant read the entire piece in ten minutes and then read it again. The group of Vietnam vets hadn't let their lack of legs stop them from starting their own business, finding love and raising families, all while flying around the country.

They'd been through a hell of a lot more than he had. Yet they still managed to create the life they wanted. Brant pulled the gift box out of his pocket, regretting his decision not to deliver it in person. Then, like a shot of adrenaline, it hit him and he knew what he had to do. He pressed his call button and when the flight attendant arrived, requested paper and pen and spent the next hour pouring out his heart and soul. When he was done he reread every word and signed it, "Love, Brant". This could be one of the biggest mistakes he'd ever made or the smartest thing he'd done in a long time.

Emotionally drained, Brant folded up the letter and closed his eyes. With images of Jessica dancing in his head like sugarplum fairies, he fell asleep for the remainder of the flight.

* * * * *

Jessica had been at a client's office all day and was exhausted when she finally walked into her living room at eight p.m. Monday night. The message light on her phone blinked rapidly, signaling that she had several messages. Jessica ignored the machine until she had changed out of her work clothes and drank half a bottle of beer. Merlin squawked loudly to be freed and her stomach demanded to be fed. Finally, with Merlin running around on the kitchen counter and a piece of cold pizza safely deposited in her stomach, Jessica hit the play button as she prepared herself a small salad.

The first message was from her brother asking what time she was showing up at Dad's for Christmas. The second call was from Cath, wishing her an early Merry Christmas since she was going to Santa Barbara with Pete to meet his parents.

"And don't forget were hitting the mall on Saturday for the day-after-Christmas sales. I should be back in plenty of time. I'll call you."

And then there was a message from Brant. She hadn't heard from him since Saturday evening when she'd dropped him off after the Christmas party. When she first heard his voice she lit up like a Christmas tree, until she heard his message and then felt like someone had just pulled the plug on Christmas.

Going home for Christmas, she thought. "Well, good for him," she said out loud. "Guess we'll be having another Singer family holiday at Dad's, complete with lots of Scotch, football and bad food."

Merlin wasn't offering up any sympathy so she put him back in his cage and went to bed early. Her last thoughts as she drifted off to sleep were of Brant sitting outside among snow-covered pine trees somewhere in Connecticut.

* * * * *

Tuesday morning, from the comfort of his parents' house in Connecticut, Brant called for a FedEx pick-up so he could send both the letter and the bracelet to Jessica's work for a Thursday morning arrival, just in time for Christmas. The last line of the letter contained the phone number of his folks' house, and the line, "Please call me. I'm placing my heart in your hands".

* * * * *

It was Thursday morning, Christmas Eve, and the employees of McMannon & Fitch were in a festive mood. Everyone except Simon Fitch. After the disastrous Christmas party, he had been written up yet again. If he had been an ordinary employee and not a partner with the company, a pink slip would surely have been in Simon's immediate future. With the acquisition deal in Oregon weeks from closing and several key accounts tied directly to him, Simon felt secure in his position despite his troubles with Jessica. The berating he had received Monday morning from McMannon was still fresh in his mind as he swept into the office on Thursday like a bad weather front, causing everyone in his path to run for cover. As he passed Claire he asked if FedEx had arrived yet.

"Yes. He came at ten after ten. Everything was taken to the mailroom," she answered in an even tone, hoping not to give Simon a reason to bite off her head.

"I'm expecting important documents from the Oregon office. They were supposed to be here yesterday. I want to get out of here early, too—I can't wait for some stupid mail clerk to deliver important papers to my door."

Claire stood up. "I'll go see if I can find it," she offered.

"No," Simon barked. "You have work to do. I need that Fetterman contract ready so I can mail it out before we break for the holiday."

And with that Simon took off to the mailroom, wearing his frustration like a heavy coat. He entered the small room ready to lay into the unsuspecting clerk but was disappointed to find no one around.

"Figures," he said under his breath.

Simon couldn't remember the last time he'd been in this room and had to search around to find the day's pile of FedEx packages. There was a login sheet on a clipboard next to the pile, which Simon glanced at and then ignored. He started going through the envelopes and boxes until he found a heavy, oversized envelope with his name on it from the advertising agency in Oregon.

As he picked up his package, he glanced at the next box in the pile and noticed it was for Jessica. For a fleeting moment he considered delivering the package to her office, giving him a chance to wish her Merry Christmas. But upon closer examination, he saw the return address was from Brant Wilson. It had just arrived that morning.

His jaw clenched as he mouthed Brant's name, looking quickly back at the door before picking up the box. He gave the package a good shake and heard something sliding around inside. Just then the mail clerk returned.

To cover his guilt, Simon turned around and blasted the unsuspecting young man. "When my clients spend the extra money to get a package to me before ten a.m., it means I want it by ten a.m., NOT when you get around to delivering it to me!"

And with a show of anger and frustration, Simon tucked both Jessica's box and his envelope under his arm and stormed out of the room, leaving the mail clerk in stunned silence.

Jessica rolled into work that morning two hours late, hoping to avoid running into anyone. She made her way straight to her office, told Kim she didn't want to be disturbed and closed her door. There she stayed until Kim knocked on her door around noon.

"Jessica? Everything okay?" she asked, as she stepped into the office.

"Sure. I just wanted to get stuff organized in here. You know, start the New Year off right."

"Good idea," Kim said, looking around at all the boxes, storyboards and oversized envelopes scattered around the office. "I'm taking off now. We have a half day today. Remember?"

"I know. I'm going to stay and get this taken care of before I leave. I have no reason to rush home anyway," she said, feeling just a little sorry for herself.

"Are you sure you're okay? You seem a little down."

"It's just the holidays and the prospect of spending the day sitting around with my dad and brother. Ever since my mom died, Christmas hasn't been the same — my family hasn't been the same. Dad doesn't seem to care about anything anymore. I was hoping this year might be different, but apparently not."

Kim wanted to dig further but looking at Jessica's somber face, she decided to drop it.

"All right then. Don't stay too late. Want me to close your door again?"

"Sure...and Merry Christmas, Kim."

Kim turned to leave but then remembered something. "I almost forgot," she said, leaving the door open and walking back to her desk. She opened the lower drawer and pulled out the frame Jessica had given to Brant at the Christmas Party. "You guys left in such a hurry that you forgot to take this with you."

Kim walked into Jessica's office and placed the frame on her desk.

Jessica looked at the frame but didn't touch it. "Thanks Kim. I'll give this to Brant the next time I see him."

Kim couldn't help herself. She just had to ask. "So you're not getting together for Christmas?"

"He went back east to be with his family. Connecticut or some such place. I hope he has a better time with his family than I do with mine."

Kim picked up a pad of Post-its and a pen and wrote her phone number in large, bold numbers before peeling off the note and sticking it on the center of Jessica's computer screen.

"If you'd like to join my family for dinner you're more than welcome. It's crazy, loud and a bit scary, but it sure is fun. We would love to have you join us."

Jessica forced a smile. "That's very sweet of you, Kim. I really appreciate the offer, but I'm afraid if I don't attempt to cook something for Christmas dinner my dad and brother will eat chili straight out of the can...cold."

"Men," Kim declared trying to sound light and cheerful. "They would starve without us. Okay then. I'm going to run. I have a few more gifts to pick up on the way home. Merry Christmas, Jessica."

"Merry Christmas," Jessica called out as Kim closed her door.

She opened her desk drawer and tossed in the frame, letting out a long sigh before picking up a fresh pile of files and returning to her organizing.

Down the hall, Simon was finishing up one last email before calling it a day. His office was tidy and neat with everything in its place. As he gathered his coat and briefcase, he scanned the office, making sure everything was where it belonged before locking up. That's when he spotted the FedEx box on the credenza. For the second time he was tempted to walk the box down to Jessica's office, using the delivery as an excuse to see her one more time before the holiday break. But then he thought about what McMannon had said. "Keep away from Jessica for a while. Let things cool down. I don't want this to explode in our faces."

As he looked at the return address label his anger flared up again, remembering who the package was from.

Probably a Christmas gift or something, he thought.

The bruises on the backs of his legs were still tender from where Brant had rammed his wheelchair into him. If Jessica didn't have that jerk in a wheelchair in her life she would be more open to his charms. Thoughts of Jessica stirred up equal parts lust and anger. Simon didn't know whether he even liked Jessica anymore. He had been attracted to her from the start, was used to getting what he wanted. Now that he had competition in the battle for Jessica, he was even more determined to win—at any cost—just for the sake of winning.

"Screw him," Simon snarled out loud as he slid the package into his in-box and placed several files on top of it. "Whatever it is will have to wait until Monday."

A deliciously wicked smile spread across his lips as he stood in his doorway looking down the hall in the direction of Jessica's closed door.

Merry Christmas, Jessica.

* * * * *

As Brant looked out the picture window of his parents' house in Weston, Connecticut, on Christmas morning, he couldn't help but think how different this view was from the one off the back of his boat. The snow that blanketed the huge expanse of lawn and flocked the trees and shrubs had created a living Christmas card overnight. His mom brought him a mug of hot coffee and kissed him on the top of his head as if he were still five years old.

"I'm so glad you decided to come," she said, holding back tears of happiness. "You shouldn't have waited so long." Then she squeezed his shoulder before returning to the kitchen to start breakfast.

Brant was glad he'd come as well. He had missed his family over the past few years and now felt foolish for letting his pride get in the way of returning home.

By eleven in the morning, aunts, uncles, cousins, nieces and nephews began to arrive and the quiet, cozy Christmas morning he had shared with his mom, dad and sister was shattered with loud greetings and laughter.

After the frenzy of opening gifts had subsided and the kids were off playing with their new video games, the adults gathered in the living room to talk and take a breath before getting dinner ready. Brant's mom and dad still held hands as they sat side by side on the overstuffed couch, and his Uncle Lloyd and Aunt Patricia still teased and poked at each other after forty-nine years of marriage. Seeing his parents and relatives together made him feel alone, and not for the first time, he wondered when or if Jessica would call him.

When he couldn't stand it any longer he excused himself to make a call. He dialed Jessica's number, realizing he didn't have the slightest idea what he was going to say after "Merry Christmas". When the answering machine picked up, he panicked and hung up.

No point leaving some pathetic message, he thought, as he rolled into the family room where his cousins and nephews were engaged in a four-way tank battle video game.

"Hey, Uncle Brant. Want to play?" his twelve-year-old nephew asked without missing a shot or taking his eyes off the television.

"I'll just watch for now," he said, pulling his chair into a better spot. "Maybe later, after I figure out what you guys are doing."

When Lindsey, his four-year-old niece came into the room, she climbed into his lap and made herself comfortable as if she did it every day.

"Whatcha doin?" she asked.

"Watching the boys play their new game."

"Want to read me a book? Santa brought me three really good ones."

"Sure."

With that, Lindsey hopped down and went running into the living room to retrieve her books. Brant rolled out to follow and met her in the hallway.

"Let's go in here," Brant suggested, turning into his father's study. "It's a lot quieter and we can sit by the window and watch the snow fall."

The study was paneled in dark wood, with one entire wall covered in bookshelves from floor to ceiling. Brant's love of books and all things literary had its beginnings in this very room.

Brant positioned his chair at an angle to the window. Now they could use the window light to read while looking out at the yard. Lindsey scrambled up into Brant's lap and wiggled around until she felt just right.

"Here. Read this one first. It's 'bout a train and Christmas."

Brant picked up the book.

"*The Polar Express.* I've heard of this one," Brant said, and opened the book reverently to its first page. "On Christmas Eve, many years ago, I lay quietly in my bed…"

Brant's mom, Connie, was walking down the hall to check on the kids in the family room when she heard Brant's melodious voice coming from the study. She paused at the open door, leaning into the doorjamb, arms crossed, listening as Brant changed his voice slightly for each character just like Brant's father used to do. Brant looked up and smiled at his mom without missing a line and then turned the page.

Brant would have made such a wonderful father, she thought, as she wiped a tear from her eyes and moved down the hall toward the sounds of screaming boys and machine-gun fire.

* * * * *

Christmas in California was nothing like a Currier & Ives painting. It was more like a postcard from Hawaii, complete with palm trees swaying back and forth in the offshore breeze. As Jessica drove north up Pacific Coast Highway toward her dad's house, she noticed that even though it was Christmas morning, dozens of surfers were sitting on their boards waiting for the next set to roll in. Jessica had bought a heavy red sweater with a white snowflake appliqué on the front to wear for Christmas, but it was too hot for sweaters—even at eight in the morning. So it sat in the backseat of her truck, in its original bag, ready to be returned after the holidays.

By nine-thirty, Jessica, her dad and Matt were done with their holiday festivities for the day and the television was turned on in search of a pregame show for the upcoming football game. Jessica had made everyone bacon, eggs and toast, cleaned up the dishes and then started thinking about what she should do about dinner. Her dad had sent Matt to the store with a list of random items, so now she sat staring at sacks of groceries with no clue as to what to make out of a five-pound sack of potatoes, bags of frozen vegetables and a turkey that should have been defrosted the day before.

Six hours later, after overcooking the vegetables, making lumpy mashed potatoes, and creating a turkey that was burnt on the outside and not cooked on the inside, Jessica looked around at the poor excuse for a meal she had prepared and burst into tears. Jessica's dad found her sitting on the kitchen counter, drinking a beer and sobbing.

"What's the matter, sweetheart?" he asked, his voice a little thick from the Scotch.

"You know I don't know how to cook. Look at this mess. We can't eat this for Christmas dinner!"

Jessica's dad looked around the kitchen as if seeing it for the first time and seemed to understand why she was really crying.

"I miss her too, Jess. I miss her every day."

Jessica looked at her dad in surprise. He hadn't mentioned her mother in years.

"What are we going to do, Dad?" Jessica asked, feeling like a little kid again.

"Guess we're going out to dinner. Matt!" he yelled. "Get the car keys. Your sister messed up dinner again. We're going out for Chinese."

Then he put his arm around Jessica and gave her a big hug.

For the two hours they were at dinner, Jessica actually forgot to be miserable. A couple bottles of Chinese beer and Matt's sick jokes had both Jessica and her father laughing so hard that tears rolled down their cheeks. Matt drove them back to the house, where the two of them helped their father up the stairs to bed. Coming down the stairs, Matt put his arm around his sister's shoulders.

"Thanks for coming. Christmas wouldn't be the same without your home cooking," he teased.

"Anytime," she replied and poked him in the ribs. "Can I ask you something?"

"Sure. Want a beer?" he asked as he headed to the kitchen to grab a bottle for himself.

"Yeah, I'll take one." Jessica followed her brother into the kitchen and pushed herself up onto the counter, her legs hitting the cupboards below.

Matt handed her a bottle and then sat on the large tiled island across from Jessica.

Matt took a long pull on his beer before asking, "So what's up, lil' sis?"

Even though she wanted to talk, she hesitated before beginning. "I'm dating this man—" was all she got out before Matt cut in.

"You want sexual advice from your big brother—"

"God, no!" Jessica looked at her brother's big smile and relaxed. "You're kidding."

"Well, yeah. Unless you really do need advice…"

"No, but thanks anyway. Actually, what I need is to talk to your friend, the one in the wheelchair. What was his name?"

"Shay. What do you want to talk to Shay about?"

"That guy I'm dating…he's in a wheelchair and I really like him, maybe even love him, but I think I've blown it somehow and I'm not sure if it's a normal 'blown-it' or something to do with him being in a wheelchair. Now he's gone home for Christmas and I'm afraid I'll never see him again and won't have the chance to apologize, although I have no clue what I'd be apologizing for—"

"Whoa. Take a breath there, Sis. I'm sure everything will work out fine. I'll call Shay tomorrow and see if he's up to the task of talking with a crazy woman."

"Thanks. I really think that will help."

Matt jumped down off the island, walked over to Jessica and scooped her off the counter into his arms as if she weighed nothing at all.

"What are you doing, you big idiot? Put me down," Jessica protested, but didn't struggle as Matt carried her into the living room.

"We're going to drink our beers and watch one of those sappy Christmas movies you love so much and then I'm going to carry *you* upstairs and tuck you into bed. You're staying here tonight and I don't want to hear any arguments."

Jessica giggled. "Okay, Dad."

Ten minutes later Jessica was snuggled up on the couch in the crook of her brother's arm watching *It's a Wonderful Life*, as she listened to the rhythmic snores of her brother and thought about Brant somewhere in Connecticut.

Chapter Eighteen

Cath considered the day after Christmas as much a national holiday as Christmas itself, and each year dragged Jessica to the mall to brave the crowds and do battle for bargains. At eight o'clock on Saturday morning, Cath was banging on Jessica's door with a chai tea latté in one hand and a large black coffee in the other.

"It's open," she heard Jessica shout from somewhere inside.

"I can't. My hands are full," Cath shouted back.

A minute later Jessica opened the door wearing a towel on her head and another around her body.

"I knew you wouldn't be ready," Cath announced as she handed Jessica her tea. "You know I like to get to the mall as soon as the stores open and before everything is picked over."

"Relax. We still have an hour."

Merlin squawked a greeting and Cath went over to his cage to free him.

"There's going to be traffic and the parking...it'll be like bumper cars at the pier."

"We could just stay here, relax and watch a movie..."

"Out of the question. There's shopping to be done, Ms. Singer, and we are just the two women to do it. So get dressed, do something with that hair and we're out of here."

A half hour later they were cruising up and down the parking lot looking for a parking space.

"I told you it was going to be crazy. We should have gotten here earlier."

"Next year we could come the night before and sleep in the car," Jessica suggested.

"Not a bad idea."

Jessica just rolled her eyes.

Once inside they began their quest for bargains. While Jessica stood in line to return her sweater, Cath pulled sweaters, skirts and dresses from the fifty-percent-off rack and draped them over her arm.

Walking past Jessica, who was still in the return line, Cath called out, "Meet me in the line for the changing rooms. I have stuff in your size, too."

Jessica waved her acknowledgement and moved one person closer to the front of the exchange line. By the time she made it over to the changing rooms, Cath was next in line to go in.

"That worked out well," Cath said, handing Jessica half the clothing. When she got a dirty look from the woman behind them, she added, "Don't worry, sweetie. We're sharing a stall. Lesbians, you know," making the woman look away in embarrassment.

Jessica just shook her head and kept staring straight ahead until it was their turn to enter. Sharing a dressing room was a squeeze but part of the day-after Christmas shopping tradition, as well. As they dressed and undressed over and over again, they told each other about their holidays. This year the conversation was very one-sided.

"Pete was such a doll. You know what he bought me?"

"Not a clue," Jessica replied as she pulled another sweater over her head.

"A digital camera, a very sexy black teddy, ten scented candles and this Tiffany heart necklace," she said unbuttoning the blouse she was trying on so Jessica could see.

"Very nice."

"He says the gifts all go together, if you catch my meaning."

"I have a pretty good idea how he expects to benefit from his collection of presents."

"So what did you get? How was your Christmas?" Cath asked as she stripped off her pants to try on a short little plaid skirt.

"Well, let's see...Dad gave me a hundred bucks for this shopping spree, and says 'Hi' by the way, and Matt bought me two beautiful journals for my writing, which I thought was very thoughtful. We were officially done with Christmas before ten o'clock, when Dad wanted to know what was for breakfast and Matt started flipping through channels looking for football games."

"What about Brant? Didn't he give you something special?"

"Nope."

"He called you on Christmas Day, didn't he?"

"He didn't have my dad's number."

"Then there was a message on your machine when you got home, a sexy email, something?"

"No. Just the one he left Monday morning before he took off for his parents' house. Haven't heard from him since." Jessica sighed as she looked at herself in the mirror. "Why did you pick this ridiculous dress for me? I look like a Jackson Pollack painting."

Cath looked up at the orange, red and yellow dress with the ruffled neckline.

"It's a steal, reduced from two-hundred seventy-five to one-fifty, and then half off that."

"I don't care if it's free. It looks like a clown costume."

"Okay, but try on this jacket. It's real suede, marked down from one-fifty to thirty-five." As Cath tried on a little black evening dress she added, "Your professor isn't too smart if he thinks he can skip town and avoid the whole Christmas thing. I'll be interested in his next move after this disaster, if he even has a next move."

Jessica tried to turn around in the cramped space to see the back of the jacket, ignoring Cath's remarks about Brant.

"I think I like this. See anything wrong with it?" she asked.

"Not a thing. New clothes are just the thing to cheer you up."

"Who says I need cheering up?" Jessica asked, trying to sound chipper.

"Trust me. You do," Cath said. "After this, let's hit Macy's and then get lunch. By then, you'll have so many new outfits and fun accessories, you'll be flying high on shopping euphoria."

By the time Jessica returned home she was exhausted. She threw all of her packages on her bed and drew a hot bath. She poured herself a glass of Merlot and sank into the steamy hot water to wash away her thoughts. After her bath, she wrapped herself in her heavy cotton bathrobe, slipped into some oversized socks and curled up in a corner of the couch with every intention of jotting down some ideas for another chapter in the tale of Princess Anne and her knight, Sir William. But despite the calming effects of the wine and hot bath, every word that came out of Lady Anne's mouth sounded harsh and extremely pissed off. So Jessica put her pen aside and opted for the mind-numbing drug of daytime television.

* * * * *

Leaving his parents' house had been like trying to walk out of the ocean, with wave after wave pulling him back out to sea. Brant's mom must have come up with a dozen different ways of suggesting that he should move back home, little hints of how nice it would be for him. The last day had been the worst of it.

"You know, there's a high school here that could use a good English teacher. I know the vice principal and could set up an interview for you."

"I like teaching college-level classes, Mom. But thanks."

And then thirty minutes later...

"We have colleges on the East Coast, too, you know. Some very prestigious colleges, in fact. I never understood why you needed to go all the way to California to go to school."

"The weather is better?" Brant suggested, knowing that had nothing to do with it.

"If you'd just stayed here, none of this would have happened."

There it is, thought Brant. If he had just stayed closer to home, maybe even lived at home, then he never would have been out riding a bike in the damn California sunshine where some idiot could send him flying through the air like a rag doll.

"Things happen wherever you live," Brant said, knowing logic didn't matter when his mom was on a roll.

"I just think it would be better if you moved back here. You'd be close to family and we could all help you out and get together more often. It would be just like when you were a kid."

The more she talked, the more Brant felt the urge to get away—the faster the better—before he was sucked back into the womb.

"Leave the boy alone, Connie," Brant's dad said. "He's doing just fine where he is."

Brant smiled a silent thank you to his dad.

"You've got to watch her, Brant. If your mom had her way all you kids would be back living under one roof, God forbid."

"Oh, Frank," Connie blurted out and left the room before they could see her crying.

Brant followed his mother with his eyes as she rushed from the room but before he could go after her, his dad held the back of his chair.

"Let her go. She just needs a good cry and then she'll be right as rain. It's hard for her to see her little boy in a wheelchair," Frank explained.

"I know. That's why I waited so long to come home. I wanted to be in the best possible condition, have my life in order, you know...I didn't want her to worry."

"Mothers would be out of a job if they couldn't worry about their kids."

"I'm not exactly a kid..."

"You are and always will be to your mother. Come on. I'll help you get your stuff together. We need to leave for the airport soon. The traffic going into New York will be a nightmare."

"Sure." Brant started to head toward the kitchen door, his dad following behind him.

"And Brant..."

"Yeah?"

"Don't wait so long before you visit us again. We really do miss you."

"I'll try. But you know, planes fly in both directions," he said with a smile, trying to lighten up the moment.

"You always were a bit of a smart ass," his dad said, giving Brant's chair a good push.

On the flight home, Brant couldn't help but wonder why Jessica had never called. At first he imagined the worst—she had been in an accident just like that dumb movie with Cary Grant that his wife had loved. All that pain and feelings of rejection and hurt when all the woman had to do was call and say, "Sorry I didn't show up. I was hit by a car." Any guy worth being in love with would understand that.

What if Jessica had read his letter and had been terrified by his sudden outpouring of feelings? What if she didn't feel the same? What if he had moved too fast and frightened her off? What if, at this very moment, she was changing her phone number and email address, and putting Brant on a "no call" list at work? Or maybe the package was lost in the Christmas onslaught and never arrived. That would be better than an accident or just plain rejection.

I need to stop torturing myself with these thoughts.

When the flight attendant came by with the drink cart, Brant ordered a double Scotch in hopes of numbing what was left of his feelings and shutting off his brain at least for the remainder of the flight.

* * * * *

The Monday after Christmas the work force dragged itself back into the office after three days of holiday cheer. The only upside of the week was that Thursday was going to be a half day for New Year's Eve, followed by another three-day weekend for New Year's. Simon had flown out to Las Vegas for Christmas to visit his sister's family and her noisy, out-of-control brood and just returned Monday morning at seven. He was feeling quite happy, having won a five-thousand dollar jackpot on a dollar slot machine the day before, which put a silver lining on his annual visit to the insane asylum.

Simon preened like a proud cock in front of Claire, waiting for her to comment on the new suit he had purchased with his winnings. Right on cue, Claire looked up.

"Is that a new suit, Mr. Fitch? It's very sharp," she said and meant it.

If she didn't already know what an ass Simon was, she might have been attracted to him in just such a suit.

259

"Why thank you, Claire. I bought it in Las Vegas with my winnings," he said, hoping she would ask how much he had won.

"You must have hit a nice jackpot."

"This suit," he said admiring his reflection in the glass of a huge photograph on the wall behind Claire, "barely put a dent in what I won."

"Wow," Claire said, knowing she needed to act impressed.

"Five thousand bills on a dollar slot."

"Must have been your lucky day. I never win on the slots. I do better at blackjack. I only go once or twice a year but I have a great—"

With the conversation taking a turn away from him and his winnings, Simon was instantly bored and cut her off.

"Yes, well, we can't all be lucky or Vegas would be out of business. Now about the Allen account. I need all the information on what we did for them three years ago. They want a new campaign and I'll be handling the creative on this one."

Without waiting for a reply, Simon strode into his office. Once seated at his desk he began to pull files from his in-box and came across Jessica's package. As he sat wondering whether or not to toss the package in the trash, Claire came in with several files. As she went to place the files in Simon's in-box she caught sight of the FedEx box with Jessica's name written in big bold letters, and picked it up, puzzlement evident on her face. Simon was quick with an explanation.

With a casual smile, he lied, "The incompetent mail clerk must have delivered this to my office by mistake. It's been sitting here since last Thursday. Idiot. I have half a mind to fire him. Take this down to Ms. Singer's office. I hope it wasn't important," he said, trying hard to keep the sarcasm out of his voice.

Jessica hadn't arrived yet so Claire gave the package to Kim. When Jessica came in fifteen minutes later, the package was the first thing Kim handed her after she sat down.

"What's this?" Jessica asked, confused that Kim was just standing there waiting for her to open a FedEx box.

"Look who it's from," she prompted. "Now look at the date."

Jessica looked up at Kim. "This should have arrived before Christmas."

"I know. Claire just dropped it on my desk saying Simon had told her some lame story about the 'incompetent' mail clerk. I bet he had it all along. Aren't you going to open it?"

"Well, yeah," Jessica turned the box around and around, looking for the pull tab.

Kim couldn't stand it any longer. She took the box away, found the tab and ripped it open before handing it back to Jessica.

"Thanks," Jessica said, looking at Kim like she was nuts. "Why are *you* so excited?"

"I just have a hunch, that's all. Now open it, will you?"

Jessica pulled the cardboard box open to reveal a small square box wrapped in shiny red paper and a gold ribbon, as well as an envelope with her name on it. She pulled out both and set them on the desk, tossing the cardboard FedEx box on the floor.

"I'll bet it's jewelry," Kim said with glee.

"Will you stop it or I'll make you leave."

"Okay, but open the box first."

Jessica picked up the gift and looking right at Kim with a mischievous smile, tested the weight in the palm of her hand, then brought the box up to her ear and shook its contents, listening to the sound of metal cascading on metal.

"Sounds like jewelry, all right," she said, teasing Kim even more.

"If you don't open that box right now, I'll open it for you," she said, reaching out as if to grab the box away.

Jessica held the box out of reach before relenting. "All right, you win," she laughed and pulled off the ribbon and tore off the paper.

When she opened the lid, Kim was hovering over her and saw the contents at the same time.

"Oh, it's lovely," Kim exclaimed.

Jessica held up the sterling silver bracelet with two dangling charms—one a tiny typewriter and the other a little silver book.

"The charms have to do with that novel you're writing, right?"

"Yes," Jessica said, draping the bracelet over her wrist.

"Here, let me put that on for you."

Kim opened the clasp and slipped it over the silver ring.

"And look," she said, spinning the bracelet around so Jessica could see. "This little piece of chain that extends beyond the clasp has a tiny silver heart. I wonder what *that* represents…"

Jessica held up her wrist and admired the thoughtful gift. "Could just be a part of the bracelet's design."

"Maybe he explains himself in the letter," Kim suggested, looking at the envelope on the desk.

Jessica picked up the envelope and ripped open one end. Out slipped three sheets of paper, precisely folded in thirds, with Brant's neat handwriting covering both sides of each sheet.

"Oh my," Kim said. "The man had a lot to say."

Jessica read the first line.

"My dear, dear Jessica. I hope you can forgive me for being such a coward and running to the safety of my parents' house just as we were starting to connect on a deeper level."

"Ummm. I think I want to read this in private," Jessica said, looking up at Kim who was peering over her shoulder.

"Right. I'll be at my desk if you need me," she said, stooping to pick up the discarded box on the floor before she left.

Jessica took her time reading Brant's love letter, amazed at the depth of his feelings and his openness. She realized that up until this moment, she hadn't had a clue as to what the man was thinking. Now all his longings and desires, his hopes for children, to be a father, to fall in love and his concerns about finding a woman who could love him and his limitations were laid bare across page after page. He told her about his first marriage and how his wife had left him because he would never be the kind of father or husband she had envisioned.

Jessica cried for his pain and hers, remembering how hurt she had been when her husband had left her for another woman because her body was incapable of making him a father.

Brant's manhood had been bruised almost as badly as his body. No wonder he had isolated himself. When Jessica came to the end of the letter she let out a curse.

"Oh, shit," she said loud enough for Kim to hear.

When Kim came rushing back she found Jessica with her head cradled in her hands.

"What's wrong? He couldn't have broken up with you. He gave you that bracelet."

"It's not that. Listen to this." Jessica read, "Please call me. I've placed my heart in your hands."

"Oh dear," Kim said, understanding what Jessica was worried about. "By now he must think you're not interested."

"Or worse. I could be the second woman who walks out on him," Jessica said, waving the pages of the letter in the air.

"So call him right now," Kim suggested, making herself comfortable in the client chair.

Christie Walker Bos

"You think?"

"Don't be one of those stupid characters in books I've read where if she'd only explained what happened there would have been no need for all the misunderstandings and heartaches that follow. I hate movies and books like that." Then Kim thought a moment. "That book you're writing...it's not like that is it?" she asked, afraid she had just put her foot in her mouth.

"No, of course not. My heroine is strong, determined and takes matters into her own hands."

"Just like you," Kim smiled.

"Just like me," Jessica echoed, although not as sure as she sounded. "I'll try him at his parents' house first."

While punching in the phone number Brant had given her in his letter, Jessica's stomach began to do somersaults and flips as she wondered what she was going to say when she heard his voice. She only had to wait two rings before someone picked up.

"Hello?"

"Hi. This is Jessica Singer, a friend of Brant's from California. Is he still there by any chance?"

"Oh, hello Jessica. I'm Brant's mother, Connie. You just missed him," said the soft female voice. "We just got back from dropping him off at the airport. He had a one o'clock flight. You could try him on his cell phone in a couple hours," Connie suggested, trying to be helpful. "Do you have the number?"

"Why yes. Thank you, Mrs. Wilson."

"Oh please, call me Connie."

"All right. Well, thank you again. I think I'll just leave him a message on his home phone."

"That sounds fine, dear. I hope to meet you someday..."

"And I you," Jessica replied before saying goodbye.

Jessica looked at Kim and tilted her head.

264

"That was odd. Brant's mom seemed so happy to hear from me, although I've never talked to her before."

"Maybe Brant said something about you," Kim suggested.

"Maybe."

* * * * *

Three thousand miles away, Connie Wilson was full of smiles as she hurried out to the garage to find her husband.

"Frank, you'll never guess who I just talked to," she said, and before he could answer she rushed on, "Jessica Singer!"

"Who?"

"Jessica Singer. Don't you remember? Brant mentioned her once or twice."

"So?"

"So? She called *here*," she said with unsuppressed glee.

"What did she want?" Frank asked as he kept stacking up the Christmas boxes.

"To talk to Brant," she said, exasperated with his inability to find meaning in what she was telling him.

"So what's the big deal?"

"I swear, you are so dense sometimes."

Frank just gave her a blank stare, waiting for Connie to fill him in as he knew she would.

"If Brant gave her *this* phone number that means he's serious about this woman. It means that Brant has a woman in his life."

"About time," Frank said, before returning to his boxes, much to his wife's frustration.

Frank smiled as he listened to his wife's huffing sounds as she stomped out of the garage.

Good for you, Brant. Good for you.

Chapter Nineteen

ဢ

Brant caught a cab outside the terminal and asked the driver to stay off the freeways to avoid the beginnings of rush-hour traffic. The sunny warm weather, blue skies and palm trees were doing nothing for his mood, and he had a hard time believing it was still winter. All he could think of was getting home, changing into sweats and going for a ride along the boardwalk. After seven days cooped up in his parents' house and then almost six hours on the plane, Brant was ready to get in some exercise and work up a sweat. Brant hoped that by pushing his body hard he could shut down his mind and stop thinking about why Jessica hadn't responded to his letter.

After tossing his luggage on the bed and changing into sweatpants and a sweatshirt, Brant was on the boardwalk cruising past moored sailboats, seafood restaurants and grassy parks. By the time he pushed his chair back up the gangplank, all he could think of was how good a hot shower was going to feel. Sitting on a hard plastic shower chair, Brant lathered up and then let the hot water wash away the sweat, suds and all his thoughts.

It wasn't until he was sitting in front of the television with a glass of Scotch in his hand that he noticed the red blinking light on his answering machine. Rolling over to the machine, Brant let a small spark of hope flitter into his conscious mind before hitting the play button.

"You have four new messages," said the recorded voice.

The first message was from Mitsy, wishing him Merry Christmas and inviting him over for dinner like she did every year. Every year he politely refused, making up some excuse why he couldn't join them. At least this year his excuse would have been legitimate. The next message was from UCLA's curriculum coordinator, Mrs. Hewlett, letting him know about next semester's set of classes and asking him if he wanted to teach a summer school class on creative writing like he did last year. The third message, he was disappointed to learn, was from his mom, with the usual worried-mom stuff about arriving home safely. He was just about to hit erase when she surprised him with her next comment.

"Oh, and Jessica Singer called here looking for you. Sounds like such a nice girl. I told her when your flight left and suggested she call you on your cell. Please call me later and fill me in on who this Ms. Singer might be."

Brant was so happy to hear that Jessica had called that he didn't even feel the slightest irritation at his mother's nosy question. So Jessica had called after all. So she had received his package, but why then wait so long—almost a week later—to call him.

That can't be a good sign, he thought, as the next message began to play.

"Message four, sent on Monday at eleven thirty-five a.m."

"Hi Brant. It's Jessica. Welcome home. I just finished reading your letter. It was so beautiful and sad and moving and the most wonderful letter I've ever received. And the bracelet…it's just perfect. I'm wearing it now. Listen…"

Brant could hear the tinkling of the silver charms.

"I'm so sorry I didn't call you sooner…"

Here it comes, thought Brant. The big "but". His body tensed as if ready for a gut punch.

"But the package just arrived this morning. Somehow it ended up in Simon's office over the holidays. Sounds suspicious to me. Anyway, I feel so awful that I wasn't able to call you over Christmas. You must have thought terrible things about me. I know I would have if you hadn't called me. I'm rattling now and using up all your tape. So call me when you get this message. And Brant…I love you, too."

Brant let out a huge sigh of relief.

"She said she loves me," Brant said out loud before downing the rest of his Scotch. "Damn!"

Not sure he could control how he sounded on the phone right now, Brant decided to send Jessica an email. Once he hit SEND it was like a heavy weight had been lifted and he felt light, happy and extremely tired. By nine o'clock he was sound asleep and didn't move until nine the next morning.

* * * * *

When Jessica walked into her house late Monday evening after work, Merlin greeted her with excited squawks and squeals. Dropping her bag and attaché case on the floor the moment she walked in, Jessica went to his cage to let him out. He jumped onto her outstretched finger and moved in short quick steps to her wrist to investigate the shiny new bracelet hanging there.

"You like my new bracelet, Merlin? My professor, or should I say my boyfriend, gave this to me," she said as she picked up the little typewriter and showed Merlin, who pecked at it appreciatively.

Then out of habit she flipped on the computer before walking into the bedroom to change. Clothes were thrown everywhere around the room and her new outfits were still in their bags.

"We need to do some laundry," she said to Merlin, who tried to keep his balance perched on her shoulder as she bent over to gather all the clothing into one huge pile.

From the bedroom, Jessica heard her computer telling her she had mail, so when she came back out she glanced at her in box. As soon as she saw Brant's name she pulled out her chair and sat down. She took a deep breath, not knowing what to expect but hoping it would be good. After a quick double-click, the message opened to five simple words.

Tomorrow. Your place or mine?

From a three-page letter to five little words. Brant had quite the range. Jessica looked around at the mess that was her small home and had no problem deciding how to respond to the email.

Your place, six-thirty, she typed and then hit SEND. Then she shrieked in delight, sending Merlin into a panicked attempt at flight, feathers flapping furiously accompanied by loud screeches.

* * * * *

Jessica had prepared for Tuesday evening that morning by showering and then dressing in black knee-high boots, a black lace bra and matching panties covered by a short gray skirt and topped with a tight V-neck sweater. Kim noticed her stylish, sexy outfit and the radiant smile on her face the moment she arrived at work.

"Have an important appointment today?" Kim asked as Jessica passed her desk.

"You could call it that," Jessica called over her shoulder as she breezed into her office.

Jessica had two year-end reports she wanted to finish before she left, so she ate her lunch at her desk. She hadn't come up for air all day, until Kim stepped into her office to tell her she was leaving.

"It's five o'clock already?" Jessica asked in surprise.

"Guess you had better wrap things up if you're going to make that 'appointment'," Kim teased.

"See you tomorrow," Jessica said, before returning her attention to her report.

After waiting a second to see if Jessica was going to tell her more, Kim left for the day. A half-hour later, Jessica finished up and began gathering her stuff to leave. When she was halfway to the door she turned around, remembering something. She went back to the desk and bent over to open her lower desk drawer. She pulled out the frame she'd bought for Brant and set it on the desk. Then she began searching around for bubble wrap and paper to rewrap her gift.

Standing at the door to her office stood Simon, transfixed by the sight of Jessica bending over in her short skirt and black boots. His mouth twitched and his breathing became short as he let his eyes travel up the length of her legs, beyond the boundary of her skirt. He watched as long as he dared before pulling himself away. He left the client folder he had brought down for her on Kim's desk and hurried away before he was discovered.

Jessica turned toward the door at the sound of retreating footsteps. She walked over to her open door and stuck her head out, looking down the hall in time to see Simon's office door closing behind him. A chill ran down her neck and she had to physically shake herself to make it disappear.

By the time Jessica pulled into the marina parking lot, all thoughts of Simon had been replaced by a growing excitement to see Brant. Carrying just her purse and Brant's gift, Jessica found the key Brant had hidden for her, opened the gate and walked with eager steps along the dock until she reached Brant's gangplank, where she gave the bell rope a good hard tug. Brant appeared almost at once to greet her, a red rose lying across his lap.

As Jessica reached the top, Brant held out the rose and when she reached out for it, he grabbed her by the wrist and pulled her onto his lap.

"I missed you terribly," he said before covering her mouth with a powerful kiss. His fingers played with the hair at the back of her neck, which sent shivers down to Jessica's toes. Her returning kiss was hot, moist and breathless, sending a soft heat flooding through his senses. Their kiss would have lasted even longer had it not been for the playful shout from Brant's neighbor, Ron.

"Way to go, Professor!"

Slightly embarrassed, Brant pulled back.

"Let's go inside," Brant suggested. "And GET SOME PRIVACY!" he shouted for the benefit of his neighbor.

Jessica stood up, smoothing her short skirt back into place. When Ron gave an appreciative whistle, Jessica smiled and waved at him as she followed Brant inside. Once in the galley, Brant turned his chair around to face Jessica and gave a low, long whistle of his own.

"So where were we?" he asked, not able to take his eyes off her.

"You like what you see?"

Brant smiled and patted his lap and Jessica sat down with her legs hanging over the side.

"I most definitely like what I see, but I like what I feel even more," Brant said in a rough whisper that revealed his deepest desires.

"And what do you feel, Professor?" Jessica whispered back, dragging her fingernails along the length of his exposed arm.

Brant closed his eyes to better focus on all that he felt.

"I feel warmth and desire here," he said, taking Jessica's hand and moving it to his lower belly. "I feel excited and scared here," he continued, moving her hand so that it cupped the side of his face. "But most of all, I feel tenderness, understanding and love," he said as he moved her hand to his chest, where he curled his fingers around hers and pressed them hard against his heart.

Jessica took her other hand and caressed the side of Brant's face, causing him to open his eyes.

"I feel the same and I would add one more feeling…"

"What's that?"

"Happiness—a deep, quiet happiness of just being here with you. A happiness like I've never felt before."

"Yes," Brant whispered before pulling her in even closer, wrapping his arms around her and holding her tight against him.

After a few moments Brant loosened his embrace and the two of them looked into each other's eyes and smiled.

"I hate to break this magical moment," Jessica said, "but I'm starving. I only had a soda and some chips from the vending machine for lunch."

Brant burst out laughing.

"I'm glad you said it. I'm starving too. That's one of the many things I love about you—nothing gets in the way of food."

"I wouldn't say that," Jessica said a bit defensively.

"Come on, admit it. Almost every time we've been together food has been involved. Even your short story centered around food."

"If you think that story was about eating rice, then we need to talk," Jessica said, standing up and crossing her arms over her chest as if she was mad.

Brant just laughed before wheeling his chair over to the refrigerator to pull out two cold bottles of beer, handing one to Jessica.

"Of course I got the imagery. A sixth grader would have figured that out. I was just pointing out the fact that you used food to convey your message."

Jessica took a long pull from her beer before answering. "Speaking of food, are we ever going to have any or are we just going to talk about it."

Right on cue, Brant's gangplank bell came to life with two sharp clangs.

"I do believe dinner has arrived."

Brant grabbed a wad of money off the kitchen counter and disappeared down the hallway. When he returned he had two white bags sitting on his lap. Jessica brought plates and forks to the table while Brant pulled out a half-dozen small white boxes from the bags.

"I hope you like Thai food. This place has the best egg rolls and Pad Thai noodles."

"Smells good enough to eat," Jessica said as she pulled up her chair to the small table.

As they filled their plates and then their stomachs, Brant shared stories of what going home for the first time since the accident had been like. Jessica hit the highlights of her holiday with her dad and brother. After an hour Brant looked inside each of the little white boxes.

"So much for leftovers," he said as he began to gather up the trash.

Jessica cleared the dishes and helped herself to a second beer. "Do you want another?" she asked.

"Sure."

While Brant finished straightening up, Jessica set the wrapped frame in the middle of the table. "You forgot this."

For a second Brant couldn't remember what he could have forgotten. Then as he held the wrapped gift in his hands it came to him.

"I'm sorry I forgot to take this the last time you gave it to me. I wasn't thinking clearly that night."

"Neither was I. I was so pissed off at Simon I didn't consider how what happened made you feel," she said.

"If you must know, I felt like a fool," Brant admitted, looking at the frame in his hands. "And then I took it out on you when it wasn't your fault at all. I guess I ruined the evening." Jessica took Brant's hand and he looked into her eyes. "I can be a jerk."

Trying to ease his pain, Jessica smiled and said, "I shouldn't have stepped in between you and Simon. You were handling the situation just fine. If I had just left it alone, Simon never could have kissed me like that."

"That's what made me feel so helpless. There I was, but I couldn't do a thing about it. And after all that, you still have to work with the guy. Can't you file sexual harassment and get him fired or transferred?"

"I've been emailing the other partner, John McMannon, about that very thing. He assures me that everything will be resolved within a month and asked me to hold tight until then. He really doesn't want to lose me."

"Neither do I." Brant brought her hand to his lips and kissed the back.

When Brant began to speak again, his voice was full of emotion. "You've given me such hope and have made me look at the way I've been hiding away from friends and family. If it weren't for you I never would have gotten on that plane. For the first time since the accident, I feel I have something to live for…a future. And even if you and I don't work out or it's too hard on you to be with me, it won't matter. You will have still given me a wonderful gift, a new outlook on life and love, and for that I thank you."

Jessica didn't know what to say. She knew Brant expected her to reply, but all that came out was an awkward, "You're welcome" before a nervous laugh seeped out of her.

"I pour my heart out and you laugh," Brant said, wadding up the wrapping paper from the frame and throwing it at Jessica.

The paper ball would have hit Jessica in the head if she hadn't ducked out of the way. "Sorry. I'm not laughing at *you*. I think you're an amazing person. I guess I find it funny that you would need me, or anyone else for that matter, to help you realize that."

Jessica looked deeply into Brant's warm eyes and sighed. "I'm the one who should be thanking *you*. You've so inspired me Brant, in ways I'm just beginning to understand. To me, you are my knight in shining armor, a partner, a friend, a lover…the yin to my yang. We've brought out the best in each other. Good stuff that has always been there, but just needed a little confirmation, a mirror into which we could see our true selves."

"I don't know what's more beautiful, your mind or your body," Brant said, leaning in to kiss her. "Why don't we finish this discussion in bed?"

"I guess I know which one you decided is more beautiful," Jessica laughed before kissing him back.

After over an hour of lovemaking, Jessica laid in the crook of Brant's arm smiling.

"I'm sure this is going to sound terrible but there are some definite advantages to making love to a man who can't move from the waist down."

"I've got to hear this."

"I like that I can bring you to the edge and then ease off. I like how you use your tongue, your mouth, and your fingers to tease and torture me sweetly until I can't stand it any longer. I like that while I'm on top of you, I can control the rhythm and pace of our lovemaking, making it last and last. You seem to savor every touch, every caress, every taste leading up to the grand finale, as much as the final climax."

"Keep talking like this and we'll be starting all over again," Brant whispered as his body sank a little deeper into total relaxation.

"I guess I just like being a more active participant and not just a 'sperm receptacle' as my first husband treated me."

"Sperm receptacle?" Brant managed to ask before drifting off.

Jessica used a single finger to pull aside an errant lock of brown hair that was lying across Brant's forehead. "Good night, good knight."

Brant mumbled something that sounded like good night before his breathing took on the slow, deep rhythm of sleep.

* * * * *

Jessica had planned on getting up early with the idea of running home to change clothes but the warmth of Brant's body and his arm wrapped possessively around her waist kept her a willing captive for longer than she planned. As she was brushing her teeth and trying to do something creative with her hair, she heard Brant getting up.

"Was I dreaming or did you say something about a sperm receptacle last night," Brant called out as he pushed his legs off the side of the bed with his hands and then pulled himself into his chair.

"Must have been a bad dream," Jessica said as she walked out of the bathroom, not wanting to discuss her previous marriage on such a beautiful day. "This is a good look," she said as she stared at Brant sitting naked in his chair with a raging hard-on.

"You want to come sit on Santa's lap, little girl? I've heard you've been very, very good."

"Very funny."

"Well if you don't want to play, at least move out of the way so I can get in the bathroom," Brant pleaded as he maneuvered his chair around so he could back into the bathroom.

By the time Brant finished his morning routine and joined Jessica in the galley, it was time for Jessica to go.

"I'll call you tonight when I get home from work," Jessica said as she grabbed her purse and then bent over to plant a soft kiss on his lips.

Brant placed a hand at the back of her neck and pulled her in closer for a deeper kiss. Jessica responded with a deep lingering kiss before pulling away.

"I'm going to be late," she said and kissed him one more time on the cheek before leaving.

*   *   *   *   *

Jessica was late by half an hour, but Simon was in a closed-door meeting and was none the wiser. Kim was the first person to notice that Jessica was wearing the same clothes she'd worn the day before.

"Didn't make it home, I see," Kim said with a raised eyebrow.

"Nope," Jessica said, quite pleased with herself. "Can't imagine anyone here noticing but you. I rarely left my office all day yesterday."

But Jessica was wrong. There was one other person who noticed. As Jessica was standing in front of the microwave waiting for her tea water to boil, Simon walked past the break room door. The short skirt and boots caught his attention once again and he paused long enough to take in the rest of the scene.

Jessica's hair was up in a high ponytail, but other than that she was dressed in exactly the same clothes as the day before. Simon knew all too well what that meant. He left just before Jessica turned around.

Sensing someone was behind her, Jessica turned but no one was there. She walked to the door and, like the day before, looked out in time to see Simon's office door being slammed shut. This was the second time this week that she felt Simon had been watching her. Claire looked from the closed door to Jessica and shrugged her shoulders. Then the familiar sound of darts being hurled at the wall began.

Chapter Twenty

ɞ

New Year's Eve morning, Jessica had packed an overnight bag for her evening on Brant's houseboat, including the pages she had written so far for her novel. Her hands had shaken as she'd placed the typed pages into the side pocket of her overnight bag.

What if he hates it? Or worse, what if he says he likes it because he likes me *but really hates it? How will I know?*

Brant would be the first person to read her book. Although she would never admit it to him, this was a test. Not of her writing skills, but for Brant. Would he, could he, be honest yet supportive? Could he give her the advice she needed without breaking her spirit? Could she share her dream of writing full-time and would he support such a risky endeavor? All these thoughts and a dozen more raced through Jessica's mind like cars jockeying for position on the 405 Freeway, as she tore around her house getting ready to leave for work.

Once at work, Jessica spent the last day of the year putting the finishing touches on cover letters that would be mailed out with year-end reports to her clients. She was just about to call Kim into her office when she appeared in the doorway as if summoned by Jessica's thoughts.

"Excuse me, Jessica. But Mr. McMannon just arrived and has asked everyone to meet in the conference room in ten minutes. Have any idea what this is all about?" Kim asked, since it was highly unusual for McMannon to come into the office, let alone call a company meeting at the last minute.

"Not a clue," Jessica said honestly. "Guess we'll mail these out after the meeting."

Ten minutes later, the employees of McMannon & Fitch filed nervously into the conference room. Everyone seemed a little tense except Simon, who looked extremely pleased with himself. The hushed whispers and stolen glances at Simon all ceased the moment John McMannon walked into the room. Every seat was filled and there were people standing at the back of the room as well. Jessica and Kim stood with their backs against the wall, along with a couple of the graphic artists — arms folded, ready for bad news. But John was full of smiles, which seemed to mean they were all going to keep their jobs. The only thing that bothered Jessica now was how much Simon was smiling.

If Simon is happy, thought Jessica, *it could mean trouble for the rest of us.*

She watched as Simon adjusted his tailored suit and stood even taller than before.

"Thank you all for joining me this morning for this surprise announcement. I wanted you all to hear it from me first. We have purchased another agency in Oregon," John said with obvious pleasure. "Simon just received the final paperwork yesterday. It's a done deal. Simon, why don't you fill everyone in?" And with that John stepped aside as Simon commandeered the position at the head of the table.

"After several months of painstaking negotiations, we have purchased Reynolds, Allen & Wesson out of Portland, Oregon. We'll be taking over the operation, using their location as a base for working into Washington and Canada. Some of you will become useless and be fired," he said with a straight face and since Simon rarely joked, everyone believed him, including John McMannon.

"Now wait a minute! That's not true," said John, moving back toward the center of the room. But Simon put up his hand to stop him.

"I was just kidding. If anything, we'll be hiring a few new people. There will be opportunities for those who want to move to Oregon, but if you prefer to stay, that won't be a problem either."

John moved back into position at the front of the room and addressed the group again.

"Next year promises to be very exciting, profitable and full of new opportunities," he said with a twinkle in his eyes. "So take the weekend off…"

Everyone chuckled.

"And come in on Monday morning ready to create the best year ever. Happy New Year everyone and be safe tonight."

A few employees echoed back "Happy New Year" before filing out of the conference room.

John stayed at the front of the room, shaking people's hands, addressing them by their first names and wishing them a pleasant evening, until Jessica made her way to the front.

"Jessica, can I see you in my office?"

"Sure," Jessica said, wondering what McMannon needed to say to her alone. Her initial thought was that somehow she'd forgotten to do something important. Her mother would always say, "Jessica, I need to see you in the kitchen", right before she was reprimanded. But John's mood was happy and upbeat and so Jessica put that thought aside as she followed John into his office. He asked her to close the door behind her. When she turned around, she found him sitting behind his desk with a wonderful smile on his face, which put her at ease. Without preamble, John began.

"Jessica, I want you to head up the new company in Oregon," he said with enthusiasm. "What do you think?"

Jessica was flabbergasted. "What?"

"The new office is going to need a leader and I thought this would be a wonderful opportunity for you. That is, if you want to move. Otherwise I'm sending Simon and you can take over his position here. Either way works for me," John said, quite pleased with the entire plan. "Don't you see? This is the perfect solution. I separate you and Simon, solving that little problem, without losing either of you. And you move up in the company, which will mean a promotion and a substantial raise."

"I don't know what to say," Jessica stammered.

"Say Oregon or L.A. and it's yours."

"What will Simon say? Doesn't he have a choice in this?"

"Not really. His only choice will be whether he stays with the company or not. After his ridiculous behavior he should be thankful I'm still keeping him onboard. It's just that he *is* damn good at what he does. The whole Oregon thing was his idea. He made it happen from start to finish—a real genius. I have to give him credit for this one."

Jessica was aware of the beating of her heart and how her mouth felt like dryer lint.

McMannon chuckled. "Well, this just might be a first…Jessica Singer speechless. My, my."

Jessica blushed. "I'm just a little overwhelmed," Jessica managed to squeak out.

"It's okay, dear. I didn't expect an answer today. Take the weekend to think about it and get back to me on Monday. Things are going to move quickly once the New Year starts and I'd love to have you at the helm."

"Thank you so much, Mr. McMannon. I will definitely give this some serious thought."

Jessica walked over and shook John's hand before turning to leave. By the time she reached her office, her heartbeat had returned to a normal rhythm and she could move her lips again. Once seated behind her desk with her feet propped up on an open drawer, the full weight of the proposition finally hit her.

A promotion, a raise, maybe even a move—something she would have jumped at a couple years ago, even a couple months ago. But now it just didn't create the kind of euphoria she'd expected. Instead of feeling joy, she felt anxious. Was this the path she wanted to take—longer hours, more stress, more travel, a plane ride away from her dad and brother? Where would her writing fit into this new work scenario? It was hard enough already carving out time to write.

And what about Brant? Her relationship with him was just beginning to blossom and what it needed to grow was *more* time together, not less.

Before she knew it, it was noon and she hadn't accomplished a thing. She could hear Kim packing up her stuff, getting ready to leave. Just then the phone rang and she heard Kim take the call.

"Yes, Mr. Wilson, she's here. Okay, Brant. I'll put you through. Happy New Year to you, too."

Then Jessica's phone rang.

"Hey sexy," she said in a deep, sultry whisper.

"You think I'm sexy?" Brant laughed. "Well that's a first."

"I highly doubt that," Jessica cooed.

"Okay. Maybe not a first, but let's just say I haven't heard that in almost a decade."

"Probably because you haven't been rolling around naked. Trust me, if other women had seen what I saw they'd be lined up down the dock waiting to ring your bell."

"Flattery will get you anything your heart desires," Brant replied, the pleasure obvious in his voice. "So when are you coming over?"

"Officially we're off right now, but I have to finish up a few things and get some reports in the mail. I should be done in a couple hours."

"Great. Could you stop at a liquor store and pick up a couple bottles of champagne? It's the one thing I forgot."

"Sure. Any particular brand? I'm not much of a champagne person."

Brant rattled off a couple brand names and ended the conversation with "Hurry home, dear!" which sent odd chills through Jessica's body.

Even when he's being a smart ass, he made her heart skip a beat or two.

Three hours later, Jessica was climbing aboard Brant's houseboat with her overnight bag and two cold bottles of champagne from Trader Joe's. Brant was sitting out on the aft deck facing into the sun, catching the last rays of the year. He heard Jessica climb aboard and when he saw her in the galley, waved her outside.

"Can you believe this weather? December 31st and it's sixty-five degrees. I can't imagine living anywhere else."

Jessica bent down and kissed him fully on the mouth before pulling up a deck chair and joining him. She turned her chair into the sun as well, rested her head on the back of the chair and closed her eyes.

"Ahh. This is what I needed after today," Jessica sighed, as the warm sea breeze caressed her cheeks and sent wisps of blonde hair flying around her face.

"Bad day at the office?"

"I wouldn't call it bad," Jessica said without opening her eyes.

"What would you call it then?"

"Monumental. Scary. A career maker-or-breaker kind of day."

Jessica still didn't open her eyes or move but Brant was sitting up a little straighter and had turned his chair around to face her.

"So? Are you going to tell me what happened or keep me in suspense?"

"It was nothing. Just the possibility of a promotion, a raise and a move."

All Brant heard was "move".

"A move? To where?"

"Oregon," Jessica said as casually as she could, even though her heart was racing.

"Oregon? You can't move there," Brant said, louder than he'd intended, causing Jessica's eyes to pop open.

"What's wrong with Oregon?" she asked, trying to sound surprised, even though all she felt was joy. *He doesn't want me to move.*

"Well," sputtered Brant. "To start with, the weather is lousy. It rains all the time and when it's not raining, it's foggy. They don't have a single authentic Mexican restaurant in the entire state and I hear they don't think much of Californians, either."

"Oregon was just offered as an option. I can take over the new office in Oregon or the Santa Monica office—my choice."

"So which did you choose?" Brant asked, trying to act like it wasn't important to him.

"I chose to make that decision after talking to you," she said with a brilliant smile on her lips and a twinkle in her eyes. "I had a feeling you would have some very definite opinions about Oregon. I told McMannon I'd give him my decision next year."

"Good decision," Brant said with obvious relief. "So tell me about the promotion and raise."

Brant and Jessica sat on the deck watching the winter sun creep closer and closer to the horizon as Jessica explained the details of the possible promotion and her misgivings about taking what was being offered.

"It just doesn't feel right. Just when I've decided to spend more time writing creatively along comes this opportunity that I would have jumped at a couple years ago. I just don't know."

"I'm glad you didn't jump into something you'd regret," Brant said, staring at the setting sun. "How about we open one of the bottles of champagne and toast the setting sun and your possible promotion?"

Jessica followed Brant inside and while he grabbed a couple champagne glasses, Jessica pulled out one of the bottles from the refrigerator. Before returning outside, she took her manuscript out of her bag. Once outside, she tucked the seventy-five-odd typed pages into the side of her seat before sitting down.

Brant rolled up beside her with the glasses.

"You want me to open that?" he asked, gesturing toward the champagne bottle.

"I can do it. I like opening these things almost better than drinking the stuff. I can open a bottle of champagne without losing a drop."

Jessica peeled away the foil wrapper and untwisted the wire cage secured over the cork. Then, with the bottle held between her knees, she wiggled the cork back and forth with small twisting motions.

"The secret is to ease the cork out just a little bit at a time, creating a small opening to let off the pressure, so by the time the cork is off, there's only the merry popping of bubbles left."

And with that, the cork flew off and champagne exploded into the air.

Jessica screamed and leapt from her chair. Champagne dripped from her nose and forehead and soaked her jeans—and had splashed all over her carefully typed pages.

"Oh shit."

Brant couldn't help himself. He burst into uncontrollable laughter. When he could breathe again he managed to ask, "How did I know that was going to happen?" He wiped the tears from his eyes.

"Look at my novel. It's soaked," Jessica said in dismay, picking up the pile of wet pages and shaking them frantically.

"They'll dry," Brant reassured her. "Come here."

Jessica looked down into Brant's warm smile and inviting eyes and clutching her novel to her breast, sat across Brant's lap.

"I'm a little wet," she warned.

"Doesn't bother me in the slightest." And he took her face between his hands and kissed away most of the liquid. "Now this is how everyone should drink champagne."

Jessica stuck out her tongue but pulled it back in before Brant could bite it.

"The champagne must have been shaken up from the drive over. I can usually open a bottle without spilling a drop."

"If you say so."

"I am *not* a klutz." Jessica pretended to pout, wiping another drop of champagne from her forehead.

"That's what you keep telling me and I really do want to believe you."

Jessica leaned her shoulder into Brant's chest. "I'm not *usually* a klutz. Only around you."

"Look, the sun is setting." Brant angled his chair so that Jessica had a better view. "The last sunset of the year…"

They watched in silence as the sun kissed the horizon and then began to melt into the blue-black water of the Pacific. Brant wrapped his arms tighter around Jessica, willing her to feel what he felt just by the passion of his embrace.

You just can't move to Oregon. Not now. Not without me, was his last thought as the final golden sliver of light disappeared into the water.

Jessica let out a long, satisfied sigh.

"This is my favorite part of any sunset…the changing of the guard from day to night. The way the colors blend from pinks, oranges and reds to pale blues, then to deeper blues and purples then turning black. If I could paint, I'd paint big scenes with huge expanses of sky like this." Her sweeping arm gestured toward the western horizon, sending several pages of her novel sailing into the air.

Leaping up, Jessica scurried around the deck, snatching up pages before they could fly overboard. Three pages escaped her grasp and ended up floating down to the water like autumn leaves.

Hugging the stack of paper tightly to her chest, Jessica leaned into the railing and watched the escapees drift away on the outgoing tide.

"Tell me that isn't your only copy," Brant said with just the right amount of concern.

"Of course not. The entire thing is saved on my computer. But now there will be pages missing when you read it."

"Come on. Let's go inside. You're dangerous out here. I've made some hors d'oeuvres and we can actually drink some of that champagne."

"Funny man," Jessica said, leading the way into the galley.

Once inside, Jessica took her usual spot in the only chair and laid out the pages of her manuscript, putting everything back in order.

"I'm missing pages ten, fourteen and fifteen."

"So tell me about this. Is it something you want me to read for you?" Brant asked as he placed a ceramic plate on the table filled with crackers, a wedge of Brie, miniature shrimp plus some scallop shish kabobs.

"This," Jessica said with a dramatic flourish of her hand, "is my first attempt at a novel. It's not the entire thing, mind you, but it's a start, a first draft. This is what I wanted to ask you about. The favor. I want your opinion."

There. She had said it and now there was no taking it back.

"Do you want me to read it like I'm your professor or —"

"No," Jessica blurted out. "Well, yes. Sort of."

Brant looked at her and smiled.

"Should I read it like your lover? Because in that case, it's brilliant, amazing, earth-shattering…"

"I get your point. Yes, I want an honest opinion, but seeing how I *am* your lover, can you be kind and gentle and if it sucks, think of a nice way of saying so?"

"I'll do my best," promised Brant, knowing that this was going to be like walking through a minefield. Brant hoped Jessica's novel had merit so he could honestly tell her so.

Brant picked up the stack of paper with reverence and placed it on the counter away from the food, placing a heavy wooden bowl filled with fruit on top of it.

"So the pages don't blow away," he explained.

After a sumptuous dinner of angel hair pasta with sun-dried tomatoes, basil, olive oil and petite medallions of beef wrapped in bacon, Brant led Jessica into the bedroom where he had candles ready to be lit, scattered around the room. A dozen tall crystal vases filled with a variety of roses—red, yellow, white and peach—made the small space look like a garden.

"Oh, Brant! They're lovely," Jessica exclaimed with delight, as she looked around at all the flowers placed on the floor and perched on the dressers. The smell of the scented candles and roses created a thick, intoxicating perfume.

"I thought you should end the year and start a new one surrounded by roses. Hope you don't mind, but I thought we'd usher in the New Year in bed."

Jessica didn't know what came over her, but she was just so happy that she felt like a little kid. She eagerly dove stomach first onto Brant bed, rolling over on to her back and giving Brant a mischievous smile. "Jump in, the water's warm."

"Naked," Brant said. "In bed *naked*. Without our clothes on. Or shoes," he said, looking at her boots resting on his comforter.

"Ohhhhh. Naked. I get it. Flowers, candles, champagne, dinner…so you think you're going to get lucky, big boy?"

"God, I hope so," he moaned.

"Me too," Jessica replied, sitting up and pulling off her boots.

Brant rolled around the room lighting all the candles before he undressed and pulled himself up to the bed. Jessica snuggled down under the comforter and nestled into the crook of Brant's arm. Brant stroked her hair, moving his fingers tenderly through the long strands from her scalp to where the ends laid curled on her shoulders.

Maybe it was the champagne or maybe it was the complete feeling of bliss that put Jessica into such a giggly mood. Brant's gentle caresses made her squirm and laugh out loud at one point.

"You know, it's not very romantic when your partner starts laughing every time you touch her," Brant said, half seriously.

"I'm sorry. But you were tickling me. Aren't you ticklish?"

"No. Not in the least."

"We'll just have to see about that."

Jessica dragged a single fingernail up Brant's side, from his waist to his armpit, gently poking him along the way, testing him for ticklishness. When he managed to contain himself, Jessica intensified her efforts, tracing circles around his nipples, moving lower to his stomach and toying with the line of hair running from his navel to the dark curls between his legs.

"Tell me when you can't feel my fingers," she said as she teased his flesh with the softest touches of her fingertips.

"Can you feel this?" she asked, as she traced figure eights around his navel.

"Yes," Brant said, barely above a whisper.

"How about now?" she queried as her fingers trailed down his thigh.

"No."

Jessica moved her hand between his legs and cupped his balls. "And here?"

"Yes," Brant's ragged voice replied.

"And how about this?" Jessica asked with the innocence of a child, before ducking her head beneath the comforter. She didn't wait for his reply and took his sudden change of breathing as a positive sign that he had plenty of feeling left where she was touching him now.

Soon Brant was on the brink of release and pulled Jessica up from below the covers.

"You're a little too good at that," Brant managed to say. "So unless you want a repeat of your champagne-opening episode, we need to change the focus to you."

Jessica smiled at Brant, happy with the reaction she'd evoked and ready to see what he had in mind. Everything was still so new between them that Jessica still wasn't sure what Brant was and wasn't capable of doing.

Brant reached over and pulled Jessica's face in closer to his. He paused, staring into her candle-lit features, taking everything in, inhaling deeply, before pulling her closer for a kiss. First, he nibbled her bottom lip before sucking it into his warm mouth. When she tried to respond he would pull back, out of range, and then start over again, nibbling, sucking and exploring her mouth. Then using his tongue to create a trail over her chin, he moved down to her throat, planted kisses lighter than the flutter of a butterfly's wings all around her ears, exhaled deeply before sucking on her meaty ear lobe and pulling a moan from deep within her. Suddenly Jessica wasn't ticklish anymore. Any resemblance to the playful bedmate that had dove into bed an hour ago was long forgotten.

Jessica arched her back with pleasure as Brant continued to make his way excruciatingly slowly to the hollow of her neck, where he licked the indentation there like a kitten lapping milk from a bowl. All the while, Brant's hands were not idle. As his lips continued their journey south along Jessica's body, his hands were free to explore the curve of her belly, the insides of her thighs and the silky soft tuft of hair between her legs.

As Brant worked his way down the length of her body, he said, "Can you feel this?"

"Hmmmm."

"How about this?" he asked, as he dragged his fingers from one thigh across to the other, grazing the top of her mound as he passed.

"Oh, yes," she murmured.

Jessica's eyes were shut, her lips moist and parted, and her body tense with a feverish anticipation of what was coming next.

"And what about this?" Brant asked before bending his head to taste Jessica's sweetness for the first time.

Jessica ignored the question completely and let her body answer for her.

* * * * *

The sound of explosions woke Brant up from a deep sleep and he opened his eyes to flashes of red and orange light filtering in through the curtains. He turned his head to look at his alarm clock. Midnight. He touched Jessica on her exposed shoulder before whispering in her ear.

"Happy New Year."

"Happy New Year," she mumbled in sleepy tones.

"Open your eyes," Brant suggested, pulling aside the curtain over the porthole window next to the bed.

Just then another set of fireworks exploded over the water, creating a shower of blue and purple sparkles cascading like a waterfall, down the black veil of night.

"How beautiful," Jessica said in a soft, dreamy voice as she propped herself up on one elbow to have a better view. "Look how it lights up the water."

"Yes, it's the most beautiful thing I've ever seen," Brant said, watching as the light created a halo effect around Jessica's shoulders and hair.

When the light show was over Jessica rolled over to face Brant.

"Can I drape my leg over your hip?" she asked.

"Sure."

Brant was on his side with his arm folded under his head and his legs stretched out straight. He used his top arm to make his legs bend at the knees so he wouldn't roll onto his back from the pressure of Jessica's leg. Once both of them were settled, Brant moved his arm until it rested in the valley of Jessica's waist. Their faces were inches away from each other.

"Do you think we can sleep like this?" Jessica wondered out loud.

"One way to find out." Brant leaned in to kiss her on the nose before closing his eyes and falling easily back to sleep.

Jessica lay awake for some time listening to the rhythmic sounds of Brant's deep breaths and the lapping of water against the side of the boat. Somewhere down the dock she heard the high-pitched sound of female laughter, the clinking of glasses, the hoots of plastic horns and shouts of "Happy New Year" being called out from boat to boat.

I've got my happy New Year right here, Jessica thought before drifting off to sleep as well.

Jessica awoke to the sound of drums beating and trumpets blaring, punctuated by the scream of a seagull and the low moan of a foghorn off in the distance. It took her a moment or two to put everything together and figure out where she was.

Then it came back to her in a wonderful rush of emotions and feelings. The gentle rocking of the boat, Brant's delicious body, a manly arm draped across her waist, the smell of salt water, the flash of brilliant colored lights in a night sky — every intimate moment came back, making her feel deliciously warm all over. But she still couldn't figure out what the drums and trumpets were all about until she remembered what day it was.

"Rose Parade," she said out loud, as she moved to the edge of the bed. This time she had come prepared, bringing a pair of heavy duty sweat pants and a sweatshirt. But she still pulled on Brant's extra pair of Ugg boots, which he had left on the side of the bed for her.

When she entered the galley after washing her face and brushing her teeth, she found it quite deserted except for the voice of Bob Eubanks announcing the President's trophy-winning float. She made herself a mug of hot tea and pulled back the blinds to reveal a foggy morning. Sitting on the back deck with her novel in his lap was Brant, a cup of coffee cradled in his hands.

When Jessica opened the sliding door, Brant looked up and smiled.

"I thought you were going to sleep until noon."

"It can't be that late," Jessica said as she stretched her arms over her head.

"It's almost ten-thirty. You missed most of the parade," Brant replied.

Jessica looked at the pages of her novel sitting neatly in his lap. Just as she was about to ask, Brant turned his chair and headed toward the door.

"Let's go inside. It's too cold out here. You like waffles?" he asked over his shoulder as he moved inside.

"Sure. As long as you're making them, I'll eat them."

Jessica watched as Brant placed her novel back on the counter out of harm's way.

This can't be a good sign. If he liked it he would have said something right away. Putting it off must mean he hates it and is just trying to figure out a way of telling me without pissing me off.

Jessica slumped down into her chair and stared at yet another flower-covered float as it moved past the cheering crowd. As an afterthought she asked, "Can I help?" and was surprised when Brant said yes.

Jessica found herself squeezing oranges for orange juice and cutting up bananas and strawberries for the waffles, which Brant was pulling out of the waffle maker all golden brown. By the time they sat down to eat she couldn't contain herself any longer.

Brant had barely gotten his lips closed around his first bite when Jessica blurted out, "So? What do you think?"

Brant looked up, startled, chewed quickly and swallowed.

"Well, considering I've just had my first bite, I'd say it's okay, although I like the waffles at the corner café…"

"No, not the waffles. My book. What do you think about my book? You read it, right?"

"Ah. The book," Brant said, taking a sip of his orange juice and then very deliberately wiping his mouth with his napkin.

Jessica wanted to reach across the table and strangle him at that very moment but she forced herself to be still.

"Let me ask you something first. What type of market are you looking at here? Contemporary fiction, serious literature, historical fiction…"

It took her a few seconds but then Jessica understood why he needed to know. While her book would never cut it as serious literature, it might have enough substance to make it in a subgenre.

"I was thinking adventure-romance. Something fun. A woman's book," Jessica said hopefully.

"Perfect," snapped Brant, relieved that Jessica didn't have false expectations of winning a Pulitzer Prize. "That's just what I was thinking as well. Of what I've read so far, I thought it was very entertaining. Remember, I'm not your target audience here, so you should have your girlfriends read it too. But the basic writing mechanics are all very professional and with a little editing and polish, this will be a good start."

Jessica was thrilled but wary.

"You're not just saying that because I made you moan with pleasure in the bedroom last night?"

"As your professor, I can honestly say your novel has potential."

"Do you think if I invest more time in my writing that I have enough raw talent to make it as a writer in this field?"

This was the career-changing question. Even if he had hated her first attempt, which he didn't, she still needed to know if he thought she was talented enough to become a novelist full time.

"What do you mean by that?" Brant asked, sensing the gravity of the question.

"In your opinion," Jessica started out. "Would it be foolish to quit my job and just concentrate on writing?"

"That would depend on what you expected. Do you expect to be able to pay your bills and write novels full-time starting tomorrow?"

"Of course not. I'm not *that* naïve."

"Do I think you have the potential and talent to get to that point someday? Maybe. Sometimes success is about hard work and commitment, and not just talent."

Jessica let out the lungful of air she had been unconsciously holding in ever since she saw Brant on the deck with her work.

"You just have to make writing a priority while figuring out a way to stay off the streets while you find an agent, a publisher, capture an audience, and then write your second, third and fourth novels…"

"That's the real trick of it, isn't it? The writing is the easy part."

"Sounds like you're on the right track. I don't know why you were so worried. You passed my class with flying colors and that was before you were sleeping with the professor."

Jessica relaxed enough to smile and take her first bite of waffle before speaking.

"So many parts of my life are on the brink of drastic change. It's all happening at once and while writing has been a longtime goal, it wasn't until this very moment that I saw clearly what I was going to do about it. I just needed an objective opinion to help me come to the same conclusion."

"I don't think you could call my opinion objective, not after last night," Brant smiled.

"You're objective enough for me. I might even hire you to be my editor, clean the work up a bit."

"And how will you pay for my services, my little starving artist?"

"In the usual way, of course," Jessica said with a flirtatious wink.

Chapter Twenty-One

ಐ

After the relaxing weekend aboard Brant's houseboat, walking into the high-energy environment of the office was like walking into a tornado. Jessica's briefcase hadn't even hit the floor when her phone began to ring and Kim was at her door waving a handful of messages at her.

The first two hours were a blur of calls and emails. At eleven o'clock she got a call from Cath, and since they hadn't talked since right after Christmas, she took the call and asked Kim to hold all others. "My God, how are you? I haven't talked to you in forever. Where have you been hiding?"

"I was about to ask you the same thing. I called you four times over the weekend at home and on your cell," Cath replied.

"I was on Brant's boat," Jessica whispered into the phone so Kim couldn't hear. "It was a wonderful weekend. I never wanted it to end."

"Let's plan to have lunch this week or take a walk or something so we can catch up," suggested Cath. "Although there is one thing I just have to tell you now."

"Sure."

"I'm engaged," Cath blurted out.

Jessica screamed with delight, causing Kim to show up at her door. Jessica mouthed the words "Cath" and "engaged" and pointed to her ring finger.

Kim clapped her hands in a silent applause before returning to her desk.

"When did this happen?"

"New Year's Eve. It was so romantic. Pete took me out on a gondola ride in Balboa Bay, complete with champagne, roses and Italian opera music. With fireworks going off overhead at midnight, he pulled out a black velvet ring box and asked me to be his lover, his companion, his wife."

"How wonderful."

Before she could say anything more, Kim stuck her head in the door, said "McMannon" and pantomimed "line one".

"I've gotta go, Cath. The boss is on the other line but I want to hear all the details over lunch. How about tomorrow?"

"That sounds great. I'll let you go. See you tomorrow," Cath said before hanging up.

With a press of a button she was connected to McMannon. "Jessica here."

"Jessica. I was wondering if you'd made a decision about what we discussed on Thursday?"

Jessica hesitated long enough that McMannon continued on.

"Why don't you come down to my office in thirty minutes and we'll talk. I'm meeting with Simon at two this afternoon and I want to let him know what I've decided by then."

"Okay. I'll come down at eleven-thirty," Jessica agreed before hanging up. Then she hit the intercom button. "Kim, could you hold all my calls for the next thirty minutes? I need some thinking time."

Jessica heard Kim close her office door but didn't open her eyes. She had her head tilted back, resting on the top of her chair and her legs stretched out with her feet balanced on her open desk drawer. She used her breathing technique to clear her mind and bring herself to a relaxed state.

She thought about what Brant had said concerning her writing, how she couldn't just quit her day job and expect to survive. But if she took the promotion, work would eat up even more of what little free time she had. Instead of moving her closer to her goal, it would make it harder to achieve what she wanted. There had to be a way to work and write, and if someday she was good enough, transition over to just writing. She knew she didn't want to move to Oregon and she didn't want to manage the L.A. office either, but what would she tell McMannon she *did* want? Her mind was still juggling possibilities even as she turned the door handle to McMannon's office thirty minutes later.

McMannon's office, although seldom used, was warm and welcoming. Jessica's heels sank into the plush green carpeting as she made her way to the huge, overstuffed distressed leather chair. The deep reddish-brown mahogany furniture glowed in the afternoon light coming in from the picture window that looked out over downtown Santa Monica.

McMannon motioned to Jessica to have a seat while he wrapped up a phone call. Jessica pulled her gray skirt down straight before sitting. The large chair was so soft that on a different occasion she might have allowed herself to sink into its comfortable embrace. But today she sat on the edge, back straight, hands on her knees. She still had no idea what she was going to say. Once McMannon hung up the phone he started the conversation.

"Did you have a pleasant weekend?" he asked, hoping to get her to relax a little.

"Oh yes. It was wonderful. Very relaxing."

"Mine was as well. The Mrs. and I took a trip over to Catalina Island and welcomed in the New Year at the Casino Ballroom."

"I've always wanted to go to Catalina," Jessica said, relieved that they were engaging in a little small talk first.

"It's only twenty-six miles off the coast. You can go for just the day or stay a few nights. You should make a point of going. It's very affordable, too."

As McMannon was talking about Catalina, Jessica realized what she was going to say. She leaned forward in her chair, happy to finally have a way to make her point.

"You know you're right. I really should go to Catalina some day, I just never seem to have enough time—time for travel, writing, enjoying myself. I never seem to get everything done I want to…which is one of the reasons I must regretfully turn down your most generous offer. The raise and promotion sound great, of course, but they also sound like a bigger time commitment just when I'm thinking about working less, not more."

McMannon leaned forward in his chair and placed his elbows on his oversized desk, resting his chin on the top of his interlocked fingers. "Let me get this straight," he began. "You don't want a raise or a promotion?"

Jessica shook her head, hearing how ridiculous that sounded.

"And I can guess you don't want to move to Oregon then, either."

"Well no. My family is here and my friends…"

"And that nice fella you brought to the Christmas party…what was his name?"

"Brant. Brant Wilson," Jessica answered, a bit surprised.

"I'm not totally out of the loop on these things, you know," he said with a knowing twinkle in his eyes. "I'm very observant, even for an old guy. So, Ms. Singer, are you quitting then?"

"Oh no, Mr. McMannon. I like working here and especially working for you. Except for Simon, it's a great job."

"A job, not a career," he said as a statement. "That explains your decision. Why don't you tell me what you *do* want? Then maybe we can come up with something that will make us both happy."

So Jessica told him about her desire to write fiction and how she'd taken a writing class, which lead to meeting her professor. Then she explained her plans for the future.

"Right now I need to keep working until I've made a name for myself as a writer, and that can take years or it may not happen at all, but I have to try. It's hard enough finding time to write with my current job responsibilities. If I take over this office, I'd never have any time to write and then my dream will never have a chance of getting off the ground."

"I can see you're very passionate about this and I admire people who have the courage to go after their dreams. I did," he said thoughtfully. "But I still think you should take the raise and the promotion—"

"But—"

"Hear me out, Jessica."

Ten minutes later, Jessica left McMannon's office with a smile on her face as she practically skipped down the hall to her office, her feet barely touching the floor.

"That must have been a good meeting," Kim commented, noticing the change in Jessica's mood, the smile on her face and the lightness of her steps.

"The best," she replied, before closing her door, kicking off her heels and doing a dance of joy, consisting of a small leprechaun leap and shaking her ass, before sitting on the edge of her desk and punching in Brant's phone number. Brant answered in two rings.

"Are you free tonight?" Jessica blurted out, so eager to tell him her news.

"I don't know. I have such a full social calendar. What's going on?"

"I have great news and I want to celebrate. Can you come over to my place? I'm going to cook for you."

"This *must* be a special occasion. You've never cooked for me or invited me over before. Can I bring anything or pick up something on the way?"

"Nope. Just come hungry. I'm making my specialty."

"And what would that be?" Brant asked, remembering the eggshells in the scrambled eggs.

"It'll be a surprise," Jessica said with such enthusiasm that Brant felt he could handle whatever she made.

"What time?"

"How about seven? That will give me enough time to straighten up a bit and have dinner started."

"Okay. I'll see you at seven."

"I love you," Jessica said automatically without thinking, as if she said that every day of her life, and then hung up quickly when she realized what she had said.

"Oh dear," she whispered to herself. "Hope that didn't shock the shit out of him." It was one thing to say "I love you" on an answering machine or at the end of a letter, and quite another to say it to someone directly. *The real litmus test will be to say it to his face, in person*, she thought.

* * * * *

Brant looked at the phone. *Wow, she said it again*, he thought. *God I hope she means it.*

And he did a happy dance of his own, whirling his chair around in a quick circle.

* * * * *

Simon was in a great mood, dressed to impress and cocksure of what McMannon wanted to see him about at their two o'clock meeting. He even said "thank you" and smiled at Claire when she brought in the reports. Claire was instantly wary. Simon was way too happy—something was bound to go wrong very soon. And when it did Claire wanted to be out of the line of fire, so she told Simon she would be doing some filing in the storage room should he need her.

At two o'clock sharp, Simon rapped three quick times on McMannon's open door before striding into the office. Without being told, Simon took a seat in the overstuffed leather chair and let himself sink in, confident in what was coming — praise for his brilliant plan, a substantial raise and maybe even a move into this office. He looked around at the large room with the great view and began making plans for how he would redecorate.

"Simon," McMannon began. "I have to congratulate you again on the Oregon acquisition. It was brilliant. Couldn't have done it better myself."

Couldn't have done it at all, you old coot, Simon thought, while keeping the pleasant mask of a smile securely in place as he nodded his head.

"So now I want to make you an offer."

Here it comes, Simon thought, sitting up a little straighter.

"I want you to head up operations in Oregon."

"*What?*" Simon exploded, dropping his mask of pleasantry and leaping to his feet. "Oregon? I don't think so! That was never the plan," he protested. "You can't send me to Oregon. It's a cultural wasteland!"

"Sit down, Simon," McMannon said as if he was speaking to an unruly child.

Instead of sitting down, Simon began to pace back and forth in front of McMannon's desk, arms gesturing as he shouted out his objections.

"What can you be *thinking*? This place will fall apart without me! You're never here. There are a thousand little details that need seeing to every day that you aren't even aware of. This whole place will come crashing down around you without my guidance. Oregon doesn't need ME. Pick someone else to take over there. Anyone but me!"

McMannon let Simon vent a bit before deciding he'd had enough.

"If you don't sit down, you will force me to fire you," he said with a powerful voice.

That got Simon's attention. "You couldn't," he stammered. "You *wouldn't*," he challenged.

"Don't underestimate me. That would be a huge mistake on your part. I still own fifty-one percent of this company. Now SIT DOWN."

Like a petulant child, Simon dropped into the chair and stared at his reflection in his highly polished shoes.

"Now listen good, young man. I'm only going to say this once. I'm moving you to Oregon. You'll take over operations there, grow the business and be a huge success. This accomplishes two goals—I have a competent person in Oregon who understands the business and how we work, and I separate you and Jessica Singer, solving *that* little problem."

Simon's head snapped up. "Jessica Singer? What's she got to do with this?"

"After your inappropriate behavior on that business trip and again at the Christmas party with a room full of witnesses, I'm surprised you have to ask. Where Jessica is concerned, you are a liability. So it's move to Oregon or resign. Those are your options. Your *only* options."

"Why don't you make Jessica move? I'm a partner for Christ's sake," Simon demanded, the color rising in his face.

"I gave her the option first and she chose L.A., so that leaves Oregon for you."

"You let *her* choose? You let her decide MY fate?" he sputtered, his voice rising again.

"Frankly Simon, you chose your own fate the moment you tried to force yourself into her hotel room. You're lucky she didn't file charges and sue the company. I'm not taking any more chances with this thing. Either accept the Oregon position or I'll expect your resignation," McMannon said in a calm voice meant to counteract Simon's rage.

Simon was furious. He clasped his hands together to stop them from shaking. He willed his breathing to return to normal as he forced himself to stand.

"I'd like until tomorrow to think about this," Simon said in an unemotional monotone.

"Sure. I'd like your decision by tomorrow afternoon. I want to finish up the paperwork by the end of the week. If you decide to move, we will of course pay all your relocation costs. I suggest taking a week off to go up to Oregon and get the lay of the land, scout out some apartments or town homes. One way or another, I want someone in Oregon starting in two weeks," he said with a pleasant smile.

Simon turned around and walked to the door as if a single misstep would shatter him into a million jagged pieces.

* * * * *

Jessica had left work at five and made four stops on her way home—a local fish market where she picked up two pounds of fresh shrimp, a small French restaurant, the corner liquor store and a flower stand for two mixed bouquets. Arms full of bags and flowers, Jessica burst into her house like a whirling dervish as Merlin began to scream for attention.

"Sorry Merlin. You're just going to have to wait. This is going to be a night to remember and I want everything to be perfect. Not only am I cooking—which is an event in and of itself—but Brant Wilson is coming over for the first time. My God, what was I thinking," Jessica sighed, and Merlin gave a long, low whistle. "You can say that again."

Dumping everything on the kitchen counter, Jessica began unloading bags. The white wine went straight into the refrigerator, along with an amazing cream sauce she had picked up at the French restaurant. The sauce was her secret ingredient. Back in college, Jessica had dated a foreign exchange student who went on to become a chef of some renown and eventually the owner of Cafe Sur La Mer. Whenever Jessica wanted to impress someone, Jon Marc slipped her a quart of his award-winning champagne sauce. All Jessica had to do was boil water for pasta, cook either chicken or shrimp to add to the sauce, heat it in the microwave then pour everything over the cooked pasta.

For tonight, Jessica had purchased two pounds of shelled, raw shrimp that the boiling water would turn into delicious pink chunks of meat, ready to be added to the sauce. She would top off the dish with freshly ground pepper, Parmesan cheese and a sprig of parsley for color.

"*C'est bien*," she said out loud, feeling quite continental.

She placed the shrimp in the sink, the flowers in a couple vases and two wineglasses in the freezer before filling two pots with water and setting them on the stove—one for the pasta and one for the shrimp.

With forty-five minutes to go, she moved her attention to cleaning. First she moved around the living room picking up all the loose clothing—a blouse here, a pair of socks there. Then she moved into the bathroom and her bedroom, where she crammed the growing pile of dirty clothes into the laundry hamper, which she then stuffed into her closet.

She made her bed and gathered up books and magazines into one neat pile. She threw away a month's worth of Sunday papers, half of which she had never even opened, and then ran a rag over any piece of furniture that was noticeably dusty, leaving anything above Brant's head for a later day. On a second sweep through the house she removed Post-it notes from the back of the front door, the refrigerator, her computer, and both the bathroom and bedroom mirrors.

In the bathroom, she cleaned the sink and mirror, straightened all the towels, checking both the toilet and shower to make sure they weren't embarrassingly dirty—both passed inspection. Once back to the kitchen, she turned on the heat under both pots and poured the sauce into a bowl. Next she pulled out the vacuum and in ten minutes was done.

Taking a moment to catch her breath, she glanced around to find the place looked descent. Now for the ambiance. She turned on and off lights until she had just the right amount of indirect and direct lighting. She set the table with burgundy placemats, matching napkins and six candles. Next she put on a CD of instrumental guitar music and went into her bedroom to change her clothes. She had just slipped into a tight pair of jeans and an oversized off-white sweater with a plunging neckline when she heard someone knocking at the front door.

She glanced at her alarm clock—six forty-five. *He's early. Must be anxious to see me.*

That made her smile. She checked her hair in the mirror before heading for the front door.

"You just couldn't wait to see me, could you?" Jessica said as she pulled open the door—only to come face to face with Simon Fitch.

Chapter Twenty-Two

ဢ

Brant started getting ready around six, changing into a pair of Dockers and a long-sleeve pale blue shirt. It was still winter, even in Southern California, so he pulled on a heavy cable-knit sweater over his shirt and then re-combed his hair. The cab he had called was waiting for him at the end of the dock when he rolled out the door. The driver opened the door so Brant could slide in before collapsing his chair and placing it in the trunk.

Brant gave the driver the address and added, "I'd like to stop along the way and get some flowers."

"Sure thing. I know just the spot."

Unfortunately the first shop they went to was already closed. They tried another and it was closed as well.

"I can take you to a grocery store. They always have flowers," the cabbie suggested.

"Never mind. Let's forget the flowers. I don't want to be late."

But two blocks from Jessica's house the driver spotted a woman selling bouquets of flowers on a street corner.

"Will that do?" he asked, pointing her out to Brant.

"That would be great."

So the driver whipped a U-turn and pulled up alongside the curb. The woman turned out to be a young girl with short-cropped brown hair and deep brown eyes. She approached the cab with several bunches of roses and held them up to the back window.

Brant rolled the window down. "How much?"

"Twelve dollars a dozen," she answered with only the slightest Spanish accent.

"Okay. Give me two dozen. Red and yellow."

As Brant was pulling money out of his pocket, he heard a knock on the other window. He looked up to see the dark face of a young boy with jet black hair holding up a huge bag of oranges.

The cab driver opened his window and yelled in Spanish, "*Bete*", but the boy didn't move.

"*Cinco por cinco*. You want?" he asked, ready to run if the cab driver opened his door.

"What am I going to do with five pounds of oranges?"

But it was obvious the boy didn't understand Brant's question since he just repeated his sales pitch.

"*Cinco por cinco*."

"Okay, sure," he said, handing the kid five dollars.

The boy pushed the bag up to the window and then gave it a big shove from the bottom, so that it fell through the window onto the backseat of the cab. After paying the woman for the flowers they were off again.

* * * * *

"Simon, what are you doing here?" Jessica asked, still in shock from finding Simon at her door instead of Brant.

"I need to talk to you about Oregon," he said as if they were having a casual conversation in the break room at work.

"Can't this wait until tomorrow?"

"No. I'm not allowed to talk to you at work and this thing needs to be settled now. You've ruined everything and now you're going to fix it!" Simon said, raising his voice and shedding the illusion of calm professionalism.

"I think you should leave, Simon," Jessica said as gently as she could, even though her internal alarm was screaming "danger, danger!"

She began to close the door but Simon was too quick and lunged into the opening, forcing his way into her house.

Jessica backed away quickly, keeping her eyes locked on Simon while mentally negotiating her way around her furniture toward the phone on her desk. Simon was pacing back and forth like a caged tiger, ranting on about how it wasn't fair that HE had to move to Oregon to keep HIS job when HE was a partner and she was nobody.

"I can't believe McMannon would give you the option of staying in L.A. *You!* What have you done to deserve this? *I'm* the one who worked this deal. *I'm* the one who deserves a raise and promotion, not *you!* You need to fix this, Jessica," he said, turning to face her. His face was flushed with color and his eyes shone bright with anger, making Jessica back away even farther.

"Tomorrow you are going to go to McMannon and say you've changed your mind. You are going to tell him that you want to go to Oregon. Do you understand? *You* have to be the one to go, not me!" To emphasize his point, Simon slammed his hand on the top of the end table, startling Merlin into a flurry of activity and squawking.

"I really want you to leave, Simon. You shouldn't be in my house. Please go or I'll call the police." Jessica felt the edge of her computer desk against the back of her legs and knew the phone was within reach.

"You're not listening to me!" Simon shouted, his voice cracking as he stepped toward her. "I'm not leaving here until you agree to talk to McMannon and take the job in Oregon!"

At the sound of Simon's angry voice, Merlin began screaming as well, causing Simon to turn his anger toward the bird. Jessica used the momentary distraction to turn around and pick up the phone.

"Shut up, you stupid bird!" Simon shouted back.

Simon turned back to Jessica just as she was trying to punch in 911 on the phone.

"What are you doing?" he shouted and lunged forward, grabbing her by the wrist and yanking the phone away.

* * * * *

At two minutes before seven the taxi pulled up to Jessica's house. A silver Porsche was parked directly in front of the house so the driver pulled into the only open spot four houses down. As Brant was pulling out money for the driver he asked, "Could I interest you in some oranges?"

"Don't think so," the cabbie replied before getting out of the car to retrieve Brant's chair from the trunk.

"Guess I'll make orange juice," Brant muttered to himself, wondering what Jessica was going to think when he showed up with five pounds of oranges.

The driver had Brant's chair out and ready when Brant opened the door. Once Brant was in his chair, the driver reached in and pulled out the roses, handing them to Brant.

"Where do you want these?" he asked, holding up the bag of oranges.

"Lay them across my lap, I guess."

And so, under the yellow glow of the streetlamps and the soft white light of Christmas lights still twinkling on several of the neighbors' houses, Brant pushed his chair up the sidewalk to Jessica's house.

When he rolled up in front of her house he noticed a problem right away that had been obscured by the white picket fence—two cement steps connected the sidewalk to the narrow walkway that lead to another set of steps leading up to her front porch. Brant was getting ready to call her on his cell phone when he heard shouting coming from inside. He strained to hear.

A loud male voice roared out, "Shut up, you stupid bird!" And seconds later, "What are you doing?"

Brant recognized Simon's voice just before he heard Jessica let out a scream.

Jessica's in trouble.

Forgetting about everything except Jessica, Brant made a beeline straight for the walkway, slamming hard into the cement step, knocking the bag of oranges on his lap to the ground.

"I have to get in there or…bring Simon out here," he said out loud, his rage simmering dangerously below the surface.

Seeing the oranges on the ground, he reached down, picked up the bag and placed it across his lap. Then he tore a hole in the red plastic and pulled out an orange. Cocking his arm back, he hurled the orange at Jessica's front door. The orange hit hard, making a loud bang before falling to the porch with a heavy thud.

* * * * *

Simon had wrenched the phone away from Jessica, clicked it off and tossed it onto one of the overstuffed chairs. Then he sat down on the couch and turned to face her, a calm, dangerous mask covering his face.

"There's no need to call the police. I'm not going to hurt you," he said evenly. "I just want you to talk to McMannon. You can call him right now. I have his home number. Tell him you want to go to Oregon. Tell him you think I would be better here in L.A. I don't really care what you tell him. You can quit for all I care. All I know is, I'm not the one moving to Oregon!"

As if to emphasize his point, something banged against the front door.

Simon jerked around at the sound.

"What the—"

Then another bang, and another. Merlin started flying around his cage, screaming at the top of his birdie lungs with each loud crash.

Simon yelled at the bird to shut up as he headed for the door.

* * * * *

Brant kept throwing oranges, hoping curiosity would pull Simon out of the house and away from Jessica. After the sixth orange slammed into the house, the door swung open to reveal a very pissed-off Simon.

Brant was ready with another orange. Before Simon understood what was making all the noise, he was hit hard in the chest by the flying fruit.

"What the fuck?" he said, ducking out of the way of another orange that missed his face by inches and slammed into the front of the house.

"Come on down here, Simon. Let's settle this once and for all. I bet I can kick your ass even from this wheelchair."

It was then that Simon realized who his assailant was. When his eyes adjusted to the dark, Simon could make out Brant sitting at the end of the walkway.

"I'll be more than happy to take care of you right now," he hissed as he started down the porch steps toward Brant.

Now Brant threw the oranges even harder, one after another, aiming for Simon's head and stomach.

Simon had to duck and use his arms to block the shots. He managed to catch one of the oranges and let out a loud "HA!"

"You're not the only one with an arm," he sneered as he cocked his arm back to hurl an orange at Brant.

With his arm pulled back his head was exposed, and Brant threw a fastball that connected squarely with Simon's nose, sending him falling back hard on his tailbone on the concrete walkway.

Simon wailed in pain. "I think you broke my nose, you asshole!" Simon sat holding both hands over his face as the blood began to seep between his fingers.

"Good," Brant spit out, breathing hard.

Just then Jessica came out the door and almost tripped on one of the many oranges that littered her front porch. When she saw Brant, a smile lit up her face and she raced down the steps and walkway, making a wide berth around Simon who was now examining the blood on his hands. Seeing the bag of oranges on Brant's lap, Jessica shook her head in amazement.

"I can't believe you took him out with oranges," she said in astonishment.

"I was a pitcher in high school with a seventy mile-per-hour fastball. I'm afraid from a sitting position my pitch is a lot slower."

"Good thing," Jessica said, looking back over her should at Simon. "A seventy mile-per-hour orange could have killed him."

The sound of police sirens could be heard getting louder until a pair of police cars turned the corner and came barreling down the street, stopping in front of Jessica's house.

"As soon as Simon went to the door, I called the police," Jessica explained before turning and walking toward the four officers who were now out of their squad cars and walking toward them.

"I'm Jessica Singer, I'm the one who called you. This is Brant Wilson, my boyfriend, and that," she said, pointing at Simon, "is the man who forced his way into my house and threatened me."

As the officers approached Simon, he tried to stand up.

"Stay on the ground, sir," said the tall thin officer who stood off to his right.

Simon looked up and showed him the blood on his hands. "Do you see what he did? I'm bleeding! I think the asshole broke my nose! What are you going to do about *him*?" he demanded, pointing at Brant with a long stiff arm. "You should be arresting *him*, not me. I just came here to talk to my employee, Ms. Singer, and this lunatic starts pelting me with oranges. *Oranges*, for Christ's sake! What kind of person carries around a bag of oranges? He's crazy, I tell you! He should be the one locked up, not me. He's a dangerous cripple. Dangerous!" Simon shouted.

"That will be enough, sir," said the officer with the gray hair peeking out from under his hat. "Do you need an ambulance?"

"What do you think, shit-for-brains? I'm bleeding all over the place."

That was the wrong thing to say. Both officers grabbed one of Simon's arms none too gently and helped him to his feet. Then they led him to one of the squad cars, reading him his rights as they walked.

As Simon was led past Brant and Jessica, he spat out a glob of blood and one word. "Dangerous!"

The other two officers approached Jessica and Brant to get their statements. Ten minutes later an ambulance arrived and Simon was helped into the back, accompanied by one of the officers. While the police were finishing up their paperwork, Brant had a moment to talk to Jessica alone.

"So he just pushed the door open and walked right in?"

"I thought it was you, so I didn't even look out the window first. That's the second time I've made the wrong assumption about who was at my door."

"It couldn't possibly have been me," said Brant.

Jessica was confused.

"How did you expect me to get up to the front door?"

Jessica turned around and, as if for the first time, noticed the steps.

"Oh, dear. I never even thought about the steps. I'm so sorry!"

"I guess I should be flattered. You seem to have forgotten that I'm in a wheelchair."

"Here I thought I'd considered everything. I wanted this evening to be so perfect— Oh shit! The dinner!" Jessica turned and ran back up the path to the house.

Brant just laughed as he watched her maneuver her way around the obstacle course of oranges and race through the front door.

"Hey guys. I'm going to need a hand here," he called out to the two police officers who were getting ready to leave.

Jessica was busy turning off the stove when she heard a knock at the door. This time she peeked out the window first. There sat Brant with two dozen red and yellow roses. The officers who had helped him up the stairs were walking down the path.

Jessica opened the door and called out to them, "Thanks, guys."

They waved without turning around and Brant tilted his chair back enough to clear the threshold before rolling into the living room. Jessica took the flowers and sat down on Brant's lap.

"Let's start this evening over," she suggested before kissing him, holding his face in her hands. "My hero. My knight on a black and silver steed comes to my rescue with oranges, of all things. You'll have to explain to me later how you happened to have a huge bag of oranges with you."

"It's the newest weapon of choice, my lady. Not only are they biodegradable, but after the battle is won, the victors can eat the spoils."

Jessica let out a warm relaxed laugh and this time Brant pulled her in tight and kissed her long and deep. When they came up for air, Jessica looked Brant in the eyes.

"I really do love you, Professor Wilson."

"So I've heard," he teased, before kissing her again. "And I love you, Jessica Singer, a.k.a. Princess Anne, former student, future author, sometime klutz—"

"Hey!"

"Just kidding. So what are we celebrating besides my breaking your boss's nose?"

"I guess the first thing would be that he's no longer my boss. Let's go into the kitchen. We'll have some wine and I'll tell you all about it," Jessica said as she tried to stand up, but Brant wouldn't let her.

"Let your knight carry you on his faithful steed, My Lady, so you can reward him with a feast fit for a king for saving you from the treacherous Simon LeStrand," Brant said, playing the part.

"Very impressive. Maybe you should be writing my novel instead of me," Jessica laughed as Brant maneuvered his way through the living room to the kitchen. As they passed by Merlin's cage, he started screaming for attention with a series of squawks and whistles.

"Who's that?" Brant asked, checking out the bird as he wheeled by.

"This is Merlin, my roommate and, up until I met you, my steady date for Friday nights."

"Lucky bird," Brant said, moving them into the kitchen where Jessica dismounted and went to the freezer to pull out the wineglasses.

She handed Brant the bottle of wine from the refrigerator and a wine opener before unwrapping the roses and arranging them in a glass vase. Then she began the final steps of preparing their meal, talking the entire time.

"You should have seen the look on his face when I told him I didn't want a raise or promotion. I guess not too many people would say no to that. I explained to him about my writing, and he guessed about you, and then I told him how I wanted to work less and not more..." Jessica had to pause to catch her breath.

"You can slow down. I'm not going anywhere. Here," he said, handing her a glass of wine.

Jessica drained her glass in three large swallows and then continued. "I'm a little wound up, what with the Simon break-in, you being here for the first time, trying to cook a meal, the promotion —"

"I thought you turned down the promotion?"

"I did. But he gave it to me anyway, plus a raise. He wants me to take the promotion for the next six months, and during that time I'm to look for my replacement and then train him or her. Once the new manager is in place, I can go back to my regular position but work only three days — Monday, Wednesday and Thursday, eleven hours a day. That still keeps me at full-time status as far as benefits are concerned, but gives me two full days to write, plus the weekends if I want. It also frees me up for an occasional four-day weekend. Isn't it perfect?"

"Sounds wonderful," Brant agreed.

"Oh. I forgot the best part," Jessica continued, pulling the sauce out of the microwave and adding the shrimp. "Simon is being moved to Oregon. That's why he was so mad. That's why he came charging over here, to try to change my mind. I've never seen him so angry. I thought he was going to burst a blood vessel."

Jessica drained the pasta, which was a bit overdone but she hoped Brant wouldn't notice once it was covered with the shrimp and sauce. As she put together their meal and brought it over to the table, she never missed a beat recounting the events that led up to Brant's arrival.

When Jessica got to the part where Simon had grabbed her to get the phone, Brant could feel his blood pressure rising again. "Now I don't feel bad at all about breaking the guy's nose. Should have kept pummeling him when he was down." Brant took a deep swallow of his wine and then refilled Jessica's glass. "I'm just glad you're okay."

"Like I said, you came to my rescue." Jessica bent over and kissed Brant on the cheek before motioning him to the small dining room table. She moved one of the four wooden chairs away so he could pull his wheelchair up to the table. "Do you mind if Merlin joins us? If I don't let him out he'll scream at us throughout the entire meal."

"Fine with me."

Jessica opened Merlin's cage and put out her finger. Merlin hopped right on. Then she moved him to her shoulder where he happily began playing with her hair. Before she sat down she turned off the kitchen and living room lights and hit the play button on the stereo to restart the CD from the beginning. The candles on the table and around the room created a soft glow. Finally seated, Jessica let out a long sigh.

Brant raised his wineglass. "A toast."

Jessica raised her glass as well.

"To being in love again, this time to an amazing woman who loves me just the way I am, chair and all."

"So you're in love? Anyone I know?"

"Yes," he answered, his eyes transfixed on her face.

"I have a toast as well," she said. "To a most amazing man who I love dearly, chair and all."

Merlin chose that moment to squawk loudly and half fly, half fall off Jessica's shoulder onto the table.

"Yes, I'm sorry to say Merlin, but you've been demoted. I have a new man in my life now."

As if he understood what that meant, he flew up to perch on the edge of Brant's glass and dropped a little present into his wine.

Brant let out a hearty laugh and put his finger out for the bird. "I don't think he approves of me."

"Bad bird," Jessica scolded, as she got up to get Brant a fresh wineglass.

After dinner, Brant moved to the couch while Jessica lit more candles and put on another classical guitar CD, turning it down low until it became soft background music. Brant was seated in the corner of the couch and Jessica curled up next to him, her legs tucked under her and Brant's arm wrapped around her shoulder.

"That was an excellent meal. I thought you couldn't cook?" Brant teased, as he combed his fingertips through her blonde hair.

"I wouldn't call it cooking. More like boiling a lot of water."

"The sauce was amazing. Gourmet quality," Brant persisted.

"It's a secret recipe that goes back to my college days," Jessica explained as she rubbed her hand over Brant's thigh. "Too bad you can't feel this."

"I'm sure it would feel wonderful. Just sitting here next to you is such a great feeling. It feels like we're a normal couple...I feel normal for once."

Jessica pressed into Brant, happy just to be with him, too. They were both silent for a few minutes, Brant still playing with Jessica's hair, Jessica still stroking Brant's thigh.

"Jessica," Brant said barely above a whisper.

"Yes?"

"Wouldn't it be wonderful if we could do this every night?"

"Yes," Jessica sighed, melting into Brant's warmth.

"Then why don't we?"

Jessica turned in Brant's arms so she could look him directly in the eyes.

"What are you saying?" Jessica asked, afraid he didn't mean what she thought.

"I want to be with you every day. I think you should move in with me." He pulled her in close and kissed her like he'd never see her again, parting her lips and taking her tongue into his mouth with such love and longing that it made Jessica want to cry.

When at last the kiss came to an end, Brant was the first to break the silence.

"I don't know what I did to deserve you, but I'm glad I did," he whispered in her ear, inhaling deeply as he nuzzled her neck. "You are an incredible woman."

Jessica just smiled. For once she wasn't going to argue with him.

Epilogue

All the single women were jostling for position to catch the bouquet while friends and family gathered around shouting encouragement. The wedding photographer gave the signal and the bouquet flew into the air in a high arc—right into Jessica's outstretched hands. Cath whipped around in time to see her maid of honor catch the bouquet of baby white roses and soft green ferns.

"Why do I have the feeling that was planned?" commented Sandy, as Cath came over and gave Jessica a hug.

"Guess you're next," Cath said happily to Jessica before moving to a chair in the center of the dance floor where Pete was waiting for her.

Cath looked amazing in her flowing white gown. The halter-top neckline left her entire back bare until the material from the front of the dress came together to wrap tightly across her bottom. Cath didn't care how many times she'd been married—she still liked wearing white, each and every time.

Making a big deal of slowly lifting Cath's wedding dress inch by inch, Pete inched his hands up her thigh until he came to a white and blue garter. The obligatory whistles and catcalls accompanied the tradition and Pete grinned like the Cheshire cat. All the single males wasted no time in gathering out on the dance floor, jumping up and down, yelling at Pete to aim high. Brant wheeled himself out to the front of the pack, with several of Pete's CHP buddies crowded close behind him.

Pete posed for the photographer before turning around and, not even attempting to disguise his intention, shooting the garter like a rubber band right into Brant's outstretched hands, much to the protests of the other bachelors.

"This was rigged," Holland shouted. Not that he wanted to get married — he just liked the competitive aspect of catching the garter.

Pete grinned, wrapped his arm around Holland's shoulder and whispered, "Cath said I had to make sure Brant caught the garter."

"Married less than an hour and already whipped. I think you could use a drink," Holland laughed, leading Pete over to the nearest bar.

Brant made his way back to the table where Jessica, Sandy and her friend Wendy were sitting. Soon Holland and Dennis joined the group with fresh drinks in hand.

"Guess you two will be getting married next," Sandy said almost sadly. "Our Thanksgiving Orphans' Orgy is going right down the shitter."

"Ah, don't be sad," Holland said. "You've still got Dennis and me. We'll always be single."

"You can say that again," laughed Wendy.

"Real nice," Holland replied. And then to change the subject, he turned to Brant, who was caressing the top of Jessica's hand. "I hear you two have moved in together. Where did you guys end up?"

"We're in Venice about a mile from Dennis' place. You know those cottage houses just west of Lincoln and north of Venice Boulevard?" Brant asked.

"You mean those great little houses where all the front yards face each other without a street in between?"

"That's right," said Jessica as she pulled a couple photographs out of her purse. "It's like living in a park."

The first photo showed a wide, meandering sidewalk that separated two rows of houses, each with their own fenced front yards. The second photo showed Jessica behind a waist-high white picket fence that was overgrown with creeping roses.

"Where do you park?" asked Holland, as he looked at the third picture of Brant sitting on a deck in front of the house.

"The garage is at the back of the house and opens onto the alley. There're three or four of these little neighborhoods in that area. When you come visit you'll have to park on one of the cross streets and then walk down the sidewalk to our house," explained Brant.

"The front yard is like a jungle, with ferns and dozens of rose bushes. It's very private," Jessica added.

"It's all one level with three bedrooms and a huge open living room that transitions right into the kitchen," Brant continued. "It needed very little in the way of modifications for my chair—a couple ramps in and out of the house and it was ready to go."

"What did you do with the houseboat?" asked Dennis.

"I sold it to a friend of Jessica's brother. He's a para, too, and loved how the place was designed to accommodate a wheelchair."

"You don't miss living on your boat?" Sandy asked. "I've always thought it would be so cool to live at the marina."

"It was great," Brant agreed. "But it just wasn't big enough for the two of us and it never would have worked with a baby."

"A baby!" Sandy and Wendy exclaimed in unison.

"What baby?" Dennis asked.

"You're pregnant?" Sandy shrieked. "That's wonderful!"

Jessica held up her hands. "Wait a minute. We're not pregnant...yet."

"We've just decided to try in vitro. We've both always wanted children," Brant explained as his hand grasped Jessica's.

"We've both been given the green light by our doctors so we know it's possible." Jessica glowed with the knowledge that someday she could be carrying a child — their child — and gave Brant's hand a squeeze right back.

Just then Pete and Cath came over to the table.

"So when's the wedding?" Cath asked, giving Brant a little punch in the arm.

Dennis leaned over to Brant. "It's a conspiracy. You might as well give in."

"Already have."

* * * * *

Three months later, Jessica was sitting in the bedroom she'd converted into her office, admiring how the sunlight bounced around the facets of her diamond engagement ring. Turning her attention back to her computer, she began working on the revisions to her novel.

Brant had suggested she change the names of her main characters, worried that Simon would see himself in her novel and sue them. Jessica's agent had agreed. So now Simon LeStrand was Phillip LeStrand, Sir William was Sir Connell and Lord McGowan was Lord Roberts. Brant had liked all the name changes, as did her agent. Now she was fine-tuning various aspects of the plot when the phone rang. After three rings it was apparent that Brant wasn't going to pick up, so Jessica grabbed the phone herself.

After fifteen minutes of intense conversation with her agent, Angela Simpson, Jessica hung up the phone, her face flush with excitement. She pushed back her desk chair and went in search of Brant. First she stuck her head into his studio to make sure he wasn't recording a class before calling out his name. The camera lights were off and the room was empty.

"Brant?"

No answer. She made her way down the short hall to the living room and headed outside. The house was divided into two parts — the three bedrooms and two bathrooms, all connected by the hallway, made up the back half of the house. The open floor plan of the family room, dining room and kitchen made up the front half. There were huge picture windows on all three exterior walls, bringing the lush gardens of the front and side yards practically into the house. Merlin's cage sat next to one of these windows on a pedestal so he could pretend he was outside with the other birds. He squawked a greeting to Jessica as she entered the room.

"Hey Merlin. Is Brant outside?"

Merlin gave a long, low whistle.

Looking out one of the windows, Jessica saw Brant sitting out on the redwood deck with a stack of papers on his lap. His red pen was flying across the page, marking up some unfortunate student's essay. He was so engrossed in what he was doing that he didn't hear Jessica open the screen door. She was at his side before he realized she was there.

"You should read this one," he said, indicating the essay with all the red markings. "Then you'd realize how good you really were."

"Even though you wouldn't give me an A."

"Will you ever let that go?" Brant asked, smiling up at her.

"Probably not. It's too fun to tease you about it, especially once I become a famous author. And speaking of becoming famous, I think I've taken my first step in that direction."

"Really?"

"I just hung up with Angela and she has a publisher who's interested in looking at my novel. Isn't that wonderful?" Jessica exclaimed.

"That's terrific! I'm so proud of you, babe."

"Of course, it's just a request for the manuscript. They'll probably have a ton of suggestions and I'll have to do some rewriting, but at least it's a nibble."

"This is great. Come here, you." Brant put his papers on the short table next to his chair and made room for Jessica on his lap.

Jessica sat down and kissed him on the cheek, her face lit by the afternoon sun filtering through the palm trees of their neighbor's yard.

"So, Professor. Do I get an A-plus now?" she asked, batting her eyelashes.

"I'll give you an A-plus all right," he replied, reaching his fingers around to her waist and tickling her until she begged him to stop.

Out of breath Jessica managed to say, "You don't play fair, do you?"

Brant answered her question with a deep passionate kiss that shut her up for all of a minute.

"I'm so happy right now, I don't even care if my book gets published or not. Just sitting here with you in our own little corner of the universe with the possibility of publication is a pretty good feeling."

"I'd agree with that," Brant answered, brushing strands of Jessica's hair away from her face. "What do you say about going inside and celebrating the moment? I think we still have a bottle of that champagne left over from New Year's Eve."

"Sure. Then you could make me a special dinner and pamper me like the princess I think I am," Jessica added.

"Now you're pushing it," Brant replied before grabbing his stack of papers, turning his chair around and wheeling them both inside.

While sipping champagne and finishing off leftover Thai food, Brant asked Jessica how she had ended her novel. "The last thing I read was up to chapter twenty."

"You know Simon—I mean *Phillip* LeStrand. I can't stop thinking of him as Simon—escapes right before his execution with the help of some of his followers. So he's still out there causing problems. And then there was the whole thing with the dragon and how Sir Connell is almost killed trying to protect Lady Anne, who ends up saving Sir Connell," Jessica explained with enthusiasm.

"How do you think up all this stuff?"

"I've been writing these stories in my head since I was a kid. It's just there," Jessica said in amazement. "The more I write, the easier it flows. It's like I've tapped into this well that I didn't even know existed."

"So how does it all end? Do they live happily ever after?"

"Does anyone?"

"I think we will," Brant smiled.

"You're such a romantic," Jessica said, poking fun at him. "It's not always that easy. Lady Anne keeps taking chances in search of adventure and Sir Connell keeps vacillating between being scared to death for her safety and being frustrated with her reckless behavior, all the while falling more in love with her every day."

"Sounds like they'll make it to me," Brant said with confidence.

"You must be an optimist," Jessica remarked.

"Not until I met you, My Lady, not until I met you."

The End

Why an electronic book?

We live in the Information Age—an exciting time in the history of human civilization, in which technology rules supreme and continues to progress in leaps and bounds every minute of every day. For a multitude of reasons, more and more avid literary fans are opting to purchase e-books instead of paper books. The question from those not yet initiated into the world of electronic reading is simply: *Why?*

1. *Price.* An electronic title at Ellora's Cave Publishing and Cerridwen Press runs anywhere from 40% to 75% less than the cover price of the exact same title in paperback format. Why? Basic mathematics and cost. It is less expensive to publish an e-book (no paper and printing, no warehousing and shipping) than it is to publish a paperback, so the savings are passed along to the consumer.

2. *Space.* Running out of room in your house for your books? That is one worry you will never have with electronic books. For a low one-time cost, you can purchase a handheld device specifically designed for e-reading. Many e-readers have large, convenient screens for viewing. Better yet, hundreds of titles can be stored within your new library—on a single microchip. There are a variety of e-readers from different manufacturers. You can also read e-books on your PC or laptop computer. (Please note that

Ellora's Cave does not endorse any specific brands. You can check our websites at www.ellorascave.com or www.cerridwenpress.com for information we make available to new consumers.)

3. *Mobility.* Because your new e-library consists of only a microchip within a small, easily transportable e-reader, your entire cache of books can be taken with you wherever you go.

4. ***Personal Viewing Preferences.*** Are the words you are currently reading too small? Too large? Too... ANNOYING? Paperback books cannot be modified according to personal preferences, but e-books can.

5. ***Instant Gratification.*** Is it the middle of the night and all the bookstores near you are closed? Are you tired of waiting days, sometimes weeks, for bookstores to ship the novels you bought? Ellora's Cave Publishing sells instantaneous downloads twenty-four hours a day, seven days a week, every day of the year. Our webstore is never closed. Our e-book delivery system is 100% automated, meaning your order is filled as soon as you pay for it.

Those are a few of the top reasons why electronic books are replacing paperbacks for many avid readers.

As always, Ellora's Cave and Cerridwen Press welcome your questions and comments. We invite you to email us at Comments@ellorascave.com or write to us directly at Ellora's Cave Publishing Inc., 1056 Home Avenue, Akron, OH 44310-3502.

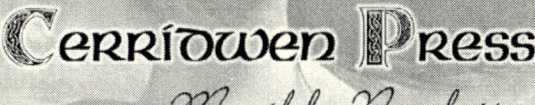

Cerrídwen Press

Monthly Newsletter

News
Author Appearances
Book Signings
New Releases
Contests
Author Profiles
Feature Articles

Available online at
www.CerridwenPress.com

Cerridwen Press

Cerridwen, the Celtic goddess of wisdom, was the muse who brought inspiration to storytellers and those in the creative arts.

Cerridwen Press encompasses the best and most innovative stories in all genres of today's fiction.

Visit our website and discover the newest titles by talented authors who still get inspired—much like the ancient storytellers did...

once upon a time.

www.cerridwenpress.com